The Fourth Vow

Richard T. Dolezal

This book is a work of fiction. The characters, the incidents and dialogue are all drawn from the author's imagination and are not to be construed as real. Any resemblance to actual events or persons, living or dead, is entirely coincidental.

ISBN: 154033712X
ISBN 13: 9781540337122
Library of Congress Control Number: 2016919058
CreateSpace Independent Publishing Platform
North Charleston, South Carolina

Charlie & Linda,
You two are great!
Enjoy the book.
Rich

For MJD, my inspiration

Isaiah 66:15–16

For behold, the LORD will come in fire
And His chariots like the whirlwind
To render His anger with fury
And His rebuke with flames of fire.
For the Lord will execute judgment by fire
And by His sword on all flesh,
And those slain by the Lord will be many.

From various news reports:

Duluth, Minnesota: Inside a sagging warehouse surrounded by weeds and empty buildings, a slab of granite engraved with the Ten Commandments awaits a buyer. The city began accepting bids this week for the monument, which once stood outside City Hall. The city agreed to remove the monument as part of the settlement of a federal lawsuit filed by the American Civil Liberties Union of Minnesota.

Berkeley, California: Residents are being asked to vote on whether to remove a Nativity scene and a Star of David from a public square because the ACLU of Northern California is threatening a lawsuit to force their removal. A man who survived the Holocaust began the citizens' opposition to the ACLU to raise awareness in the community of the assault on traditional religious values that is part of the ACLU agenda.

Arlington, Virginia: Federal agents arrested the former president of the Virginia Chapter of the ACLU on charges of possessing child pornography videos downloaded from the Internet. The complaint alleges that the videos depict graphic forcible intercourse with young girls. One of the girls on the video is seen and heard crying. Another girl is visibly restrained by ropes while being sexually assaulted.

1

MARKUS ROIST STOOD next to his rental car in the empty parking lot of the Development Authority on Treasure Island, an artificial island that sits in the bay between Oakland and San Francisco. The night was balmy—unseasonably warm for December, he understood.

He checked his watch.

He left the parking lot, crossed the Avenue of Palms, and moved to the water's edge for an unobstructed view.

He raised his binoculars and traced the San Francisco–Oakland Bay Bridge to that point where it enters San Francisco. He knew the exact location because earlier that day he had made a very special delivery to the Bay View Brewery and Pub, which was almost directly under the bridge.

While Roist was many things, a delivery man he most definitely was not. But this was an important assignment. He had been provided with detailed instructions regarding the cases of champagne he was to deliver: four cases went one place; one case went elsewhere.

He did not ask about the contents. No need, really. He assumed the one case contained a bomb. It was just a guess—albeit, an educated one, given the nature of his work and the identity of the person who hired him for this task.

When he agreed to this assignment, he was told it would not be very difficult. And it was not difficult at all. In fact, it was remarkably easy. His was one of a number of delivery trucks, almost all of them white vans, parked or double-parked in front of the restaurant that was closed in order to prepare for the night's big party. No one had pressed him for credentials, no one monitored what he was doing, and no one challenged him for moving elsewhere in the restaurant besides the bar area.

Once he gained entrance to the restaurant, it took no more than ten minutes, beginning to end. He had spent much more time trying to secure a parking space close to the restaurant. He did not want to double-park or violate any other parking laws that might have drawn attention to his white van.

Roist had never been to San Francisco before this assignment. In order to prepare properly, he had flown in from Rome three days ago, giving him time to find his way around the area before tonight's event. Planning was always key: Roist believed this, and the people he worked for excelled at it.

He wondered whether he was at the end, in the middle, or at the beginning of something old and vicious...or new and vicious. He also speculated about what part he might play going forward. Perhaps it all depends on what happens tonight.

After retiring from the Swiss Guard—where he personally protected the Pope, very much like the Secret Service in America protects the president—Roist had taken a moral pivot, for convoluted reasons he could not fully articulate. He no longer protected lives. He took them. He became an assassin: First as a mercenary sniper, killing from a distance; then as an assassin in close, almost personal situations.

Tonight, however, he was not an active assassin. He was a voyeur. Waiting. Watching. Wondering what would happen in the restaurant he had visited earlier in the day.

2

PROTESTORS MARCHED SINGLE file in front of the popular Bay View Brewery and Pub on the Embarcadero. With them were a number of musicians playing guitars and flutes. The group sang popular religious songs as they marched.

These protestors were far better dressed than the garden-variety San Francisco protestor. The individuals marching were mostly middle aged. Their placards said: "50,000,000 Babies Murdered since Roe v. Wade." Some placards said, "Jesus is the Reason," it being understood among them that Jesus was, indeed, the reason for the season—the season being Christmas—even though, technically, they were still in Advent. It was the first day of December.

San Francisco police officers stood watch along the sidewalk where the protestors peacefully continued their serpentine march. The police slowly moved the protestors off the sidewalk and across the street as vehicles arrived to drop off partygoers in front of the restaurant.

Inside the restaurant, Miguel Alejandro Maria Torres, the effeminately handsome executive director of the American Civil Liberties Union, liked what he saw: the partygoers revving it up, well into their third or fourth drinks. Over four hundred invited guests—most of them affluent, many of them exceedingly wealthy, and some indecently wealthy—filled the premises to overflowing.

Tonight will be a very successful fund raiser, he thought. What a masterstroke, having this party in San Francisco. If ever a party and an organization identified with a city, this was it.

The multi-level restaurant had the usual exposed wood, brick and mortar, with generous clumps of ferns and other greenery throughout. For this gala, the walls were covered with large photos and posters detailing the modern history of the American Civil Liberties Union and its impact on American society, with an emphasis on the Northern California Chapter, the largest chapter in the country.

Quotations from judges, lawyers, politicians, and media personalities were sprinkled throughout. At the entrance a large tableau was on display that identified the people and organizations that support the ACLU. Tonight presented a great opportunity to raise a substantial amount of money by obtaining pledges from invited guests, many of whom were already contributors.

This type of gathering energized Torres because he was in his element. Prior to his appointment as the executive director of the American Civil Liberties Union, Torres successfully raised funds for the Ford Foundation's gay and lesbian initiatives, HIV/AIDS research and prevention, and sexual-orientation discrimination. He moved on to the Rockefeller Foundation, where he did the same type of work, before becoming the executive director of the ACLU. The fact that Miguel Torres was handsome, elegantly slim, and an openly gay Hispanic man added a measure of mystique to his abundant charisma. With his Ivy League education and law degree, he moved easily in all social circles on either coast.

At the dais, Torres pounded a wood gavel to silence the room. "Good evening, good evening, my friends. May I have your attention for just a few moments? Please, may I have your attention for a few moments? Then we can party till dawn," he laughed into the microphone, waiting for the crowd to look at him…to drink him in.

Torres learned long ago, when he had no money and less influence, that he had to fake it to make it. Even then, he managed to dress in tailor-made clothing. Tonight, as he felt the eyes of hundreds of people wash over him, he exuded confidence because in his mind he *had* made it. His tailored tuxedo cost over $4000, his shoes $1200 dollars. Everything was top drawer. He had learned at the Ford and Rockefeller Foundations that rich people would rather directly give money to people who looked *rich* than to people who looked like they needed it.

Tonight Torres looked rich, and tonight he planned to ask for a lot of money from the very wealthy people standing before him. "I simply want to take this opportunity to thank all of you for attending our party this evening. This is the largest turnout in the seven years the Northern California Chapter has sponsored this event. We have four hundred guests here tonight. First and foremost, I want to thank Brandy Shugart and her staff here in San Francisco for making this event such a grand affair."

The crowd applauded in response.

"Next, we must thank our long-time friend and patron, Lawrence Perry, chairman and CEO of DataBasic Systems—one of the great companies on the West Coast—for cohosting this party. Now, Larry is a guy who knows how to party," roared Torres, giving credit to a major bankroller of the ACLU, a man whom Torres personally thought repugnant and lacking in even rudimentary social graces. However, Perry wrote big checks, and Torres loved to cash them.

"Let me just say this: if Jesus is the reason for the season, then Santa Claus will be here around midnight to give us our gifts for being good boys and girls," continued Torres in a mocking tone.

The crowd laughed some more.

"Look at Iran, Afghanistan, Iraq, Syria, Somalia, Pakistan, and other countries to see what religion has done to them. To those who call us *elite* or the *intelligentsia* and who attack us as secular humanists or atheists, know this: a secular society is the only society where your individual liberties will be protected. All this talk about moral values and belief systems bandied about during this recent election is hogwash. *Hogwash.* Now there is a good Bible Belt phrase!

"Think about it for a moment: any belief system is, by definition, *exclusionary.* How Christian," said Torres, holding up two fingers on each hand to symbolize quotation marks, "is it to deny two people in love the right to marry each other just because they are of the same gender? Or to deny a woman the freedom to control her own body?

"Herb Caen, the famous columnist for the *San Francisco Chronicle* and the *San Francisco Examiner,* loved this city and its chaos and its diversity so much that he referred to it as *Baghdad-by-the-Bay.* His name is on the street outside, by the way. How appropriate that we are here in this great city that celebrates its extraordinary diversity.

"One more thing Herb Caen said that I think bears repeating, given the protestors outside: he said that 'the trouble with born-again Christians is that they are an even bigger pain in the ass the second time around,' and Herb Caen was right!" shouted Torres.

Much of the crowd burst into tremendous applause and raucous laughter that continued unabated for thirty seconds.

Torres lived for these moments. Tonight belonged to him.

"Well, enough of my soapbox," he chastised himself publicly, knowing that everyone loved self-deprecation. "Now on to business...and then pleasure," he smiled, as his vocal inflection soothed the crowd while alerting them to important topics to come.

"As you know, the ACLU has over three hundred full time staff and five times as many volunteers and pro bono attorneys to help us protect your freedom...our freedom...even the freedom of those who disagree with us.

"We work around the clock, ladies and gentlemen. ACLU lawyers and staff and volunteers are tireless and relentless in their efforts to ensure that our civil rights—guaranteed to us by the United States Constitution—are protected against the broad reach of the government, especially this government," Torres said slowly, lowering his voice as if to suppress a gag reflex.

The crowd loved the svelte Hispanic's over-the-top acting.

"Wow," exclaimed a short blond man in black Gucci, "he's wild."

A few of the partygoers were dressed to excess in the provocative San Francisco way; however, most of the partygoers were attired in fashionable cocktail wear. Those from the entertainment industry down the coast dressed to impress, wearing the trendiest designer clothing available on Rodeo Drive in Beverly Hills. The business executives and entrepreneurs from Silicon Valley dressed the same no matter what the event: expensive jeans, black shoes, and dark T-shirts that peeked out from the expensive, untucked shirts worn over them.

"Tonight we are fortunate to have with us the two magnificent United States senators from California: two people we should thank personally for their tireless efforts in protecting a woman's right to choose, keeping religion in its proper place, and ensuring the promise of marriage to all men and women in love—irrespective of their sexual orientation. I think the entertainment industry should also thank them for their devotion to maintaining freedom of expression in film, in public libraries...and, yes, in our bedrooms. Please welcome Senator Helen Schuman and Senator Yvonne Kaplan."

The partygoers applauded enthusiastically.

"The lady in red needs no introduction. Ladies and gentleman, the most important person in the Congress: Speaker of the House Jenny Bartoli.

The crowd applauded enthusiastically...and longer.

"In fact, ladies and gentlemen, I believe we are partying in her district this evening. Madame Speaker, thank you for your presence. It means a great deal to all of us. I guess the State of California is well represented on the national level.

"We also have the elegant and politically astute mayor of San Francisco here, the man who has been described as the most influential politician in the Golden State, the man who has a Rolodex the size of Oakland—or is that simply another of the urban myths surrounding Billy Blackman?" Torres laughed.

More applause.

"In addition, we have congressional representatives gracing us with their presence tonight, as well as a number of judges here this evening. We thank them for their vigilance and persistence in the face of this aggressive right-wing administration. Thankfully, the voters have shown them the door," Torres said, reminding the crowd that a new liberal administration would be sworn in next month.

"Finally, so many of you from the entertainment industry are here that we cannot help but marvel at the star power you are generating tonight. You in the entertainment industry have long been instrumental in fighting to protect the free expression of art guaranteed by the United States Constitution. You are our heroes, and we want to be your champions. We want to work with you to keep the morality police out of our movie theaters, out of our living rooms and public libraries, and, especially, out of our bedrooms. These are not the Dark Ages. If anything, it is the hyper-Renaissance. *We* are the enlightened ones, not the extreme religious right who live in flyover red states," said Torres, raising his voice in a crescendo.

More wild applause.

Looking directly at the audience, Torres said in a serious tone of voice, "And thank you for all that *you have done.* Thank you for all that *you do.* And thank you, in advance, for all that *you will do.*

"Now, please dig deep into your pockets, and give generously tonight. We need your support. Our goal tonight is forty-five million dollars. Help us, so we can help you.

"Enjoy yourselves, my friends. And for those of you who still believe in Santa Claus...and Jesus Christ...*Merry Christmas*," Torres shouted.

The disc jockey played *Holly Jolly Christmas*, sung by Burl Ives, as the crowd burst into applause and silly laughter.

3

DAWN MEADOWS, AN athletic-looking reporter from the local CBS affiliate, and her cameraman were about to do a live televised interview with Torres, Billy Blackman, and Lawrence Perry.

"Three, two, one," the cameraman counted down as he turned on the lights, and Dawn Meadows flashed her dental-implants-perfect smile toward the camera.

"Tonight the Bay View Brewery and Pub on the Embarcadero is rocking with partygoers. We are at the Seventh Annual Separation of Church and State Gala sponsored by the Northern California Chapter of the American Civil Liberties Union. This is a fun, and a *fund-raising*, event," Dawn said through her luminous smile and landscaped lips, "with a silent auction to raise money for the ACLU to continue its important work in protecting our civil rights.

"Here with me is the executive director of the ACLU, Miguel Alejandro Maria Torres, the first Hispanic and the first openly gay person to lead the ACLU. Is that correct Miguel?" smiled Dawn Meadow, as she moved the microphone toward Torres's chin.

"Yes, I plead guilty to being both Hispanic and gay," answered Torres, bemused but confident. "Actually, Dawn, I'm Hispanic, gay, and Episcopalian...at the moment," he said winking conspiratorially to acknowledge the presence of the gay Episcopal bishop from Hartford, Connecticut.

"I'm living proof of the promise of America, provided our precious civil liberties are protected. Each year our work to protect America's freedoms becomes more urgent. This, of course, requires funding for the staff members who toil tirelessly from coast to coast, border to border, to make the American dream one that each person can realize in his or her lifetime. So, in furtherance of that effort, tonight we have this great party to help us raise money for the New Year and the new challenges that await us all."

"Thank you, Miguel," said Dawn Meadows, as Torres moved away. The reporter turned to her next interview. "Here with me now is someone who needs no introduction: the exciting and colorful mayor of San Francisco, the Honorable Billy Blackman.

"Mr. Mayor, imagine seeing you at a party!" joked Dawn Meadow, her green contact lenses twinkling almost as much as her teeth.

"My, my, Dawn, don't you look lovely this evening," gushed the mayor as he examined the clinging red dress the reporter wore. "It is really, really nice to see you again. And let me say, on behalf of the viewing audience, great dress! But we have to stop meeting like this," laughed the mayor.

"Wow, what a party! Tonight we are going to raise some serious money for Miguel and his troops. Right, Larry?" Blackman said, trying to pull Lawrence Perry into the camera's view. "Larry here has more money than he has skin cells. Right, Larry?" joshed Blackman. "He is paying for this party! How great is that? Thanks, Larry."

Squinting at the camera through European-inspired eyeglasses, visibly smudged and appearing too small for his fleshy face, a profusely sweating Lawrence Perry waited for the lovely Dawn Meadows to ask him a question or two.

Dawn Meadows moved the microphone toward Larry Perry's flabby, moist chin and started to ask him a question when, abruptly, she completely ignored him. Her attention became riveted over his left shoulder. She focused on a diminutive figure closing fast. Senator Kaplan was working her way to the camera, intent on being the first senator to be interviewed.

Meadows tried to push Perry out of the way, but he proved to be immovable, so she danced around his girth and stepped toward the junior senator from California (the one with the large mouth and no brain, according to the senior senator from California).

Brain or no brain, the petite senator from Marin County recognized that Dawn Meadows was an important reporter employed by the most watched television news program in the Bay Area.

"Dawn, how nice to see you again," said Senator Kaplan to the camera, not even looking at the reporter who moved to her side.

"Senator Kaplan, it is very nice to see you, too," Meadows said. "Are you home for the holidays?" She almost said *Christmas*, but she caught herself from committing a double faux pas since Senator Kaplan was Jewish, and Christmas wasn't a term generally used at this party.

"Yes, I am. As you know, I typically leave Washington in the middle of December; however, I left early to attend this party in order to give witness to the important work that the ACLU is doing to preserve our freedoms. I'm certain that all of your viewers will agree with me that under this Republican administration our fundamental freedoms are being eroded and irreparably harmed. A woman's right to choose, for example. Thank God for the ACLU," said Senator Kaplan to the camera.

Loud laughter erupted behind her as Billy Blackman moved into the camera shot. "Yvonne, Yvonne," he chided her, calling the senator by her first name, "you can't put 'God' in the same sentence as 'ACLU.' It doesn't compute," he laughed. "Right, Larry?"

Senator Kaplan strained at a smile, not enjoying being upstaged by the exuberant, camera-hogging mayor.

Larry Perry tried to laugh in support of his friend, the mayor, but he felt sick—so sick, in fact, he worried he might vomit. He worried he might vomit on camera...possibly *on* the camera.

But he was wrong about the camera. Instead, he vomited on the Jimmy Choo red stilettos adorning Dawn Meadows's buffed feet.

The startled reporter looked disgustedly at her feet and then at Perry. Rage and vomit left her mouth at about the same time. She tried to sign off from the broadcast but could not manage it.

At that very moment, the studio lost the live feed from the restaurant.

4

THE BLINDING FLASH of a thousand suns exploded inside the restaurant. In seconds the ambient temperature in the building raced to over ten million degrees Fahrenheit, creating a fireball that filled the entire restaurant.

A shockwave of pressurized, superheated air blew out the roof, the front of the building, and one side, quickly reducing everything and everybody to white, hot ash.

Fiery shockwaves levitated automobiles, trucks, and a passing trolley car, reducing metal to walnut-sized ingots. The outside air was sucked into the hellish vortex, packing a potent punch that hurled the molten metal ingots into the warehouse across the Embarcadero. The warehouse quickly disintegrated into smoldering rubble.

Small fires erupted inside the destroyed restaurant space, but they rapidly self-extinguished since no oxygen fueled their combustion, the fireball having consumed all available air.

The hot wind that preceded the shockwave blew over the icy water of San Francisco Bay, cooling itself into foggy evaporation before reaching the opposite shore of Treasure Island.

After a few minutes, the firestorm followed the shockwave and raged out over the same frigid water, generating exploding bubbles along the surface, creating steamy mist in the atmosphere directly above, stalling in place near Treasure Island until it consumed itself into nonexistence.

The partygoers and restaurant staff inside the restaurant died instantly, as did those revelers on the patio in front and on the sidewalk between the restaurant and the street. The powerful blast also killed all the protestors parading in front of the restaurant on the other side of the street.

Vehicles parked in front of the restaurant were flash-incinerated, reduced to the size of baseballs, and blown into the bay. Lamp poles, once in front of the restaurant, were now gone, while lamp poles across the Embarcadero were tortured, twisted, and scorched.

A trolley on its way to Fisherman's Wharf that crossed in front of the awful force of the explosive punch was transformed into a small concave piece of molten metal and soldered to its iron tracks; all seventeen people on board vaporized.

Where guests stood a moment before enjoying the festive nature of the event, sipping champagne, cocktails, wine, and beer, and making small talk…now ashen remains littered the restaurant floor, the sidewalk, and the street. Oddly, there was no blood in the horrid scene; human blood had been boiled into vapors, sucked into the fireball, and then had been moved by the shockwave.

Hissing sounds of ruptured gas pipes and gurgling, spitting sounds from wrenched water pipes filled the air for a few minutes before becoming completely silent.

The restaurant cavern yawned darkly into the diabolical night, spewing clouds of debris dust from the pulverized building materials. A steaming, black scar stretched from the base of the five-foot thick back wall of the building, over the sidewalk and street, crossed the Embarcadero, and continued along the footprint of the destroyed warehouse. It stained the concrete sidewalk and congealed every piece of remaining asphalt. Incandescent heat had etched the concrete as it fired across it, vaporized everything near it, and had scorched everything not incinerated into an unrecognizable form.

All four hundred people on the official guest list died.

The restaurant staff died.

The protestors died.

The media contingent died.

The police and private security guards managing the protestors and providing security for the party died.

Some tourists and passersby died.

The cremains of five hundred people lay spread across the landscape.

• • •

Roist threw his binoculars to the ground to save his eyesight. His eyes were already blurry from the brilliant light triggered by the explosion in the restaurant he had visited earlier in the day.

He could hardly think. His mind struggled to comprehend what he was watching.

What was in that box he had delivered? How could something so small do such extraordinary damage?

He wondered how many people he helped kill today.

5

ALL AVAILABLE SAN Francisco emergency medical teams, fire and police, converged near the corner of Harrison and the Embarcadero within five to twenty minutes following the blast. They stationed themselves a distance away from the scene of devastation, waiting for the hazmat team to appear. No one knew what horror the area might hold for them, so they held back. Within fifteen minutes the hazmat team arrived in their Technical Operations Mobile Unit, designed specifically for hazard-risk assessment and incident management.

Inside the gleaming red and white unit, which was about the size of a luxury motor coach, there were computers, telecommunications equipment, and linkages to regional and national communication centers along with medical monitoring equipment, chemical, biological, and radioactive detection gauges, as well as decontamination equipment.

A robotic device on wheels was launched from under the mobile operations vehicle, steered by remote control from inside. This tiny go-cart-type vehicle contained a mobile Geiger counter that would determine the level of radiation in the air and transmit that data to a screen inside the mobile operations vehicle. It also was equipped with air-sampling equipment to analyze the air particles to determine levels and types of contaminants.

All the members of the hazmat crew believed this was a thermonuclear explosion; however, their training and protocols required strict adherence to systematic checks to rule out and to identify a broad array of potential hazards, instead of relying on the conclusions initially reached by visual inspection alone.

The mobile device reported minor radiation levels—more elevated in some areas deep inside the cavern, but still at acceptable levels—as the four-wheeled device approached what used to be the front of the restaurant. The air outside the building was also acceptable, almost normal.

The operator directed the mobile device into the deepest recesses inside for more readings because he could not believe the readings already captured. This time the radiation level was even lower than the first reading.

"How can this be? I wonder if there is a calibration problem with the unit," the operator said.

The woman in charge of this hazmat unit also thought there must be an issue with the readings being taken and analyzed. She ordered another unit to the site.

Air samples indicated that the air quality was poor, mostly because of the extreme amount of ash in the air. Other than the ash, the analysis showed no traces of chemical or biological contaminants; however, in spite of the readings, the hazmat team believed the area had to be radioactive. They decided to do nothing until another radiation detector could be delivered to the site.

After a short wait, the new radiation detector arrived and was deployed. The operator initiated one more sweep to check radiation in the deep spaces of the restaurant. The readings from the new radiation detector were even better than the previous readings.

Finally, the hazmat team left their motor coach, wearing regular uniforms with full-face respirators. Fire, rescue, and police personnel approached, most wearing particulate masks. More gear was handed out, and when everyone was properly covered to protect against fine particulate inhalation, the group proceeded to the opening in the front of the building.

They used flashlights since the fire department had not yet rigged searchlights to shine into the building. With so many beams of light careening off ash particles, the place looked like the middle of a blizzard with careening headlights of multiple colliding vehicles.

All checks for gas leaks indicated there were none, and the hazmat team and the San Francisco Fire Department concluded that a thermonuclear explosion had created such extraordinary heat that ruptured gas pipes were cauterized by their own molten metal. The same was true for water pipes and electrical wiring. The water pipes were melted at their ends, sealing any opening. As for electrical wiring, there was none left.

A fire department team checked for structural damage. The interior of the building was larger than it seemed from the exterior. Within the building structure, all floors, ceilings, the roof, the stairs, and furnishings had disappeared. The distance from the rubble of the main floor to the top of the only remaining walls—where the roof once joined those walls—measured more than sixty feet. They were stunned to think they were inside a five-story building with all the floors missing.

6

A CONFERENCE ROOM off the presidential suite at 1600 Pennsylvania Avenue was buzzing with subdued conversation. The attorney general, director of the FBI, director of the Secret Service, director of the CIA, secretary of homeland security, secretary of defense, and their aides shared coffee, fruit, and bagels with the president, his chief of staff, and his press secretary. They were there to brief him on the events in San Francisco. It was seven o'clock in the morning in the District of Columbia—four o'clock in San Francisco.

The director of the FBI, Gary Yount, started the meeting: "Mr. President, at about eleven o'clock last night Pacific Coast Time, there was an explosion in a restaurant where the ACLU of Northern California was holding a fund raiser. We believe at least five hundred people are dead, including Senators Schuman and Kaplan, the speaker of the house, Jenny Bartoli, Congressmen Halley, Cabot, and Werner, a few federal judges, and many other media, business, and Hollywood entertainment people, as well as ACLU supporters. Most of the hierarchy of the ACLU was killed. There were protestors out in front when the place blew up, and they were all killed—as were seventeen San Francisco police officers doing security and crowd control."

"Are these numbers firm?" asked the president.

"No, they are not firm at this time," Yount answered.

"Please continue," said the president.

"San Francisco Hazmat, Police, and Fire were on the scene quickly, and we had agents there within minutes. When I last checked with the agent-in-charge, right before this meeting, he said there is every reason to believe that this was a nuclear explosion of some sort. The agent said the explosion ripped through the restaurant and, essentially, destroyed everything, including all the people."

"Destroyed?" asked the president.

"*Vaporized*. The explosion reduced everyone to ashes."

"Ashes! Oh my God," said the president in disbelief and horror. "So, it could not have been a conventional bomb?"

"No, sir. That is very unlikely, given the level of destruction.

"We checked flight information from the FAA and local airports. There is no indication that an airplane dropped a bomb or became a bomb. Nor is there any reason to believe that a missile caused this damage; so, we are left to assume that an explosion on the ground was the proximate cause."

Sandra Bridges, the secretary of homeland security, continued, "Mr. President, there is no current indication that this is the work of a foreign terrorist group. There was no increased chatter or any mention of San Francisco or the ACLU in any of the recent transmissions that have been intercepted. And, while we don't have a complete list of the guests, it seems doubtful that any particular guest would have been a target of a foreign terrorist group, since that is not how they generally operate. However, we are rechecking all chatter that may have mentioned the speaker, Senators Schuman and Kaplan, the congressmen, the judges, and anyone else we know were guests. Particularly, we are checking Senator Schuman's husband, Robert Glubman, because of his defense-contracting business in the Middle East."

"Along that same line," added Attorney General Thomas Owens, "we have no information that would suggest domestic terrorism on an organized scale. However, that doesn't mean a few highly motivated and bomb-savvy crazies acting alone couldn't have done this. Right now we just don't know. A technically sophisticated nuclear weapon, like the one this had to be, is a far cry from a crude truck bomb made by a McVeigh type, like in the Oklahoma City bombing."

The people in the room were quiet.

After a few seconds, the president said: "A nuclear explosion."

"Yes, sir."

"How will this investigation proceed?" the president asked. "I mean, here you have a nuke, and here you have the ACLU...and you have liberal United States senators and members of Congress, along with local liberal politicians and judges killed. Plus you have police officers and peaceful protestors killed, as well. This will become the singular news event around the world for months. The cable shows will have every spook-theorist talking head under contract offering gratuitous suggestions and hypothetical motives. What do we say? And who should say it?"

"You, sir, should be the spokesperson" said the president's press secretary, "and you should be on the air within the next hour. We have to go."

There was a brief discussion of what the president might say, but there was disagreement that he had to speak to the American public as soon as possible. Sandra Bridges suggested that, after the president's address, she, Tom, and Gary could hold a joint press conference to discuss their investigation of the incident and tell the media that they were working with local and state law enforcement in California.

The president agreed. "Schedule a press conference for noon today to tell the media what we know, without offering any speculation regarding the people behind this. I think it premature to exclude foreign terrorist groups at this time. Who knows? Our intelligence agencies haven't produced stellar information recently. I also think you three should make an appearance at the press conference in San Francisco later today. Call the mayor's office out there to coordinate. Keep the focus on California—not here."

7

THE NEWS OF the blast in San Francisco broke on national and international news shortly after midnight Pacific Coast Time, but without details. With the morning sun, news helicopters swarmed to the blast area to broadcast video to local and national news outlets.

Was this another 9/11 terrorist attack? Was it a domestic terrorist attack by right-wing extremists? Speculation ran across the political spectrum and ruled the morning airwaves, even though no one had any information.

CNN's top political and terrorism reporters held a panel discussion with talking heads from around the country (all from CNN news bureaus, qualifying themselves as experts because they had reported news for more than ten years). The CNN host talked about *hate* as being a possible motive for the explosion and the fires. But what, exactly, was the focus of the hate?

One panel member said, "Clearly, the fact that this was an ACLU party and fund raiser would suggest that the ACLU itself, as an organization, was the target. One can only speculate that conservative Christians might be involved because of the separation of church and state issue."

"But, Lesley, don't forget that there were Christian protestors outside the restaurant who were killed. I find it hard to believe they would be sacrificed. I saw the footage that was on the local news channel in San Francisco last night. It showed a number of men and women protesting in front of the restaurant, with a police presence to ensure nothing happened between the protestors and the arriving guests. I just don't think any right-wing Christian group would kill Christian protestors—or anyone else, for that matter."

"There were Christians *inside*. And they were killed," Norah Sullivan, another reporter, tersely added.

The host asked her, "Is this a diversion? Could it be the work of a foreign terrorist group? A group who has access to nuclear weapons?"

"The answer is yes, possibly, although it seems farfetched. I think a domestic terrorist group would be more likely: people who hate the ACLU."

"Well, based on the blogs and call-in radio this morning, it appears that the majority of Americans hate the ACLU. Maybe the sound of clapping you hear is the silent majority of Christians who hate the ACLU—all those who are pro-life and pro-Boy Scouts and so on. What do you think, Barry?" asked the host, throwing it over to Barry Solomon, a CNN political reporter.

"To me it just underscores how much bitterness there is in this country. This past election broke all records for attack ads and hate-mongering."

The host told the viewing audience just tuning in, "We are awaiting a press conference in San Francisco with the deputy mayor, the police department, and, we are told, the attorney general of the United States, the director of the FBI, and the secretary of homeland security."

The broadcast broke away to the scene in San Francisco as the press conference began.

8

"**GOOD AFTERNOON,** I am Nancy Valeria, the deputy mayor of San Francisco. With me are Chief of Police Russell Trotter, Fire Chief Douglas Pryor, and Yuri Olmar from the California Department of Justice. Also with us are United States Attorney General Thomas Owens, Secretary of Homeland Security Sandra Bridges, and FBI Director Gary Yount.

"Last night a disaster occurred in our city. Around eleven o'clock there was a massive explosion at the Bay View Brewery and Pub on the Embarcadero at Harrison. The American Civil Liberties Union of Northern California had reserved the entire restaurant for a fund-raising event and party.

"We believe, but cannot confirm, that more than five hundred people were killed by the explosion. Not only were the people in the restaurant killed, but people outside on the sidewalk and street were also killed, including seventeen police officers.

"Among those who died are Jenny Bartoli, the speaker of the house and our congressional representative for decades; the two United States senators from California, Senator Helen Schuman and Senator Yvonne Kaplan; their husbands and some staff members; three United States members of Congress: Harry Werner, Brad Halley, and Guy Cabot; two judges from the Ninth Circuit Court of Appeals, Tamika Jackson and Waylon Bergerstaff; and many in the entertainment industry, including producer David Gollum and actress Cassie Worthington. Lastly, I report with great personal regret, Billy Brown, our mayor, was in attendance and was also killed.

"On behalf of the people of San Francisco, our prayers and condolences go out to all those who lost loved ones last night.

"In my capacity as deputy mayor, I will be handling the administrative issues relating to the investigation into this tragedy; however, the investigation itself will be managed by Chief Trotter," concluded Deputy Mayor Valeria, stepping aside to let Chief Trotter move to the microphones.

"Thank you, Madame Deputy Mayor. Let me say at the outset that this investigation is just getting underway. Following the blast last night, we had fire and bomb investigators carefully comb through the site. The site itself is marked off so forensics people from the various agencies can do their work. We established a task force to work this investigation that includes the California Department of Justice, the FBI, the Department of Homeland Security, the Secret Service, and many other agencies.

"We do not yet have a complete list of victims. The deputy mayor shared the names of some of those who we know were killed in the blast, but there are many more still unidentified victims. We hope to have a fairly complete list by the end of the day tomorrow. This list will include the identities of the guests, the ACLU staff, restaurant workers, police and security, passersby, and protestors who were in front of the restaurant at the time of the blast.

"We will be holding routine press conferences as this investigation continues," Chief Trotter said, and then, looking at Nancy Valeria, he added, "Madame Deputy Mayor, I believe the time for these press conferences will be five p.m., is that correct?"

Deputy Mayor Valeria walked to the microphones. "Yes, that is my understanding. Thank you, Chief Trotter. Chief Pryor? No? Okay then. Mr. Attorney General?"

"Thank you, Madame Deputy Mayor. Secretary Bridges, Director Yount, and I met with the president this morning to brief him on this explosion. The president's first concern was for the families of those who perished in the explosion. Our thoughts and prayers go out to them.

"The president has directed all the heads of federal agencies to work with local police and state investigators to do whatever they can to help in any way. To that end, Director Yount has already deployed a significant number of FBI agents to this investigation, including FBI bomb experts and forensic experts. Thank you."

Reporters' hands stabbed the air to ask questions before he even finished saying his last word. Nothing asked was answered.

9

HE WATCHED HIS old friend, the attorney general of the United States, at the press conference in San Francisco. Tom's life was not going to get better at the end of his career in government. There would be no easy transition. Certainly the president-elect would have his people all over the Justice Department to make certain the investigation was handled to the president-elect's satisfaction—and to maintain maximum visibility for his political base.

The television inside the open-air bar only had CNN International News, but it was enough. Blake sipped his cold beer while staring at the television screen, even though the story of the bombing in San Francisco was now replaced by a piece on the Zika epidemic.

"How long has it been now?" Blake wondered. Tom had been appointed attorney general after his predecessor died of a sudden heart attack at the end of his first year in office—about six or seven years ago?

"Is Tom the reason I am here?" Blake laughed to himself, although it was bittersweet laughter. He took another pull on his cold bottle of Banks beer, locally brewed and freshly opened by a barely bikini-clad bartender. What could be better?

"My life," he thought.

His thoughts quickly turned to Annie and Connor, forever locked in his memory, never changing one bit from the last time he saw them alive. "I have grown older, but they have not."

It wasn't Tom. Of course it wasn't Tom. Blake always understood that. It happened because there is evil in the world. Sadly, it was just that simple. His wife and son were innocent, surrogate targets of a car bomb meant for him.

Staring at the nearly empty bottle of beer, Blake considered his situation: After he buried his wife and son and transitioned his law practice, he left for Barbados. He wanted to do nothing but hard, physical work to keep from thinking about what happened to them and, by extension, to himself.

He looked down at his hands: calloused, scarred, and brown as the beer bottle he held. His muscular arms were still covered with dirt and sweat, even though he had toweled off before leaving the fishing boat. There was no mirror available, so he could not see his face, but he knew what it would reflect: taut, weather-beaten skin and sun-streaked, hair—thick and unruly, salty-dirty from a day at sea.

After finishing his beer, he considered his current situation. He had come here because this was where Annie and he were married. She loved this island. Blake felt close to her here. Connor never had the chance to see Barbados. He was killed before his fifth birthday.

Blake swiveled on his barstool to focus on the turquoise water. Perhaps it was time to go home. "Maybe I can help Tom," Blake thought. "Annie would want that. Tom was her close friend, too."

A gentle ocean breeze moved through the open-air bar, filled mostly with tourists. Blake ordered another beer. Looking out at the water along a stretch of near-perfect white sand, he considered for a moment whether he could fit in again should he decide to return to Washington.

"Should I decide to return to Washington? Is there even a choice?" Thoughts raced through Blake's mind. "What will it be like without my father there? I have never lived there without him. All my life, my father was that constant presence, which I never valued for what it was until he was gone."

Blake wondered whether he had disappointed his father by leaving the firm and leaving Washington. His father said he hadn't, of course, but that was expected, knowing his father. Then his father died suddenly, and Blake was not there when it happened, although the truth was that his being there would not have made one bit of difference. Blake went back to mourn his death, but he could not have prevented it.

Jordan did not want Blake to leave again after their father's funeral. His sister missed him, especially now that she was alone without any family, except her own. Her mother was dead. Her father was dead. And her brother was lost in Barbados. Lost to her.

Blake looked at his empty beer bottle, wondering if there was truth serum mixed in with the hops, malt, and barley today. He laughed, causing tourists in new Tommy Bahama shirts and shorts to turn and look at him. He noticed it. He guessed the tourists probably viewed him as *local color.* If the tourists knew he had graduated summa cum laude from Princeton University and then second in his law-school class at the University of Virginia, if they knew he had been a JAG officer in the United States Marine Corps and then a partner in the most elite law firm in the District of Columbia, they probably would have been surprised...and then very interested in his obvious downfall in Barbados.

Blake ordered another beer.

10

SNOW HAD BEEN falling since Thanksgiving causing hundreds of flights to be canceled or significantly delayed along the Eastern Seaboard. These canceled or delayed flights, in turn, created a domino delay effect all the way to the West Coast and the Gulf Coast. Tens of thousands of travelers spent their Thanksgiving holiday stranded in airports.

Now, barely into December, it was already the greatest accumulation of snow in the Northeast since records were kept. In Connecticut, schools invoked their snow-days cancellation policy on the earliest date on record. Another record was set: more snow days than ever before. "So much for global warming," he thought.

For Justin Addison Lowell, it should have been a quiet time to work on his latest book. Lowell, professor emeritus of law and society at Yale University Law School, particularly enjoyed it when heavy snow blanketed New Haven because it made the city look, well, more livable. Today, because of the snow, he worked from home in a cozy study filled with books and sad memories of his wife who had committed suicide in the garage ten years ago, and their only child who had died in a freak skiing accident the following year.

Lowell relished the privileges and status of his position, including the stipend for travel and research paid by the foundation sponsoring his academic chair. Except for the one seminar class he taught, he had a great deal of time at his disposal to do other things—including serving on the boards of many corporations, non-profit organizations, and a number of philanthropic foundations.

To say that his was a long and distinguished career in the law would be stating the obvious. He welcomed the accolades, the honors, the deference, and the adulation. To say that Professor Lowell possessed a well-developed love of himself would be stating the truth.

Generally, he was a man of keen sensory perception, but today he hardly knew it was snowing. His concentration focused on what had happened in San Francisco.

The home phone rang, jolting him back to his surroundings. He picked it up and listened to the voice on the other end.

"No, I did not anticipate such a thing. I never would have imagined it," Lowell said indignantly, while wondering if he should have anticipated such a thing. "At least two or three years have passed, and nothing. Nothing. Now this!"

After a minute or two of listening, Lowell answered, "Yes, I will do that right away. I will schedule the meeting as soon as possible." He ended the call. He stared out the window into snow blindness. He imagined a bullet blasting through the wintry whiteout, through the storm window, and smashing into the middle of his forehead.

11

"THIS IS A Christmas gift that God gives us all," said Reverend Peterson in his commanding voice, seated on an elaborately carved and upholstered rosewood chair, surrounded by members of his television family. His silky, white hair was razor cut and carefully sprayed into place by his personal attendant. Tonight he wore a custom-tailored, midnight-blue suit of exquisite Italian wool and a crisply starched blue shirt with white collar and white French cuffs, also custom-made. A solid-colored gold silk tie from Hermès set off the colors wonderfully. Diamond-studded, twenty-four-carat gold, crown-of-thorns cufflinks punctuated the fashion statement with sparkling glimmer and a hint of devotion to a higher power.

While it might seem incongruous to some—a crown of thorns made of gold and adorned with diamonds—Reverend Peterson's brand of Christianity believed the Lord considered conspicuously embellished prosperity an acceptable way of life. It was testimony to the wearer's success in spreading the Word of God. *Alleluia.*

Ervin Peterson, pastor of the largest congregations in Texas—with the most widely viewed religious programs on television—looked more like a CEO than a minister. His financial empire was conservatively believed to be worth almost $800 million. The gold Rolex watch on his left wrist was a gift from his wife when their personal wealth passed the $100 million threshold. That had been some time ago. Many in his congregation believed that, with all his other ventures included, the good reverend was actually worth more than Oprah. *Double alleluia.*

To his right sat Ruth Peterson, his wife of more than forty years. She had been named after one of the famous women of the Old Testament. Her face had the startled look of multiple Botox injections, although her personal attendant did a fine job of applying makeup to perk up her rigid skin, giving her a few character wrinkles to enliven her countenance. Tonight, she wore lavender contact lenses. Piled like cotton-candy, her mountainous pink-platinum hair complemented her husband's pinkish facial color. Ruth Peterson always wore white. She preferred something lacy and ultra-feminine...something with layers of folds to conceal the consequences of her love of all things chocolate. Her dress tonight was an elegant mother-of-the-bride type dress. Lacy, layered, feminine...in size twenty-two. Her stockings were textured white and her shoes white satin with gold threads. She, too, was blessed by God.

Reverend Peterson began: "We are going to talk about the ACLU this evening, my friends. I want to tell you what I believe is true. I believe God exacted his vengeance upon the ACLU and their gay friends, porno friends, and atheist friends last night when the ACLU mocked the birth of our dear Lord, Jesus Christ, and our celebration of Christmas.

"But what is new? Hasn't this godless organization been doing that for years? Decades? I am just surprised God waited so long to visit his punishment on these heathens.

"Let me recap for you: Last night in San Francisco, the ACLU held a fund raiser at a restaurant. The fund raiser is called the Annual Separation of Church and State Gala...again, to mock the season of Christmas and to herald, not Jesus Christ the Son of God, our Savior, but rather the ACLU's idea of a secular society devoid of moral values and righteous principles. Pornography is their way of life. Ridiculing devout Christians is their pastime. This is evil personified in one organization.

"Now, through the grace of God, most of the leaders of the ACLU have been blown to hell—and along with them their gay friends and porn stars and their radical, anti-Christ, anti-Christian religion, anti-American agenda.

"You hear that sound, brothers and sisters? That is the sound of Boy Scouts around the country celebrating. That's the sound of Christian communities celebrating...tired of being shaken down by ACLU lawyers with endless threats of litigation. That's the sound of unborn babies screaming for life against the abortionist's knife. That's the sound of mothers and fathers celebrating their victories over the purveyors and defenders of child pornography, over the defenders of sexual perverts and pedophiles.

"Rejoice and be glad, people; this is a wonderful night. God is with us! God is with us!

"Even on such short notice, we managed to gather a panel of experts on the ACLU and other atheist organizations such as Americans United for Separation of Church and State and the Freedom from Religion Foundation, among others.

"Let me introduce our panel: Next to Ruth is Doctor Mary Ellen Gorman, a political historian from Southern Methodist University. Doctor Gorman has authored over twelve books on a variety of topics, most of them dealing with the role of religion in America. Her latest book, one that you can order online from our website or by calling the number on the screen, is entitled *In God We Trust: America United.*

"To my far right is Reverend Martin Schneider, the pastor of the largest Assembly of God denomination on the West Coast, located in Irvine, California. Reverend Schneider has written five books on the topic of church and state. Reverend Schneider debunks the myth that our constitution requires this country to rid itself of Christian symbols or symbols of any religion. It's the liberal courts that construe our constitution irrationally because—surprise, surprise—they have their own agenda, one similar to that of the ACLU.

"And, lastly, to my immediate right is Doctor Phyllis Howard, Distinguished professor of religious history and constitutional law at Texas Christian University. Doctor Howard is a true legal scholar. She has argued before appellate courts nationwide. She has argued nine times before the United States Supreme Court. Doctor Howard has a PhD in legal studies, with a concentration on the First Amendment to the Constitution. Did I say that right, Doctor Howard?" asked Reverend Peterson.

Doctor Howard nodded in the affirmative.

"What a brain trust we have here tonight," smiled Reverend Peterson. "Let me start with you, Professor Gorman. Can you give us an introduction to the ACLU, starting from its beginning? Wasn't it originally—and maybe it still is—a communist organization?"

Mary Ellen Gorman, tall and gaunt, blond hair tightly pulled back into a bun, wearing a dark pantsuit, and looking younger than anyone else on the stage, responded, "Roger Baldwin founded the ACLU in nineteen seventeen, although it was called the National Civil Liberties Bureau at the start. They changed the name to the American Civil Liberties Union in nineteen twenty. Baldwin was a communist and a socialist and a Unitarian, as well," she explained.

"Unitarian?" interrupted Reverend Peterson. "So that might explain why his organization is so anti-Christian."

"Well, yes, certainly that would be a consideration—plus the fact that he was a communist," she continued.

"And who was it that said, 'Religion is the opium of the people'?" interjected Reverend Schneider. "It was Karl Marx, the Father of Communism. It all fits, doesn't it?"

Professor Gorman calmly continued, "Baldwin came out of comfortable surroundings in Massachusetts. He attended Harvard College and went into social work. He joined the Communist Party, was a pacifist, and refused to serve his country during World War I, claiming he was a conscientious objector."

Reverend Peterson blurted, "That would explain why the ACLU is so antimilitary, including being against the Patriot Act and this country's defense ever since the Vietnam War. It's all laid out. The ACLU is the child of its father, and its father was anti-American in all his thoughts, words, and deeds—anti-Christian to his core."

Gorman hated appearing on these types of television panels because she detested being interrupted repeatedly. But this was the price she had to pay to promote her books. She had to grin and bear it, all the way to the bank.

Professor Gorman responded, "Yes, to a large extent that is true. Baldwin founded the American Civil Liberties Union with several people who were members of the Communist Party. The ACLU, at that time and continuing up to today, supported left-wing activities that were fomented by the Communist Party and leftist labor unions such as the Industrial Workers of the World, a socialist organization. Clearly he was enamored of Soviet Russia and their communist revolution."

"Did he have a family?" asked Ruth Peterson, ever a family-values person.

Gorman looked at Reverend Peterson's wife. To Gorman, Ruth Peterson looked like a pink and white marshmallow with a larynx; she quickly suppressed her errant thoughts.

"Well, he was married to a lawyer-journalist named Madeleine Doty. She didn't take his last name, and for most of their marriage, they did not live together; it would be called an open marriage today. Eventually, they divorced, and he took up with a woman named Evelyn Preston who already had two children. He and Evelyn never married but did have a child together."

"So that would explain the ACLU's negative views on the sanctity of marriage. Traditional marriage means nothing to them," bellowed Reverend Peterson. "The marriage between a man and a woman means nothing to them—nothing! That explains why they promote same-sex marriages."

"But why is the ACLU attacking the Boy Scouts?" asked Ruth.

Gorman looked down. She had had enough. She stopped speaking. She didn't think she was being rude. She had to protect her sanity.

"I can answer that," offered Professor Howard. "The ACLU has been a shill for the gay/lesbian lobby for decades now. For example, the ACLU sued Wal-Mart because Wal-Mart took a book off their shelves. That book was written by the pedophile crowd, the North American Man-Boy Love Association. Just the name makes a decent person sick.

"Now fast-forward to the Boy Scouts. Because the Boy Scouts will not allow known homosexuals to be troop leaders, the ACLU attacked the Boy Scouts of America, and they also attacked the Boy Scout oath that has *God* in it. Can you imagine that? Norman Rockwell must be rolling over in his grave!

"Gays make up a large number of donors to the ACLU, and there are gays at the highest levels of foundations that give money or grants to the ACLU. In fact, the executive director of the ACLU who was killed in San Francisco was gay. He previously worked for the Rockefeller and Ford Foundations, known for bankrolling pro-gay programs. They have gay networks and allegiances that few decent people know about. Look at Hollywood, for God's sake."

"This is God's vengeance," shouted Ruth Peterson, throwing her hands up. "This is God's vengeance! This is God's vengeance!" she cried louder, standing up and swaying her upward-thrust arms, reaching for the Almighty.

12

CABLE AND NETWORK news programs on Sunday night covered the events of the day, focusing their air time on the "ACLU Bombing," as it was being called on one cable network. Another network termed it "Terror by the Bay."

All the news programs had gripping orchestral music to accompany their segment programming titles. Notwithstanding the great music, they all reported an overwhelming number of calls and e-mails and tweets saying, in effect, that the ACLU got what it deserved. Voters on Internet polls validated those messages by affirming those sentiments and overwhelmingly agreeing that the ACLU had brought this on itself.

E-mails from viewers included bizarre and laughable statements such as "God is *gay*. She called her people home in SF," and "Unborn 400, ACLU 0," referring to the number of ACLU staff and guests killed, and so on.

Not all the e-mails were of this nature, however. Many offered solace and sympathy to those who had lost loved ones, as well as prayers for those who died and for those left behind.

One person thought it ironic that people were praying for the ACLU staffers and their supporters who died. That person said, "Hey, pray for the millions of babies murdered since Roe v. Wade;

pray for the victims of sexual predators and child molesters—all clients of the ACLU. But do not pray for the ACLU. Let them burn in hell."

Cable news programs, with their hired pundits, commented on the press conference and the ensuing investigation. One of the pundits, a former police commissioner of New York City, said, "This will be a very difficult investigation. Here's what we know so far, and it's not much: One. This was no accident; therefore, this is a criminal investigation. Period. End of story.

"Two. The investigation teams aren't certain of the location of the explosive device, but they believe it must have been in the back of the restaurant to achieve maximum forward force, given the design of the building. This was an old building. All of the walls were extremely thick—four to five feet thick along some walls. Two of the walls, one in back and one on the side, had earth behind them, and the other two did not. The blast blew out the latter two walls. Knowing where the bomb was located might provide a clue regarding who placed it there and how it might have been hidden…who would have had access. That sort of thing.

"Three. They haven't said it yet, but they are thinking a special type of nuclear weapon must have been used. Why? Because no conventional weapon, like dynamite, plastic explosives, et cetera, would have been so extraordinarily destructive. My sources tell me there was a trace of radioactivity, but it wasn't life threatening to the first responders when it was measured. The first responders have been checked by medical professionals, just in case there was some dangerous exposure, but nothing negative has been reported. Believe me, this—in and of itself—is extraordinary. This suggests a very sophisticated tactical nuclear weapon. Not a dirty bomb by any means.

"But, incredibly, these are not the only reasons why this investigation will be so difficult. It will be difficult because of the people who were killed and, of course, the organization itself: the ACLU. There could be any one of a thousand reasons why someone or some group would want to harm the ACLU or the people at that party. For starters, don't forget the role the ACLU played in the aftermath of the Roe v. Wade decision and its continuing defense of abortion on demand. I saw the footage of the protestors outside the restaurant that night. One of them had a sign that said: 'Since Roe v. Wade, fifty million children killed.' You know, there could be a vendetta on this one issue alone."

The host of the news program probed further into ACLU matters. "Do you think the fact that the ACLU had an openly gay man at the helm might have had anything to do with this?"

"Well, I certainly hope not. I mean, if you think of it in those terms, then approximately four hundred ninety-nine people died to take out one person. However, it is interesting that this explosion happened in the most gay-friendly city in the nation."

"And don't forget that the gay Episcopal bishop from New England was in attendance at this Separation of Church and State gala," a panel member stated, just letting it hang out there.

"What might be some other issues, if you were to speculate?" asked the host, ignoring the fact that they were all engaged in speculation.

"Boy Scouts; separation of church and state in all its forms—from removing the Ten Commandments from public buildings to removing a cross from the flag of the City of Los Angeles to keeping prayer out of schools—pornography, the ACLU calls for protection of even child pornography; promoting abortion on demand," another panelist pundit said, as if thoughtfully ticking off motives, one after another.

"It's God. It's about God. It's so obvious. Here it is, just a few weeks before Christmas. A recent survey showed that more than sixty-seven percent of this country's population believe that Jesus was born to the Virgin Mary in Bethlehem on or about this day, and the rest of the story—as they say—is history, religious history. Maybe somebody didn't like the ACLU screwing up their Christmas. I've got to say, having a Separation of Church and State Gala in San Francisco right before Christmas, man, that's asking for trouble," the host observed.

13

AT THE OFFICES of *L'Osservatore Romano*, the global affairs and press office of the Vatican, Stefano Del Alba copied a variety of American media articles covering the ACLU explosion. He arranged them in chronological order, placed them in a folder, and had a messenger take them to the papal residence.

Vatican City, along with Singapore and Monaco, is one of three remaining city-states in the world, after Great Britain turned Hong Kong over to China in 1997. The *Stato della Città del_Vaticano,* or the State of Vatican City, is where the universal government and administration of the Roman Catholic Church is located.

Vatican City, while having its own geographical territory and its own army—however small—exists within the larger geographical boundary of Rome, Italy, pursuant to a treaty signed in 1929. At less than a square mile, with fewer than one thousand residents, Vatican City is the smallest country in the world by area and by population.

In addition to St. Peter's Square, the Basilica of St. Peter, the Sistine Chapel and the Apostolic Palace, there are numerous other buildings within the walls of Vatican City, including its own radio station, press and media offices, libraries and museums, gardens, other churches and chapels, and barracks for the Swiss Guard, the army of Vatican City. Most importantly, this is where the Pope lives.

The Pope, the head of the Roman Catholic Church, traces his authority directly back to St. Peter, the apostle to whom Jesus Christ entrusted his church. *Tu es Petrus, et super hanc petram aedificabo eccelesiam meam*...That church, now over one billion souls strong and spread around the globe, is his responsibility. Tonight, the 265th pope in two thousand years sat at his desk in the papal apartment in the Vatican, sipping hot tea and eating a biscuit. He was alone...and lonely with his thoughts.

Could John Paul have set this in motion, Benedict wondered? Although he was close to Pope John Paul II, his predecessor to the throne of St. Peter, Benedict knew that John Paul had his secrets. Was this one of them?

Looking out over St. Peter's Square, Pope Benedict remembered that time decades ago when he first walked into the square. At that time he was a well-respected theology professor from Regensburg University in Germany. His very first glimpse of St. Peter's Basilica from the far end of the square rendered him speechless.

What brought Benedict to Rome those decades ago was a request from his bishop in Germany to assist him in planning for, and attending, the Second Vatican Ecumenical Council in 1962. The Council was convoked by Pope John XXIII, who died shortly after the Council began, leaving it to his successor, Pope Paul VI, to manage the Council to its conclusion. "More like *mismanage* it," Benedict thought.

As Benedict continued to gaze out the window, he wished he could do it all over again. If *only* he could do it over again. He would do it differently. At that time he didn't have any power, but he also didn't have many cares. Surely, he could have done something to make a difference, to change the course. Instead, it was he who had changed—and all for the greater glory of God, no doubt. Chewing on his biscuit, he considered his life then and compared it to his life now: fifty years later. Now what was he?

The leader of the Roman Catholic Church.

Was he still excited about God and God's creatures? Or was he burdened by endless arguments inside these walls, outside these walls, and all over the world?

Burdened?

Why had that word popped into his head, he wondered? "Is it a burden to do that which God has chosen for you? But did God choose this for me? Or did I? Or did *they*?"

Benedict believed that the church of his youth and early priesthood was far different from the one he now presided over. His old church had absolutes, he thought. Absolute moral values. Absolute beliefs. He wanted to dial back the clock to those old days because he believed that those days were better, although he was very much alone in that regard. *There is no going back, his advisors told him.*

At the time of his election to the Throne of St. Peter by his peers in the College of Cardinals, he was one of only three cardinals in the conclave who had not been given his red hat by John Paul. Yet, they elected him. Why? Well, he knew the real—and hardly secret—reason why: because he was very old. Those who elected him were betting on the actuarial tables that he wouldn't live very long, just long enough to give those cardinals with ambition to become pope more time to politick before his death and the subsequent papal conclave to elect a successor.

"The *next* conclave," he laughed to himself. Whereas John Paul was elected pope at a young fifty-eight years of age and lived until age eighty-four, he, Benedict, was elected pope at age seventy-eight. How many more years were left in him?

Now, at age eighty-one, Benedict was spry, alert, and intelligent. Nevertheless, the calendar worked against him. If only he could live another twenty years; that might be enough time to nudge the church into a different direction. Optimistic by nature, Benedict forged ahead with the difficult task of returning the church to what it once was.

If only he had more time.

Sipping his tea, he reflected further. He had come to Rome during the pontificate of another cardinal who was very old when he was elected pope, the thought being that he would be a caretaker pope until better candidates could work out their differences before the next conclave. Cardinal Angelo Roncalli, a jovial, portly man from the Archdiocese of Venice, became Pope John XXIII at the age of eighty-three. The world loved him. And why not? He was very humble and lovable—and exceedingly liberal, a socialist to his bones. However, rather than being the caretaker pope his electors expected him to be, he initiated the most sweeping systemic liturgical and theological changes in the church in almost a thousand years.

"What a disaster they turned out to be," thought Benedict. Too bad Pope John wasn't a bit less jovial and a bit more realistically intelligent at the time, and too bad his successor as pope—another Italian socialist—felt the need to continue John's directives, ultimately causing incalculable damage to the worldwide church, Benedict fervently believed.

"Where was God when we needed him?" Benedict wondered. "Why did God let them ruin his church?"

There was a knock on the door.

"Your Holiness?"

"Please come in."

The messenger entered and handed the folder of news clippings to Benedict, who began reading immediately, even before the messenger was out the door.

After a few minutes, he put down the clippings and rubbed one hand over his eyes and forehead. Looking up at the ceiling, Benedict wondered if the investigation in the United States would lead to the Vatican.

Drinking the last drop of his tea, the Pope stood up. It was crystal clear to him. The explosion in California was not the Holy Spirit working in mysterious ways. Such would be wishful thinking. No, this decidedly had the mark of one man, John Paul, reaching out from the grave with a vengeance.

Benedict smiled, thinking that being old might not be so bad after all.

14

THE MOOD IN the national headquarters office of the ACLU was somber because virtually all the senior people, including the executive director, had been killed in San Francisco.

Small groups of workers conversed in front of empty offices and cubicles, talking about the explosion in San Francisco and wondering if they were safe in New York. Though they all had work to do, they could not focus, preferring to yield to group depression and dismay.

The director of human resources, Donna Packer, walked around the floor trying to console and motivate the staffers she encountered, even though she herself was despondent.

It had been early Sunday morning when she received the call from FBI agents notifying her of the explosion and asking for information about the guest list. She had asked the agents to meet with her this morning when the other senior manager in the office, Angela Carr, would be available.

When she called Carr Sunday afternoon regarding the FBI request to interview them, Carr called in private lawyers to be present and advise them. She didn't have to go far for legal talent. The ACLU national headquarters is located at 125 Broad Street in lower Manhattan in a forty-story building, more than two-thirds of which housed the principal office of a large national law firm. This law firm, like many across the county, offered its hard-charging young associates and junior partners the opportunity to do pro bono legal work on behalf of the ACLU.

Angela Carr, Donna Packer, Esteban Gutierrez, Joel Wachter and Alicia George sat on one side of the table in the conference room next to the empty executive director's office. On the other side were FBI agents Lloyd Brewer, Orrin Mayes and Frank Scordich, ready to interview the ACLU employees to find out anything that might be helpful in their investigation of the San Francisco bombing.

As the parties settled in for the meeting, Scordich commented, "This is really a great view," referring to the conference room's location overlooking the East River. Helicopters flew in and out of the heliport across the road, and ferries moved to and from the ferry terminals next to the helipad. "You must be paying top dollar per square foot for this place at the tip of Manhattan," he said.

Ignoring his remarks, Angela Carr introduced herself as the director of administration of the national headquarters. She then introduced Donna Packer, the director of human resources and Esteban Gutierrez, the late executive director's administrative assistant. She also introduced Joel Wachter and Alicia George from Parton and Crownell, outside legal counsel to the ACLU.

After the FBI contingent introduced themselves, the lead agent, Lloyd Brewer, said, "Thank you for meeting with us so soon after many of your friends and colleagues lost their lives in the explosion on the West Coast. We're sorry for your loss. The reason we are here today is simple: we need information to help us in this investigation. When I called Ms. Packer yesterday she was kind enough to arrange this meeting for us to ask you some questions and get some more information. I would like to start with Ms. Carr."

"Agent Brewer, if I may," interjected Joel Wachter, "we appreciate your efforts to investigate this tragedy, and we will do whatever we can to assist you. However, my client has never viewed the FBI as its friend. In some instances, I may tell someone not to answer.

"Further, I know that you and the other agents here will be asking for documents and other written information. We will not provide you with any written information without a court order providing absolute specificity to your document request."

Agent Brewer responded, "Thank you. We will not be getting a court order to do our job. It's an odd request, but if the ACLU does not wish to cooperate, so be it. However, since we are here we would like to ask some questions, subject to your role as legal advisor to these people. Do you have any objection?"

"Go right ahead."

Agent Brewer faced Angela Carr. "Ms. Carr, what is your job? What duties do you have?"

Angela Carr recited her job description. Essentially, she was the chief administrative officer at the national level. She also worked with local field-office administrative directors in each chapter across the country.

"How long have you been in this position?"

"About five years."

"Ms. Carr, you helped the San Francisco office coordinate this fund raiser, is that right?"

"Yes."

"What did you do?"

"Wait, wait," interjected Wachter. "It sounds like you are taking a deposition, not a statement. Why not ask her what she knows about the events in San Francisco?"

Brewer ignored Wachter. "Please, go on," he said to Angela Carr.

"Every year, or at least every year for the past six or seven years, this was the biggest annual fund raiser we had. We cosponsored it with the local office in San Francisco, although they did most of the work: finding a location, arranging menus and entertainment, and providing us with their suggested list of invitees. Our office added other people to the list and arranged for national media exposure."

"Do you have files on all the invitees? Any background information? Their past and current contributions?"

Wachter tapped his fingers on the table, indicating his disgust at the pace and the questions.

"We have a list of invitees, similar in many respects to what the local office in San Francisco has. However, I don't think that we have to share that list with you," stated Ms. Carr.

"Look, we are here to help you. Well, maybe not help you as much as to ask you for your help in solving this crime."

Again Wachter interjected forcefully, "No, you look. Just saying you are here to help us doesn't actually make it so. Ms. Carr has experienced a significant loss, as have all these other fine folks. Again, this isn't a deposition. You don't need to burden these people with background questions that have no relevance to your stated purpose for being here. Get to the point."

"What did you do before coming to work here?"

"I was deputy chief administrative officer for the Rockefeller Foundation."

"How long did you work there?"

"Ten years."

"After that?"

"I came to work here."

"Why weren't you in San Francisco?"

"Are you accusing me of something, Agent Brewer? I lost many good friends in the explosion. And why didn't I die? Well, it might have been preferable to sitting here, answering your inane questions while picking up after people I—we—loved and admired," she responded indignantly.

Brewer sat stunned for a second, not anticipating this reaction. Angela Carr looked demure and soft. She was dressed conservatively in a dark skirt, white blouse, and a simple pearl necklace. She was also very pretty. And obviously tough.

"I apologize, Ms. Carr, if I appeared insensitive. But I just needed to know why you were not in San Francisco."

Wachter raised his hand and interjected, "I think we are done here, Agent Brewer. You and your colleagues can leave now."

Agent Brewer turned his attention to Angela Carr, saying, "Since you are the most senior person here, I guess you are, de facto, in charge."

Carr quickly informed Brewer that she was leaving the ACLU. Thursday would be her last day.

"Really? Are you going to work somewhere else?"

"Not right away. My plan is to travel the world for a while."

"When did you make the decision to leave?"

"I gave Miguel my notice of resignation six weeks ago."

"I see," Brewer said. "Well, I guess until a new person takes your place, you are still in charge of the office. So, we are recommending twenty-four-hour security for you until some future date. We can provide it or NYPD can do it."

"Thank you, but no thanks," Carr replied. "Our policy is clear on that topic. We maintain our own security."

"We have trained agents or local police who will provide security. You might wish to reconsider."

"The answer is *no*. There are protocols that require us to maintain our own security. We don't need any security from the FBI or the police."

15

AFTER THE FBI agents left, Angela Carr went to Donna Packer's office to talk about the awful events of the weekend.

"I envy you," Packer commented, "You are on your way out of here. I might have to follow."

"This is a terrible time, I know," answered Carr. "I can't believe what happened. It's surreal. Later this morning the new hire, Brandon Hughes, will be here. He plans to shadow me for the next few days, and then he'll be on his own."

"And you will be out of here. It won't be the same," smiled Packer. "You hired me, and now you leave. Take me with you."

Carr laughed. "Donna, you are the best thing that ever happened to this place. Now you are the most important person. You can't leave. But I can." With that, Angela stood up, embraced Donna Packer and left her office.

• • •

Sitting in her own office behind closed doors, Carr did some deep breathing exercises to calm herself. Even though the offices were chilly every Monday morning in the winter, she could feel perspiration on her back and under her arms. Her stomach quivered, and she felt faint. She bent over in pain.

After a few minutes, she stood up slowly and walked to the window that looked out toward Battery Park and the Hudson River beyond. The explosion in San Francisco had shocked her. She worried that what she did *here* may have resulted in the murder of five hundred people. How could she live with that? She had only wanted to show the information to her brother...because she needed to share it with someone...because it was devastating...because it was so harmful...because it was so evil.

Only a burst of willpower had gotten her to work that morning. "Four days left," she thought. "Four days until I am out of here.

"Will I make it?

"Who is left to kill me?"

16

BLAKE WASTED NO time. He had made his decision, and he acted on it immediately. There was no difficulty in packing to return to the United States. He sold everything, and what didn't sell he gave away or threw away—everything, that is, except his personal items and anything to do with his wife and son.

His flight on American Airlines took him to Miami, where he changed planes for a short flight to Ronald Reagan Washington National Airport. After he retrieved his checked bag, he rented a car and drove to the cemetery where his wife, child, and parents were buried. Even though it was a brisk wintry day, and all he had on were jeans and a cotton sweatshirt, he spent time at each grave site praying and wishing his family was still alive.

"What now?" he thought. He could go to his sister's house and surprise her, but he thought better of that plan. What he really needed to do was decompress. Here he was in DC, a place with recent bad memories. He needed to walk around, get used to the activity in the nation's capital, and begin to blend in, if possible.

Blake drove to Pentagon City, checked into the Ritz Carlton there, and settled in for the rest of the day and night. The next morning, he drove to the mall and purchased all he needed *to succeed in business*, he laughed to himself. Suits, shirts, shoes and everything else for business attire and business casual. The suits needed tailoring. He requested that it be done on an expedited basis: two days. He also bought casual clothing appropriate for the season.

Next, he contacted a realtor friend to find a rental unit, maybe a townhouse with a garage. A garage? He needed a car. After speaking to his realtor, Blake drove to the closest auto mall to check out vehicles. He leased a top-of-the-line Honda Accord for one year… because he wasn't certain how long he would stay. The dealership returned Blake's rental car, and he drove away in his new car.

The realtor called with listings. Blake liked the third place he visited. It was fully furnished, had an attached garage, and was in a nice residential area of Georgetown. He leased it immediately…for one year.

Blake moved in the next day, even though there was some maintenance pending. He had no hangers for his clothing, so he bought hangers at the local drugstore and off-loaded the clothes in the master closet. He ordered bundled services for television and Internet. Then he called his sister at work.

17

THE SIX PEOPLE who comprised the ultrasecret ACLU Select Board of Trustees looked at each other around the polished, burled walnut table in the conference room on the thirty-third floor in the law offices of Parton and Crownell. Sitting with them was a person who was not a select trustee. He was a union man. No one from the law firm was present.

Each of the trustees privately concluded that no one at this table was suitable for the task at hand, even though one of them had to assume the responsibility for that task, nevertheless. How it was done, or by whom, was of little consequence to them—provided something was done expeditiously and covertly and did not involve them personally.

When the voice started to speak, they turned their attention to the futuristic-looking conference phone in the center of the table.

"We cannot trust anyone, I am sorry to say," said the disembodied voice through the phone. "This is our reality. Now we must tend to business. Our very survival presses us into immediate action. Now is not the time to be squeamish. Now is the time to strike back!"

Click. The line went dead.

The tall, supremely confident Ford Foundation president, Taylor Morris, locked eyes with the patrician law professor, Justin Lowell, and commented, "We should have expected this," as if pointing an accusatory finger at Lowell.

Before The Law Professor could respond, the youngest person in the room, Andrew DuPont, disagreed. "No, no, you are wrong," he said to Morris, who leaned back in his chair, as if actually considering the remote possibility that he could, indeed, be wrong.

"Who could have anticipated something like this? It is absurd to argue about it. Besides, we all agreed on the strategy. And, for a while, it seemed to work, didn't it?" Who could have anticipated this?" DuPont repeated. "The answer is *no one*."

Over tortoise-shell framed reading glasses, The Law Professor peered at his young ally and responded, "Of course we could not have expected this! To think otherwise is madness." Turning toward Taylor Morris, he repeated, "Madness."

"Yes, of course, it is madness. And, yes, of course, we could not have anticipated it, as you say, whether it be true or not. But here we are, suffering the consequences of something none of us anticipated. What do we do? Theoretically, I suppose, we have numerous options but, realistically, I suspect our options are quite limited. Wouldn't you agree?" said Valerie Cole-Williams, dean of Harvard Law School.

All heads nodded slightly.

"Options," she continued. "What are our options?"

The Rockefeller Foundation president, W. Nash Rawlins, said, "Negotiation may still be possible, although I am not certain with whom anymore."

"Negotiation? Really?" The Law Professor responded. "You must be joking. Five hundred people were killed: ours and everyone else in the blast area. Does this appear to be a tactic to get us to some imaginary negotiation table? To me, this is a slice of Hiroshima or Nagasaki. Unconditional surrender...*after* the devastation—that's what this is all about. That is what they want. Frankly, there may be more of this coming. None of us could be safe from now on."

"Well, if that is the case, then where are the terms of surrender?" asked Claire Holder Kaufman, dean of Columbia Law School. "Nothing. No contact, whatsoever. Maybe this is something else. Maybe these are different people. We don't know."

The Law Professor leaned forward in his chair. He took off his glasses for effect, as if he were going to make a closing argument, and said, "Desperate times, desperate measures. They know who we are. They know where we live. They know where we work. Any one of us could be a target. I think our options are extremely limited. But our lives and our reputations are hanging in the balance. We need to fight back!"

"What do you have in mind?" DuPont asked.

"First, we all must make certain that we have ample security around us wherever we are. Second, we must get rid of everyone who was associated with Carson Elliott. They have too much information. Enough to destroy us still."

After discussing their options, slim to none, they agreed they must retaliate quickly.

The Law Professor said, "The FBI has already started investigating our people and our offices. I, for one, am uncomfortable with this because I do not know what incriminating documents may be in any of our offices, especially here and in Washington and San Francisco. We tried to keep Miguel Torres under control, but it has been difficult. He talks too much. Well, he used to talk too much. Not anymore."

The union leader, James Farrell, said, "I agree. You do need to fight back. Let me take care of this for you." He thought to himself, "I wouldn't want any of you getting your soft hands dirty." He knew they viewed him like something they might scrape off the bottom of their shoes, but they also needed him. And that probably irked them more than his blue-collar background.

"Plausible deniability, that is what we need," The Law Professor added. "I appreciate your volunteering, Mr. Farrell."

"Justin, I think we need *two* people to manage our response," said Taylor Morris. "I recommend you and Mr. Farrell work together on our behalf."

All the others around the table eagerly nodded in agreement.

The Law Professor knew he was trapped.

18

BENEDICT HAD LUNCH with Bishop Stefan Krybesci in the Pope's private dining room. When Cardinal Karol Josef Wojtyla from Krakow became Pope John Paul II, he invited his old friend Stefan Krybesci to the Vatican to work for him, although in what capacity it was never made clear. The gossip was that John Paul missed his homeland and enjoyed speaking Polish with the bishop, confiding in him things he would never tell anyone else.

The bishop had been John Paul's closest friend since they had attended the University of Krakow. They had entered seminary together and were ordained priests. Together they fought for the church and their countrymen by opposing their Nazi masters, and then their Communist masters, at every turn—and doing it with enough finesse so that neither one landed in prison.

Bishop Krybesci had spent the last twenty-five years at the Vatican but few knew much about him. He was just one of many cardinals, bishops, monsignors, and priests meandering about. When John Paul was alive, he and the bishop took long walks together in the Vatican Gardens, sometimes even venturing outside the Vatican's walls at night. They prayed together and often ate their meals together. Inside the Vatican there was no doubt that the bishop knew more about John Paul and what he was thinking than anyone else.

After the food was served and the wait staff had left the room, Benedict got right to the point. "Stefan, no one was closer to Karol than you. It must have been such a pleasure for him to have had you here for so long. I want to ask you something about Karol." Benedict knew that the world held many vivid pictures of Pope John Paul: the vibrant, handsome, athletic, Slavic-looking, scholar-poet-actor from Krakow who became the first non-Italian pope in five centuries and who, along with Lech Walesa, Margaret Thatcher and Ronald Reagan helped defeat Communism in his native Poland and throughout Eastern Europe. John Paul was one of the most influential men of his century. The world followed him as he traveled to countless countries, more than any other pope. They knew his signature habit of kissing the ground of the host country after he emerged from his plane and had seen pictures of the millions upon millions of Catholics who attended outdoor masses. They were well-versed in his cagey ability to scold politicians in public and lecture them in private.

He was a man strong enough to survive an assassination attempt that left him in worse health than reported, but compassionate enough to meet and to forgive the captured assassin. Near the end of his days, the public saw John Paul as an old man, appearing barely lucid, clinging to his cross-shaped pastoral staff. The world witnessed a suffering pope who epitomized humankind, a man closer to heaven than earth. The world saw a giant of a man slowly dying before its eyes.

The pictures of John Paul, ravaged by Parkinson's disease, his head tilted, his eyelids half-closed, one hand trembling uncontrollably, caused some in the Vatican who opposed his policies to start a rumor campaign suggesting that he had not, in fact, been in control of the church for years. Instead, the rumors suggested it was Cardinal Joseph Ratzinger, the conservative prefect of the Congregation of the Doctrine of the Faith who was in control—the man now known to the world as Pope Benedict, John Paul's successor.

"Stefan, I agreed with Karol in all that he did for the church. We had many, many late-night sessions discussing theology and the world gone mad and the unfortunate state of the church since the Second Vatican Council, especially in America. Even though I know he had confidence in me, and I was completely loyal to him, I also know he did not tell me many things, for reasons that, perhaps, he thought made good sense at the time. Maybe he was protecting me.

"Now he is gone to our Heavenly Father, but some of the things he may have kept from me…Well, how can I say this? Some of those things of which I know nothing may become serious problems for the church…and for me. Do you understand, Stefan?"

Bishop Krybesci weighed less than one hundred pounds. Ever since John Paul's death, he needed a wheelchair for transportation, always with an attendant pushing it. He suffered from a multitude of medical problems. He wanted to die, but death refused to come to him.

The bishop had no facility with languages, although he could speak some German, Benedict's native tongue. It made no difference, however, since old age and debility caused the bishop to garble his speech, no matter what the language. Sometimes his syntax made no sense or he would only say a few seemingly illogical words. His Italian doctors shrugged their medical shoulders and said it was old age. What could they do?

So he would not slump in his wheelchair, the bishop's attendants placed pillows on each side of him, propping him up. One pillow must have given way because the Bishop tilted to the left. Through rheumy eyes, the bishop tried to focus on Benedict's face.

Benedict wasn't sure if the bishop even heard what he just said. The bishop, for inexplicably vain reasons, refused to wear a much-needed hearing aid.

"Stefan…" Benedict started again, pushing the pillow back into place.

Interrupting Benedict, the bishop mumbled in a mixture of German, Polish and spit, "Satan…in America."

Benedict listened intently, lowering his head to hear the Bishop better. "Stefan, listen to me! What are you saying?"

"Fatima."

"Satan? Fatima?" Benedict asked. "Stefan, please listen to me carefully. Did Karol do anything *to stop* Satan? Why did he mention *Fatima*?"

It was well known in the Vatican, and to Catholics around the world, that John Paul had a special devotion to the Lady of Fatima because it was on her feast day that an unsuccessful assassination attempt was made on his life. John Paul credited the Lady of Fatima for saving his life and for his recovery.

Benedict took hold of the wheelchair and moved the bishop to the window so he could look out over St. Peter's Square where lights illuminated the throngs of people still out there. He fluffed up the bishop's pillows to make him more comfortable and upright and then used a napkin to dab away drool from the bishop's lips and open mouth.

The bishop struggled to sit higher in his wheelchair. He moved his head ever so slightly, suggesting that he was trying to focus on Benedict's face. The bishop's face grimaced in pain as he tried to make his mouth, lips, and tongue work together. With considerable effort the bishop whispered, "Evil."

"Evil? What evil? What is evil?" Benedict leaned close to the bishop's ear and said, "Karol told you that Satan is in America? Is that it? Is that what is evil? Is America evil?"

With eyes half-closed, the bishop looked at Benedict, as if he were trying to convey a message.

Benedict continued, hoping to keep the bishop focused a bit longer, "Did Karol do anything about...Satan?"

Bishop Krybesci closed his eyelids so tight that tears squeezed out. His forehead scrunched up to show waves of wrinkles belying his age. Eyes still shut, the bishop whispered painfully, "America."

Benedict looked at the bishop, who now seemed to be sleeping. After a few minutes waiting for the bishop to wake up, Benedict called to have the bishop taken back to his residence and to have his untouched food removed.

After the bishop left, Benedict sat down and closed his eyes to think. Was there any reason to believe what the bishop said? In fact, did the bishop even know what he was saying? Satan in America. What did that mean?

Benedict knew the concerns John Paul had about America. The church needed the United States for the money Americans donated so that the church could continue its mission of helping the poor. Without America where would the money come from? America was the world's most generous nation. Unfortunately, the Vatican never did fully comprehend the devastating impact of the many episodes of sexual misconduct by priests in the United States and the adverse financial consequences to the church as a result.

The fallout in America would have been worse if Americans had discovered that it was Pope John XXIII—the lovable, jovial pontiff they adored—who ordered bishops and cardinals to hide their predator priests and to cover up the messes they had caused. That was in 1961.

According to financial advisors in the Vatican, the church in America had paid more than $5 billion in settlements and jury awards stemming from the perverse sexual appetites of its priests and bishops. Moreover, and quite apart from the money paid in legal reparations, donations to the church from American Catholics declined significantly. Not only did the church have to pay extraordinary damages for the unforgivable conduct of its priests and bishops, but the collection plates were now nearly empty because Americans had become so disgusted with the way the church handled the sexual-abuse issues that they stopped donating to it.

Benedict focused his eyes on the opposite wall, on the simple crucifix—the penultimate symbol of Christianity—given to him by his father when he was ordained a priest in his native Germany. With the way of the cross came redemption: the Son of God dying to save mankind.

Benedict wondered whether it made any sense. To save mankind from what? From evil? From Satan? From itself? There was a constant battle: good versus evil. "Even with God on our side, why is the battle always so close?" Benedict thought. "But is God really on our side? If so, why would God allow so much evil in the world?" There were many questions, few answers, lots of dogma.

Satan in America. Benedict wondered what the Bishop was trying to tell him.

Fatima. What was he to make of it?

19

BENEDICT APPROACHED HIS faith intellectually. He did not spend much time considering the validity of miracles or apparitions or extrasensory observations like his predecessor John Paul had.

Benedict requested all archival information regarding Fatima.

• • •

The story began on May 13, 1917, in Fatima, Portugal, when three children—Lucia Santos and her cousins Jacinta and Francisco Marto—were guarding sheep and praying the rosary together. According to the children, Mary, the Mother of God, appeared before them six times during that year, on the thirteenth day of six consecutive months, telling them things that later became known as the *Secrets of Fatima*.

The so-called Secrets were alleged prophecies Mary told to the three children in 1917 and were written down—but not revealed—by Lucia Santos at the request of the local bishop. There were three secrets. The First Secret was a vision of hell described by Mary. It was a plea for prayer to avoid the pain of hell.

The Second Secret predicted the trouble Russia would cause the world as it became a totalitarian Communist country and the state sponsor of millions of deaths. In addition, the Second Secret prophesied another World War.

The Third Secret was not read until the year 1960. Pope John XXIII was the first pope to read the Third Secret, but he chose not to reveal it. Instead, he put it back into a vault inside the Vatican. His action only inflamed interest in the mystery. Surely, it had to be bad news, many thought, otherwise why not reveal it? After all, the other two secrets had already been revealed.

There were many who suspected that the Third Secret foretold the destruction of the church, from within, during the sixth decade of the twentieth century.

The Second Vatican Council—the purpose of which was *to modernize* the church—opened in 1962. John XXIII died at the very beginning of the four-year council. The next pope—Paul VI, elected in 1963—managed the Council to its closing. He read the Third Secret in 1966, after the close of the Council but he, too, did not reveal it.

Some believed that the Third Secret also prophesied the murder of a pope. So when an assassination attempt was made on Pope John Paul II on May 13, 1981, which was the feast day of the Lady of Fatima, many believed this event was the realization of that prophecy.

Benedict read the file on Fatima. He knew that, for centuries, the hierarchy of the church has had to deal with the ranting and raving of Mary worshippers and promoters who wanted to capitalize on such apparition opportunities. Each pope, when presented with factual details, found the stories difficult to believe and, generally, gave them no credence. Presumably, that is how his immediate predecessors reacted when they ignored the contents of this Third Secret of Fatima—or they understood fully, and chose to keep the contents from being made public.

Pope John Paul would definitely have understood the meaning of the Third Secret because of his experience as a priest in Poland before, and after, the Second World War. John Paul knew, firsthand, the horrific evil described in the Third Secret: first, the Nazis and then the Communists—systemic evil on a monumental scale, layer upon layer. Pervasive. Insidious. Soulless. Depressing. Destructive.

Benedict himself understood the appeal of such evil if properly propagandized to the masses. He was German, after all. He had grown up under the Nazis. He witnessed their brand of evil: an evil so seductive, so charming, manipulative and disarming that it permeated all of German life; an evil that abetted the organized murder of millions of Jews, Catholics, and others, while the citizens of Germany closed their eyes and shut their minds to this wickedness in their midst, until their national denial destroyed them all.

It occurred to him that he might be the only person alive who knew the Third Secret. Everyone else who had read it was dead, including the writer herself. Benedict asked himself, "Is it really a *secret* at all? Is it really *credible*?" All of this Fatima belief was predicated on an unverifiable apparition and the words of three children with too much time on their hands while tending sheep and goats, day and night. But wasn't that what made it so compelling and, in the end, utterly believable? How could the children have even imagined these prophecies? They were virtually illiterate and clueless. How would they even know there was a country named Russia, for example…or America?

Benedict scrunched his eyelids tighter. He could feel his heart beat faster. He wondered, "Am I actually considering this *credible*… and not just the fantasies of bored children spending too many nights alone, staring at the night sky, praying the rosary, and making up stories?"

20

CHATSWORTH, CALIFORNIA, IS in the San Fernando Valley of the greater Los Angeles metropolitan area. It boasts more pornography studios and adult entertainment distribution centers than any place in the United States. To say that pornography is big business in Chatsworth is an understatement. There are economists and analysts who speculate about such things, but annual revenue from porn can never be accurately verified. Some experts estimate that worldwide porn revenues exceed $90 billion annually, with annual revenues in the United States in the $40–$50 billion range. Much of it generated here, in one manner or another.

Porn profit margins are huge because expenses to produce pornography are minimal. Imagine what the profit margins in the auto industry would be if the auto companies did not have to manufacture a car but rather started with a car already built that they had only to market and distribute.

In the porn business, female and male bodies show up for work fully assembled, ready to titillate. Only marketing and distribution remain. And, in the porn business, there is consumer prurient interest driving sales revenue, so marketing is not a significant expense.

Three distributors annually jockey for bragging rights as the world's largest distributor of pornography. One is located in Holland, one in Thailand, and the last in Chatsworth.

The distribution/fulfillment center in Chatsworth had no brand name or logo on it, only numbers on the building denoting the address. Inside were the most modern robotic picking and packing machines in the industry, which were employed to ship sex magazines of every taste, DVDs, sex toys, sex aids, and provocative clothing throughout North and South America. In one area of the building, there were servers and related peripherals for online pornography, an explosive growth business.

Adjacent to this facility was a two-story building that also had no identifying information on it other than numbers for the address. Inside this building were office cubicles fighting for space and some perimeter offices with doors for privacy. The person occupying the biggest corner office on the second floor sat comfortably in an overstuffed leather chair on sturdy wheels, quite possibly the world's largest custom office chair. It supported an occupant who weighed close to four hundred pounds and on whom dazzled about ten pounds of gold bling and gold glitz: eccentricity fashioned into wearable jewelry. The rest of the body was the product of extreme-living, in a bad-diet sort of way.

According to the park rangers in Yellowstone National Park, the head of a bull bison weighs approximately forty pounds. This man's head came close, poundage-wise. It was a big sphere of bone, brain, and flesh. And, if he had a normal human neck, it would not have been able to support his head upright. Fortunately, his neck was also similar to a bull bison's neck.

"Where?" The Fat Man asked into the phone.

At the other end of the phone connection—also sitting in a leather chair, this one smaller and elegantly tufted with brass nailheads—was The Law Professor taking action on his pledge. Also on the conference call was the union leader, James Farrell, in his office in the District of Columbia.

"The Van Nuys Airport. We will be flying in tomorrow afternoon. We can meet on the plane. Again, I must stress that this is very important. And strictly confidential."

The morbidly obese porno man in the huge desk chair stared out the window at the small parking lot where his new pearl-white Cadillac Escalade ESV was parked. Why would this man be speaking to him if it weren't important? After all, their social circles spun in different orbits. They had never met before, although The Fat Man had previously worked with Farrell on a number of projects, some of them for the ACLU.

"What time?"

"Two o'clock."

"I will be there. Call me when you touch down."

"Please come alone."

"I go nowhere alone."

"Fine, fine, but only you will board the plane. Is that understood?"

"It is. See you tomorrow."

The Law Professor closed his eyes, thinking, "So this is how my life will end…dealing with scum."

• • •

After he rang off with The Law Professor, The Fat Man immediately called Farrell to talk to him alone. "Who the fuck is that asshole? And tell me why I should care about him giving me orders? Are you serious? What is this about?"

Farrell laughed at the outburst, while confirming that The Law Professor was an asshole, like the rest of them. He told The Fat Man to be polite and to listen to The Law Professor but not to take any action until Farrell authorized it. After all, it was Farrell who would be giving The Fat Man his marching orders *and* his money.

• • •

After Farrell and The Fat Man finished their discussion, Farrell sat at the desk in his office and looked out the window. He regretted working with these ACLU clowns. When times were flush, they were all right, although still puffing themselves up like proud little peacocks. But when things got dicey, they acted like circus cops, running in circles and crashing into each other. The worst one was genuinely crazy, he thought. It was his deepest regret letting her talk the others into killing the only man who could help them now. What a stupid mistake. But it had been personal for her. Now look at the mess they were in.

21

WASHINGTON, DC, IS the seat of federal power in the United States. Here, the three branches of the federal government coexist uneasily: Congress (the legislative branch); the president and his administration and all the agencies of government (the executive branch); and the Supreme Court and all subordinate affiliated federal courts (the judicial branch). In a manner of speaking, DC was one-stop shopping for lobbyists, lawyers, litigants, and liars.

The ACLU of the National Capital Area occupied offices in a nice, mixed-use neighborhood near one of the most reviled traffic roundabouts in the District of Columbia, Dupont Circle.

The two FBI agents opened the door to the office and walked into a crowded area filled with office cubicles, reams of paper in stacks and bankers' boxes, and plenty of wall posters. A tall, thin man with gray hair pulled into a ponytail sat at the only desk in the reception area.

"May I help you?" he asked without looking up from his computer screen.

"We called earlier. I am FBI Agent McMahon and this is Agent Timmons. We scheduled an appointment with Mr. Jeffords. Is he here?"

Robert Jeffords poked his head around the wall of his cubicle, which was behind the backs of the two FBI Agents and said, "Here I am."

The agents turned away from the desk and the ponytail man. What they saw almost caused them to laugh, but they struggled to maintain straight faces. In front of them was a large man wearing a bright-blue short-sleeve shirt, brown pants, black socks, and scuffed black dress shoes. His long, stringy gray hair looked unwashed, and his face sported gray and black stubble. Perched crookedly on his nose were thick, bluish-tinted glasses, the left lens fractured with half of it missing.

"Mr. Jeffords," Agent McMahon said, maintaining his professional demeanor. "Thank you for meeting with us."

"Please come and sit," said Jeffords, as he swept his arm toward two chairs crammed inside his cubicle.

Agent McMahon told Mr. Jeffords that the FBI was visiting every ACLU field office, plus the headquarters in New York, as part of the investigation that had just started. He said that the ACLU Legislative Office, only a few blocks away, refused to answer any questions or to share any documents. They had referred the agents to this office.

Outside, the afternoon weather grew more threatening. Where the chilly morning had offered sun, the afternoon only had enveloping winter clouds, bloated with the promise of freezing rain. It was a few minutes past three o'clock.

When the agents started to ask Mr. Jeffords questions, he immediately deferred, saying that the agents had to talk to the new head of the office, Margaret Reading, an ACLU senior staff lawyer from Santa Monica, California, who had just arrived.

Jeffords escorted the FBI agents down a cluttered hallway to her office. With her was another staff attorney, Henry Waxler.

"Thank you for meeting with us," offered Agent McMahon. "I am Agent Terry McMahon, and this is Agent Debbie Timmons. We are visiting all the ACLU chapter offices to gather information that may prove helpful in investigating the explosion in California."

Reading's face had a ruddy complexion that screamed rosacea. She wore round, rimless glasses, perched on the bridge of an expansive nose. Her wrinkled pantsuit smelled like it had been cured over a tobacco fire. Her gravelly voice suggested a three-pack-a-day smoker.

"Look, I just walked in the door, literally. I left Los Angeles yesterday afternoon in a hurry to get here to help out. I realize that you are trying to do your job, but so am I. At the moment, however, I just don't have the time to be helpful. And, to be honest, I just don't appreciate you being here to snoop around while we are still in mourning and trying to pick up the pieces."

Reading was a former nun who went to law school later in life. The natural aggression that forced her out of the convent turned into a valuable attribute in her role as a lawyer intent on rooting out any discrimination—real or imagined—against gays and lesbians. She was universally disliked by associates and adversaries. She knew it. So why pretend to be nice?

Agent McMahon studied her for a few seconds before responding. "I apologize for the timing. Our original appointment was with Mr. Jeffords, but he referred us to you."

Reading's blouse collar was open and above the second button a gold cross on a delicate rope chain hung. McMahon thought it incongruous that someone working for the ACLU would wear a cross, but he caught himself before going down a prejudicial path that years of experience and sensitivity training cautioned him to avoid.

"I really do not have time to talk to you today…or any day in the foreseeable future," Reading said.

McMahon sucked in a deep breath, allowing him some time to respond. He considered himself a professional lawman. He also had two teenagers at home who routinely probed the limits of his patience. "Why is it," he asked himself, "that I still have difficulty with certain people?" He answered his own question: "Because certain people are jerks, no matter what their gender. *And what is her gender anyway*?" he joked to himself.

"I understand. But one more thing, let us provide security for your office," he offered.

"No."

"Local police then," McMahon said.

Reading looked at him dismissively. "What part of *no* do you not understand?"

22

FATHER JAMES WALSH led Markus Roist to a private library in the *Curia Generalizia*, the international headquarters of the Society of Jesus, located only a few blocks from St. Peter's Basilica. Father Walsh, one of four principal assistants to the superior general, and the only American, asked Roist if he cared for something to drink. Roist declined and sat down in a familiar leather chair. Father Walsh left.

As Roist waited, he thought, "Had I become a priest, I would have become a Jesuit [as the members of the Society of Jesus were known]. No doubt in my mind. These are men of action—intellectual, certainly, but men of action always."

He knew the history of the Society of Jesus. The Jesuits were devoted to education. No other religious order operated as many colleges and universities as the Society of Jesus, numbering approximately one hundred twenty worldwide, with twenty-eight in the United States. They also operated two hundred secondary schools worldwide, with fifty-eight in the United States.

The history of the Catholic Church would inform you that the Jesuits saved the church from near extinction in Europe during the period of the Protestant Reformation in the sixteenth and seventeenth centuries by initiating a successful Catholic counter-reformation. In fact, they came into existence for that very purpose.

The Jesuits engaged in intellectual battles in Europe against the Protestants, and everywhere in the world, on behalf of the Pope.

Because of its power and influence throughout the church, and its mastery of church politics, the Society of Jesus stood alone at the pinnacle of importance of all religious orders. For this reason, the superior general of the Society of Jesus was often referred to as the Black Pope, not solely because of the black cassock he wore in contrast to the white cassock worn by the Pope, but because of his powerful influence in the church. Many inside the church believed the power and influence of the superior general was second only to that of the Pope.

No other religious order in the Catholic Church was as admired, vilified, envied, hated, praised and cursed by people inside and outside of the church—and none was as critically necessary to the preservation of the church—as was the Society of Jesus.

All three hundred religious orders in the church require their members to take vows of poverty, chastity, and obedience. Poverty refers to having no personal ownership of property, in favor of communal assets. Chastity refers to celibacy, no conjugal relationships. Obedience refers to each individual giving up his or her desires for personal fulfillment in order to follow the rules of their religious order and the church.

Because of the special relationship between the Pope and the Society of Jesus, certain Jesuits who attained stature within their order are allowed to take a fourth vow, in addition to the required three vows of poverty, chastity and obedience. This fourth vow was to the Pope himself: a vow to do whatever the Pope asked. In every respect, these fourth-vow Jesuits were the Pope's men, loyal to the Vicar of Christ on earth. Wherever the Pope would send them, they would go immediately. Whatever he asked of them, they would do faithfully and without question.

Roist considered the current father general—a fourth-vow Jesuit. Here was a man of depth, of extraordinary intelligence and courage, with energy in his convictions and steel in his resolve. He was the perfect man to lead the Jesuits at this time—far, far better than the man he replaced.

Roist knew the story of Sabino Arana's historic appointment as superior general. The previous superior general, Diego Laynez, and his assistants believed in the unleashed liberalism enunciated in the Second Vatican Council and were opposed to Pope John Paul's conservative beliefs. Laynez had managed to turn most of the Jesuits against the Pope. As a result, the Jesuits were deliberately slow, or totally disobedient, in following the Pope's directives. Inside the church there was a war between the Black Pope and the Pope.

When Laynez suffered a severe stroke, there was the need for an election to vote in a new superior general. Laynez had already chosen his successor, a person who held the same beliefs. Although a formality, the process of calling an election required obtaining the Pope's permission to proceed. Throughout the entire history of the Jesuits, every pope had given permission. But not this time.

Rather than allow an election, John Paul appointed the new superior general himself. There was no vote and no appeal. The Pope exercised his papal authority and the Jesuits could do nothing about it. The Pope appointed Sabino Arana as the new superior general. He was a man the Pope could trust, and he was strong enough to confront and manage the leftist priests in his order.

"Yes, I would have been a Jesuit," Roist concluded as he sat in the quiet library.

Five minutes later Sabino Arana walked in. He was dressed in a simple black cassock and brilliant-white Roman collar. The twenty-ninth superior general in the history of the Society of Jesus was a tall, wiry man with an aquiline nose, black hair, black eyebrows, black eyes and a charming smile.

Roist stood to greet him. He had known Father Arana for fifteen years. They had met when Roist commanded the Swiss Guard unit protecting the pope.

"The explosion in America. It is a matter of interest for His Holiness," Arana said, using as few words as possible.

Roist nodded slightly, but he remained silent, even though his thoughts were flying in many directions. After all, it was he who placed the bomb in the restaurant. He was not certain if Arana knew that, but even if he did he likely would not mention it.

Father Arana spoke ambiguously at times, using phrases that *could be* construed a number of ways, if taken out of context. "I spoke with His Holiness this morning. He wondered about the investigation in America possibly leading here. He does not want the papacy involved."

"What would you have me do?"

"Whatever is necessary," Arana replied, giving Roist broad discretion in making his own decisions.

23

NOT FAR FROM Chatsworth is the Van Nuys Airport. It is one of the busiest general aviation airports in the world.

The Boeing Business Jet on approach carried people from the Ford Foundation, plus one law professor and one union leader. After the plane landed and taxied to the executive terminal, all the foundation people deplaned, leaving The Law Professor and the union leader on board.

"Hello?" answered The Fat Man, sitting in the backseat of his elongated Escalade.

"I am at the executive terminal. Come to the vehicle gate where a white car will meet you and you can follow that car to the plane. Park by the stairway, and come up—by yourself."

"Sure."

When the pearl-white Escalade pulled next to the plane, The Law Professor was looking out his window at the SUV. He watched as the sumo-sized man struggled to get out of the vehicle. A disgusted look spread over The Law Professor's face, as if he had eaten bad tuna. As The Fat Man sluggishly started up the stairway, The Law Professor moved forward in the cabin to greet him.

It was like a solar eclipse. The Fat Man blocked out the sunlit tarmac, casting the opening of the plane into total darkness. Removing his enormous Gucci sunglasses, The Fat Man let his pudgy pig eyes adjust to the interior light. He stuck out a ham-sized hand to shake the slender, manicured hand The Law Professor offered.

The Law Professor led The Fat Man to the club chair area of the plane where they could sit comfortably facing each other. Farrell was waiting for them. He thought The Fat Man had put on another fifty pounds since he last saw him. "How far does skin stretch?" he wondered.

There were no pleasantries exchanged. The Law Professor was barely cordial.

The Fat Man did not care about pleasantries. It was money he wanted.

While The Law Professor explained what he wanted him to do, The Fat Man was calculating how much he would request for the work. He would do it only if all the money was paid in advance.

The Law Professor could not maintain a poker face when he heard the amount. His eyes were angry, his lips were tight, and his body tensed so much that he seemed to grow taller in their midst. After a few seconds, The Law Professor got himself under control. He knew there was no negotiation. The trustees would blame him, without question, but he really had no choice in the matter.

"All right," The Law Professor agreed. "Mr. Farrell will give you the details and your money. Do not contact me ever. Work through Mr. Farrell."

That was it. No handshake. No pat on the back. No goodbye.

The Fat Man worked his way to a standing position and shook the fuselage when he waddled forward to the door. He blocked the sun at the door again before slowly descending, one step at a time, like a lumbering toddler learning how to negotiate stairs.

24

FUNERALS AND MEMORIALS across the country filled the next few days. The majority were in California and New York. Because of the celebrity and prominence of the dead, every effort was made to stagger services across the country to allow as many of the same attendees to be present, plus allow time for cable and network news programs to broadcast from as many venues as possible.

In Northern California, the governor chose to have one grand public ceremony for the state's two United States senators, the speaker of the house, congressmen, and the mayor of San Francisco, Lawrence Perry, and everyone else who died in the explosion. The nondenominational memorial service was held in front of city hall in San Francisco. The vice president of the United States attended the service in San Francisco, where he was heavily booed by the throngs of people crowding the public spaces. The president-elect, on the other hand, was wildly cheered by the same people. Other individual services throughout the city started within two hours of the service at city hall.

In Southern California, services were held in Beverly Hills, Brentwood, Hollywood, and Malibu for the actors, producers, and entertainment people killed in the blast. Because their agents and family wanted maximum exposure for their dead celebrities and loved ones to stoke residual royalties, they could not reach agreement on having one service. Instead, separate, elaborate services were held, and because many of these services overlapped, guests were pressured by agents and studio executives into attending one service over another. In essence, mourners were divided into an A-list and a B-list. Some were guaranteed the opportunity to eulogize the deceased or to comment to television reporters—anything to influence their decision regarding which service to attend.

There was a rush for Vera Wang, Gucci, Versace, Armani and the newest, hottest designer funeral dresses and accessories. Funerals became great theater in the City of Angels. Hollywood embraced grief like no other place on earth.

In New York, services for all the ACLU staff members killed in San Francisco were held in Battery Park at the tip of Manhattan, close to the ACLU national headquarters. A great number of ministers, rabbis, new-age secular humanists, priests, and atheists spoke at the nondenominational service. They all spoke eloquently, from their points of view.

It was Miguel Torres's mother, however, who many thought was the most memorable of all who spoke. She sat in a wheelchair, but with some help she managed to rise and stand at the lectern. Her name was Yolanda Maria Villarosa—having taken the name of her most recent husband, a wealthy real-estate developer in Puerto Rico. She was in a wheelchair because she recently had surgery to remove spider veins in her legs. Her hair was platinum blond, and she looked younger than many of the women in attendance. Collagen injected into her lips and cheekbones filled, softened and gave dimension to her angular face.

"My son was killed because he was *gay*," she cried out. "Because he was gay. Nothing more and nothing less." She continued, her voice cracking. "What is wrong with this country?" she asked, and then answered her own rhetorical question. "Here is what is wrong: this country is filled with hate. *Hate*. My Miguel loved everyone. Now this," she stage-whispered. "Now this." She wobbled slightly at the lectern but managed to fall back into her wheelchair; two attendants rushed to ensure she hadn't injured herself.

Far in the background, along the periphery of the mourners, were a number of large, tough-looking men walking in a circle. They were quiet. They were respectful. But they were not mourners. The signs they carried said, "Boy Scouts Go to Heaven. Queers Go to Hell" and "Sodomy is a Sin" and "Merry Christmas, ACLU."

The three major news networks had their stately anchormen and elegant anchorwomen at the service in Battery Park. Dressed in dark blue or black cashmere coats, identical Burberry wool scarves, and kid-leather gloves, they used their most sorrowful voices to exalt the dead and to question the world around them—a world filled with hate, they proclaimed—even as they did their ratings-best to stoke more hatred and division.

On cable-news programs, the ubiquitous talking heads—drawn from the same stable of perennial panelists and pundits—commented on the funeral service in New York, the attendees, the meaning of it all, and even spoke a few words about the dead. Questions were posed about the hatred in this country that may have given rise to these killings. One host wondered whether the ACLU had brought this on itself. He was from Fox News. He thought it was a fair and balanced observation.

• • •

In Hartford, Connecticut, at the Episcopal Cathedral Church of St. Quentin, a memorial service was held for Bishop Roberts and his partner, Giorgio Chella, a well-known interior designer from Milan. Episcopal bishops and priests and other clergymen and clergywomen of rank from all religious denominations attended the somber service, including the archbishop of Canterbury and Archbishop Dimon Talo of South Africa, a Nobel Peace Prize winner.

In addition to clergy, hundreds of mourners filled the large gothic structure to pay their respects to the man who brought notoriety to the Hartford community and schism to his worldwide church.

The Hartford Police Department was fully deployed to ensure that there was no disruption to the funeral service from the protestors standing across the street.

Local and national news channels and cable-news outlets focused on the distinguished mourners in attendance, including local, state and federal politicians. They also commented on the protestors across the street from the cathedral. The protestors held signs that read “Jesus Had No Gay Apostles,” “Better Dead Than Alive,” and “Say Hello to Lucifer for Me.”

25

ON THURSDAY NIGHT, Reverend Ervin Peterson and his wife, Ruth, stared into the cameras and then lowered their heads in prayer. "Dear Heavenly Father, we pray for the souls, the lost souls of those who were killed in San Francisco. We know you have boundless mercy, but we ask you to look sternly on those whose souls you have before you…They are lost, yes, but they chose their paths.

"When you consider their souls for salvation, please consider also the fifty million unborn babies they helped kill, the little boys they helped sodomize, the little girls they seduced into lives of sexual craziness, and all they have done to defile your Son's birthday and to mock your Ten Commandments. In the name of your Son, Jesus Christ, we ask you to judge them harshly for their sins. Amen," intoned Reverend Peterson.

"Brothers and sisters, and all of you in our television-family viewing audience, today, thankfully, brings to a close the seemingly endless, shameless memorials to heathens that all the mainstream-media outlets have exalted and magnified beyond belief. It would have been better for those who died, at least the majority of them, to have crawled off into a filthy corner to wait for the devil to pull them into his van," he said.

"Ruth and I have with us tonight a man who once was a homosexual. According to the information he provided us, Rudy is the son of a frightfully dominant mother and a weak-kneed father. His mother was a busy business executive and his father a meek accountant. I say 'once was' because, through divine intervention and some very hard work here on earth, he transformed himself into a healthy heterosexual person. Let me introduce Rudy Smith."

The television audience applauded as a medium-sized man walked onto the stage and waved to the audience. He shook Reverend Peterson's hand and kissed Ruth Peterson on her substantial cheek. The man then sat in the overstuffed leather chair designated for solo guests.

"Rudy, your story is a real tearjerker, if I do say so," offered Reverend Peterson, looking at Rudy Smith and the camera behind him. "You've had to work hard to find salvation, son. But you did it and you can be proud. You busted the myth, didn't you? Haven't we always said that the homosexual lifestyle is a choice that people make? Sure, it may be addictive and habit-forming in an odd way, but at the end of the day, it is still a choice."

Were it not for his literary agent intent on creating interest in the biography Rudy was contracted to write, Rudy would not be on stage with Reverend Peterson. He disliked every minute of it. He wanted to be invisible. *He wanted to escape.*

Rudy Smith's eyes didn't seem quite right. The harsh glare of the klieg lights and strange angles of light beams were enough to make most guests wish they had on sunglasses. Frequently their eyelids went into protective mode by half-shutting. In Smith's case, his eyelids opened *wider.*

"Can you tell our family here in the studio and our viewing family from around the world, what it was like for you to walk through the darkness and into the light?" asked the reverend in his most sincere voice.

On television a second of dead air seems like a week. Reverend Peterson and his charming, chubby wife waited for Rudy Smith to say something. A few seconds passed, seeming more like a month of dead air to Peterson who believed on-air television time is money.

He asked again, "Rudy, I know it has been hard for you. But now you are with God's people. Please tell us the story of your glory."

For inexplicable reasons, Rudy Smith fixated on Reverend Peterson's voice. It filled his head like helium fills a balloon, leaving no room for anything else. Smith thought his head might explode. He could feel his forehead expanding, his skull stretching. Peterson's voice grew louder and louder, pumping more helium into Rudy's head.

How wide can eyelids open? A question rarely, if ever, asked. In Rudy Smith's case, both eyelids seemed to recede behind the white part of his eyeballs. Suddenly, he swayed one way and then the other and finally pitched forward onto the thick custom-made Persian rug woven with Christian symbols.

26

"WHAT CAN YOU say? They're whackos," laughed the A-list Hollywood actor lounging on the set of the popular cable-television program *Daily Grind*. "I'm convinced that the vast right-wing machine is behind this," he continued. "They have such hatred that it spills over into everyday life. Their leaders are hate-mongering radio personalities. They spew nothing but anger. What would you expect?"

"You can't be serious. No one knows who did this. You certainly don't. You're an actor. All you know is what the script says. So who wrote your script?" shot back a former Republican congressman from Orange County, California.

"Don't you understand? The American Civil Liberties Union is at work protecting our constitutional rights on a daily basis," replied the actor. "Where would we be as a nation without them?"

"Sure, let's have gay men groping Cub Scouts. Let's have porn sites for everyone, no matter their age. Let's take 'Christ' out of Christmas and let's take God out of every document our founding fathers drafted. Oh, and while we are at it, let's remove the word 'God' from every public building in the country. Our paper money can say 'In Atheists We Trust,'" responded the former congressman.

As these two where exchanging insults, the host made faces as if he were sustaining body blows in a fight. His positions were well known. He was antimilitary, pro-abortion, in favor of all gay and lesbian issues, in favor of same-sex marriage, against profiling for terrorists, and vehemently anti-Catholic because he once was one. He used this program to frequently blast the outgoing conservative administration—in particular, the president and the vice president.

"Do you all think that this nation is on the brink?" he teased his panel.

"On the brink of what?" one of them shot back.

"On the brink of civil war," the host replied. "Look, there is a movement out there to make certain that religion isn't shoved down our throats like a daily vitamin by a born-again president and some Evangelical cabinet officers," he replied.

"Isn't it a bit ironic?" he continued. "Here we have been in Iraq and Afghanistan, trying to remove 'Allah' from their everyday lives by introducing secular governments, while here in our own country we are funding faith-based activities in defiance of separation of church and state. We, as a nation, are having somebody else's values injected into our everyday lives."

"So, what are you saying about the ACLU bombing? Do you think a televangelist blew up the building? Are you saying that someone who is Christian, *an actual religion of love and peace*, was responsible?"

"No, I don't know who would blow up the building and I don't know who would kill so many innocent people. But someone did. Or some group. Someone murdered over five hundred people in cold blood."

27

SABINO ARANA WALKED alone along the *Via Dolorosa*. A black wool beret covered his head, a black wool overcoat covered his body, a black wool scarf wound around his neck, and black leather gloves covered his hands. Partially hidden from view were his black cassock with white Roman collar, black socks, and black shoes—an easy wardrobe choice for the superior general of the Society of Jesus.

Anxious with his thoughts, he walked in the waning sunlight of the late afternoon.

He could not work.

He could not pray.

So he went for a walk…to think.

He thought about his religious order and himself. In a way, it had come full circle. In 1540 a Basque soldier, Ignatius of Loyola, had founded the Society of Jesus. He established this new religious order in the form of a military organization, with the eager permission and blessing of a besieged Pope Paul III whose papacy was reeling from the onslaught of the Protestant Reformation.

Ignatius, the first superior general of the Society of Jesus, became the Pope's chief strategist as they began the task of fighting the Protestant Reformation at every turn. The Jesuits, as they were known, became the Pope's intellectual religious warriors in mind, heart, and spirit. Their mission was to do whatever the Pope wanted in order to save the Catholic Church.

Now, more than four hundred years later, another Basque—this one from the Arana military family—was the twenty-ninth superior general of the Society of Jesus. His job was to restore the Jesuits to their former prominence and their special mission to work on behalf of the Holy Father.

As he walked through the darkening light—oblivious to the world around him, except for the soft wind that caressed his face with a chilling touch—he reflected on his personal journey. Then he quickly caught himself. "Ah, the personal-journey seduction," he thought. "Always about me—me, me, me. In truth, I am of no consequence. I am here to serve God and his leader on earth, the Pope, and to guide and nourish our religious order."

Arana needed this walk in cold air to refresh his body, to clear his mind, and to calm his soul. He had one troubling thought that took him back a few years. It had been a difficult time for him and for Dominic Pacelli. They felt personally responsible for causing one man's death. But now five hundred people were dead in America. "Am I responsible for setting this in motion?" Arana wondered. "It was Pope John Paul who introduced me to his friends from the University of Krakow; and, later, I introduced them to John Palmer."

28

THE WEATHER IN the nation's capital was turning winter-miserable. Freezing rain covered the streets and sidewalks of the District of Columbia, followed by heavy snow. In the neighborhood of the ACLU of the National Capital Area near Dupont Circle, only a few Yellow Cabs were out sliding about.

Harry Waxler turned off the desk lamp, got up from his Herman Miller desk chair—one of the ergonomic luxuries he permitted himself—and put on his wool-and-cashmere jacket—the one Todd, his current life-partner, had given him five years ago for their second anniversary. He was exhausted. At age sixty-three, he didn't have the energy anymore to pull an all-nighter. And, frankly, he didn't see the need. His work was done. Why hang around, especially with weather conditions getting worse by the minute? His new boss, Margaret Reading, had gone home six hours before. She was from California, but she wasn't stupid. She knew bad weather was coming.

It was close to midnight when he walked out of his cramped office, leaving the door open in case someone needed to use any of his files filling the shelves and stacked on the floor in his office. Since childhood Harry had disciplined himself into saving electricity as if it were the scarcest of commodities. He turned off his desk lamp and office lights before leaving.

As he walked down the corridor, Harry marveled that people were still working, especially on a terrible-weather night like this. He knew that most of them were working on the important lawsuit—guaranteed to embarrass the administration—that would be filed on Monday morning in federal district court in Washington. Those working so late were volunteer interns from local law schools who shared the same ideological views as the ACLU.

The principal reason they were working such long hours, Harry chuckled to himself, was that a "leaked" copy of the ACLU court filing would be dropped off at CBS News on Sunday morning, just in time for its Sunday-night *60 Minutes* program. The interns were proofreading the briefs, checking citations, and so on.

The ACLU was working in concert with CBS News and the *New York Times* to portray Raleigh Thornton, a thirty-seven-year-old artist, as a victim of the current Republican administration's religious beliefs when it pulled *all* funding for public art programs after he depicted Jesus Christ on the Cross submerged in urine and feces. It was a First Amendment case, according to the ACLU. Thornton was the president's nephew. The ACLU was requesting a restraining order against defunding the public art program.

Only a handful of staffers knew about the *60 Minutes* setup. Harry, being one of them, had arranged a small dinner party on Sunday night with the *60 Minutes* television piece as a surprise event for his guests. He didn't even tell Todd because he knew Todd adored surprises.

Since Harry was taking a cab to the Adams-Morgan district where he lived, a stop in the men's room before leaving the building would make the trip more comfortable. "Discipline and comfort," he thought to himself as he opened the door to the men's room.

As he stood at the urinal thinking through the complex legal argument he had fashioned in the brief that lay on his desk, he heard the restroom door creak open. Everything creaked and groaned in this old building, he often said. Since the ACLU office occupied the entire space on this secure floor, Harry figured that someone working late needed to use the restroom, too.

But Harry was wrong.

He didn't see the two men enter the restroom and position themselves behind him. The taller one smashed Harry's head against the wall above the urinal. He then braced the back of Harry's neck with one arm, while he pulled Harry's head backward with the other. Excruciating pain exploded in Harry's neck. After a few seconds the man let go and watched Harry crumble to the floor, urinating on himself.

The second man stomped on Harry's head. He took a few steps backward, pointed a pistol at Harry's head and pulled the trigger. The silencer on the pistol muffled the report. Blood squirted across Harry's forehead from the bullet wound, spraying splintered bone and tissue fragments into the red river pooling on the floor.

"You didn't need to do that," said the man who broke Harry's neck. "I already killed him."

"I needed some action. Grab his office keys, and let's go."

The men walked out, leaving Harry with blood draining from his head and his arms jerking spasmodically. Harry's blood splattered the wool and cashmere jacket from Todd and continued to puddle under his brain-dead head until his heart stopped beating.

The men tried the main door to the ACLU office. It was unlocked. The shorter man threw Harry's keys into a trash can by the door. They proceeded into the empty reception area where they split up, each moving down one of the two parallel hallways. They looked into all cubicles, office spaces, conference rooms, and libraries. Each man carried a pistol with a silencer attached. Walking quickly and quietly down the corridors, they coldly executed everyone they encountered, reloading as they walked farther along each corridor.

It surprised them that it was so easy. No fight or flight. The interns did nothing. Even after it appeared that everyone was dead, they checked each body to make certain no one was alive.

Inside the mailroom they discovered a young woman hiding behind a large Konica photocopy machine. "Don't shoot me. Please don't shoot me. I didn't do anything," cried the young woman hysterically. "Please, please," she moaned as the taller man grabbed her hair and pulled her from her hiding place. The woman shouted, "Please, don't...don't shoot me...please!"

The man aimed the gun at her head and pulled the trigger.

Next, the shorter man found the wall safe, opened it, and threw the contents onto the floor. The men planted incendiary devices at certain places throughout the office, timed to go off in thirty minutes. Then they quickly left the building through the stairwell, disappearing into the District of Columbia night.

• • •

Miles away in New York City, the bodies of security guards were being dragged to a utility closet on the main floor. The desk that they had recently occupied had a bank of security monitors. The screens were black. All the cameras feeding the screens throughout the building had been disconnected from their electrical source. In addition, all related security-monitoring devices were shut down—including fire sprinklers, heat sensing devices and remote alarm units designed to send out warnings to local law enforcement and fire departments.

All the doors into the building had been locked. No one could get in through the normal entries, not even with key cards that authorized entry twenty-four hours a day. With this worsening weather, the late hour, and the weekend, it was unlikely anyone would want to get in. However, it was likely that individuals might still be working in the law firm occupying the top twenty floors. After all, this was New York, the city that never sleeps—and neither do young associates in large law firms who are intent on billing out their required hours. A list of current occupants at the law firm, with their names and floor numbers was on the sign-in sheet at the empty security desk.

On the eighteenth floor, in the headquarters office of the ACLU, a team of three men moved into the office space through the double doors they pried open. They spread out to reconnoiter the entire floor. Encountering no one, they began opening doors to offices and storage rooms. They opened file cabinets, spilling documents, memos, and other paper around the floor. The team leader went into the corner office of the executive director. The artwork hiding the wall safe had already been removed. The safe was visible. He opened the safe with an electronic device and then pulled out all the contents and tossed them on top of the desk.

While the leader worked in the corner office, the other men double-checked the security devices and fire-protection devices to ensure they were not servicing this floor. They then began wiring the explosive charges they had with them. They spoke little—each of them an expert at his work. Silence was the rule.

The team leader walked among them to check their work. If he was satisfied, he tapped the shoulder of the man responsible for that part of the wiring, and the man was redeployed to work elsewhere on the eighteenth floor or to provide security on the main floor.

After a short while, the leader attached all the wires to control mechanisms with timers. He carefully set the activation time. He propped open the double doors and then he rode the elevator down to the main floor to join his men there. He walked out of the elevator and saw that his men were in the shadows, watching the doors and the other banks of elevators. They gathered together and fled the building, disappearing into the raw, windy night.

• • •

The front door to the offices of the Northern California Chapter of the ACLU is on the street level at 39 Drumm Street, across from the

Hyatt Embarcadero Hotel. Only a small brass sign indicates that the ACLU is upstairs. The ACLU office space sprawled over the upper floors of three different buildings, with doorways through common walls to allow movement for the staffers working there.

Of the fifty-three ACLU-affiliated offices around the country, this one was the largest. It had more than eighty full-time staffers and hundreds of volunteers, not only in San Francisco but also at satellite offices in the region, including a legislative office in Sacramento. The cubicles and offices had no inhabitants since everyone in this ACLU office had died in the explosion. Some cubicles and offices had been picked clean by loved ones who came by to gather mementos and personal effects. Most of the cubicles and offices remained in the condition they were in before the fatal fund raiser.

Inside the office, in near darkness except for handheld flashlights, a group of skilled men methodically trashed the place, overturning desks, dumping books and manuals from bookcases, and scattering paper everywhere. Working off blueprints of the buildings, the men positioned incendiary devices in optimal areas to create maximum damage over the entire office footprint.

The team leader double-checked the wiring to his satisfaction. He made certain that the incendiary devices were properly in sync and correctly placed to ensure rapid acceleration of the impending fires.

After approximately twenty-five minutes, the men went down the back stairway to the alley, stepped over one dead security guard, and dispersed in different directions through the foggy San Francisco night.

29

AT TWO O'CLOCK in the morning, Eastern Standard Time, electrical current from carefully placed control devices raced through the wiring in the ACLU office space at 125 Broad Street in Manhattan. Flashpoints exploded along the inside perimeter of the office where the wiring had been strung, creating intense fires that sped along ancillary routes, crisscrossing the interior office space. Where office walls and cubicles might have prevented easy access for the fires, small explosive charges blew away all impediments.

Within minutes a conflagration engulfed the entire eighteenth floor. Ravenous flames fed on paper, wood, plastic, and all available combustible material, including carpeting and ceiling tiles, not as flame-retardant as advertised.

Even as the air temperature grew colder outside, the air temperature inside the National ACLU office grew hotter—the flames destroying all paper files, computer equipment, all paper on desktops, in desk drawers, in filing cabinets, and all books. In particular, the documents formerly in the safe located in the executive director's office lay in smoldering ashes on the scorched desktop.

The sprinkler system did not respond to the smoke and flames because the arsonists had shut off the water valves feeding the sprinklers. Every other emergency-detection warning system had also been disabled. It took more than two hours from the time the fires ignited until lawyers working at Parton and Crownell on the upper floors smelled smoke and called 911 before escaping down the stairwells. Many windows on the eighteenth floor had expanded to the point of fracturing, blasting free of their frames and sounding every bit like heavy-caliber gunfire.

Waves of fire trucks from different stations responded to the call in the predawn hours. The battalion chief onsite laid out the tactical plans before the firefighters entered the building. A few firefighters raced through the upper floors to alert any lawyers working there, while others went directly to the eighteenth floor.

Upon learning that the location was the ACLU office, some of the firefighters joked among themselves that they should just piss on the fire to try to put it out, thereby prolonging it.

As they worked to get the fire under control and to keep it from spreading to other floors, it was evident to all the firefighters that this was a case of very sophisticated arson. It took more than six hours before all flames were extinguished. The only victims found at the scene of the fire were the security guards who had been shot to death and hidden in a utility closet on the main floor.

• • •

In Washington, DC, the fire started at approximately the same time as the fire in Manhattan. The first 911 call came about one hour after the fire started, called in by a passing cab driver.

The fire burned through the ceiling tiles and spread to the floor above, where offices of the Legal Aid Society of the District of Columbia were located. The fire engulfed two floors in the building and threatened a third floor.

Ice glazed the streets around Dupont Circle so that when fire trucks and command vehicles began arriving on scene many of them slid obliquely across the roundabout, hitting parked cars, damaging a drugstore front, and destroying the entrance to the Metro station below.

By daybreak firefighters had control of the flames, and by midmorning they extinguished the fire completely. The firefighters easily spotted the places on the floor where the fires were ignited. The wiring was destroyed, but the control boxes were partially intact: clear evidence of arson. But worse, the firefighters discovered charred bodies throughout the smoldering debris on the floor that housed the ACLU offices. The crime scene now escalated beyond arson to homicide.

• • •

At the ACLU office in San Francisco, the fire started shortly after midnight in the Pacific Time Zone. Tiny explosions throughout the floor facilitated the progression of the flames in all directions, so that maximum damage was done in a very short time frame.

When the fire truck sirens began screeching through the concrete caverns created by the numerous buildings within the Embarcadero office complex, police on duty at the nearby explosion crime scene blocks away perked up, becoming more vigilant. They called their command post to find out what was happening. After finding out that it was the ACLU office only a few blocks away that was on fire, their commander sent squad cars to the crime scene for their protection and to the site of the fire, just in case there was another attack.

Because of the recent explosion at the Bay View Restaurant, the battalion fire chief on the scene at 39 Drumm Street was reluctant to have his firefighters enter the building. He ordered all vehicles away from the front of the building, not wanting them to turn into molten nuggets in case there was another nuclear explosion.

Time passed as the fire consumed more and more of the buildings, soon reaching adjacent floors and businesses. Tongues of flickering flames licked the outside of the building through windows that were blown out by the intense heat. Still, the firefighters' only activity was setting up hoses to spray water on the fire from a distance.

A few firefighters volunteered to take the hoses up ladders close to the building to direct the water with more accuracy; however, the battalion chief would not permit this. He wanted assurance from the hazmat team on scene and police personnel that it was safe for his firefighters to get close to the building.

As he waited for word that his firefighters would be safe from explosives, the battalion chief continued to look at the flames lapping along the broken windows. For reasons he could not fathom, his mind went to a program he recently saw on Fox News where the host, Bill O'Reilly, called the ACLU "the most dangerous organization in America." The fire chief thought to himself, "Right, *dangerous*, for a number of reasons."

30

THE J. EDGAR Hoover FBI Building was an odd-looking building on a street of mediocre, copycat Federal architecture. It did not fit in. "Just like the person it was named after," Blake thought, walking toward the Justice Department located on the opposite side of Pennsylvania Avenue.

Blake believed the air temperature must have dropped more than twenty degrees since his morning run. He briefly thought about the warm sun in Barbados. He looked at the Robert F. Kennedy Justice Building ahead of him, another example of bizarre architecture. It looked like a giant concrete bunker with enormous bronze doors and disproportionately tiny windows. "This might just be the worst-looking building in a town of bad-looking buildings," thought Blake. Thankfully, justice is blind; otherwise, Lady Justice might be looking for new digs. That was the inside joke.

"The general will see you now," said Mrs. Arnison, the senior administrative assistant who was working for her fifth attorney general. In the Federal Civil Service, seniority is the name of the game, and Mrs. Arnison had been around for a long time—as evidenced by her anteroom office, large enough for an executive vice-president in private industry.

"Blake," bellowed Thomas Owens, Blake's closest friend and the nation's chief law-enforcement officer, "thanks for coming." He shook Blake's hand and hugged him the way men do.

"It's my pleasure, Tom," smiled Blake, following Owens back into his office. "You're looking successful," Blake tweaked his old friend.

"Yes, I am very successful. Thank you for noticing. But I would leave it all tomorrow and flee to Barbados, if I could, and never wear a suit and tie again, and never deal with the White House and the press at the same time. Man, you look great. Is that a real tan? I think you've lost about twenty pounds. Suddenly I feel very pudgy. That's odd; a few minutes ago I thought I looked surprisingly lean and mean."

Blake responded, "Yes, it is a real tan, but I had to work with my hands outside in the sun to get it—you know, physical labor."

"I do physical labor. Many times a day I raise an imaginary gun to my head and squeeze its imaginary trigger. I do about ten reps each time."

"Well, let's get to it. Please, have a seat," said Owens, nodding to his conference table which was almost completely covered by stacks of files. "I can use your help on this ACLU mess. Thanks for contacting me. I am sorry that you had to leave your island paradise to come back to Washington."

"I'm happy to be here. It would seem that the ACLU has fallen on hard times."

"Well, yes, I would say having your people and donors killed and your three main offices set on fire would qualify as 'hard times,'" answered Owens.

"What can I do that hundreds of people aren't doing already?" asked Blake.

"Blake, this is the government, remember? We are redundant at every level. After 9/11 we've actually started to talk to other agencies, but it is baby talk and the steps are baby steps. To answer your question: I am not certain what you can do. I just think I can use your innate abilities on this. Besides you can make some money, and it might be interesting."

"Everything involving you is interesting," Blake said. "If you want one more body, I would be happy to help you."

Owens laughed. "Blake, I don't know how many people we have working this thing. There are probably thousands, not hundreds. There are agencies working on this that I didn't even know existed, but apparently, there still aren't enough investigators because we aren't even close to naming any legitimate suspects.

"Unless you've been living in Tibet or *Barbados*, you may have noticed that the media is killing us. The president's people are calling me four or five times a day. I keep telling them they will be the first to know. They have no patience. I guess having a nuclear explosion in our country killing five hundred people will have that effect on you," Owens said, smiling but still looking less than cheerful.

He continued, "Things were bad enough before last weekend's fires and murders in the ACLU offices in Washington, New York, and San Francisco.

"We have so many leads that we have no leads. You know what I mean? Apparently, more people hated the ACLU than even I imagined.

"Now we're tripping over local police and fire departments, and they're tripping over us. This whole thing has taken a crazy turn. Before the fires and murders, we had offered security to the ACLU for all their offices, but they declined. They didn't want our protection. They said they had their own security. Well, guess what? Even though they turned us down, who gets blamed? We do. Read the papers."

"Okay, Tom, what do you want me to do that your skilled investigators aren't doing already?"

"I just want you to look at everything we have and tell me what you think. In fact, that is exactly what I want you to do: *think*. Think about the categories of these stacks and how they sliced and diced the files in each stack. Just tell me where we should be looking.

"We're having a difficult time finding any information about the original bomb. Apparently we have similar weapons in our arsenal, and there may also be two or three other countries that might have the same thing, but we do not know if any rogue groups have something similar.

"I've been told that all the good guys' weapons are accounted for, but can I believe that?

"We have a couple hundred people, many of them nuclear physicists and scientists, working on that part of the investigation. They all have higher-than-high, super secret clearances, although this is such a poorly kept secret that even I know it. Now you do, too. I think that brings the number to over six thousand," Owens said, facetiously.

"Blake, I asked John Palmer for his help. The nuke people on our side trust him; plus, he knows all the players worldwide. I have him briefing me separately. He speaks *English* to me."

Professor John Palmer had been one of their law-school professors at the University of Virginia, and he was like a family member to Blake. One day in class, when Tom was having a difficult time explaining a legal concept involving intellectual property, Professor Palmer sarcastically asked him whether English was his second language.

"We also have the CIA, the NSA, and others working this, as well as our allies around the globe. What allies, right? Even that whack-job from the U.N., the guy who runs their nuclear-investigation agency called to offer his help. You know what? We are so hard up we accepted his offer. Can you believe it? He is an idiot. A self-absorbed idiot. The Norwegians gave him the Nobel Peace Prize, for God's sake, but then, they gave one to Jimmy Carter and the original Palestinian terrorist, Yassar Arafat."

"I think you are losing your mind," observed Blake. "Can you hang on until the new guy takes your place?"

"Blake, I really meant it when I said thanks for offering to help me. I know it must be very difficult for you. What has it been? About three years? More? I know I was responsible for getting you involved with that money-laundering case. I am sorry to my bones for what happened to Annie and Connor, and I will take that to my grave. I think of them all the time."

Silence filled the room as the two close friends sat at the table, lost in their own thoughts, each filled with regret. Blake looked at Tom and recalled how Tom had arranged a blind date for Blake with Annie Watson and had later served as his best man at their wedding.

Tom said, "Look, Blake, we may have rushed this. You're right. There are thousands of investigators working on this case. You don't need to get involved. I think I just wanted to see a friendly face. I am so happy that you offered to help me. Since I never get to leave this office, I had to invite you here," laughed Owens, in his self-deprecating fashion. "You should go back to Barbados before you lose your tan."

Blake knew Tom Owens rarely asked for help because Tom Owens rarely needed help. Tom had mastered division of labor and delegation 101 when he was in grade school, Blake thought, so this must be quite a burden. Surely, Tom just wanted to leave this office without any major matters pending for the new administration and his successor at the Department of Justice. Now this.

Blake smiled and said matter-of-factly, "What do I have left to lose, except my tan? My life has been on hold for years. I worked on a fishing boat in Barbados, thinking I could distract myself and ease the pain of losing Annie and Connor. But it doesn't quite work that way, I guess. The pain continues," Blake said. "At least let me be useful, Tom."

"Thanks," said Owens, looking intently at his old friend, wondering if he had done the right thing in accepting Blake's offer to help. He wondered if he was being unfair. But he took Blake at his word, thinking that working here might help Blake as much as it would help him.

"I need you to look at the ACLU and figure out who would do this and who might have the capability of pulling off this explosion. I can't rely on people finding where this bomb was made or how it got here. I already have all kinds of background on the ACLU. If you would just look at this situation…the bomb, the ACLU, the guest list, anything you want…use or discard the information available right now or ask for more," Tom said, looking down at the table.

"Blake, I don't expect you to do anything miraculous. Just let me know what you think. I trust your instincts and your judgment."

"All right, I can do that," replied Blake, wondering what, if anything, he could add to this investigation. Blake stood and shook Tom's hand. Then Tom moved back to his desk.

"You'll be working with a few other people," Tom said, his eyes cast down, feeling safe behind his desk.

Blake looked at him as if he didn't understand him, thinking that maybe English was, indeed, Tom's second language. "What?"

"I know, I know. That's not how you prefer to work, but I have no choice, Blake," Tom said, throwing out his arms. "The White House says time is of the essence, and the scope of this investigation is enormous. Blah, blah, blah, blah. I need something to feed the press, and I need it ASAP. So, please go along with me on this. It's not my idea, Blake. I honestly have no choice."

"Tom," scolded Blake, "you know that as soon as people start introducing themselves around a table you have something akin to a 'committee' being stillborn—dead on arrival, Tom, DOA. The only way to avoid it—is not to do it. What is the chance of strangers being completely in sync from the start?" asked Blake.

Tom did not respond.

"Who will be working with me?" asked Blake, unhappy at this turn of events.

"The president has someone in mind," answered Tom, "and I have a couple of great people I will give you."

“The president?” Blake exclaimed. “Please tell me it’s not a political appointee or some public-relations person—or worse, some son or daughter of a big donor out to make a difference.”

“Blake, I don’t know who it is,” explained Owens. “When I told the president about you and how I wanted you to work with us, it was like a light turned on in his head. It was a cartoon moment. Before I could finish my sentence, he told me he was going to have someone else work with you, but that you would still be in charge. Whoever it is will be here tomorrow morning. Then we’ll both know.”

“How did you ever get to this office?” asked Blake. “You still can’t tell a decent lie. The president never said I would be in charge, did he? He never said anything of the sort. What if a four-star general shows up tomorrow? Do you think I’ll be in charge?”

“I’ll tell the general that you *are* in charge,” smiled Tom, “that you actually have one more star than he does. Wow, five stars! That should provide you with a decent pension.”

Tom knew he was asking his friend for a big favor. Blake was brilliant and clever, but he preferred to work alone. He was an individual contributor who did not enjoy being part of a group. At times he seemed brusque or rude, which was not his character at all. He just did not have much patience because his mind worked so quickly, and if you couldn’t keep up, you were a drag.

“Tomorrow, then?” Tom said. “On the chance that you would agree to help me, I reserved the conference room down the hall for you. Very spacious.”

31

SHE LOOKED LIKE an exotically beautiful Victoria's Secret model with Asian genes and an IQ near genius level. She was tall, well-developed and exotically beautiful. She moved with athletic grace. Her full name was Samantha Ann Rhodes, but all her friends called her Sam.

Samantha was an orphan toddler in Hong Kong when a wealthy married couple, who were part of the British diplomatic corps there, adopted her. As a result, she grew up in different countries all over the world, wherever her adoptive parents were posted. Her first university degree was from the National University of Singapore. She also had a doctorate in applied mathematics (game theory) from Oxford, plus advanced degrees in other academic disciplines from universities in the United States.

Samantha backed her Range Rover out of the garage and began the drive to the Justice Department. It was six o'clock in the morning. She stopped at Starbucks for coffee and a cranberry scone, and she drank full-bodied Verona Blend and ate her low-fat scone during her drive. The outside temperature gauge in her vehicle showed it was only a few degrees above freezing. The forecasted snow hadn't materialized yet, but the morning air felt saturated with moisture.

After finding a place to park, she walked into the visitor's entrance of the building. The paunchy security guard checked her list of visitors, found the name Samantha Ann Rhodes on it, and sent her through multiple screening devices and into the hallowed halls of the Department of Justice.

A more agile security guard gave Samantha a visitor's pass and escorted her through hallways to an elevator, up to the top floor, and then down more hallways until they reached a conference room close to the office suite of the attorney general of the United States.

Opening the door, Samantha entered a spacious room with a large conference table, a number of chairs, wall charts, telephones, laptops and piles of file folders. Seated at one end of the table was a ruggedly handsome man looking up at her.

Blake stood to introduce himself. "Hello, I'm Blake Elliott."

"I'm Samantha Rhodes," she responded with a hint of a British accent, moving closer to shake Blake's outstretched hand. She felt the strength of his calloused hand, quickly scanned his tan and the highlights in his hair, and wondered what he was doing here. He certainly did not have the typical Washington-bureaucrat winter pallor and squishy handshake. "Please, call me Sam," she said to Blake.

Samantha put her coffee cup on the table, took off her wool-lined Burberry raincoat and hung it on a coatrack in the corner. Blake watched her, struck by her beauty and grace. He caught himself staring, so he lowered his gaze to the papers in front of him but that lasted only a few seconds before he stole another glance. She turned back to the table and sat a few chairs up from Blake, facing the door. She sipped her coffee as she scanned the table. She could feel Blake's eyes on her. Finally, she looked at him and asked, "Who are you?" Then, realizing how awkwardly she had phrased her question, she hastened to add, "Are you with the Justice Department?"

Blake smiled, "No, I'm working for Tom Owens on the ACLU investigation. Are you with the Justice Department?"

"No, I'm not. I was sent over here by the White House to work on the ACLU investigation, too."

"This is the first day for both of us, then. All these stacks of files are investigative material or summaries gathered by state and federal investigators or other individuals with relevant information. I spoke with Tom yesterday. He wants us to become familiar with these files," said Blake. "Based on my meeting yesterday here is what I know. Other investigative agencies are trying to track the explosive device. There are a number of countries in the world that either have such a nuclear device or can produce one. According to the information provided, every country with such nuclear capability is being, or has been, contacted."

"Even our country?"

Blake looked at her. "Our country? What do you mean?"

Samantha responded, "Does the United States...*our country*... have such a weapon?"

She looked at him wondering if his good looks and suntan masked someone with a dull mind, since he seemingly didn't understand what "our country" meant.

"Yes, our country does have such a weapon," he smiled at her, as if reading *her* mind. "They are all accounted for." At least now he knew she claimed to be an American citizen.

"What is in these files and how is the information organized?" asked Samantha, looking at the stacks of files on the table and on the counter running halfway around the room.

"I don't know. I've only been here for about a half an hour. I quickly paged through some of these stacks before you arrived. Someone's obviously been busy compiling a great deal of information about the ACLU. They look very complete, at least as far as the information I reviewed. Whether it will be helpful, I don't know."

"Are the fires at the ACLU offices connected?"

Before Blake could answer Samantha's question, there was a knock on the door. It opened, and in walked Tom Owens with a man and woman carrying more files.

"Good morning," said Tom cheerfully. "Here is a sketchy file relating to the fire and homicides at the ACLU office here in the

District. I also managed to free up the two best people I have to help you: Leon Wilson and Sapphire Wilson.

"Leon and Sapphire, let me introduce Blake Elliott and… Samantha Rhodes, I presume? While I am at it, let me introduce myself. I am Tom Owens.

"So, you were sent over by the president," Tom said to Samantha, stating something everyone already knew, but saying it as a compliment.

"Leon and Sapphire, this man is actually a long-time friend of mine, Blake Elliott. I don't know how much longer we will stay friends but, as luck would have it, we are still friends as of this very moment."

Everyone smiled, even Samantha, instantly recognizing a close connection between the attorney general and the man with the tan.

"Ms. Rhodes, you and Mr. Elliott can exchange biographical information later, if you haven't already—although I would guess that Leon and Sapphire can tell you things about yourselves only your closest friends know. They really are that good.

"My time is limited right now because of the president's scheduled press conference this morning regarding the investigation, the media coverage of the ACLU bombing, and the fires and murders this past weekend," Owens said, looking at Samantha, and obliquely at Blake, using friendship body-language encryption to send him the message: *you lucked out!*

"Leon and Sapphire have done a great job summarizing the investigation material. They can tell you about all the files you see on this table, and they can help you find more information, if needed. They've been around long enough to know where to get information without wasting time.

"Samantha, I had the chance to meet with Blake yesterday. I told him the investigation into the explosive device itself is well underway, employing scientists, military personnel, and others. So, you don't need to concern yourselves with that, unless you trip over some enriched uranium that is relevant to this investigation.

"I want you to focus on the ACLU as a target—including its leaders, its benefactors, and its current staff. Leon and Sapphire developed a great deal of historical and current information concerning the ACLU. What made them a nuclear target? Why torch their offices?

"I know you will have questions. You can direct those questions to Leon and Sapphire for answers. My office is a few doors away, and I will be checking in on your progress often. Thank you for helping us," Tom said, as he left the room.

32

FOR A SECOND or two it was quiet following the departure of the attorney general of the United States. Leon and Sapphire Wilson sat down opposite Samantha.

"The first thing we need is coffee," said Leon. He got up and walked to the corner of the conference room where he opened a cabinet and pulled out a coffeemaker, filters, ground coffee, dry creamer and sugar.

"Leon and I are real partners, like husband-and-wife partners," Sapphire offered, "Leon is with the FBI and I work for the general, but now we are assigned to work with you two. Leon gets everything from the bureau and local law enforcement, plus homeland security and I get everything from Justice, the Secret Service and every other spooky agency.

"We started working on this right after the explosion in California. At that time, our job was to ensure that the general had absolutely all current, relevant information. We have many more files that are the source documents for these summaries.

"The files I carried in are from the district police regarding the murders that occurred the other night at the ACLU office over by Dupont Circle. We will be getting information from NYPD and the folks in San Francisco regarding their investigations as soon as information is available."

Sapphire looked at Leon, who was filling the coffee pot with water, and then at Blake. She said to Blake, "We know all about you from the general."

Blake smiled and replied, "Really? What did he say?"

"Well, he said that you are fascinating to work with and some...other...things," Sapphire laughed. "You're a lawyer, although you don't practice law at the moment. However, the firm where you were a partner is named after your father, and just happens to be the most powerful law firm in Washington. You graduated from Princeton where you were an All-American lacrosse player and from the University of Virginia Law School where you and the general were roommates. He says you're one of the most brilliant people he knows, but he also said that he's a better tennis player. In fact, Leon, honey, weren't the general's words a *much better* tennis player?" Sapphire quipped, as she turned to Leon.

Leon said, "Yes, but the general said you probably think you're the better tennis player."

Leon sat down next to his wife. The Wilsons looked at Samantha, and Sapphire said, "This will be a new experience for you, Samantha. My sources in the West Wing tell me you recently returned from North Korea, where you've been working on yet another nuclear nonproliferation treaty. Well, I don't know if this investigation will be as much fun as dealing with that crazy little man in North Korea," she laughed. "But you must have impressed the president and his people with your work, otherwise you wouldn't be here. This must be your very first criminal investigation, right?"

"Yes."

Her first investigation. Blake wondered why she was here. If time was of the essence, why send a rookie...unless the rookie was good, very good.

"We know that you, too, are brilliant, with a doctorate in applied mathematics and other advanced degrees. You've lived all over the world and speak a number of languages. Before starting your own consulting firm, you were a professor at Stanford University. Most of your work now is done for the government, but you do have other large clients in what we government employees refer to as the *private sector.* And you also play tennis."

Samantha smiled slightly, "Well, that's me in a nutshell."

Blake and Samantha looked at each other with more interest. She asked the Wilsons, "You have the advantage. Tell us about yourselves."

Sapphire smiled, canted her head toward Leon and said, "We're happily married."

Leon smiled and added, "Very happily married. No children. No pets. Maybe that's why we're so happy."

Blake liked their rapport. He asked, "Okay, apart from your personal happiness, what else will you share with us?"

"We're both lawyers—University of Maryland Law School and former FBI agents; well, Leon is still with the bureau. We work on special assignments with numerous agencies, most recently homeland security. We always try to work together because we like to think that we complement each other," Sapphire said. "Plus, we can use the car-pool lane."

Leon laughed. So did Blake. Samantha smiled.

Sapphire continued, "The general told us to help you in any way we can. For starters, we will be updating all information as it comes in. We will track down whatever you need or want. We also have a full-time assistant to help with things like conference calls and copying."

"Then we're set," said Blake. "Have you two reviewed these files?"

"Thoroughly," answered Leon. "We don't have photographic memories like you two, but we have pretty good short-term memories. Plus, we know where to find the information."

Samantha asked them, "Where do you think this investigation is at this point?"

"Nowhere and everywhere, like the general said," answered Leon. "We have so much information about so many people with so many motives to damage the ACLU that it is sadly bewildering."

• • •

Leon and Blake went to the basement cafeteria to get some bagels and fruit. When they left, Sapphire talked with Samantha in the conference room. "Please call me Sam," said Samantha. "I really appreciate all that you and Leon have done already. I feel like the proverbial fish out of water, since I've never been involved in an investigation."

"I can imagine," replied Sapphire. "That's why we have all of your bio info. The general needed to know your background before he would allow you to work on this investigation. He doesn't just roll over for the White House."

"So you know all about me? And I know a little bit about you, at least what you and Leon shared. However, I know nothing about Blake, except what you told us."

"He's not a civil servant or an executive appointee or anything like that. He is a private citizen, just like you. What he also is, though, is the general's best friend.

"Shortly after the general took office, he brought Blake in to work on a very complex criminal investigation involving Fortune 100 companies and a few governments in South America. The federal agencies investigating were making little headway until Blake came in and managed to see patterns of business transactions that no one else realized existed. He even went undercover in South America to gather evidence. It was amazing to say the least, and a little embarrassing for the agencies involved. From that assignment, he went on to do work for other agencies involved in criminal investigations—but no more undercover work because the general did not want him in danger."

"So he was a consultant, then, working for the government?" asked Samantha.

"Yes," answered Sapphire. "He was a…*contractor*…We don't like the term *consultant* in government. At that time, Blake was a partner at Elliott and Morgan."

"I know the name. Some of my corporate clients use that firm for their litigation. It's a powerhouse firm, I understand."

"Right, a powerhouse firm. Actually, that's probably an understatement. Basically, it's a white-glove firm with brass knuckles under the white gloves: aggressive and extremely competent. Blake started with the firm after he left the Marine Corps."

Before Samantha could ask why Blake left the firm, the door opened. Leon and Blake each carried a tray with bagels, yogurt and fruit to share.

At around five o'clock, Leon and Sapphire left for the day. The Wilsons explained that their days started around four-thirty in the morning when they got up, worked out, compiled information received overnight, and sent that information to their computer printers in the Justice Department and FBI buildings.

After the Wilsons had left, the room was quiet. Samantha had her head down and was scribbling on her legal pad. Blake looked at what she was writing from his side of the table. He saw was a number of circles and lines, with writing at various places on the page. Although he didn't know precisely what patterns she was using, Blake was certain that patterns were taking form in her mind. Even with his limited knowledge of her background, he understood that she was engaged in some sort of nonlinear thinking…lateral thinking…whatever the term. It certainly looked outside the box. "Tom would be pleased," he thought.

Blake's own experience as a marine officer and litigator helped him immeasurably in thinking and prioritizing. He learned how to adopt a clinical detachment from the chatter of politics, office intrigue and professional jealousies that hampered all law-enforcement agencies in doing their jobs. Blake, like Tom Owens, knew that law-enforcement personnel all attended the same schools for investigative skills, and—even though many of them had investigated the biggest crimes of their time—being human, their natural inclination was to complicate things. Sheer numbers of agencies and personnel added layers of complexity to solving criminal investigations. A single piece of evidence could take on all sorts of different meanings after the involved agencies reviewed it, discussed it, theorized over it and summarized its usefulness.

For all these reasons, Blake preferred to work alone.

33

BLAKE AND SAMANTHA spent the rest of the week reviewing files and information already available, plus some redacted files from homeland security regarding domestic and international terrorist groups. They discussed their thoughts and theories, and they worked off each other's skill sets. In the process, they were becoming comfortable with one another. Blake even had to admit to himself that he and Samantha synced well when they worked together.

With the weekend approaching, Leon and Sapphire said they would not be in the office because they were going to a wedding on Saturday in Towson, Maryland, and on Sunday they were attending the baptism of their seventh nephew in Baltimore.

Around noon on Saturday, while they were eating sandwiches from the vending machines in the basement of the Justice Department, Blake told Samantha that he would be leaving in the afternoon to attend a concert at the National Cathedral. He explained that it was the Cathedral's Christmas concert and that his niece and nephew were singing in the choir.

Samantha asked a number of questions about the concert and told Blake she had sung in Christmas concerts when she was a child and a teenager. She was raised in the Anglican Church by her adoptive parents who were members.

Listening to Samantha talk about her childhood and the memories she had of singing in the choir on Christmas, Blake wondered whether he should invite her, although he knew tickets were limited. He wondered what his sister and brother-in-law would think. "Wouldn't it be an intrusion on Jordan and David? Besides, how could I get a ticket for her?"

When they finished their sandwiches, Blake excused himself and left the room to call his sister, Jordan, to inquire about another ticket.

When Blake returned to the room he said, "Sam, you are coming with me this afternoon. We are going to the National Cathedral to pray for divine guidance so that we know what the hell we are doing in this investigation. If *seasonal* singing should break out while we are there, that will be a good sign that we are on the right track."

• • •

Dominating the intersection of Massachusetts and Wisconsin Avenues in the northwest quadrant of Washington, DC, is the Episcopal Cathedral Church of Saint Peter and Saint Paul, more popularly known as the National Cathedral. Gothic in design, the cathedral is the seventh largest in the world and second largest in the United States, after St. John the Divine in New York City.

The National Cathedral complex includes three schools: Beauvoir Elementary, St. Albans for Boys, and the National Cathedral School for Girls. It occupies sixty prime acres on Mount St. Alban in the District of Columbia, close to Embassy Row and up the road from Georgetown University.

Blake managed to sneak Samantha into the cathedral with him since Jordan could not get another ticket. They arrived to find Jordan and David sitting in their reserved space near the front, protecting their territory from aggressive church members looking for seats. Jordan had finagled good seats so that they would have a clear view of Jennifer and Paul, their children. Because the concert was sold out and Jordan hadn't been able to get another ticket for Samantha, the four of them squished together in a space meant for three.

The Choir of Men and Boys and the Choir of Women, all dressed in red gowns and white surplices stood on terraced risers facing the congregation. They began with a favorite Advent hymn:

O come, O come, Emmanuel
And ransom captive Israel
That mourns in lonely exile here
Until the Son of God appear
Rejoice! Rejoice! Emmanuel
Shall come to thee, O Israel.

The interior of the gothic cathedral was vast in length and height: the length to the high altar almost a football field and a half for God's team and the vaulted ceiling ten stories closer to heaven. Voices and musical instruments filled the holy space with joyful noise.

Samantha sat between Blake and Jordan. Jordan leaned over and whispered to Blake, "Dad was the only person I knew who liked Advent more than Christmas. I wish he were here to see Jennifer and Paul."

Blake did not respond, just nodded, but as was often the case with his sister, he was thinking similar thoughts. Blake also wished his father were alive because he missed him so much. His father frequently helped Blake think his way to clarity on many legal issues—and human issues, as well. He often thought his dad was the quintessential problem solver—not so much because he had a solution to every problem but because he redefined the problem, using some mental sleight of hand that was humorous, surprisingly rational and, generally, effective.

"I agree. He loved the notion of things unfolding, like Advent. We certainly know his feelings about Christmas."

"Right. *Santa* and *Satan*," Jordan said quietly.

"*Fungible*," added Blake, in a whisper. "That's what Dad would say."

They smiled, remembering their father's annual observation that the true meaning of Christmas had been lost to irrational gift giving, needless debt, and depression.

Samantha couldn't help but hear Blake and Jordan talk about their father. It prompted her to think of her father. She knew he would have enjoyed this moment very much. She made a mental note to call him tomorrow and tell him about the lovely concert. Should she mention Blake? Her father might jump to a wrong conclusion. He might think his daughter was on a date. Well, at least Blake wasn't an academic. Her father would appreciate that.

When the concert ended they moved into the choir area at the front of the cathedral to congratulate the singers. Because Blake and Samantha had arrived just before the concert began, Blake only had time to introduce Samantha to his sister and brother-in-law. Now Blake told Jordan and David about Tom Owens, the ACLU investigation, and Samantha having been sent over by the White House. Samantha thanked them for allowing her to intrude on their family afternoon.

Blake could see that Jordan was doing a preliminary sisterly evaluation of Samantha. When Jordan looked back at Blake, she was smiling approval. Blake just shook his head.

The choir members fanned out across the front of the cathedral as their families and friends swarmed over them. Jordan and David hugged their son. Blake shook Paul's hand and introduced him to Samantha. Paul thanked his uncle and Ms. Rhodes for coming. Samantha liked him immediately. What manners! They told Paul they would meet him in the Gathering Room.

Jordan kept looking for Jennifer amid the throng of people. She finally saw her with some of her girlfriends. She worked her way over to Jennifer and gave her a hug and invited Jennifer's friends to join the family for refreshments.

34

IT WAS DUSK when they exited the cathedral. Snow flurries whirled through frosty air creating halos around the streetlamps and requiring car windows to be brushed clear of snow accumulation. The weather forecast called for colder weather and heavy snow over the next three days. "Maybe a white Christmas this year," the adults thought. "Maybe school will be canceled," Jennifer and Paul hoped.

"Blake, will you be joining us for dinner? We haven't seen much of you since your return," Jordan said. "We're eating Italian tonight: pasta, meatballs, red sauce, salad, great bread and a little red wine. Life can be good, especially if you embrace it," Jordan hugged her brother. "I think you need some lessons."

Samantha smiled at Blake's sister having a little fun with her brother.

"Samantha, do you eat pasta? Do you like wine? How about a *fun family*?" Jordan said, as she put an arm around Samantha's waist in a welcoming gesture.

Blake said to Samantha, "Jordan cooks like she was born in Bologna."

"Really? I spent a little time at the University of Bologna. I think I gained ten pounds the first week because I loved the food so much. But I really don't want to impose. I had a lovely time already, and I very much appreciate your inviting me."

Blake prevailed on Samantha to join them. "It's a perfect night for pasta and red sauce. Plus David has an outstanding wine cellar, and now Jordan has a standard against which to be judged: someone who knows Italian food."

"I did not say I *knew* Italian food, I only said I loved Italian food," Samantha laughed, agreeing to join them for dinner, thinking Blake seemed very interested in having her stay longer. Or did she misread his interest? Maybe it wasn't interest, just good manners. She wondered which it was as she drove to Jordan's house, following Blake's car.

She reflected on the past week and, catching her reflection in the rearview mirror, she found herself smiling. She even looked again in her rearview mirror to confirm that she was smiling—and to check her makeup. "Get a grip," she scolded herself. "This is purely social. Above all else, you are a *disinterested* professional," she continued telling herself. "Disinterested," she repeated. "A disinterested professional from the White House," she repeated again.

The evening was comfortable for everyone, particularly Samantha, who appreciated Jordan and David's easygoing nature and the courtesy and attentiveness of their children. Blake came alive in this group. He was vivacious, funny, self-deprecating and a joy to be around, she thought, even comparing him to other men she had dated. But wait, she caught herself. This was not a date. However, it was comfortable, she had to admit. And it had proved to be a great evening.

As the others conversed before the fireplace that was crackling and spitting from the hardwood fire, Jordan and Samantha chatted in the kitchen. Jordan, without any prompting, gave her a synopsis of her younger brother. She talked about their childhood, the fact that each had attended the Cathedral schools, and the fact that her children were going to the same schools now.

Jordan talked about herself. She had gone to Princeton University as an undergraduate and then Stanford for her PhD in forensic psychology.

Samantha discussed her life, mentioning that she had been adopted in Hong Kong by a wonderful couple. It was a singular life-changing event for her. Otherwise, she might still be in Hong Kong. Since her new parents were British diplomats, she traveled all over the world as they went from assignment to assignment; the fact that they were independently wealthy meant she could attend the best schools anywhere. Because she loved mathematics, she gravitated toward academic disciplines that were based on mathematics. Pursuing this interest, she went on to get multiple advanced degrees, including a PhD, very much like Jordan.

When they discovered they had both been at Stanford University, they laughed together like old friends, talking about favorite hangouts and restaurants, beautiful weather and the proximity to the ocean and San Francisco.

"I was a visiting professor at Princeton, Oxford, and Trinity College in Dublin, and then on the faculty at Stanford, when my father finally persuaded me to abandon *the inbreeding of academic life*, as he called it. He knew I hated the politics. He hated all my male friends because he thought they were all liberal academic phonies and fakes and other terms I probably shouldn't mention," laughed Samantha.

"What did you do then?"

"Well, although I did not immediately credit my father with sage advice, I did take stock of my life and my relationships, and I ended up agreeing with him. With my father's support, I left my secure, academic cocoon and started my own consulting practice. One assignment led to another and it became successful, and I am much happier."

"Is that how you got this assignment to work on the ACLU investigation?"

"In a roundabout way, yes."

Jordan grew to like Samantha even more during this conversation. She sensed a budding affection that Samantha had for her brother. She told her about Blake's wife and son, mentioning the role Tom Owens played as Blake's close friend, his best man, and the one who got him involved with his current work.

When she told Samantha what a great family Annie, Connor, and Blake were, and about the depression Blake fell into following their deaths, she choked up, remembering how it was for Blake when he found out his wife and son had died because of the case he was working on for the Justice Department.

"I mean, no one could have anticipated what happened. Poor Tom Owens. He went into a funk, too. It was a horrible time for so many of us," said Jordan. She explained that Blake had quit the law firm and left the country. "Then, about a year later, my father was killed in a mugging downtown, close to his office. That added another incredibly sad episode to our lives. It was terrible."

"Is your mother still living?"

"No, she died a few months before Annie and Connor were killed—maybe four years ago. She had a stroke about twelve years before her death that left her severely paralyzed and with impaired brain function. She could not be rehabilitated."

"Was she in a nursing home?"

"No, no, my father had a special room designed for her in our house to accommodate her wheelchair, special bed and other medical equipment. He also had around-the-clock nursing care."

"I am so sorry," Samantha said. "That must have been a very difficult time for your father, Blake and yourself."

"Yes, it was a very trying time; however, as the years passed by, we adjusted to the reality of our lives."

Samantha listened intently as she helped Jordan with the dishes. "Jordan, as you know, I only met Blake a few days ago. This is my first experience with a criminal investigation, and I've never had a chance, really, to speak with him about anything except our work." After a moment of silence, Samantha asked, "How is Blake now?"

"Ah," Jordan smiled warmly, "that's the question we all want answered; although he seems quite happy tonight."

35

MONDAY MORNING, AFTER everyone got settled in, Blake discussed his knowledge of the ACLU. "Our law firm…my father's law firm…was that rare group of lawyers who did pro bono work *against* the ACLU. At that time, my father believed that the ACLU was trying to undermine the values and beliefs of this country by attacking foundational groups in the United States—such as Christian and Jewish religious organizations and schools, patriotic organizations, the military, and even the Boy Scouts. He also believed that the ACLU was all about destroying moral values by promoting pornography—including child pornography—under the guise of artistic expression, a First Amendment right, according to the ACLU.

"During and after the Vietnam war, the ACLU defended burning the American flag as another example of freedom of speech, and by doing so they were intent on diminishing a symbol of American patriotism over the centuries: the American flag. It was an attack on a foundational group: active-duty military and their families, not to mention the millions of American veterans who served under that flag.

"My father believed these attacks by the ACLU were tactical in nature, part of an overall plan. Virtually everything they did was inescapably related. The conclusion was that all ACLU activity is a controlled, concentrated, and concerted effort to destroy traditional American values in this country, under the guise for protecting Americans' civil liberties."

Blake sipped from his bottle of water and continued, "The ACLU has offices all over the United States—around sixty of them. Each year more and more of its money arrives in the form of donations from foundations—now more than ever before. That was the great benefit Miguel Torres brought to the ACLU. He knew how to open the money spigots of philanthropic foundations. As a result, money poured into ACLU coffers. In addition, he tapped Hollywood and the adult-entertainment industry for bundles of money. His fund raising prowess was legendary.

"Look at the party in San Francisco and the guest list. The ACLU planned to raise more than forty-five million dollars that night alone. Politicians would kill each other for a fraction of that kind of haul in one night.

"The guest list and the attendees at that fund raiser speak volumes about the stature of the ACLU in the twenty-first century: United States senators and members of Congress, judges, mayors, prominent lawyers, college presidents, bishops, priests, heavy-hitting movie producers and A-list actors, top-notch business billionaires and multimillionaires, foundation executives, and union leaders.

"Contrast that to the time period the ACLU was founded and during its early years. No one could have imagined that one of their lawyers would sit on the Supreme Court. How utterly improbable. Right? Then it was a gutter organization, managed by radicals—marginal, to be polite. But now they have one of their own on the Supreme Court and others on the same court who are card-carrying members. And more embedded throughout the judiciary.

"When the ACLU started out, no self-respecting lawyer would have anything to do with it. Then, under new leadership, the ACLU developed a plan, and that plan has been carried out meticulously. Right now, the ACLU has lawyers from major law firms doing pro bono work. This did not happen overnight. But it did happen. And it continues today.

"The average citizen has no idea how slick an operation the ACLU is—to the extent that the average citizen thinks about the ACLU at all. Most people do not know and do not care. They believe what they choose to believe or what the mainstream media tell them, and they do not want facts getting in the way of their belief systems."

Sapphire commented, "The ACLU is clever. It portrays itself as wrapped in the Constitution while it is burning the American flag. It feeds off certain groups for notoriety and for money—such as gays and lesbians, feminists, pro-choice advocates, union workers, teachers and librarians and, of course, their old standby: atheists, secular humanists, and socialists, all at home in the Democratic Party. I am not condemning Democrats. I am only pointing out how the ACLU has closely aligned itself with, and is largely protected by, the major political party in this country."

"No doubt about it," said Leon, "the ACLU is one slick operation."

"Right, and they are also a moneymaking legal machine. They sue little towns around the country over some alleged constitutional violation, forcing them to settle because they don't have the money to fight lawsuits. The ACLU has free legal talent from pro bono lawyers, and they get their legal fees from the government," said Sapphire. "How sweet it is!"

"That's right," answered Leon. "Pure profit for the ACLU. Just recently a judge in San Diego awarded two million dollars in attorneys' fees to the ACLU, even though the pro bono lawyers litigating the case for the ACLU told the judge they were working for free. Pure profit: money from the taxpayers to the ACLU. Thank you very much."

36

LATER THAT MORNING, Samantha and Sapphire were ready to discuss the ACLU guest list they had been reviewing. Sapphire said, "We categorized the list and put numbers in each category:

National ACLU staff from New York: thirteen
Local ACLU staff in California: twenty-eight
California ACLU volunteers and pro bono lawyers: twenty-six
Other lawyers in private practice, mostly criminal defense: twenty-two
Law school deans and professors: twenty-one
Judges of state and federal courts: seventeen
United States senators from California, their families and staff: fifteen
Congressmen and women, their families, and staff: nineteen
Pornography industry producers and distributors: twenty-one
Hollywood producers and actors: twenty-three
Unions: the National Education Association, American Library Association, AFL-CIO, Teamsters, United Auto Workers and National Actors Guild: thirty-two Colleges and universities, a few presidents, along with faculty members: twenty-eight

Clergy, including ten Catholic priests and one bishop from Hartford: eighteen
Business and industry: thirty
Foundation leaders and grant makers: thirty-three
Private donors: thirty-six
Local, state and federal government officials: twenty

"That adds up to a total of four hundred and two people," Sapphire said.

"Priests?" Blake was surprised, "*Catholic* priests?"

"Right," answered Sapphire. "Some were presidents of Catholic universities. But maybe it is not so surprising. I mean, the Catholic Church is socialist, isn't it? *Social justice, liberation theology,* and all of that."

"Do you have the guest lists from previous years?" Blake asked, wondering if previous ACLU fund raisers had the same guests in attendance.

"No," Sapphire said. "The FBI requested that information from Angela Carr, the director of administration for the National ACLU headquarters, but counsel for the ACLU demanded a court order."

37

LEON TOLD THEM the FBI could not find Angela Carr.

"Does Brewer suspect she was murdered?" asked Sapphire.

"He doesn't know what to make of it, at this point. All the other people in that ACLU office are accounted for. Carr is the only one missing," answered Leon. "Brewer is interested, obviously. He has agents looking for her, talking to friends and family. It may be nothing. Who knows? I told Brewer to keep us informed."

Blake asked, "Tell me about her again. Obviously, she didn't attend the fund raiser, but what else do we know about her?"

Leon said, "We know she worked for the Rockefeller Foundation before she went to work at the ACLU. I'll call Agent Brewer and have him give us whatever else he's got on her."

The Wilsons left early so they could stop at the FBI Building across the street to pick up some information for their nighttime reading. Blake suggested to Samantha that they grab a bite to eat someplace quiet and continue discussing their work.

• • •

Samantha drove them to the Ritz Carlton in Georgetown. They sat in the lobby lounge, close to the fireplace, and ordered draft beer and steak sandwiches from the menu. When the waiter left them, Blake noticed his father's closest friend—and Blake's old law school professor—walk into the room. Blake excused himself and went to greet John Palmer, professor emeritus at Georgetown University.

"Blake, nice to see you," said Professor Palmer with a kindly smile, shaking Blake's hand and examining him closely. "It has been awhile. How are you doing? I did not know you were back in town."

"I'm doing fine," answered Blake. "I came back about three weeks ago. I asked Tom Owens if I could help him on this ACLU investigation."

"I see. We have something in common then as Tom contacted me shortly after the explosion, but it was the Department of Defense who actually hired me. I'm working with their bomb experts and weapons experts to track down the origin of the nuclear device."

"Can you join us for dinner or a drink?" asked Blake. "My colleague and I just left the Justice Department to grab a bite to eat. Please join us."

"I would love to, Blake; however, I am waiting to meet a friend to discuss…who knows what?" smiled Palmer, looking over Blake's shoulder. "Besides, it looks to me like you may not want company," he said, nodding his head toward the lovely woman sitting near the fireplace. Then he looked again, studying the woman over the top of his glasses. "Is that Samantha Rhodes?" he asked, almost to himself.

"Yes, that is Samantha Rhodes. She's working with me on this investigation. Do you know her?"

"I was in Korea with her. Well, actually, we were there with about two hundred other people from the State Department, Defense, and the administration, working on nuclear disarmament discussions with North Korea and our allies over there."

"Really?" asked Blake. "I knew she was over there, but I didn't know you were there, too."

"Blake, not only is Samantha beautiful, but she is beautiful *and* smart. Very smart," offered Professor Palmer. "She provided an excellent analysis of variables that gave all of us a number of probable scenarios to work with and consider during the negotiations. She and I became drinking buddies. We even ate *kimchi*—but not until we had a few beers first," he laughed.

"Would you mind if I said hello to her?"

"No, of course not," said Blake.

John Palmer approached Samantha, who was looking intently at her notes. Sensing that someone was in front of her, she looked up and, seeing Palmer, smiled broadly. "John, what a pleasure seeing you again," she said, as she stood to hug Palmer. "You are looking well. Can you join us?"

"Blake told me you two are working together on the ACLU investigation. I didn't know this was something you did, Sam," said Palmer, adding, "not that you wouldn't be excellent at it."

"I try to stay out of Blake's way and not slow him down," Samantha replied, smiling at Blake. "The White House asked me to help in any way that I can, but so far I feel like a potted plant."

"I cannot imagine you slowing down anyone," smiled Palmer. "Most of us had a hard time keeping up with you in Korea." Then turning to Blake, he said, "Blake, she may appear to be a slow starter, but when she understands the terrain, she accelerates fast. Most people stand by in awe. I know I did. Hardly a potted plant. Far from it."

After a brief conversation in which Professor Palmer discussed his long friendship with Blake's father, his involvement with the ACLU investigation and his admiration for Samantha's and Blake's work, Palmer noticed that his friend had arrived. For a moment, he seemed distracted, like his mind jumped someplace else. Then, after a second or two, he added, "Look, if you have a chance, come by my office tomorrow morning around eleven thirty, and we can talk more about the investigation."

Samantha and Blake said good-bye to Palmer and returned to their own conversation. Blake quickly glanced over at Palmer's friend, a man he did not recognize, and the man looked toward their booth. Blake watched as the two of them left the bar without having a drink. That seemed a bit odd.

Over their second draft beer, Blake told Samantha more about John's friendship with Blake's father that had started decades before. "John and my father were law school classmates who became close friends. They worked for the Department of Commerce before going into private practice. John gravitated toward teaching and consulting, and my father left to start his own firm. Actually, it was John who encouraged my father to start his own firm. John, in fact, sent legal work his way.

"John became a world-renowned intellectual property licensing and technology expert. He worked with my father's small firm because of their friendship. At that time, I believe there were only three people in the firm. My father often said John was one of the principal reasons the firm survived and prospered."

"All I can say about John is that he made Korea more interesting than I could ever have imagined," said Samantha. "If I could say more, I would, but I signed a confidentiality agreement and other documents prohibiting me from discussing anything that took place in Korea."

"Under pain of death?" laughed Blake.

"I believe so," smiled Samantha in return.

38

AS SOON AS Blake arrived at the Justice Department the next morning, he called John Palmer's office number to confirm their meeting. Blake's call went directly to voice mail. He left a message stating that he and Sam would be there at eleven-thirty.

The main campus at Georgetown University in the northwest quadrant of Washington occupies approximately one hundred acres above the Potomac River overlooking northern Virginia. Georgetown University is one of twenty-eight colleges and universities that the Society of Jesus established and continually operate in the United States.

Professor Palmer served on the faculty of the Edmund Walsh School of Foreign Service, the oldest school of foreign service in the United States and one of the most prestigious in the world. For Palmer, it was a nice change from teaching law students at the University of Virginia, plus it kept him in Washington full time to pursue his lucrative consulting work.

Palmer's office was in the intercultural center on the campus. Samantha and Blake walked from the parking garage to the quadrangle of buildings at the intercultural center. The air temperature hovered around freezing, with snow falling heavily as they walked to Palmer's building. They opened the lobby door, checked the directory and entered the elevator.

When the elevator doors opened on the fourth floor and they exited, a man ran into them, throwing them back into the elevator car. The man was able to maintain his balance and continued running down the hallway. Blake helped Samantha regain her footing while he watched the man leave through a stairwell door at the end of the hallway.

"What was that?" Samantha exclaimed, straightening her clothing.

"A man in a hurry, I guess," answered Blake, not knowing what to make of it.

They walked down a long hallway to Palmer's office and knocked on his door. No response. Blake tried the doorknob, and the door opened into an anteroom with comfortable-looking leather sofas and armchairs. Photos of cathedrals adorned the few strips of wall that were not covered with floor-to-ceiling bookshelves, filled to capacity.

"John," Blake called out, as he walked toward the closed door to Professor Palmer's interior office. Blake knocked on the door. No answer. He tried the doorknob. It was locked. Checking his watch, Blake confirmed that it was precisely 11:30 a.m. "That's odd," thought Blake, since one of John Palmer's legendary attributes was his punctuality.

"Listen," Samantha whispered. "I think somebody is in there."

They both put their ears to the door. It sounded like labored breathing inside. Blake pounded on the door, but there was no response. He kicked at the door until the frame broke away from the door jamb, and he was able to push in the door.

"Oh my God. John! John!" Blake shouted.

Samantha came in and looked. "Oh, no. Please, God, no."

They found Palmer lying face down, a bloody puddle collecting on the surface of the desk next to his head. Samantha grabbed her cell phone and called 911 while Blake tended to Palmer. She then called Leon who told them to stay put, saying he would come over immediately with another FBI agent.

With tears in his eyes, Blake felt for a pulse on John's neck. It was faint. He twisted John's head slightly to see part of his forehead. Blake inhaled sharply when he saw what looked like a bullet hole in John's forehead. He used his handkerchief to try to stop the blood flow, but the linen handkerchief quickly became soaked and did nothing to stanch the blood leaving Palmer's head.

Blake squeezed Palmer's hand to let him know he was there and to console him.

Samantha joined Blake. She was crying. "John, please stay with us. Please."

The campus police were the first to respond, arriving minutes after the call.

Emergency medical technicians arrived next, closely followed by the District police. The EMTs worked on Palmer, eventually moving him to a gurney. In no time they had him hooked up to tubes, bags and monitors, then they wheeled him out of the office to their ambulance. They told the police and Blake that his condition did not look good. The police taped the area to preserve the crime scene for forensics.

While the EMTs worked on Palmer, Blake noticed the office day planner on the professor's desk. It had "Blake and Samantha" written on that day at eleven-thirty. The only other entry was "MP" at ten. Blake wondered whether it was "MP" who did this. He showed Samantha the entry, and they looked around the office to find anything that might offer a clue as to MP's identity.

They told the police how they found Palmer and at what time. They also described the man who bumped into them before he disappeared into a stairwell at the far end of the hallway.

Shortly after the EMTs left, Leon and two men walked in. Blake quickly explained to Leon what had happened. Leon and the two men introduced themselves to the police and explained that there was a chance Professor Palmer's attack might be linked to their ongoing investigation of the ACLU bombing and fires. They exchanged cards and information. Leon and the two men walked back into the anteroom, closely followed by a detective from the District.

"I am Detective Seiden of the District Police. I'd like to ask you two some more questions," he said, nodding to Samantha and Blake.

"Sure," responded Blake, as Samantha looked on, saying nothing. "But first, may I speak with my associates?" asked Blake, looking toward Leon and the two men.

"Sure, sure," allowed the detective, as he moved back into the office.

"Leon, John Palmer is a close friend of mine and my family. He is Sam's friend, as well. I'd like to think this was a burglary gone wrong; however, it doesn't look that way. I believe John has an apartment on campus here somewhere. Can you find it, and can we get into it?"

"Sure," Leon said. "These are FBI agents Jesus Martinez and Fred Ecker. They will coordinate with the local police, and we'll get you into Palmer's apartment."

39

PALMER LIVED IN the recently completed Jesuit residence center. The complex was originally built for Jesuit priests who were faculty members at Georgetown; however, because there were fewer Jesuit professors than anticipated when the building was erected, the space became available to other professors. John Palmer, who had been living in a townhouse nearby, decided to move on campus.

A Georgetown University police officer was waiting for Leon at the door of the building. He led them into Palmer's apartment on the first floor. Leon spoke with the officer while Samantha and Blake walked into the apartment.

Palmer's apartment was spacious. There was an office, living room, bedroom, and a bathroom but no kitchen since the residents ate their meals in their communal dining room. Similar to his office in the foreign-studies building, Palmer had floor-to-ceiling bookcases lining much of his living room and his office.

Samantha and Blake walked around the living room together. There were numerous photos and memorabilia, plus a small entertainment center with a flat-screen television and audio equipment. Overstuffed leather furniture, including a well-worn recliner, and a few coffee tables stood on a wood floor covered with oriental rugs.

There were also floor lamps and table lamps. Where there were no bookshelves, the walls were covered with bamboo-like wallpaper that had textures and woven materials in rich autumn colors. Overhead indirect lighting was integrated into the decor so as to illuminate select areas of the room, giving the entire space the feel of a men's club.

A few bookshelves were devoted to photo books on cathedrals and European churches. Colorful, contemporary religious artwork was on wall spaces where there were no bookshelves. Blake didn't think this unusual since this was, after all, a Jesuit University, and he knew Professor Palmer was a devout Catholic.

On the coffee tables were framed photos of Palmer and Blake's father, including some in front of European cathedrals, monasteries and parts of the Vatican. In some of the photos, there was another man Blake did not recognize, although he looked vaguely familiar.

Blake viewed the photos with surprise. He didn't remember his father being in Europe to visit cathedrals. It didn't seem like something his father would do. Plus, he knew his father never traveled for pleasure, certainly not by air.

Observing Blake looking closely at a grouping of photos, Samantha asked, "What is it?"

"I don't know. I mean, I do know, but I'm surprised."

"Surprised?"

"Yes. My father is in some of these photos with John and another person. From the background, I would guess that these photos were taken in Italy. It doesn't look like these photos are very old."

"Why is it surprising?"

"I was very close to my father, and I don't remember him traveling to Italy or anywhere in Europe in the years before he died. If he did, he never mentioned it to me. And that alone would be odd."

Samantha examined the photos. She said, "Your father is quite handsome."

As they moved along the wall looking at the other photos and memorabilia, Samantha noted they were from all over the world. She remembered John taking photos in Korea when she was there. He always seemed to have a camera nearby.

Blake snapped pictures of the framed photos that had his father in them.

They moved into the office where Blake opened the drawers of the professor's desk. He found supplies, cough drops, gum, and a loaded handgun. The gun was no surprise since Blake knew the professor went to some scary places around the world, plus he lived in the scariest of them all: the District of Columbia.

Blake examined everything on the top of the desk, starting with junk mail and correspondence, all neatly organized. Lying front-side down under a stack of magazines was a large envelope. Blake picked it up and looked at the front. It had bold capital letters written on it: IN CASE OF MY DEATH OR INCAPACITATING INJURY (SO THAT I CANNOT COMMUNICATE), PLEASE CONTACT HOLLY WATERS IMMEDIATELY. Three phone numbers, two of which had local area codes, were listed.

"Holly Waters?" Blake thought, "When did I last see her? My father's funeral?"

Inside the envelope Blake found copies of John Palmer's last will and testament, health-care directives, health-care power of attorney and another power of attorney. The professor also had two pages of funeral instructions and requests for his funeral service. Blake checked the dates on these documents. Everything had been executed within the past week. Palmer named Holly Waters his executor of his last will and testament and his attorney-in-fact for the health-care directives and the general power of attorney.

Three filing cabinets were arranged along one wall to the right of the desk. Samantha said, "One file cabinet is mostly school-related: lesson plans, tests, papers and so on, along with copies of some legal documents. The other two cabinets contain files for his consulting clients."

Blake and Samantha went through the file drawers. In one folder Blake found another last will and testament, along with health-care directives, health-care power of attorney and general power of attorney. Blake noted the dates on the documents: eight years ago, when his father was still alive. In these documents, John Palmer had named Carson Elliott as his executor and attorney-in-fact. On the outside of the folder was this handwritten advisory: old documents, superseded by new documents, with last week's date, also handwritten.

From the office they moved into the bedroom. It was also neat and well-organized. Samantha searched his closet while Blake went through the drawers of the two dressers in the room. Nothing seemed out of place, or of particular interest, until Blake found a blank postcard.

The photo on the front of the postcard showed the Bay View Brewery and Pub in San Francisco.

40

JORDAN SAT IN the waiting room at the Georgetown University Medical Center where Palmer was in surgery. Along with her were two uniformed police officers.

She had gone to the hospital as quickly as possible after Blake's call in the afternoon. Jordan wanted to be there for the man she called Uncle John.

Palmer had never married and had no living relatives. She wondered who she should contact. She had already tried to reach Holly Waters, leaving a voice-mail message to call Jordan's cell phone immediately.

Jordan figured that the attack on John Palmer would be on local news, and tomorrow morning it would be in the newspapers. Once the word was out, John's friends would be visiting him in the hospital.

Samantha and Blake joined Jordan after they left Palmer's apartment.

"How is he?" asked Blake as he hugged his sister, who had been crying, tears still on her cheeks.

"He's barely alive," Jordan replied, as she hugged Samantha. "I've been here about two hours. I spoke to one of the surgical nurses not long ago. There's nothing to report, except that he is in critical condition."

"This is horrible," Samantha said. "Who would do such a thing?"

Together they waited. Jordan told Blake that she had called Holly Waters but no one answered, so she left a voice mail. Blake, in turn, told Jordan about the large envelope and John's instructions to call Holly if something like this happened to him.

Doctors and nurses and aides went in and out of the surgery area.

Another hour passed.

Then another.

Finally, a doctor came out and walked over to them. He asked if they were family members of Mr. Palmer. Jordan said they were his closest friends and that Mr. Palmer had no family.

The doctor spoke to all of them. "We could not save him. Mr. Palmer died a few minutes ago. I am very sorry for your loss."

41

CNN'S ROUNDTABLE DISCUSSED current events but mostly focused on issues surrounding the ACLU incidents. Panelists included print reporters from the *New York Times, Washington Post, Chicago Tribune* and *Los Angeles Times.*

"What can I say? Events make news. When the pastor of a megachurch in Colorado—I think there are over eleven thousand members, I'd say that qualifies as a megachurch—is linked to drug-fueled trysts with a known homosexual prostitute, that is news. It's news not only for the obvious reasons but also because this pastor, married and the father of five, is the leader of an Evangelical Christian group that is publicly opposed to homosexuality and homosexual marriages. Really, could a Hollywood scriptwriter top this?" the political reporter for the *Washington Post* asked.

"From homily to sodomy. Isn't that what we are talking about? Add some illicit drugs to the sex and you've got a scandal of evangelical proportions. Where is Jimmy Swaggart for God's sake?" laughed the reporter from Los Angeles. "At least he did the heterosexual prostitution thing."

"Is there a pecking order?" asked the female reporter from Chicago, sarcastically. "And, by the way, what does this have to do with the ACLU?"

"Plenty. These are the type of prominent *religious* people who attack the ACLU because the ACLU promotes social justice with respect to gay men and women that these hypocrites attack. This is a great example of the *holier than thou* being brought down," answered the political reporter for the *Washington Post*.

"This is like a sidebar to the attacks on the ACLU. Still, it is very telling that these right-wing religious people do not practice what they preach. Worse, they go out of their way to condemn a lifestyle that is doing them no harm. Look, there are wonderful committed same-sex couples out there—much more committed than the good pastor, apparently," the reporter from the *New York Times* stated.

"Speaking of right-wing Christians, there is one sitting in the White House at the moment. It will be interesting to see if his administration finds the killer or killers of the five hundred in San Francisco. Right now it would appear they are not working too hard to solve this crime."

"Okay," said the host. "We need to take a commercial break, but when we return I want to ask you to consider this: the Boy Scouts don't want homosexuals to be troop leaders, and now maybe they should add Evangelical ministers to that list, as well."

The panel laughed as the screen closed.

The viewing public watched a commercial about erectile dysfunction—ED, as the suave, masculine man with white hair called it, as if referring to a friend.

42

"HOLLY WATERS IS nowhere to be found. We called all her phone numbers and spoke to housekeepers at each address. The one in Arlington said Holly had not been there for a month. The one in Palm Beach said Holly had been there for the past few weeks, but she left immediately after John Palmer called her," Blake said. "According to the housekeeper, no one knew Holly was leaving. And no one knows where she went."

Sapphire had information that she had gathered the day before about John Palmer—including credit-card history showing his travel during the past year, a good portion of it in Korea, Europe, Singapore, India and Hong Kong.

Blake requested information about Palmer's travels in Italy during the past four years. He told Sapphire and Leon about the photos of his father, Palmer, and another man in front of cathedrals and other places that suggested Italy. He showed them the photos on his cell phone.

Leon suggested getting travel information on Blake's father and cross-referencing it with Palmer's travels to find out if they were in Europe at the same time and, if so, where. Blake requested that Holly Walters's travel information be added to the mix.

When Leon and Sapphire left the conference room, they went to Sapphire's office and closed the door. "Are we all on the same page?" wondered Sapphire. "We're supposed to be working on the ACLU investigation. I'm sorry about Professor Palmer, but this is outside the scope of our project here. Don't you agree?"

"Maybe it is just a coincidence, Blake and Samantha running into him in Georgetown, but it was no secret that Palmer was working on this investigation. He has contacts all over the world. Even the general wanted his help in finding the bomb maker."

"Okay, but I think we should waste no more than a day on Palmer's murder. I don't really mean *waste*. However, we have no reason to believe this is related to the ACLU."

"But we don't know for sure," cautioned Leon.

• • •

Later that afternoon, Leon joined them in the conference room. He told Blake that the police had asked faculty and staff at Georgetown University who knew Palmer to review the photos from Palmer's apartment. The other man in the photo with Blake's father and Palmer was Monsignor Dominic Pacelli, a professor of moral theology at the university. He was a close friend of Palmer.

"Is Monsignor Pacelli in town?" asked Blake. We need talk to him."

"*I wish*," Leon said. "You're not going to believe this, but there is another dead body at Georgetown University: Monsignor Pacelli. They just found him in his apartment in the same building where John Palmer lived. He's been dead a day or two. They've got forensics over there now."

Blake and Samantha looked at each other. Sapphire looked at Leon. Everyone was quiet for a moment. Everyone was thinking the same thing: "What is going on? Could this possibly be another coincidence?"

"How did he die?" asked Sapphire.

"He was shot in the face. Like someone took aim at his nose. No one missed him because they thought he was visiting his brother in Maryland."

"Do the police have any ideas?" asked Sapphire.

"Well, they believe he just opened the door and was shot. There is no sign of a struggle. It's too early to know much more."

Blake said, "The monsignor may have been lying dead in his apartment when we were in John's apartment."

Samantha observed, "Blake, everyone in that photo with your father has been murdered. Recently murdered. My sense is that whatever prompted the killing of John and the monsignor may be related to the ACLU bombing."

Leon objected. "That's a stretch, isn't it, Sam? I mean, the ACLU bombing and the murders of Palmer and Pacelli may be unrelated, as much as related. We have nothing linking the two at this time."

"The postcard is a link. Sapphire, we need everything you can find on Monsignor Pacelli. And Leon, please add the monsignor to the cross-referenced travel information on John Palmer, my father and Holly Waters," said Blake.

"Certainly. Here is one question, Blake. The photos of your father, John Palmer, and Monsignor Pacelli. Who took the photos? That person may be in danger," Sapphire said.

"My bet is that Holly took the photos," Blake responded. "We need to find her...and fast."

43

LOOKING OUT THROUGH the dirty windows of the Russian-made sedan, which had been converted into a cab, Roist stared at the garbage heaped alongside the highway leading into the city. He saw frozen carcasses of dogs, cats, goats, and other livestock, mingled with odd pieces of furniture, appliances, broken television sets, and everything else one could imagine finding in a landfill, but not usually along a major highway.

"This is my third trip here and my last," he thought. "What a pigsty, Bucharest." He walked through a small park to University Square where he sat in a coffeehouse until the late afternoon. Dressed like an older graduate student, he blended in with the students in the coffeehouse, as well as those roaming about outside.

The coffeehouse faced a large, concrete building that housed the science departments of the university. Roist thought the building was like every other public building the Russians erected during their time in power. He wondered why the Russians built big ugly buildings. Why not small, if they were going for ugly? Keep the ugly small.

He drank coffee and browsed through a textbook he had picked up. From his table by the window, he watched two specific windows on the seventh floor of the building.

As the sun slowly set, the lights inside those two windows grew more distinct. Lights in the other windows on the seventh floor, and on other floors, were being turned off. Classes were over for the day. The students were gone. The professors were gone.

From his backpack he took out a pair of glasses with a thick black frame and put them on. Next, he tugged a red knit ski hat over his head. Slinging his backpack over one shoulder, he put on his gloves and walked outside. In the below-freezing weather, the ski hat warmed his head, and the thick black-framed glasses punctuated his new look and changed his appearance.

He went into the science building and climbed the stairwell to the seventh floor. Once there, he moved down the hallway to the office whose lighted windows he had been watching from the coffeehouse. He hesitated, waiting for a student to pass. When the hallway was empty, he opened the office door.

"Professor?" he asked, looking straight at the old man sitting in an armchair reading. Roist quickly scanned the small office to make certain no one else was in it. He quietly locked the door behind him and turned his full attention back to the man, who now appeared irritated.

"Professor Blodnisky?"

"Yes," replied the professor, putting down his book to concentrate on Roist. "What is it? Who are you?" he demanded.

Roist rushed the professor, pulling out a sturdy plastic bag from his jacket pocket. He grabbed the professor's throat in a strangle-grip to keep him from screaming and put the plastic bag over his head.

Blodnisky smashed his fists and forearms against Roist's shoulders, hitting him as hard as he could, realizing in horror that this man was trying to kill him. *Was killing him.*

Roist thrust one knee into the professor's stomach to weaken him. He pushed Blodnisky back into the chair and continued the death grip around the man's neck. His left hand held the bag tight over the dying man's head.

When he was finished, he cleaned up around the office, straightened the professor's clothing, put the book the professor was reading back on the professor's chest and closed the dead man's eyelids. With a mortician's attention to detail, Roist made certain that the professor looked good…in death.

Once satisfied with the appearance of the office and the professor, who appeared now like a man who died peacefully while reading, he took a folded piece of paper out of his backpack and put it on the desk, laying it on top of other pieces of mail.

Next, he unlocked the door and peered into the hallway. Seeing no one, he let himself out.

44

ANGELA CARR SAT alone on the spacious veranda, soaking in the moist warmth of the Caribbean sun, her face and body glistening from the sunshine reflecting off the tiny beads of perspiration that seemed to float on her skin.

In front of her lay powdery-white sand etched against the turquoise-blue-green water that was gently stroking the beach. Above her, against an aquamarine sky, white clouds billowed in ever-changing formations fashioned by upper air currents. She thought she could pass the rest of her days simply looking at the fascinating sky, the colorful water, and listening to the gentle waves lapping the beach. What's the worst that could happen? Sunburn?

New York seemed a galaxy away—a bad memory, fading slowly. In retrospect, she marveled that she had ever agreed to do it in the first place. She rebuked herself; after all, she was the one who had brought the documents to her brother's attention. "Pure happenstance, finding those documents," she thought. Now look what had happened. Over five hundred people dead since she gave that information to her brother years ago.

Maybe it was because her world was ending that she agreed to do something so daring, so out of character, as to stay on at the ACLU at her brother's request. After all, she had been questioned three times when they were searching for a mole. How did she manage to avoid suspicion? It seemed improbable. How had she survived? Was survival even the best thing for her? Maybe she could have forced her own death, had she spoken out. Now here she was. She thought about her circumstances, her life as it was:

Her wonderful husband was gone.

Her medical situation was terminal—or not. She was in remission.

She was in hiding.

She was scared they would find her and kill her. But, honestly, how much life did she have to lose? Now, looking out at the multi-hued water and glorious sky, she realized how happy she was just to be alive *for this moment*. How long would she have? No one knew, not even her doctors.

Remission. It was a funny word, pregnant with hope and possibility...and dread. The sands of the hourglass, and all of that.

Life. Living. But for how long? How long?

First she had lost her husband, who loved life to the fullest and loved her more than anything. Why did God take him away? She grieved; she became angry. She hated her life alone.

It was her brother who gave her a purpose again, knowing that her medical condition might worsen at any moment.

Living day by day. That was how she existed during those years in New York after she discovered the documents. Living day by day.

45

ROIST FLEW TO Belgrade, Serbia, where he had a short layover, and then on to Zagreb, Croatia. He slept on both flights and washed and shaved in the airport bathrooms.

From the Zagreb airport he took a bus to the center of the city. He walked through light snow flurries to the Upper Town to exercise his legs after sitting so long in cramped airplane seats. He walked until he found a place to sit across the street from the Science and Technology Research Institute bordering Zagreb University.

Students passed in front of him, ignoring him, not even wondering why anyone might be sitting on a bench in near freezing weather. The snow grew heavier as it kept falling. Roist figured bigger snowflakes acted as a blanket against the cold. Every so often he dusted the snow from his clothing.

Bucharest had seemed much colder and damper, but that was Romania—only suitable for vampires. Still, vampires notwithstanding, Bucharest provided a good start. Since he knew Professor Blodnisky's office location at the university there, it proved quite easy to get in and out without any trouble. This place might not be as easy because he did not have current office information, only the building number.

In the late afternoon, when most of the students were gone for the day, Roist put on his black-framed glasses and a bright-blue ski hat this time. He walked across the street and entered the building. To his dismay the walls inside the lobby were plastered with posters and notices in a language he could not read. He finally found what he thought was a directory for the building. As he stood there trying to find the one recognizable name he needed, a young woman tapped him on the shoulder. He turned to hear her speak unintelligibly. His blank stare prompted her to speak in recognizable French, a language he knew well. She simply wanted to help him because he looked lost.

He replied in French, telling her that he was from Grenoble, France to surprise his Uncle Vlad who was a professor in this building. Could she help him find his office?

Thirty minutes later, Roist left the building and into a snowstorm. Even with the wind howling and the snow crunching loudly beneath his footsteps, he could hear his heart racing. His head was drenched with sweat under the ski hat.

Uncle Vlad had surprised him with his strength and his will to live. Roist tussled with the old man longer than he expected, trying to keep him quiet while suffocating him—not that easy today. Roist meticulously cleaned the office before leaving. It had to look like the old man only wrestled his heart, thrashing around the room but losing the match in the end. Another death by natural causes.

As he had done before in Bucharest, Roist pulled a piece of paper from his backpack and put it on the dead man's desk prior to leaving the office.

Walking through the near-blizzard, Roist thrust his hands into his jacket pockets to keep them warm. He felt the moist plastic bag in one pocket—moisture from the professor's mouth and his dying breath. He threw away the plastic bag.

"It should be easier than that to kill an old man," Roist thought. Then, he regretted that thought and said a prayer for Uncle Vlad.

46

BLAKE TOLD JORDAN about the envelope found in John Palmer's apartment.

"Did you reach Holly?" asked Jordan.

"No. We can't find her," answered Blake. "We have her address here and in Palm Beach, but she isn't at either location. We're checking other sources, so maybe we will be able to find her soon. Holly has no family anymore, and I don't know about her circle of friends, other than John and Dad."

"Dad used to say Holly's circle of friends included the wealthiest people in the country and the world, and some of the most powerful. He often wondered why she worked at all, much less working for the firm. But the answer was obvious. She *loved* him," Jordan declared. "She wanted to be with him every day."

Blake looked at his sister quizzically.

Jordan returned a steady gaze. "It's true. Women know these things."

Samantha nodded her head.

They were at the funeral home making arrangements for John Palmer's memorial. When they were finished, Blake and Samantha walked Jordan to her car. They hugged goodbye, and she drove away.

• • •

"Buy you a drink?" Samantha asked, as she and Blake walked to their car.

"Sure, but only if it is a very large drink," smiled Blake in return.

Samantha drove them to the Ritz Carlton in Georgetown, her favorite place, and the last place they had seen John Palmer alive. Inside, they found a leather sofa by the fireplace in the intimate Lobby Lounge and ordered their drinks. In the background, Nat King Cole sang:

> Chestnuts roasting on an open fire
> Jack Frost nipping at your nose
> Yuletide carols being sung by a choir
> And folks dressed up like Eskimos

When the drinks arrived, Blake asked, "What do you think? Would you take this assignment again?"

Samantha looked at Blake and answered, "In a nanosecond. This is interesting. Very challenging. 'Why would I do it again,' you might ask? Because, unlike my regular work, in this investigation there is no entity or person on the other side to analyze and project future actions. Here, we have to solve *for the identity* of the other side. Plus, in this situation everything *has already happened*. To solve the problem, you need to use experience, intuition, investigative skills, a little luck, and then maybe you'll find the solution. If we could find the origin of the nuclear device, that would help tremendously.

"Right now, we're in a fact-gathering mode, focusing on the ACLU. However, we also have the murders of John Palmer and Monsignor Pacelli to consider, along with the disappearance of Angela Carr and Holly Waters. Are these related or unrelated events?"

"Do you think the murders of John Palmer and the monsignor just might be a bizarre coincidence?" asked Blake.

Samantha looked over the rim of her glass at the flames flickering in the fireplace. She slowly put down her glass and turned fully to face Blake. "That is the question of the moment, isn't it?" She said this as much to herself as to Blake and then added, "I think it's unlikely that John's murder is a coincidence—something unrelated to the investigation. Why? Because John was working on the ACLU investigation as well, and he was murdered after we saw him but before our meeting with him to talk about the ACLU investigation. When we saw him here he said he had something to share with us, so he invited us to visit him. I believe that was the reason he was killed. Which means he must have been followed when we last saw him."

"I agree with you. I don't believe in coincidence," Blake said. "I think your conclusion may be right on target."

Samantha enjoyed sitting next to Blake. She appreciated his intelligence, certainly, but there were intangibles that, well, thrilled her about him. Yet, she could not quickly describe what they were. She chastised herself for thinking about such things while Blake was explaining his thoughts on a serious matter.

Blake shrugged his shoulders ever so slightly and said, "Italy may be the key to this. But why?"

47

ROIST RAISED THE wineglass to admire the ruby color of its contents. He swirled the glass, noting the liquid fingers clinging to the inside. Next, he brought the glass to his nose. He inhaled the vapors once, twice, three times. Then he drank deeply.

After continuous travel over the past four days, Roist rewarded himself with an excellent meal at a first-class restaurant that was close to the Parliament buildings in Zagreb. His body ached from lack of sleep in a decent bed, but tonight he would be in a comfortable bed at an airport hotel.

Pouring more wine into his glass, Roist was thankful he would not have to go to Estonia to visit another scientist. Blessedly, natural causes—the kind he tried to stage—had intervened in his favor. The scientist was dead.

Roist celebrated his good fortune with a bottle of vintage Bordeaux. Good fortune smiled on him, he thought. These scientists were well into their eighties. So, if each one were to be found slumped over his desk or in his favorite chair, it would be assumed that a fatal heart attack or stroke was the natural cause of death—the normal end to a long life. Nothing suspicious. Just old age inexorably at work. No autopsy needed. Death comes. Life goes.

"Tomorrow I leave for Prague. Then it is over."

• • •

At the airport in Prague, Czech Republic, Roist boarded a bus to the subway that took him to the train station. When the train arrived in Pilsen, he took a cab to the area of the Great Synagogue. He registered at a local hotel, telling the desk clerk that he was a tourist from Slovenia. The desk clerk gave him a map of the immediate area, one that included cultural sites and other information a tourist might find useful. More useful to Roist, however, were the names of the streets on the map.

In his hotel room, Roist pulled out the note he had in his coat pocket. He found the street on the map that corresponded to the street name written on the note; however, he could not determine where the actual numerical address was on the map. Still, it was enough for him to get started. He would find his way.

Roist pulled his ski cap down over his ears and pulled up the collar of his coat to protect his neck from the savagely cold wind. He thrust his gloved hands into his coat pockets to keep them out of the wind. Underfoot, the icy snow on the sidewalk creaked as he walked to the street named in the note. Streetlights came on, even though the winter sky still offered some lingering natural light. He looked at his watch. It was only three-thirty in the afternoon. The days were quite short this late in the calendar year. Soon it would be dark.

When he arrived at the desired street, Roist didn't know which way to turn to find the address he needed, so he jumped on a tram heading in one direction, hoping it might be the correct one. It was a good call. He got off one block past the address. To his surprise, the location turned out to be a nursing home or hospice. He could not determine which, as he stood in front of the building. "Now what?" he thought. This was an interesting development. Maybe the man was dying. Maybe he was already dead.

His face was being assaulted by the frigid wind. He angled his body so that his back took the brunt of the bitterly cold, blustery weather, giving his face some momentary relief. But almost immediately he felt cold daggers stabbing their way across his shoulder blades and lower back. He just wasn't dressed properly for these frigid conditions. Every part of his body ached from the icy assault.

"Tomorrow," he thought. No need to rush this.

That evening he ate in the dining room of his hotel and drank the famous local beer. Later, in his room, he opened his shaving gear and found the small bottle. He put the bottle on his nightstand, cranked the knobs on the tepidly warm radiators as far as they would turn, and tried to fall asleep.

Overnight the temperature plunged well below freezing. The wind gusting from the north created a deadly wind chill. The radiators under the windows in his room knocked incessantly, irritating Roist. Even more irritating was the screeching wind that hammered the windows. He could not sleep. Two hours before dawn he was up and already dressed. He looked outside through the frosted window panes. The dark street was empty.

He used his tactical knife to cut open the top of his fleece ski hat, which he then pulled down over his head and face to cover his throat and neck. He tugged some of it up to cover his nose. He put on the other ski hat and pulled it down over his ears. He already had on tightly knit long underwear—the type used for skiing in the Alps. His trousers were wool. He put on a fleece jacket and a fleece vest under his coat.

Roist left the hotel by the back stairwell. Outside, the wind blasted his body and sucked his breath away. He had taken a wool blanket from his hotel room. He pulled it over his shoulders and the back of his head and neck and, even though he had on gloves, he wrapped the blanket around his gloved hands to keep them as warm as possible. His toes and feet were already becoming numb. He had failed in the shoe department, having only casual shoes and cotton socks. It felt like all his body heat was escaping through his feet.

No cabs. No buses. No vehicles on the street. It was predawn. Roist jogged to the address he found last night. It took at least twenty minutes. By then he had lost all feeling in his toes.

He entered the building through a rear delivery entrance that had a broken lock. Inside, he stood in place for five minutes to allow his body to warm up and his hands and feet to feel more comfortable. He could not remember ever being so cold. He exercised the fingers of both hands, including moving his wrists back and forth. He did toe stands to get blood moving and to generate warmth in his feet.

Next, Roist folded the blanket and hid it. He walked down a hallway that led him to the reception area on the main floor. He knew the building had three floors. Somewhere inside this building was the man he would kill.

The reception area was empty. No one attended the front desk. Roist assumed it was too early to have it staffed. He found the room directory, and using the man's last name, Roist found the man's room number. It was on the first floor, back the same hallway he had just walked through.

Roist found the room he wanted. Slowly, he pushed open the door and entered the room. Modest illumination from a nightlight plugged into the wall socket near the bed was sufficient for him to see that only one person was sleeping in the room. He noticed another bed pushed up against the far wall, but it was empty.

As he stood close to the bed, listening to the man's heavy breathing, Roist pulled on a pair of latex gloves from his pocket and took out a handkerchief and the small bottle. He unscrewed the top and poured all the liquid from the bottle into the handkerchief. Then, using both hands he pressed the handkerchief over the sleeping man's nose and mouth, holding it hard as the man's head and body jerked awake.

The deadly handkerchief muffled the man's last gasps at life. After a minute, Roist removed the handkerchief and rearranged the man's countenance to approximate sleeping. He screwed the top back on the bottle, wrapped the bottle in the handkerchief, and put them in his pocket.

No one was in the hallway. He moved to the exit door and peered out the small window. No one was approaching. Roist pulled the blanket back over his shoulders and opened the door carefully so the wind wouldn't catch it and bang it against the handrail. Everything had gone perfectly. He didn't want a clanging sound to alert anyone.

Roist left the warmth of the building to rejoin the frigid world he previously occupied. As he retraced his steps, wind swirled around him, lifting the blanket off his shoulders. "Could it get any colder?" he wondered, as he clutched the wool blanket around the back of his neck and head.

Sleep deprivation, coupled with the bitter weather conditions, made for an unhappy man. He could not will his legs to jog back to the hotel, so he settled for a quick walk, although he didn't think his legs were moving very fast. He peered over the makeshift scarf covering his nose and saw no one in the streets ahead.

The blowing snow obscured the definition between street and sidewalk as he plodded forward, sometimes on the sidewalk and sometimes in the street. "What does it matter?" he thought. "There are no vehicles out in these conditions." He felt frigid but oddly ebullient because he was finished with killing scientists.

May they rest in peace.

48

BY THIS TIME, all the attendees, staff, protestors, and police officers at the ACLU fund raiser had been identified and investigated. The FBI agents, and all the other law-enforcement departments and agencies assisting, reached the inescapable conclusion that the ACLU *itself* was the target, not any particular individual or small groups of individuals, such as politicians or judges. In addition, those investigating domestic hate groups found nothing to support spending any further time digging deeper. Certainly hatred and motive existed, but no group had the means to create such a sophisticated explosive device.

Homeland security and related agencies that focused on international terrorists could not find any actionable evidence pointing to any terrorist group as having had a role in the explosion in San Francisco. While some groups claimed responsibility, there was nothing to support their involvement.

Law enforcement worked by their rules, comfortable in their routine activities relating to finding factually accurate information and evidence to support criminal activity, intent, motive, means and opportunity. In short, all the checklist items needed to prove a simple homicide case were followed, only the scale of the crime was supersized. The obvious impediment to their routine was the total lack of evidence available to them at the crime scene.

FBI agents and all law-enforcement investigators are, first and foremost, human beings. Even the most experienced among them are able to maintain a clinical detachment for only so long before passion trumps objectivity. As a result, the heads of agencies, including the director of the FBI, had to continually remind their people to stay focused on the elements of the crime and not to be biased by the work the ACLU performed.

Most of the investigators were Christian, to varying degrees, and it soon became apparent that they held a group belief that the ACLU was attacked because of its continual assault on Christianity in the United States. The fact that the explosion happened close to Christmas only served to reinforce that belief, and the reinforcement of that belief made the investigators less interested in solving the crime, although they would never admit it.

Human issues aside, the lack of evidence of any sort was dispiriting. There was so much pressure put on the investigators to find something, anything, that their work habits and long hours fueled a feeling of angry depression and increasing lethargy.

Matters were not quite as bad for those investigators searching for the origin of the explosive device. Their starting point was far better because they had databases and historical knowledge available to them going back decades regarding nuclear tactical device manufacture and the ingredients needed for such a device. There were names, biographies, locations, and other information, all of which helped the investigators ramp up their work quickly. While this information wasn't evidence of any sort, it offered pathways *to* evidence.

John Palmer was part of the investigation team looking into the history of the Soviet Union nuclear-technology programs: the players, their work and what happened to that technology and those scientists and their work *after* the collapse of the Soviet Union. He had responsibility for tracking key nuclear scientists, including the four scientists who had been friends since their days at the

University of Krakow. In fact, John Palmer knew each of them and had worked with them during the past three to four years.

Because of the high-level sensitivity of this part of the investigation into the origin of the explosive device and the need to maintain secrecy, the information disseminated to those involved *in the other part* of the ACLU investigation was only carefully filtered summaries, without specifics. The information about John Palmer knowing and working with the four nuclear scientists, for example, was never disclosed.

49

SAPPHIRE OPENED THE door and walked in. "All right, here's what I have," she said. "Background on the dead priest, Monsignor Pacelli, and travel information on John Palmer, the monsignor, and your father, Blake. I also have information on Holly Waters. Do you want to discuss this now or wait?" asked Sapphire.

"Now," answered Blake. "Maybe we can find something that will link us to the ACLU, particularly since John Palmer was hired to help in finding the origin of the bomb."

"Dominic Anthony Pacelli was born in Providence, Rhode Island, in 1952. He graduated from Boston College and then entered the Jesuit seminary in Massachusetts. He was ordained in Rome and studied there for a number of years, during which time he received several degrees, including a doctorate in moral theology. When he returned to the United States he taught at the Jesuit School of Theology in Berkeley, California, and at the University of San Francisco. For the past seven years, he has been teaching at Georgetown University.

"The Monsignor was one of five children. His four siblings are still living, although his parents are not. He has two sisters and two brothers. One sister lives in Virginia, and the other lives in Rhode Island. One brother lives in Kentucky, and the other one lives in a veteran's hospital near Annapolis."

Sapphire continued, "Monsignor Pacelli traveled extensively to Europe, often taking student groups to visit cathedrals and the Vatican. According to Georgetown administration, Monsignor Pacelli and Professor Palmer were good friends. They often traveled to Europe together. They shared the same interest in exploring the famous cathedrals of Europe."

"Leon, can we get into the monsignor's office and his apartment?" asked Samantha, surprising everyone by the request.

"Well, yes, I suppose we can, but we may have to do it under the radar," answered Leon. "Why?"

"I have a hunch," Samantha smiled, knowing that intuition wasn't the reason she was in this group. "Here is what I am thinking," she continued. "When we ran into John the night before he was killed, he was waiting to meet someone. When that person arrived they left the premises immediately. My hunch is that the man meeting John was the monsignor.

"For the sake of argument, let's say that John knew something important regarding this investigation. When he saw us together and learned we were working on the same investigation, maybe he became alarmed," offered Samantha, looking over at Blake.

No one commented, so she continued, "Okay, we have no idea if or why John became alarmed, but let's assume he did and that it had to do with the investigation, and/or maybe it had something to do with knowing both Blake and me. Remember, I worked closely with John in Korea for about one month not that long ago."

"But if he were alarmed," said Leon "as you suggest, why would he invite you to meet with him the next day? Was he going to tell you something? Why did he want to see you? And why in his office?"

Blake added, "I don't know. Maybe he wasn't alarmed. Maybe he was concerned for our safety. Besides, these are all suppositions."

Sapphire then said, "Maybe he was neither. Maybe we, you, are grasping at straws."

"If the glove doesn't fit, you must acquit," Leon whispered.

Smiles around the table.

"O.J. Simpson trial. Right?" Samantha said. "But wait. Think about it. John is murdered and it doesn't appear to be a burglary. This happens the day after he saw us and learned of our involvement in the ACLU investigation. He asked us to meet him the very next day, and he was killed immediately before he was to meet with us. Then his friend Monsignor Pacelli is murdered at about the same time that John is killed.

"When we visited John's apartment, we found a number of photos with Blake's father and the monsignor in them. What, if anything, might those photos have to do with the ACLU? And then Holly Waters disappears after she gets a phone call from John. It may all be coincidence; however, I doubt that it is. There are too many linkages. Don't forget the postcard we found in John's dresser. Isn't that in the category of a terrific clue? If only we knew what it meant."

"We may be dealing in suppositions, but that postcard is real. It *is* a terrific clue, and it directly points to Palmer's involvement with the ACLU bombing," Leon said.

"I know, I know," Samantha continued. "What is the likelihood that these recent events are *not* connected to the ACLU? Don't forget, in John's office, in his day planner on his desk, he had the initials MP written for a meeting shortly before our scheduled meeting. 'MP' equals Monsignor Pacelli. That's my bet."

"What is the likelihood that they *are* connected?" asked Blake. "We can't ignore the fact that someone killed the monsignor and John Palmer. I agree with Sam on that. I also agree that their murders are surrounded by a number of possibilities—many relating to the ACLU investigation, and some not. I don't want to waste any of our time, but until we get more information about John Palmer and the monsignor, we won't know enough to make a decent judgment call."

Leon and Sapphire looked at each other the way married couples do when they are sending telepathic messages back and forth. They nodded in agreement.

Sapphire added, "We have the professor's telephone records around the time of his attack. One call was to Holly Waters at nine-thirty the same night he ran into you two in Georgetown."

"We saw him no later than eight, I would guess," said Blake.

Sapphire shared information about Palmer and Monsignor Pacelli, including their insurance and banking data. Palmer had never married. His parents died years ago. He had no siblings. His banking and investment information showed that he had over $8 million in investments and savings. In his will, he set aside $1 million in trust for Jordan's children and one million for Blake; the remainder he gave to the law school at the University of Virginia and Georgetown University School of Foreign Service.

The monsignor's checking and savings accounts only had $34,000 in them. He gave that money to his siblings. The beneficiary of Monsignor Pacelli's modest $20,000 life-insurance policy was Gethsemani Abbey in Kentucky.

"Kentucky?" asked Blake, picking up on the named beneficiary of the monsignor's life-insurance policy. "Kentucky is where one brother lives. Do we have an address for this brother?"

"Right now all we know is that he lives someplace in Kentucky," answered Sapphire.

50

LATER THAT AFTERNOON they were able to get into the monsignor's office in the religion building on campus. A university police officer opened the door for them and stood inside.

Leon found a desk calendar that showed a ten o'clock appointment with Professor Palmer the day the monsignor was murdered. There was no computer in the office, even though there was a modem connected to a cable outlet in the wall next to the desk. A slight imprint on the desk mat suggested the previous weight of a laptop.

Blake and the others looked through Monsignor Pacelli's books and desktop papers. There were a number of photos on the walls, bookcases, and credenza, along with religious artwork. One photo showed Monsignor Pacelli with a woman, a man, and a number of children. "Maybe the monsignor's older sister, her husband, and children," Blake thought.

The file cabinets were locked, but Leon quickly opened them with something he pulled from his pocket. He smiled at Blake as he opened the top drawer.

Three of the four file drawers contained teaching materials, student papers, grading information, and related source materials for theology classes. The fourth file drawer was filled with travel information—including photos of churches and cathedrals, all of which appeared to be located in Europe.

The photos on the wall showed Monsignor Pacelli with a number of other priests, students, bishops and cardinals, along with photos of the monsignor in Rome with Pope John Paul and one photo with John Paul's successor, Pope Benedict. Sapphire pointed out that among the photos of the monsignor, there were a number with Cardinal Ratzinger before he was elected pope and took the name Benedict.

Sapphire remembered from her workup of the monsignor that he had lived, studied, and worked in Rome for more than a decade after he left Boston College. She made a note to herself to find out whether the monsignor worked in the Vatican when he was in Rome.

When they were finished, the university police officer closed the office, locked the door and gave Leon the key to the monsignor's living quarters in the Jesuit residence building.

The monsignor's apartment could have been John Palmer's apartment, it was so similar. Bookshelves filled most of the walls, and there were photos on walls and horizontal surfaces. There was a photo of the monsignor, John Palmer, Blake's father, and four other men on one bookshelf. The men were seated at a rectangular table located on a sun-drenched, vine-covered patio. On the table were platters of food, loaves of bread, and bottles of wine. All of the men in the photo were dressed in casual attire. It was either Napa or Italy.

More photos showed the monsignor with the last pope, the current pope, and other priests. All these photos were taken inside. One photo must have been of the monsignor's mother and father. Other photos appeared to be of family members. There was one photo of a young woman in cap and gown and the monsignor, dressed in a black suit, with his arm around her shoulder. There appeared to be a family resemblance.

Samantha checked the bookcases, desktop and desk drawers for mail, papers, or anything of interest. Twin wooden file cabinets were in the apartment's office, but the drawers were locked. Leon quickly opened them with the same device he used in the monsignor's teaching office. The file cabinets held lesson plans and documents pertaining to one subject matter or another, and folders of information relating to cathedrals and monasteries in the United States, Europe, and around the world. Everything was very similar to what they found in his office in the religion building, except for one file drawer that held a number of photos that appeared to be family photos, some quite old. The photos showed a mother and father and their five children, all elementary-school age or younger. The three boys looked like their father, and the two girls looked like their mother.

There were other photos of the same children wearing school uniforms, at various ages, and photos of parents—growing older. There were group photos of priests and other photos, including some with John Palmer and Blake's father.

The photos of the monsignor with Blake's father were of great interest to Blake because he had no knowledge that his father even knew Monsignor Pacelli. Of course, Blake realized his father knew hundreds of people, and Blake only had knowledge of a fraction of them. It still seemed odd to him that his father never mentioned going to Italy. Perhaps Jordan knew about this. Maybe his father *had* mentioned it to him at a time when Blake was in deep mourning over Annie's and Connor's deaths.

The monsignor's bedroom was as simple as a monk's cell: a narrow bed with a thin mattress, a table and chair, a nightstand with a lamp, an inexpensive wooden chest of drawers and an overhead light. His closet contained very little clothing.

The walls of the bedroom were painted white, and each wall had religious artwork on it. On one side of his bed was a small piece of carpet, almost like a carpet sample from a flooring store. There were worn imprints that suggested he used the carpet to kneel on by his bed to pray. The wall behind his bed held a crucifix. The opposite wall held a carved wooden plaque that said: *Ad Majorem Dei Gloriam.*

Sapphire said, "That's the motto of the Society of Jesus from its founder St. Ignatius of Loyola. It is Latin and means 'for the greater glory of God.' This is what the monsignor looked at every night as he fell asleep."

51

THE NEXT MORNING Blake called his father's law firm and spoke with the managing partner, a person he knew well. Blake explained the circumstances regarding the investigation. He asked to review his father's files and travel logs for anything pertaining to travel to Europe.

Blake then called Jordan. He asked her about their father's travels to Europe, either on business or pleasure, and whether he might have known Monsignor Dominic Pacelli. Jordan remembered their father going to Europe a few times with John Palmer, but she had no knowledge of Monsignor Pacelli.

"What was Dad doing there?" asked Blake.

"I think it was work-related. That was why John went with him or met him there. You were gone at the time, or we didn't know where you were. I remember because Dad wanted you to know where he was, in case you needed him. But no one knew where you were," she repeated, gently poking him with her intonation.

"How long ago?"

"Three years, maybe. Shortly after Mother died, I think. What is going on?" asked Jordan.

"I really don't know," answered Blake, honestly. He told Jordan what he had learned about Monsignor Pacelli, about the photos with their father, and the fact that the priest was murdered about the same time as John Palmer. He mentioned the day planner on John's desk with the initials "MP" written in for the meeting earlier the day John was killed.

Jordan could not believe there had been another murder on campus at Georgetown University. She was stunned.

"I'm going to the firm this afternoon to find out what I can about Dad going to Europe with John, and anything to do with Monsignor Pacelli. I'll let you know," said Blake, ringing off.

• • •

Midmorning Leon came into the conference room with a sheaf of papers in his hand. "Okay. First, the good monsignor. Agents contacted most of his siblings. There is the sister living in Providence, Rhode Island: Her name is Rose Montebello. She is married, with three adult children. Her husband works for the Rhode Island Department of Revenue. She operates a children's day care in her home. The last time she had contact with the monsignor was a few weeks ago. He called to tell her that he might be going to Italy and, if so, would not be back for Christmas. Mrs. Montebello mentioned a younger sister whose name is Maria. No one has heard from this sister for almost seven years. The last place she lived, according to Mrs. Montebello, was someplace in Maryland or Virginia.

"Agents contacted the brother who lives in a veterans administration nursing home outside of Baltimore, close to Annapolis. His name is Franco Pacelli. He is suffering from multiple strokes. He never married. He retired from the navy and went to work for the Social Security Administration until he retired again. He is seventy-one years old. He did not know when he last spoke to the monsignor, although the nursing-home records show that the monsignor saw him the same day he called Mrs. Montebello."

Leon continued. "Monsignor Pacelli has a twin brother—an identical twin. He is a monk at the Abbey of Gethsemani in Kentucky. Remember Gethsemani? That was the named beneficiary of the monsignor's life-insurance policy. The monsignor's brother has been there for about thirty years.

"And get this. He isn't there right now. His abbot doesn't know where he is. The monk's name is Father Leo Pacelli. He has cancer, and he received permission from the abbot to travel here for a cancer clinical-trial research program at George Washington University Medical Center. He left the monastery six days ago. His scheduled appointment was four days ago, but he never showed. According to the abbot, Father Leo was going to stay in a guest apartment at Georgetown University, which was to be arranged by his brother, the monsignor."

Blake started to say, "Call over there and—"

"I already have someone checking Georgetown University to find out if Father Leo ever arrived. According to the head man at his monastery, the abbot, Father Pacelli does not have a cell phone. In fact, this was the first time Father Pacelli left the monastery in thirty years, except for local doctor and dentist appointments.

"The abbot said that Father Leo does not have a driver's license but he did have some other form of identification, plus some cash. No credit cards. The people at the abbey drove him to the airport in Louisville and got him through security and onto the plane. According to the abbot, the monsignor was scheduled to meet Father Leo at Reagan National Airport, take him to Georgetown University where he was to stay, and then take him to George Washington Medical Center the next day."

"Did the agents get any recent photos of the siblings?" asked Blake.

"No, Mrs. Montebello had no recent pictures of her brothers or her sister, but I do have some old photos," answered Leon as he passed around copies of the photos sent to him.

One group of photos showed Mrs. Montebello, along with family pictures that she had in her house. The photos included one with all the siblings, although it was more than thirty-five years old and was very grainy, making the figures look like they were covered with gauze.

Blake asked Leon if there was an autopsy done on Monsignor Dominic Pacelli. "We need to confirm that the dead person is really the monsignor."

Sapphire looked at her husband and said, "This is getting weird."

"Weirder," Leon corrected her.

52

SAPPHIRE COMPLETED REVIEWING a cross-reference of travel information involving Carson Elliott, John Palmer, Monsignor Pacelli, and Holly Waters. The data came from multiple sources, including credit-card-processing bureaus, travel manifests, and customs information, among others.

"There are a number of dates where John Palmer and the monsignor were on the same plane—mostly to Italy, but also to other places in Europe, including Eastern Europe. Your father and Holly Waters were not on any of those flights.

"It was about three years ago that your father started flying to Rome, always with Holly Waters but never with John Palmer or Monsignor Pacelli.

"Your father and Holly Waters never flew anywhere else in Europe, as far as we can determine. It was always Dulles Airport to Rome Fiumicino Airport. Their time in Italy never lasted more than four days. In Rome they stayed at the same hotel as John Palmer. There is no record of the monsignor staying there."

Blake sat silent, his mind filled with questions. He knew that his father wouldn't have cared about visiting cathedrals. He didn't even go to church. He also didn't care about visiting Europe—or anywhere else, for that matter. He didn't like to travel. While many members of the firm racked up hundreds of thousands of travel miles, Carson Elliott was content staying in Washington.

• • •

Leon walked over to Blake, Samantha, and Sapphire with a photo in his hand. "Look at this," he said. "This woman worked in the New York office of the ACLU. We got these photos of her from the ACLU website. She helped arrange the party but didn't go to San Francisco. She's the one who disappeared after the fire. This is Angela Carr."

They each looked at the photo being passed around. Silence filled the room, as the four of them looked at one another.

"There's a family resemblance surely, don't you think?" Samantha said, referring to the photos from Monsignor Pacelli's apartment and the photos of Angela Carr. She placed them on the conference table for Blake, Sapphire and Leon to view.

Sapphire responded, "There absolutely is. She looks like her mother."

Leon said, "She may just look like a member of the family. All Italians look alike, right?"—trying to inject a little ethnic humor in the mix. "As I recall, when the police and FBI interviewed the sister in Rhode Island after the monsignor's murder, she made no mention of an Angela Carr. She called her younger sister by a different name."

• • •

In the early afternoon, more information came in regarding Angela Carr. Sapphire held copies of investigative reports, plus her own notes. "Here is a headline! Angela Carr's maiden name is Pacelli."

Everyone stopped their work and looked at Sapphire.

"Her full name is *Maria* Angela *Pacelli* Carr. She's a widow. Her husband Bradley Carr died of cancer ten years ago. No children. She never remarried. She started work at ACLU National Headquarters about five years ago. She lives alone in an apartment on Staten Island.

"Pacelli?" asked Samantha.

"I guess there was no reason to tell anyone her maiden name," Sapphire continued. "According to these reports, she had a number of friends at the ACLU office in Manhattan. Her work was outstanding, and she seemed to be a trusted team member. The people the agents spoke to said she was full of fun and very intelligent. The human resources person remembered only one photo on Carr's desk, a wedding photo. They all knew she was a widow because they often tried to play matchmaker, but she was never interested. No boyfriends that we know of."

"So this is the sister Mrs. Montebello called Maria?" Samantha said. "She is the monsignor's sister. He is dead, or his brother is dead. She may be dead. Or they are all dead."

53

AT FIVE O'CLOCK Blake began getting ready to go to his old law firm. This would be his first visit there since Annie and Connor died...and his first visit there without his father's presence. Blake debated taking someone with him; he thought it would be helpful if Samantha went along since she brought a different skill set. Or was he kidding himself? Did he just want her to go because he wanted her with him?

Blake *and* Samantha took a cab to the law firm. They spent only a minute or two in the reception area before Peter Babcock, the managing partner, came out to greet Blake warmly and to be introduced to Samantha. He guided them back through wood-paneled hallways and past sharp-looking lawyers—many of whom greeted Blake as he walked past—and into a familiar corner office, the office that had once belonged to his father. It surprised Blake that no one had moved into his father's office.

Sensing this, Babcock said, "Blake, as you may remember, I was the fifth lawyer your father hired for this firm. Now we have over three hundred lawyers—small by many standards, but that is by design. Your father created this firm. He molded it. He developed and nurtured our loyal client base. He also educated most of us in how to be the best lawyers we could be.

"This office held magic for all of us when he occupied it. He was everything to this firm. We wanted to honor him by keeping this office as it was when he was here. For special occasions, we use his private conference room. This is where we have his files and the other information you requested," Babcock said, leading Blake and Samantha through the spacious office to a door that led into a moderate-sized conference room.

Standing inside the door was another person who Babcock introduced as Sheila Cohen, a paralegal in the firm. Babcock said she was the person instrumental in pulling all the files together. Sheila would be available to answer any questions regarding the files, to the extent she was permitted by client confidentiality and attorney-client privilege. Babcock excused himself, saying he would check back later.

The firm had no records of any clients of Carson Elliott in Europe. Cohen could not find anything indicating that his father traveled to Europe to meet with clients of the firm. In addition, the law firm's travel agency had no record of Carson Elliott flying to Europe.

It was one of the anecdotes the firm enjoyed about its founding partner. Whereas other lawyers relished the idea of flying on a client's new Gulfstream or the latest Boeing Business Jet, the most important lawyer of them all flew first class on a commercial airplane, the bigger the better. Carson Elliott preferred to meet his clients in his office.

Blake asked Sheila about Monsignor Pacelli. She said she had never heard of him, except what she had recently read in the local paper about his murder at Georgetown University. She called someone to check the monsignor's name in the law firm's index of names. After a few minutes, a call came back to say the firm had no record of his name in any capacity—not a client, not a party to any litigation or commercial matter, not even as a visitor to the firm.

After reviewing the files, Samantha and Blake wrapped up their business at the firm. Peter Babcock came in to tell them that if they needed any more information, the firm would do what it could to provide it.

Blake asked Peter if he had seen Holly Waters recently. Babcock told Blake that Holly retired about a month after his father's death, staying only long enough to transition files and to finalize other matters. That was the last time Holly was at the firm, as far as he knew.

Babcock and Blake spoke for a few minutes, and Babcock told Blake how much the partners would welcome having Blake back in the firm. Blake thanked Peter and Sheila for their assistance. After Samantha put copies of the few documents they thought helpful into her briefcase, they said their farewells.

• • •

Snow flurries greeted them as they exited the building on Twelfth Street. Finding a cab proved difficult, but they finally caught one to take them back to the Justice Department. Once there, Blake walked Samantha to her car on the third level of the parking ramp, where they discussed the day's revelations for a short while.

Blake was parked on the second level, and as he walked down the stairwell, he realized he needed to give Samantha the few documents he had taken from the law firm. He hurriedly ran up the stairs to catch Samantha before she left.

As he pushed open the stairwell door, a deafening car-horn blast assaulted his ears. He saw Samantha struggling with two men on the driver's side of her vehicle. She must have hit the panic button on her key fob. He ran to help her.

When the men saw Blake coming at them, they shoved Samantha to the ground, tore her briefcase away, and started toward Blake like they were going to attack him. After looking at each other, they decided to run away instead, each peeling off in a different direction.

Samantha was on the ground when Blake reached her. He helped her up and saw a trickle of blood from one corner of her mouth. Her face was flushed and puffy, her hair mussed, and her clothing disheveled.

"Sam, are you okay? Let me look at you. Stay still for a second."

Blake examined her, and then helped her stand up. "Can you walk?"

Samantha was shaking, so Blake wrapped his arms around her and held her close, calming her. He had her sit in the passenger-side front seat until help came. Then he sat in the car, started it and turned on the heater to warm her.

"What happened?"

"They were parked next to me, waiting for me, I guess. I couldn't see them in the dark. As soon as you left and I opened my car door, they jumped out and grabbed me. They wanted my briefcase. It had copies of everything we took from the law firm, plus some background information on the ACLU that Sapphire gave us. I didn't want them to have it, so I fought back."

Blake called Leon to tell him Samantha had been attacked. He asked Leon to get EMTs to the parking garage to take care of her, and he also wanted FBI forensics to check out her vehicle and the one parked next to it. Blake told Leon not to alert local police.

The EMTs arrived and examined Samantha, cleaned her cuts, checked her bruising, and then insisted that she be taken to the emergency room, fearing that she might have a concussion and possibly internal injuries. Blake followed them in his car.

When the crime-lab technicians arrived, they did their work onsite and then towed the assailants' car to the FBI garage for further inspection.

Blake stayed with Samantha while she was being examined by emergency-room physicians and staff. They determined that she did not have a concussion or internal injuries, only scrapes and bruises. When she was released, Blake took her home. Leon already had security at her house, inside and outside. But Blake stayed with her overnight anyway, sleeping in a guest bedroom.

54

FARRELL HATED HIM. He always had. The phony bastard. "But, hell," he thought, "they're all phony bastards, what with their Ivy League bullshit educations and jacked-up snobbery." He knew they looked at him as lower rank and file, someone to be tolerated but never invited inside their tent. Fuckin' jerks. So full of themselves.

Farrell popped more antacids into his mouth and started to chew. "These guys are bad for my stomach," he thought. "How many bankers, lawyers, judges, philanthropists, and academics can I stand in a twenty-four-hour period? No wonder my stomach spits up acid.

"Listen to this asshole pontificate," he thought, looking over at The Law Professor. Farrell could see The Fat Man's eyes darting about, trying to figure out what The Law Professor was saying.

They were in a conference room at the Chicago law firm used by Farrell's union. Just the three of them.

"Are you certain the police or FBI will not find out their identities?" asked The Law Professor, for what seemed like the tenth time.

Fingering an oddly shaped piece of gold bling on his sausage-like pinky finger, The Fat Man hunched forward and looked at The Law

Professor the way a tired teacher would look at a stupid student. "Listen, I know what I'm doing. My guys"—referring to the men he had hired to do the work The Law Professor had requested—"are beyond professionals. They are *elite*. There is no way anyone will ever find out anything." The Fat Man leaned back in his chair, straining its structural integrity.

Farrell smiled at The Fat Man, who moved his pudgy pig-eyes in acknowledgment.

"Your people don't seem that elite to me," challenged The Law Professor. "They killed the wrong person, for God's sake. We wanted the monsignor dead—not his brother."

"Identical twins. Go figure," said The Fat Man, refusing to accept any blame. "You should have told us. *Or maybe you didn't know.*"

Farrell added, "Identical twins. Give me a break. That's like out of *Twilight Zone* or something. How can you fault anyone for a mistake like that? Even the Justice Department was surprised about the twin brother. My source told me that."

"So you admit it was a *mistake*," The Law Professor shot back.

"I hope you don't think you are cross-examining me," snapped Farrell.

"Then your *elite* thugs roughed up the girl but didn't *dispatch* her," The Law Professor continued, ignoring Farrell and focusing on The Fat Man.

"*Dispatch her?* You mean *kill* her? Man, you can't even say the word. You wanted the information from the law firm. You wanted to scare her. You did not tell me you wanted her killed. If you had, then she'd be dead. *Dispatched*, as you say," The Fat Man responded, enjoying the verbal interchange with this pompous Ivy League ass, thinking it was worth the trip to cold Chicago.

The Law Professor's manicured fingers drummed the tabletop. "If your thugs are so elite, then what happened at the ACLU office in Washington? Did your *convicts* enjoy killing those law students before starting the fire? They killed one of our key staff lawyers, too. We could have closed the office in advance. We did not tell you to kill them."

"Convicts? You must be joking," The Fat Man exclaimed, hunched forward again. "We had to do it this way. Maybe you forgot that four hundred of your friends were blown away. Had you closed the office that would have been highly unusual, and it would have drawn unwanted attention from the police and the FBI. Please, let me do my job. You just sit back and enjoy your life."

Farrell agreed with him. "There was no other way. All the documents were destroyed, including everything in the safes. I got this information directly from the Justice Department; you know that. While killing those people was unfortunate, it had to be done. Collateral damage."

There was momentary quiet. Each man's eyes searched the grains of wood in the highly polished table, as if to make sense out of the swirls...and this conversation.

It was The Law Professor who broke the silence. "Forgive me if I offended you," he said, disingenuously, to The Fat Man, even though he was looking obliquely at Farrell. Alone on his side of the table, The Law Professor could not help one more jab: "Our report says the girl and Elliott saw your man leave Palmer's office. Fortunately, he wasn't caught. Even I, an amateur, would think that having two people for the job would have been better. At the very least, your henchman should have had a lookout."

Unlike Farrell, the up-through-the-ranks union lifer, The Fat Man had a master's degree in cinematic arts from the University of Southern California. "*Henchman? Lookout?* What is this, a western movie? Stick to teaching law, old man," he thought. The Fat Man bit his lower lip to keep from erupting.

The Law Professor continued, "It has been a while. When will we learn where the other two are: the monsignor and Holly Waters?"

Farrell headed off The Fat Man before he said something nasty. "Our source tells us that the Justice Department cannot find them either."

"*I know that*," said The Law Professor, disgustedly, "but that is not what I asked you. We need to find them for reasons far different than the Justice Department's."

55

HE KNEW SHE did not like it when he called her at work, so he waited until she was home.

"I am in Chicago talking to Farrell and his obese friend from California. I let them have it, Ruth. I told them how unhappy we are." The Law Professor went on to summarize his afternoon.

"Justin, this whole issue with identical twins is incredible. I tend to agree with The Fat Man's point. No one knew the monsignor had an identical twin brother."

Not liking what he was hearing, The Law Professor interjected, "Ruth, these people are *scum*. You don't have to deal with them. I do. You have no idea what it is like."

"I know. I know. But they are *our* scum, Justin. They are all we have at the moment. Let's be realistic. Hold your nose when dealing with them."

He disagreed with her. "Surely there are others we can find," he thought, although he had no idea how to go about finding them. He could prevail upon Farrell for help, but The Law Professor viewed Farrell as part of the problem. Union jerk.

"Justin, I have been thinking about our situation."

Now what? The Law Professor worried and waited.

"We need to take bold action."

"Yes, Ruth. What do you have in mind?" The Law Professor held his breath. What now?

"We must kill the Pope."

The Law Professor couldn't believe what he just heard. "Kill the Pope! Ruth, have you lost your mind?" He knew she would get angry when challenged this way, but so be it. She was acting insane. Call a spade a spade. Call crazy talk...*insanity.* This was insanity.

"Ruth, we have no idea if this Pope had anything to do with the bombing. I, for one, would think not. This is something John Paul might do, but he's dead. Besides, I cannot imagine a holy man killing five hundred people. It makes no sense. There's no precedent. There's no evidence."

Before The Law Professor could further explain why he thought her idea was crazy, Ruth Bergman continued, "Of course we cannot kill the Pope, at least not at this juncture. However, we can kill his representative here in Washington. The Vatican's ambassador to the United States, the *papal nuncio*, lives on Embassy Row."

There was no response from The Law Professor. "Didn't she hear what I just said?" he wondered.

"Justin? Are you there?"

"Yes, Ruth, I am here listening. Is this something we want to do? Draw attention to ourselves? Do we want to rely on Farrell and The Fat Man to carry out an assignment like this, trusting they won't make more mistakes?"

"Justin, I think Farrell and The Fat Man need to redeem themselves. They should be happy to do this for us. Justin, these are the people we must rely on. There is no time to find someone else at this point."

No response.

"Killing the papal nuncio will send a strong message to the Vatican. If nothing happens in return, then we can assume our bold action was effective."

"Ruth, you seem to be forgetting that we are killing a prominent figure here in Washington. There will be an immediate response on many levels, not just local police but also the State Department, FBI and international law enforcement, among others. Ruth, this is not like killing a private person. This will draw national and international attention. The papal nuncio is an ambassador, for God's sake."

"Yes, Justin, I know. That is the beauty of it."

"Ruth, we will be killing an ambassador! Did you not hear me?" The Law Professor hated her sometimes. This was one of those times. When would it end?

"Contact Farrell and The Fat Man. Tell them what you want them to do and how you want them to proceed. This time, give them precise instructions, so there will be no mistakes. Make certain they have enough people."

The Law Professor raised his voice, "How many people have you killed, Ruth? I don't know what to tell them. Do you? How many murders have you planned? I have planned none. What shall I tell them? For starters, I will probably have to explain to them who the papal nuncio is and where he lives."

• • •

Twelve years before, Pope John Paul appointed Archbishop Alberto Baccari to be papal nuncio to the United States. Baccari had served previously in diplomatic positions in the Middle East, Lebanon, Israel, Nicaragua, Honduras and Panama in Central America.

John Paul had absolute faith and trust in this career diplomat. The fact that Baccari knew world history and global politics and embraced the church with the same conservative ideological fervor as the Pope sealed his appointment to this important post. What kept him in the position was the fact that Cardinal Joseph Ratzinger, now Pope Benedict, had recommended Baccari to John Paul for the position in the first place.

In addition to his responsibility as a diplomat, the papal nuncio also served as liaison between the Vatican and the hierarchy of the

Catholic Church in the United States. Among other things, it was Baccari's obligation to report his observations regarding the life of the Catholic faithful in the United States directly to the Pope.

Baccari's long career as a diplomat had taken him to many of the world's most dangerous geopolitical hotspots and danger zones. He had never felt his life was in danger in any one of them. Now, living in Washington, DC, in the shadow of the National Cathedral, in the most stable country on earth, his life was in danger. And he didn't know it.

56

"SHE IS HOME now, and everything checked out okay. Only bruises. Plus the obvious scare of being roughed up in a parking garage," Blake said. He sat across from Tom Owens who knew about the assault on Samantha and had already received concerned calls from the White House for letting such a thing happen.

"Do you believe this? What am I supposed to do, personally stand guard in parking ramps? Why the assault and theft of documents—documents that can be replaced in an hour? Are these people stupid?

"The White House wants me to assure them that what just happened will be kept under wraps. Right. What are they smoking over there? This administration is a *sieve*.

"This investigation is driving me crazy. The White House calls multiple times a day because the media vultures are all over them. This *freedom of the press* thing is too much. But worse, we have nothing to report. We can't even find out who made the nuke. What a sad state of affairs when you can't figure out who made a nuclear weapon. What kind of world is this?" the attorney general ranted.

Blake agreed.

"And we can't figure out who started the fires and killed the ACLU people and the security guards," Owens continued.

"Right."

"Even though there are thousands of people working on this investigation, we are nowhere. Nowhere!

"We cannot disclose what happened to Ms. Rhodes under orders from the White House. However, once the *journos* find out, as they inevitably will, I cannot say that I was acting under orders from some assistant to the assistant press-secretary stooge in the White House. I'm on my own, Blake, shucking and jiving.

"The media jackals already think we are either deceiving them or we are too inept to figure this out."

"Right."

"The press corps. What the hell is a press corps? Oh, let me answer that. The press corps is a figment of the devil's imagination. They, along with their readers, watch too many crime dramas on television since they apparently think crimes should be solved in an hour, give or take a few commercials. But we know the harsh truth, don't we? Some crimes are never solved, no matter how many investigators are assigned."

Blake interrupted, "Look, Tom, the investigation is just taking time. Last night we had to make a slight detour. But we're on track. The press has its teeth into this because the ACLU is one of its darlings, and this administration is not."

"Ah, my friend Blake always had a penchant for stating the obvious."

"I think you need to say The Serenity Prayer every hour of the work day."

"I don't have time."

"Have someone draft an executive summary of it."

"Sure. I'll put Mrs. Arnison right on it."

"Okay, listen to this." Blake changed the direction of the conversation and told Owens about his thoughts regarding John Palmer, Monsignor Pacelli, the new information about Angela Carr's maiden name and relationship to the monsignor, and his father's possible involvement.

"Tom, this is way beyond coincidence. These events are all connected. I want to continue looking into this, at least for the short term. I believe we have hit on something. Exactly what, I can't even speculate, but we are locked onto something—something important, I am certain."

"Okay, go figure it out. Hell, you may be the only one who might solve this thing."

"I don't know where this will lead."

"I don't care, at the moment. Follow it wherever it takes you. Just hurry," said Owens. "And, for my sake, please protect Ms. Rhodes."

57

"MY BROTHERS AND sisters," intoned the Reverend Peterson, "Do you think it is possible...do you think it is even conceivable... that the Lord, our God, has his divine hand in this ACLU matter? Could he be the prime mover behind it?

"Yes, yes, I know; it is difficult to believe such a thing, but at times our God is a ferocious God—unforgiving, angry. Look at the Old Testament for examples. Could this be an angry God at his most destructive?"

Mrs. Peterson nodded in agreement, first toward her husband and then to the studio audience and television viewers worldwide. For those watching the broadcast from the comfort of their homes, a prayer-line phone number crawled across the bottom of the screen inviting viewers to call in and make donations to the program.

The reverend continued, "As if abortion—the ruthless killing of innocent babies—wasn't enough to stoke the wrath of a righteous God, the ACLU and its minions have sought to destroy the sanctity of marriage between a man and a woman—a blessed arrangement from the dawn of time—by gagging us with same-sex marriages. The ACLU, through its legions of lawyers, has fought to overturn every state referendum where the people have voted to prohibit such offensive same-sex unions."

Tears welled up in Mrs. Peterson's eyes, something that was caught by the well-practiced cameraman and broadcast over the airwaves. After the money shot, she reverently bowed her head.

The prayer lines were flooded with donations shortly thereafter. Volunteers scrambled to move the donors along to the credit card verifiers so they could answer waiting calls.

"Judges…brothers and sisters, we think of judges as decent human beings called on to act wisely in dispensing justice. We think of Solomon. We think of wisdom. We think of the scales of justice. But, unhappily, we all know the sad truth, don't we? There are many judges sitting on every court who do not believe as we do. Many of them are card-carrying members of the ACLU—even a few on the United States Supreme Court!

"What are we to think? Is Satan at work in our legal and judicial systems?

"Yes, of course, he is. Yes. Yes. Yes!" shouted the Reverend Peterson.

"Now you can understand why I believe that our Lord, God Almighty, may be responsible for what happened in San Francisco," the Reverend Peterson concluded, as the studio band played and the studio choir sang the "Battle Hymn of the Republic":

> Mine eyes have seen the glory of the coming of the Lord;
> He is trampling out the vintage where the grapes of wrath
>   are stored;
> He hath loosed the fateful lightning of his terrible swift
>   sword;
> His truth is marching on.
> Glory! Glory! Hallelujah! Glory! Glory! Hallelujah!
> Glory! Glory! Hallelujah! His truth is marching on.

Money poured in over the prayer lines. The volunteers couldn't keep up. They were concerned the phone system might go down. They prayed, and the phone system survived to process credit card after credit card after credit card. Hallelujah!

58

A LEISURELY FORTY-MINUTE trip took them across calm, multitinted blue water to another country. After the yacht docked at the marina in Marigot, they walked to a pâtisserie where they purchased freshly baked croissants and strong dark coffee.

They sat outside facing the marina and the open water beyond. Since this side of the island was not a port for large cruise ships, the marina was tiny and the small town still quaint: sea gulls, sailboats, yachts and very few people.

The two women had new hair color, new hairstyles and new makeup. Behind large sunglasses and underneath sun hats, they believed even friends would not immediately recognize them. Of course, the chance of encountering a friend here was very unlikely. They leaned back in their chairs and tried to relax. It was the first time they had left their compound since arriving in Anguilla a week ago.

"I'm so nervous. And there is no one around," Angela said.

"I understand. But I think we are quite safe here," Holly answered.

"No, no—please, forgive me. The world is a big place. Who would look for me here? It seems so far away from New York. Everything I did for the past few years was in preparation of leaving without a trace. Unless I slipped up somewhere, there should be no trace. I shouldn't be nervous," she said, trying to convince herself of the truth of her statement. "On the plus side, this will be my first Christmas in a warm place."

Holly smiled at Angela, thinking, "What a courageous woman. Here she is, nervous in the Caribbean. What must it have been like for her in New York? How nervous must she have been there every day?"

She knew almost everything about Angela from information John and Dom had given her. In fact, when they told her what Dom had asked Angela to do, Holly could not believe it. Without even knowing Angela, Holly had been praying for her for years. Her prayers must have been answered because here Angela was, sitting across the table from her on the French side of St. Maarten.

Holly did not tell Angela that her brother and John had been murdered in Washington. Why should she? Angela didn't know John at all, and any link to her own situation would only cause her greater concern. As for her brother's murder, there was nothing she could do about it—nothing that anyone could do. Why tell her now? Let her rest a bit more. There was so much sadness in Angela's life. How much more could she take? Holly knew about Angela's illness and worried that any more psychological stress might trigger a return of her cancer. She wanted to tell her about her brother. It would be the humane thing to do. But wouldn't it be *more* humane not to tell her at this time?

After a few more minutes of silence, Angela told Holly she was sick to death about what had happened in California. She wondered if she had anything to do with it. It could not be a coincidence. The explosion must have been caused, in one way or another, by the information she gave to her brother. Tears trickled down her cheeks.

Holly knew all about the information Angela discovered at the ACLU. She also knew that Angela had no idea how that information was put to use, initially. Then they had asked Angela to stay on at the ACLU to ferret out any additional information that might be useful once negotiations began.

Watching Angela drink her coffee and enjoy her croissant, Holly's heart swelled with affection for her. Again, she thought, "What a magnificent woman. How could we ever repay her?"

We?

Holly's mind hurt with a savagely ironic thought: but for Angela accidentally finding those ACLU documents, Carson would still be alive.

Holly could hardly breathe; her lungs felt paralyzed. It was not a panic attack—more like a death wish seeping out of her mind and into her breathing. Such was her life after Carson. It was not much of a life. He was her whole world...and every thought in it.

She gathered herself and focused on the moment.

After walking around the marina, they left the area to stroll past dress shops, perfumeries and jewelry stores before returning to their yacht.

Holly's RavenRock security detail guarded them every moment. RavenRock Limited, the world's preeminent security and risk mitigation organization, was the only company in which Holly personally had a minority ownership interest. It was a wise choice.

59

EVERYONE STOOD WHEN Samantha walked into the conference room. Except for a few discernible bruises, she looked great.

"Welcome back," Blake said. "We missed you."

"How are you feeling?" Leon asked.

"A little banged up, but otherwise okay."

"Were you able to identify the guys who attacked you?" Sapphire asked.

"Not really. I gave the FBI what I could remember. It was dark, I wasn't paying attention, plus it happened so fast. I know they were white men."

"Ah, white men. Difficult to ID," Leon joked.

"I am really happy to be back here," Samantha said. "I'm ready to work. What's new?"

Leon responded, holding a report in his hands, "It was the monk. Not the monsignor."

"How do they know?" Samantha asked.

"Traces of chemotherapy drugs. Father Leo's oncologist in Kentucky provided the information, and the crime lab here confirmed it. We also contacted Monsignor Pacelli's personal physician who said he was a picture of good health. Since they were identical twins, they had the same blood type. We couldn't use dental records because Father Leo's face was destroyed by the gunshot. The crime techs lifted fingerprints to ID the body, but nothing came up. Apparently, neither Father Leo nor the monsignor ever had their prints taken. This was the best forensics could do," Leon said.

"Okay. Was there a billfold on the body?" asked Blake.

"No. The university police found all of Father Leo's belongings in the guest room he was occupying: a small suitcase, toiletries, and a billfold. Well, I guess it wasn't much of a billfold. He had his money and some identification in a plastic sandwich bag," answered Leon, flashing a sad smile.

"Why kill Father Leo?" Samantha asked.

"Mistaken identity?" Sapphire said. "The monsignor was probably the real target."

"The monsignor is linked to John Palmer and my father, if that means anything. Certainly it must," Blake offered.

"Father Leo hadn't left the monastery in thirty years, except to visit doctors and dentists nearby. When he does leave his quiet, holy neighborhood to fly here, he gets whacked. That's bad for tourism in the District," Leon observed.

"We don't even know if the monsignor picked him up. Someone at Georgetown University might know. In any event, within a day or two of his arrival, Father Leo is killed.

"The question remains: is the monsignor alive or dead? If dead, who killed him? If alive, where is he?" Blake wondered.

"We really have nothing on the monsignor so far. We can only assume someone tried to kill him but ended up killing his brother by mistake," observed Sapphire.

"I wonder if Father Leo had any idea he was in danger. Who knows, maybe he chose to help his brother, even though it might mean his death. He knew he was in terminal medical condition—irreversible and painful. If he did make the choice to stand in for his brother, maybe it wasn't that difficult of a choice to make," said Samantha.

"I mean, you can look at the killing from two sides: The killer or killers may not have known the monsignor. Father Leo was in his brother's apartment, so they could have mistaken Father Leo for the monsignor. The flip side is this: the brothers may purposely have set up Father Leo as a target in place of the monsignor."

"Greater love hath no man than this, that he lay down his life for his brother; is that what you think?" asked Blake.

"Possibly. Or it could be pure happenstance: the monk visiting at the wrong time, being in the wrong place. However, the abbot said the monsignor was going to meet his brother at the airport and take him back to Georgetown University where he had a room for him. Could it be that the monsignor stayed in that room while his brother occupied the monsignor's apartment?" questioned Samantha.

"This notion of a brother giving his life for a brother…that's premised on what?" asked Leon.

"The knowledge that the one brother was in danger of losing his life, while the other brother was *already* losing his," Samantha responded.

"Sapphire, we need more information about the monsignor from the time he was in college to now. How did he get the 'monsignor' designation? Contact the Jesuits to find out everything you can about him, his friends, his private affairs, anything that might explain why he was a target," said Blake.

"We also need more on our other missing persons. Angela Carr—we need something on her whereabouts. Maybe she and her brother, the monsignor, are in hiding together," offered Blake. "And Holly Waters. We need to find her."

"What can you tell us about Holly Waters?"

"After college she worked at the Commerce Department where she met my father and John Palmer, who were working there. When my father left to start his firm, Holly went with him.

"Holly is not a lawyer. She graduated from Vanderbilt University with a degree in history. She is very intelligent. My father often said she was the smartest person in the firm. She is an only child. Her father founded International Advanced Technologies. When her parents died, she inherited billions and billions of dollars, plus controlling interest in a global-tech giant. She never had to work a day in her life. But she did. At the firm she was the business development director. For want of another term, she was a *rainmaker*, along with my father.

"Holly had connections all over the world. She used them to steer business to the firm. Her father's company was one of the firm's principal clients. She traveled with the firm's lawyers around the globe. As I've mentioned, my father didn't like to travel very much. That's why seeing him photographed in Italy with John was a surprise," Blake responded.

Leon observed, "This is turning into a missing-persons bureau. When we get back from across the street, tell us what you want us to do about Holly Waters. No, no, don't bother. I will put the FBI on her again, this time for real. If she isn't dead and buried somewhere, they should find her." Leon paused for a moment and then continued, "I shouldn't have said that. I'm sorry. We have a lot of dead people—over five hundred, plus, John Palmer and the poor monk. Plus, we have three *missing* people: Holly Waters, Monsignor Pacelli, and Angela Carr. And we don't know if they are involved with the ACLU explosion."

"We need to go over to the FBI building first and then work the phones to find out more information about our missing folks. See you later," said Sapphire.

When they were alone, Samantha looked at Blake and asked him, "Was there anyone in the firm who knew more about your father's activities than Holly Waters?"

"No," Blake said.

"Remember how Jordan told me Holly was in love with your father? That's why she stayed with the firm," Samantha said.

"I learned early on never to correct my older sister. If Holly was in love with my father, I never saw anything that was unprofessional pass between them. Clearly, they enjoyed each other. The partners in the firm thought Holly was special. She made them quite wealthy through the work she brought to the firm. Holly was well-respected because she knew business and how corporations worked. Her insights were valuable when it came to developing a discovery strategy in commercial litigation. It wasn't just her social connections that made her unique, but rather it was her intelligence and vision. And, the most amazing thing of all was that she was a very charming and likable person—not a phony bone in her body."

"Do you think your father loved her?" asked Samantha.

Blake looked at her for a moment. A trace of a smile developed as he gazed at her. "This isn't the type of question I'd expect from a chaos-theory wizard who could stare down the North Koreans."

Samantha smiled in return. "I didn't exactly stare down the North Koreans. I just got cold over there. My eyes were frozen in place."

"All I can say is this: if my father didn't care deeply for Holly, I doubt she would have stayed at the firm. But he was devoted to my mother, who for years was in a near-vegetative state because of her stroke. If my father and Holly ever expressed their love physically, I just don't know," Blake said, shaking his head.

"I thought she was brilliant and very kind," Blake continued. "She dressed nicely, but never out of step with the women partners in the firm. She frequently prefaced her keen observations or arguments with 'I am not a lawyer, *but...*,' and then she would nail whatever issue she was discussing. My dad would sit back, smile, and then he would say that we had all been sprinkled with 'Holy

Water.' Maybe I was slow on the uptake," Blake confessed. "Maybe it was quite evident how they felt about one another."

"Was Holly close to John Palmer?"

"Oh, absolutely. They were best friends. Holly tried to act as a matchmaker for John, finding him suitable women to date, but John was a confirmed bachelor. He loved working and traveling and living alone. It was that simple."

"Assuming she is alive, where do you think she might be?" asked Samantha.

"I hope she is alive," answered Blake. "Where she might be... honestly, she could be anywhere. She has so much money that she could buy her own island and fortify it with a large army if she chose. The only two places she owns that I know about are here and in Palm Beach. Jordan might have some idea. She works on different levels than I do. She has more information, I am certain."

Samantha said, "John called Holly within hours after he ran into us. At least he spoke to someone at her residence in Florida for almost twenty minutes. The next morning John was murdered and Holly was gone. Assuming John spoke with her, what did he tell her?"

"I've thought about it, Sam," he responded. "When we found out that John called Holly, I am certain it was to report that I was back in Washington and involved in this ACLU investigation."

"John was...what...simply informing her that you were investigating the attack on the ACLU? Alerting her? Warning her? What could it be? And then she vanishes. At least, I would like to think she intentionally disappeared," said Samantha.

Blake raised his eyebrows. "Is your theory about her intentionally disappearing based on years of study in applied mathematics?" He smiled at her.

"No, it's based on having two X chromosomes. You know, women's intuition."

60

BLAKE WENT ALONE to his father's law firm for a meeting he had scheduled with Peter Babcock after Samantha was attacked. He also picked up replacement copies of the documents that had been stolen from Samantha.

"Blake, I am sorry to hear about what happened to Samantha. Crime in this city keeps getting worse. Please give her my regards and best wishes for a speedy recovery.

"As far as your request, I can only do so much. You know that," explained Babcock. "Even though he is your father, we still have ethical and legal obligations to the firm's clients."

"All I need is a clue. What was my father doing in Rome if he wasn't there on firm business? You know he hated to travel. The fact that he was with John Palmer tells me he was there on behalf of a client. Plus, Holly was with them."

Babcock looked out the window. He wanted to help Blake. What were the obligations he referred to? In actuality there were none, other than a gentlemen's agreement between the man he revered, Carson Elliott, and himself. He had pledged he would never divulge what he learned from Carson. But were these present circumstances so extraordinary that Carson would understand if he gave the information to his son?

Turning away from the window to face Blake, he asked him to sit down. "Your father was my role model and my mentor, Blake. He took me into his firm. He made me an excellent lawyer, all modesty aside. He also tried to make me into a decent person, with ethics, morals, and a sense of honor—just like he did for everyone else in this firm. It sets us apart from other law firms. We are the most highly selective firm in the city in recruiting new lawyers. Being a decent person and a good lawyer in Washington is no small feat. You know that."

Blake listened intently, understanding that Babcock was struggling mentally and emotionally, although not displaying it physically. "A good lawyer, indeed," Blake thought.

"Your father and Holly took some vacation time. I know they met John in Italy. What they were doing there, the firm has no record. We have no client information involving your father in Italy. John, of course, provided separate legal services to the firm's clients all over the world, including Italy, so I cannot comment on any work he performed on behalf of any of the firm's clients, since we were never privy to such information."

"Is that it?" asked Blake, waiting.

Babcock looked down at his folded hands on the table. He sat quietly for a moment. Then he said, "Your father seemed...different...after he returned. He seemed *distracted*, which, as you know, was never the case. He always focused like a laser. Nothing distracted him. Well, that changed when he came back from Italy. Maybe distracted isn't the right word. *Preoccupied* might be more like it."

"When did he go to Italy?"

"About three years ago."

"What do you think he was doing there?"

"I don't know. As far as we were concerned, he could do whatever he wanted. Who was going to stop him? He was our founder, a man of impeccable character. He was no rogue lawyer. He was one of the most respected lawyers in the country. If he chose to do something off-line, outside the firm, that was his business. We have no record that he ever took advantage of firm resources. It simply was not in his nature."

"What about Holly?"

"Holly?" laughed Babcock, "She could buy the firm and all the other firms in the District and still have money to buy a country or two in South America. Are you kidding? We all concluded that the only reason Holly worked here was...your father. She loved him. Platonically, we believe. But she did love him. Everyone knew it. But it was professional."

"Professionally platonic," smiled Blake.

"Yes. It does seem odd to be discussing their relationship this way, but that about captures it. She was wealthy beyond measure. She was brilliant, clever. She was a tremendous asset to the firm. She brought in business from all over the world. As you well know, she helped make all of us wealthy. And, yes, she could have done anything she wanted with any man she wanted. But she chose to stay here. Why? Because of your father."

Babcock stopped for a moment. He looked straight at Blake. "After your mother died, your father told me he was going to ask Holly to marry him. He thought they would elope. I remember it so well because I thought your father's idea of eloping would be taking Amtrak to New York for some Broadway shows."

"Life is interesting," observed Blake. "I only wish they had had the opportunity...two people who were perfectly suited for one another."

"So true. They were perfect for one another. Best friends. Enjoyable people. Kind and generous. Life isn't often fair."

"What did Holly do here after my father died?"

"She and I went through all of your father's files, appointments, and scheduled court appearances. You know the drill after a lawyer dies or leaves the firm. We parceled his work out among the partners and associates. We contacted clients. We billed clients for his unbilled time. And so forth. Many of us were already working on legal matters with him, and so we knew quite a bit about his files and client expectations. Holly knew the rest. It took us about a month to deal with everything. She packed his personal belongings in boxes and took them to Jordan for you two to determine what you might want."

"Did you ask Holly to stay?" Blake asked.

"Did we ask her to stay? Yes, we asked her to stay. Actually, we begged her to stay. But she said she couldn't. We all understood. With your father gone, Holly had no reason to be here. We were worried about her. John spent a good deal of time consoling her and she him."

61

LEON AND SAPPHIRE sang along with the Christmas carols playing on the radio in their car as they drove to Georgetown University. The absence of students, gone for the Christmas break, made finding a parking space easy. They walked a block to the administration building, one of the older buildings on campus.

"We have an appointment with Father Shea," Leon said to the young lady behind the desk. The door to an office beyond the desk was open, and out of it emerged a scholarly looking man with a gray beard and gray hair, round eyeglasses and brown eyes over a warm smile. He wore a black turtleneck, a gray cardigan sweater and black corduroy slacks.

"Let me guess, you must be Leon and Sapphire Wilson," he said. "Right on time. Ah, punctuality. *Deo gratias*, thank God, that some people still practice punctuality. Please, please come in," he gestured. "I am Timothy Shea."

Leon and Sapphire walked into an office that looked like a bookmobile in heat. Books were everywhere—not just doubled up on heaving bookshelves, but in stacks on the floor all around the room, behind Father Shea's desk, in piles on the credenza, on the windowsills, and on the chairs where Father Shea motioned the Wilsons to sit.

"Just put the books on the floor. I apologize for the mess. I'm not married and have no wife to take care of me," he laughed. He said it so effortlessly that Leon and Sapphire figured he had said the same thing many times before. They liked him immediately.

Before Leon or Sapphire could say anything, Father Shea offered them coffee and tea. "Our campus is struggling with the fact that two murders took place here, a place dedicated to learning. I knew Professor Palmer personally and loved the man: brilliant and totally unpretentious. In all respects a magnificent human being. And that is high praise these days."

Leon took the lead, "We came here to discuss Monsignor Pacelli, but if you have anything to add about Professor Palmer we would welcome any insights."

"Well, I cannot add much more about John. He was great company. He could talk about anything. I know he was a good friend of Monsignor Pacelli."

"What can you tell us about Monsignor Pacelli?"

"Dominic and I go way back, to the seminary in Rome. We were ordained there. We both stayed on for advanced degrees at Gregorian University, the Jesuit university in Rome. I left before Dominic and went to South America for a number of years. We kept in touch and saw each other, oh, maybe every other year at some conference somewhere. I went back to Rome for a while, but by then he was gone. After Rome I came here, about nine years ago. Dominic came here about seven years ago, I think," Father Shea said.

Sapphire inquired, "Did Monsignor Pacelli ever talk about his family?"

"We all have families, you know," he smiled, "although some of us are happier to be away from them. That may be an exaggeration. Yes, Dominic did talk about his family over the years. But, you know, as time moves us along, we end up replacing one family with another. Surely, if there were an emergency in our family we would be there instantly, of course. I remember that Dominic came from a large family, but I don't remember details about any of the family members except for Father Leo. Dominic spoke of Leo all the time. I think Dominic wished he had Leo's life in the monastery."

"Had you ever met Father Leo?" asked Leon.

"No, I never met him. I knew he was coming here for medical treatment. Dominic told me. I had hoped to meet him before he returned to the monastery. What a tragedy."

"During the time that Monsignor Pacelli lived here and taught classes here, were there ever any problems?"

"What kind of problems?" asked Father Shea, warily.

Sapphire answered, "Problems of any type."

"No."

"We understand that he routinely took students on tours in Italy. What can you tell us about that?" asked Leon.

"Because he had spent so much time in Rome and in Italy he knew the country very well, and he was fluent in Italian. The university offered travel tours to Rome and to other places in Italy for our students during their breaks. They lasted about two weeks, from beginning to end."

"Did you know that John Palmer and the monsignor often traveled together in Europe?" asked Sapphire.

Father Shea smiled at them. "May I ask, is either of you Catholic?"

"We are both Catholic," said Leon.

"Okay. You know then that we priests are supposed to be celibate. What that means these days in the modern church is this: it makes no difference whether you are heterosexual, homosexual, or whatever, as long as you are committed to your vow of chastity," offered Father Shea. "Maybe I am overreacting to your question or reading too much into it. For the record, I am quite certain Dominic is a heterosexual celibate priest. I know John was a heterosexual man. They were friends. They shared the same passion: cathedral architecture, Gothic cathedrals, principally, and other majestic cathedrals. As far as I am aware, that was the only passion they shared."

"I am sorry, Father," said Leon, "We had to ask. We simply need to know facts. We are not passing judgment on anyone. Facts are important for obvious reasons, like solving crimes."

"Touché," said Father Shea, "you are correct. Here are some facts for you: Monsignor Pacelli is a moral theologian. He teaches undergraduate and graduate classes in that subject. He is among the highest-ranked professors at Georgetown, as determined by the students, a teacher's toughest critics. On a nonacademic level, he goes to the Marine Corps Base at Quantico, Virginia every weekend to hear confessions and to say Mass. They love him, too. He looks like he could be a marine."

"By the way, what did he do to get the 'monsignor' title?" asked Sapphire.

"Dominic worked for powerful people in Rome," said Father Shea. "It is an honorary title that was bestowed on him by Pope John Paul for the work he did on the new Catholic catechism that was introduced about ten years ago. Dominic was embarrassed by the title of monsignor, but he could not say no to the Pope."

"Father Shea, we are in an odd situation, to be honest. We believe someone wanted to kill Monsignor Pacelli but mistakenly killed Father Leo Pacelli instead. Our optimistic assumption is that Monsignor Pacelli went into hiding either before or after the murder of his brother. We have no way of knowing which is accurate, at this point," Leon said.

Father Shea listened intently, hoping his friend Dominic was alive and safe.

"Since you know Monsignor Pacelli so well, where would you guess he might go for his own safety?"

Without hesitation, Father Shea replied, "Rome."

Leon asked, "Not the Vatican?"

"The Vatican is *in* Rome," grinned Father Shea.

Sapphire smiled, and said, "My husband did not study geography in college. He studied football."

Father Shea let out a belly laugh that took Leon and Sapphire by surprise. "To answer your question, yes, I believe he would be safe there. Of course, Dominic could be safe anywhere in Italy, since he knows the country so well. If he were in this country, I do not know where he might be. California could be a choice, since he spent time there," answered Father Shea.

"Would other Jesuit universities or churches offer to hide him?" Leon asked.

"Yes, of course. We have many universities in this country and around the world. We also have seminaries and schools of theology. Dominic could be at any one of them. But, unless he told them, no one would think that he was hiding."

"If he were to reach out to anyone about his situation, who do you think he would contact?"

"Sabino Arana, our superior general."

62

"YES, MY BROTHERS and sisters, it has been a few weeks since the hand of God swept the deck clean by exorcizing four hundred unrepentant sinners from our presence.

"We pray for those who protested against those sinners and for those police officers who provided security for them. We believe that same hand of God delivered them to paradise and their eternal reward," the Reverend Peterson said into the camera.

"Christmas: the birthday of our Lord and Savior, Jesus Christ. A time we celebrate with great joy and happiness because here is the beginning of our salvation. Out of humble circumstances to prove solidarity with our flesh, the child Jesus was born a King such as the world had never seen before and would never see again. The King of Kings," Reverend Peterson continued. "With us tonight is a choir of young boys and girls from God's Love Baptist Church in Lubbock—the best singers West Texas has to offer. This very choir has sung in all the major cities of Europe, in New York, and in Washington, DC. Please join me in welcoming them here."

When the choir started singing, the Reverend Peterson moved across the stage to sit with his wife on the velvet sofa. He whispered to her, "You look lovely tonight, my dear."

She responded, "As do you."

The audience settled in to enjoy the pure voices of children who would be singing traditional Christmas carols in the manner in which they were intended to be sung. No embellishments. No riffs. No soloists. Just the simple pleasure of Christmas music to glorify the birthday of Jesus Christ.

Midway through the first song, a man stood up in the center of the small television theater. No one paid much attention to him at first, until he brandished an automatic weapon. He yelled something inaudible and then started shooting. He sprayed the stage area with hundreds of rounds, hitting rows and rows of young singers, painting their chests and stomachs and heads with red flowers, red blossoms, red spots, *red blood*.

No one in the audience stopped the man. They all ran for cover. Even the security guards ran away, as the man changed magazines and kept on firing from his location.

Screams, yells, the smell of gunfire, the irregular bursts of an automatic weapon, sounds of things breaking, the whimpering moans of dying children: an audible agony inside the television studio.

It was the Reverend Peterson who ran at the man. He alone. While it took him a few seconds to understand what was happening and to get up from his overstuffed sofa, once he was fully engaged he turned into a brawny, well-dressed missile honing in on the man with the gun.

The man was disrupting *his* Christmas program.

How the shooter didn't see the good reverend rushing at him so he could direct fire his way, no one could figure out. Maybe the Kevlar hand of God guarded Reverend Peterson. Whatever the reason, the shooter failed to act before Reverend Peterson leapt over a row of cushioned seats and grabbed the man by the front of his neck.

"My God," Reverend Peterson yelled. It was Rudy Smith! No longer just a former homosexual. He was now a killer! An active shooter.

While the reverend was choking Rudy Smith to death with fingers of steel, strength developed from years of counting money, the muzzle of the rifle got trapped in a seat cushion in a downward position. It kept firing, ricocheting bullets off the cement floor.

As Reverend Peterson squeezed the last breath out of his former guest, only then did Rudy's finger release the trigger. And only then did Reverend Peterson realize he was in terrific pain. He looked down at his bloody, shredded legs and feet...and fainted.

63

BLAKE TELEPHONED HIS sister. "Did you know that Dad and Holly were going to get married?"

Jordan answered, "Yes, I knew. Holly told me. We met for lunch one day. She wanted me to know how much she loved Dad and how much she loved you and me. She was so happy, Blake; I cannot tell you how happy! She radiated joy. It sounds like a greeting card, but it is absolutely true. I don't know that I ever saw a happier woman in my life."

"Was this on a 'need to know basis'? Why didn't you tell me?" Blake asked.

"Well, you were gone. And then. Suddenly, Dad was gone…I don't know. I put it out of my mind, I guess."

"What about Dad? Did he say anything to you?"

"He called me that night after I met Holly for lunch. I told him before he told me. We both laughed. I could tell he was very excited and happy," Jordan said, adding, "He cared for our mother for a long, long time. Now it was his turn to celebrate and enjoy his life. What an awful shame their happiness was short-lived. Dad died before they could get married."

Blake heard sadness in his sister's voice. He understood the loss of one's love.

“Peter Babcock told me about it. Even he was excited for them, and he rarely gets excited about anything,” said Blake. “When was the last time you saw Holly?”

“It’s been too long,” answered Jordan. “The last time I saw her was at Dad’s funeral. She was grief stricken. We consoled one another, I remember. When was the time before that? It must have been our lunch date. Before that…I’ll have to think on it. Certainly, it must have been at the firm. Maybe I stopped in to see Dad or pick him up for lunch or something.”

“Holly is still missing,” said Blake. “When I spoke to Peter Babcock he didn’t have any idea where she might be.

“We checked all the general aviation airports in the Palm Beach area and found nothing. We also checked the business jets owned or leased by her companies. We know she often flew to places in the Caribbean, Bermuda, the Bahamas and Cayman Islands. These were places where she would go for long weekends to get away from Washington weather.”

“Maybe she’s hiding in plain sight in Washington,” Jordan said.

“We are looking for her here; however, she would likely think twice about it since John was killed here.”

“Maybe she’s still in Florida,” offered Jordan. “Or she could be in Tennessee. She went to school there and still has a number of friends in and around Nashville. Maybe you should check with her sorority sisters to see if they kept in touch with her.”

“Warm weather,” Blake declared, ignoring his sister for the moment, “Holly loves warm weather, so on that fact alone, my bet is she is somewhere warm. That would rule out Nashville at this time of the year, along with a good portion of the United States.”

“I think she’s in Florida somewhere. She has many lifelong friends living there. Did you check with them?”

“We have the FBI looking for her there. Right now, all we know for certain is that she’s missing,” Blake said, adding, “Angela Carr is missing. The monsignor is missing, although we have a corpse in his place: his twin brother. John is dead. Superimposed on all this is the ACLU investigation."

"Plus, Dad may have been involved," added Jordan, as if Blake were missing that important fact.

"Right. We need to connect the dots and find someone soon before there's another murder."

64

"WE THINK SHE is in the Caribbean," Sapphire said. "Our contacts in the Caribbean circulated digital photos of Holly Waters, and there appears to be a match on the island of Anguilla. If it is her, the name she is using is Sarah McKenzie, complete with a British passport."

"Who gave us this information?" Blake asked.

"The Brits. They control Anguilla."

"Ask them to watch her. I will get there as fast as I can, but first I need to tell Tom where I'm going."

Leon and Sapphire suggested that Samantha go with Blake. There was enough work for the Wilsons to do without flying to Anguilla.

Blake met with Tom to tell him the news regarding Holly. He explained how important she was in helping them understanding why John Palmer was murdered, as well as the mystery of the monsignor's disappearance.

Tom agreed. He told Blake to make it fast—to get down there and get back. "We have an investigation to finish. Take one of our planes. Have one of my paralegals, Taryn or Barbara, arrange it."

Blake could not find Taryn in the building, and Barbara was out. Because he needed to get to Anguilla as quickly as possible, he asked Mrs. Arnison to arrange the flight to Anguilla.

• • •

The next day Blake, Samantha, and two FBI agents flew out of Washington to the tiny island of Anguilla, a British dependency approximately 250 miles west of Puerto Rico.

They arrived midafternoon on a sun-drenched day in the Caribbean. When they emerged from their plane, they experienced a sixty-degree change in temperature and perspiration-producing humidity.

Inside the airport terminal a tall, thin man with tobacco-colored skin, wearing seersucker business-casual clothes, approached them. "Good afternoon. I am Roscoe Albins, senior attaché of the British government. You are Mr. Elliott, I presume? I spoke with your colleague, Mrs. Wilson. I am here to assist you in any way that I can."

Blake shook hands with Mr. Albins and introduced Samantha and the two agents.

"Anguilla has the best beaches in the world," said Albins. "If you have time, you must enjoy them. I will tell you my favorites."

"Thank you," answered Blake. "But we don't have time. What information do you have regarding Sarah McKenzie?"

Albins wished he could chat a bit more about Anguilla. Maybe later. "We compared the photos your FBI circulated with photos from surveillance cameras in our marina. We check all the photos against passport photos. The principal features of our Sarah McKenzie compare favorably to those of your Holly Waters."

"How long has Sarah McKenzie been here?"

"She has been on island a week, I believe—maybe more than a week, possibly less. Well, whatever the time frame, we know she is on island."

"Do you know where she is staying?" asked Blake.

"Yes. I will take you there. The property she occupies is gated and has security guards."

Albins took their bags to his Toyota Land Cruiser. One FBI agent, Blake and Samantha rode with him. The other agent followed in a car with a driver Albins provided.

They drove over poorly paved winding roads until they reached Maunday's Bay, which Albins declared one of the most beautiful beaches in all the Caribbean. Along the beach were villas, most of them with Moorish architecture, all of them white with red tile roofs. The beach stretched for over a mile, and the villas appeared more elaborate and more secluded farther down the beach.

Albins turned onto a gravel road running parallel to the beach. He continued on to where the beach was at its widest, and then he stopped his vehicle.

"Ahead of us is the compound. It used to be a private resort until ten years ago. According to property records it is owned by T. L. Holdings, LTD. They have been remodeling for the last three years. I know the general contractor. He said that the place was being refurbished and turned into an executive retreat for people in the company," he said.

"Who hired him?" asked Blake.

Albins replied, "An architectural firm from the States."

"Okay, let's go," said Blake, as Roscoe moved slowly on the gravel road until they reached a closed gate. A sign on one of the columns read "Private Road. No Access."

"Can you go off-road to get us to the place?" Blake asked, peering at the compound in the distance.

Albins backed up, cranked the wheel toward the beach, engaged four-wheel drive, and slowly moved from the gravel road to the powdery sand, sinking in. The vehicle jostled its occupants as it crept over the sand toward the compound. After a short distance, two Jeeps painted the color of the sand approached the vehicle—one from the front and the other from the side.

Albins stopped as the Jeep directly ahead continued its approach and eventually pulled up to the Land Cruiser's front bumper, where it parked. Three men got out; the driver remained. The Jeep approaching from the side continued until it stopped directly behind the Land Cruiser. No one emerged from that Jeep.

The FBI agent with Blake and Samantha removed his gun from its holster. The other agent was back on the gravel road because the car he was in could not negotiate the sandy beach.

"Stay here," Albins said, as he opened his door and got out, walking toward the three men in front. He showed the men his identification and continued speaking to them. One of the men walked to the vehicle and looked in at Blake. He took out a mobile phone and shot photos of Blake and Samantha.

After a few minutes, Albins turned and walked back to his vehicle, passing the man who took the photos. Albins looked dejected.

The Jeep in the rear moved backward, giving Albins room to backup. The Land Cruiser backed away from the Jeep in front, turned around, and headed toward the gravel road.

"I think it is fair to say that whoever is in that compound is quite keen on security," Albins said. "The gentlemen were straightforward with me, though. 'No entry,' he said. I did not tell them who you were, even though he asked me. I told him you were friends of mine and that I had no obligation to tell him your names. When I asked him who was in the house, he smiled and told me he did not have to disclose that, either. A stalemate, I would say."

"So now what?" Blake asked.

"I take you to your hotel."

65

TRADE WINDS, WARM and steady, enveloped Blake and Samantha as they sat on the hotel patio overlooking Shoal Bay. It had been over two hours since the incident with the guards at the compound. They had changed from their Washington, DC, clothes to comfortable tropical attire, mostly lightweight silk. Their security detail, wearing business-casual clothing more suited for Washington, sat nearby in the shade.

Blake turned to the approaching waiter who handed him a folded paper. On it was written, "Dinner at seven o'clock—a car will pick you up. All of you." No signature, no name. "This is getting interesting," Blake thought.

At seven o'clock a white Mercedes SUV pulled in front of the hotel. A large man emerged from the driver's side and walked into the open-air lobby where Blake and Samantha were standing, along with their FBI security.

"Mr. Elliott?" the man asked.

"Yes."

"Please come with me," the man said, as he escorted all of them to the vehicle. One FBI agent sat in front with the driver, and the other sat in back.

The Mercedes sped off in the opposite direction from the compound where Albins had taken them earlier. After ten minutes the vehicle pulled onto a road that was nearly undetectable. Trees, shrubs, and walls obscured almost everything except the road itself. After traveling through the dense foliage, they reached an opening and saw a very large, well-landscaped, lighted courtyard with fountains and hundreds of flowering shrubs. It looked like an elegant resort property.

The driver escorted them to a building on the left, one that was attached by a walkway to a much larger building directly in front. He led them up a short stairway onto an expansive deck covered by the roof line of the building and open on three sides. The open space had numerous outdoor sofas and chairs, all in vibrant colors. There was a single dining table covered with a white linen tablecloth, napkins and place settings for three. An exotic flower display was in the center.

Four men stood along the back wall. They looked like the men Blake had seen earlier in the day, except that now they were better dressed. They wore white trousers and light-blue shirts, with the word RavenRock stitched in red on each shirt.

The driver led them to a small bar on one side of the deck. "Please, have a drink," the man said, leaving them with the bartender.

With chilled glasses of champagne in hand, Blake and Samantha walked to the railing along the front of the deck. The dark-blue sea below them massaged the shore. It took their eyes a few moments to adjust, but soon they saw groups of men standing at intervals along the beach. It appeared that the men had assault rifles in their hands and something bulky on their foreheads. Night-vision goggles?

Blake and Samantha stood drinking, talking, and watching the beach below. Their FBI agents sat on one side of the deck with their soft drinks, watching them and everyone else.

"My dear Blake," said a female voice behind them.

Blake recognized Holly's voice instantly. He turned and saw that her hair color and style were different from the last photos Blake had seen. She looked thinner than he remembered, but still classically beautiful. Blake set his drink on the railing and hugged Holly. Seconds passed as they held their embrace in silence, lost in private thoughts. When they uncoupled, Holly held one of Blake's hands in hers and looked at Samantha.

"Holly, this is my good friend and colleague, Samantha Rhodes," Blake said. The way he said it conveyed more than mere friendship, he realized. He saw both Samantha and Holly pick up on what he just said.

Holly walked to Samantha, pulling Blake with her. She reached out with her free hand to hold Samantha's hand in such a natural way that it seemed like old friends reacquainting.

"Samantha, it is my pleasure," said Holly, who remained standing between them, still holding their hands for a few seconds silently.

"Well, I didn't think you would find me. At least that was my hope. I should have known. John warned me," Holly said, looking at Blake with adoring eyes.

Blake smiled back at her and said, "Holly, why are you here?"

"You mean I can't enjoy the sun and the sand?" laughed Holly, deflecting the inquiry, as the bartender brought her a chilled glass of champagne.

Samantha said, "You are here for a reason other than sun and sand. Florida has sun and sand." Had someone other than Samantha uttered those words, they would have seemed rude; but Samantha spoke so matter-of-factly that there was no edge to her words.

Holly smiled again, saying, "Yes. I have another reason. In fact, I have a number of reasons. But having you two here changes everything…unfortunately." Her smile faded.

"Does it have something to do with John's murder?" asked Blake.

Holly looked at Blake intently, saying, "Yes it does. But, please sit down. We should have something to eat. You have had a long travel day, I am sure."

At the table, Blake continued, "We know John called you at your home in Palm Beach the night before he was killed."

"That is true," replied Holly, a note of sadness in her voice. "He was such a dear man."

"You disappeared after John called you."

Holly looked at him, her eyes registering affection for Blake and sadness at the same time.

"You went into hiding, not wanting anyone to find you. It's fortunate that we did," Blake finished.

"That is a matter of opinion, Blake. However, the mere fact that I went into hiding, as you say, is not really at issue here, is it? John told me that Tom Owens hired you to help investigate the attack on the ACLU. When he saw you with Samantha"—Holly turned in Samantha's direction—"for whom he had high regard and admiration—he became concerned."

"Why?" asked Blake. "John was working on the investigation, too."

"He was being protective. He did not want anything to happen to you or to Samantha. John was murdered, and I understand Samantha was attacked the other day. Wouldn't you agree that John had reason to be concerned?"

"Where did you get that information?" asked Samantha, surprised.

Holly turned to her and said slyly, "I have my sources."

"In John's apartment we found photos of my father, John and a priest named Monsignor Pacelli—taken in Italy, apparently. But I can't find out why Dad was there. The firm says it has no information, or they won't share it. We thought the monsignor was murdered, but it was his twin brother instead. Now we can't find the monsignor. He could be dead. We don't know. And then you disappear. What is going on?"

Ignoring his question, Holly said, "My immediate concern is whether you have been followed here."

"We took a private plane here," Blake answered.

"A private plane," asked Holly, "or a *government* plane?"

Blake realized he had just been sprinkled with Holy Water. "A government plane. Thanks to Tom."

"How is Tom?" asked Holly. "He has done a fine job as attorney general."

Blake told Holly about the earlier incident near the compound where Roscoe's vehicle was stopped. "I assume that is where you are staying," stated Blake.

Holly did not respond to Blake's question. She looked at Samantha and then back to Blake. "It would be better for all of us if you two would leave the island immediately."

Blake and Samantha looked at her, neither one of them saying a word.

"Listen to me. Go back tonight. You are in danger here. And now so am I."

Blake dashed a quick look at Samantha, who was focused on Holly. He scanned the deck. One FBI agent was looking at them; the other was looking at the four armed security men who stood quietly along the back wall. The bartender was motionless behind the tiny bar. Ceiling fans whirred overhead, circulating humid air. Water lapped against the shoreline. The night smelled of fragrant flowers. Danger? Here, in paradise?

"I think we need to know—" Blake started, when bursts of automatic gunfire shattered the tranquility of the night. The wood railing where they had just been standing blew apart into lethal slivers; bigger pieces of wood went flying high into the air above the deck.

Suddenly it was daylight. Security lights turned on everywhere, illuminating the beach area with overlapping cones of bright, white light.

Blake could see men in black wet suits lying face down along the beach, their legs being awkwardly moved back and forth by the wave action. They must be dead. Were boats offshore? He saw dark shapes low in the water at the extreme periphery of illumination provided by the security lights.

He turned around to locate Holly and Samantha. They were huddled in different corners of the open-air deck. Holly's guards moved her along the wall to the stairway and disappeared down it.

Then he heard it. A rocket-propelled grenade hit the wall directly above Samantha and the FBI guards who were shielding her. He saw Samantha collapse as the FBI agents fell on top of her.

Blake ran to them just as another grenade landed behind him.

66

ROIST SEARCHED ALONG seemingly endless corridors looking for coffee. He had quit smoking decades ago, but he could never quit drinking coffee. He was addicted. He admitted it to himself. "So what?" he thought. "My teeth are not yellow, and I feel great after a strong cup of coffee."

He wasn't familiar with this island but marveled at the size of the airport. "There could not be that many people flying out of here on business," he thought. Therefore, it must be a tourist destination or a transfer hub for the many islands in the Caribbean. The airport was the only part of the island he would get to see. The places he traveled always interested him. He wished there were more time to investigate Puerto Rico.

The United Airlines flight to Dulles Airport pushed back from the gate twenty minutes late—no explanation given. It sat on the tarmac another fifteen minutes. Finally, the plane taxied to the designated runway for takeoff. Before the plane was airborne, he was asleep.

As the plane began its descent over the Northern Virginia countryside, Roist opened his eyes and slowly stretched in place. He popped a mint in his mouth to freshen his taste and breath. Outside his window the gray gloom of a wintry afternoon spread across rolling hills and housing subdivisions. His watch said two-fifteen. He had been sleeping for almost three hours.

Roist had enjoyed the last few days of sunshine and warm water in Anguilla, lying on a sugary beach and giving shape and meaning to billowing white clouds passing overhead. He knew this downtime replenished his physical energy, but equally as important, it cleansed his mind so he could better compartmentalize his thinking and his memories. This was how he had learned to care for himself mentally and emotionally. Above all else, he absolved himself for killing the scientists. He put their deaths, and his causation, into a mental compartment and closed the door.

He was surprised by the vicious attack on Holly. It happened while he was staying at the compound miles away. He heard the gunfire but did not know the cause until the helicopter swooped in and dropped off Holly. She told him what had happened. But for RavenRock, Holly might have been killed. It was a war, after all. His part was to be a nameless assassin.

Before he left Anguilla, he went to see the restaurant where the attack took place. Holly's security told him that seven attackers had been killed. The two visitors from the Justice Department had sustained injuries. RavenRock medical technicians attended to them immediately after the fire fight and then flew them back to the States. Both FBI agents, however, had been killed. The Justice Department plane returned their bodies to Washington. Two men on Holly's security team had serious injuries but were expected to live. They were being treated in St. Maarten. Five of the resort staff had been killed, caught in the cross fire.

Roist was in Washington to determine the planned activities of the Papal Nuncio over the next two weeks. He was under specific orders not to meet with the Papal Nuncio or any of his staff. His job was to gather information and relay it to Holly.

67

SAMANTHA AND BLAKE suffered concussions and lacerations from flying shrapnel during the attack at the resort in Anguilla. The RPG blasts had rendered them unconscious, and Samantha's life was saved by the FBI agents who shielded her, even though it cost them their lives. As for Blake, he lived because the grenade that landed behind him rolled under a steel-framed, overstuffed outdoor chaise lounge that took the brunt of the exploding shrapnel.

Following the attack, RavenRock emergency medical technicians attended to the wounded. Holly wanted Samantha and Blake stabilized and their injuries dressed as soon as possible so they could be flown back to the States. Once they were ready to fly, she had her Gulfstream G650 transport them to a private airport in Northern Virginia, close to a trauma hospital. RavenRock medical personnel went along to monitor them. An ambulance met the plane on the tarmac and took them to Falls Church, Virginia, where the best trauma hospital in the region was located.

• • •

Blake woke up to see Tom Owens staring down at him. Blake looked around at the tubes attached to him and the machines to which the tubes were attached. No one else was in the room besides Tom.

"Where do you think I am?" Blake asked Tom, who laughed at Blake's question. "This doesn't look like Anguilla. Where is Sam? Is she hurt?"

Tom told Blake what happened to him and to Samantha in Anguilla and how Holly had sent the two of them back for expert medical care. They had both suffered minor concussions and assorted cuts and bruises—nothing life threatening for Blake but Samantha was in critical condition because she had severe lacerations to her neck and shoulders. The doctors thought one or two days in bed would see Blake back on his feet and fully functioning; however, Samantha would need a longer recovery time.

Tom also explained that the two FBI agents were dead. Their bodies had been returned on the Justice Department plane.

"I am so sorry," Blake said. "What happened to Holly?"

"We have no idea. She disappeared after the attack. The British authorities do not think she is on their island. Again, no one is certain where she is. Tell me what happened there."

Blake described in detail what they experienced from the moment they arrived in Anguilla all the way up to the attack at the resort. He summarized his conversation with Holly Waters and mentioned her concern for his safety.

Tom asked if Taryn had handled the flight arrangements for them. Blake said that it was Mrs. Arnison.

"So, if Holly is correct, the attack is related to the ACLU investigation," Tom said.

"That's right."

"This investigation is turning into an ugly affair for you and Samantha and, sadly, already a fatal one for John Palmer. What the hell is going on? We now have an investigation within an ongoing investigation. Is that it?"

Blake replied, "Yes. I believe that's accurate."

Tom stood silent for a minute or two before saying, "Tell me if you want off the ACLU investigation and this bizarre, apparently related, investigation as well. I'm concerned for your safety. I'm going to talk with Samantha too, once she is fully lucid, and offer her a chance to roll off. What do you think? In fact, let's do this: think about it; you don't have to answer me now," Tom said.

"Tom, I'm in for the duration. We need to see this through. I want answers."

"This isn't a morphine-drip response, is it? You do not have to answer me now."

"I'm in," Blake said. "Now, please, let me enjoy the morphine."

68

HOLLY SWAM LAPS until her arms and legs could no longer propel her through the water. She got out, toweled off, poured herself some lemonade, and sat in a comfortable chair under the large umbrella. From her vantage point, she could see Angela running on the treadmill inside.

She picked up a mobile phone and punched the speed dial. A slight smile slowly spread across her face. The voice-mail message said that Blake and Samantha were back in Washington. Although Samantha was still in serious condition, Blake was recovering from a concussion and shrapnel wounds from the exploding grenade.

Holly leaned back against the cushion, closing her eyes for a moment to consider her options. But her thoughts quickly shifted to Carson Elliott, the man she loved above all else. She had been so close to her dream of living out her life with him. She knew that he, too, longed for that time when they could be together twenty-four hours of every day. They were on the verge of escaping into their own world, living their shared dream…and then John had invited Carson to Rome.

"How bizarrely life has treated us," Holly reflected. "Who would have thought that a visit with the Pope would condemn us to this hell?" Well, that's how she looked at it now. Carson had different thoughts at the time, as did she. But her point of view now was from a life shattered by events none of them could have foreseen.

Holly could feel the air leave her lungs. After a minute, she inhaled deeply and exhaled fully, again and again, until her breathing returned to normal. She sipped more lemonade. Tears spotted her cheeks. She was hardly aware of them.

"Carson, my dear Carson, I loved you more than even you could have imagined. I would have died with you, if only I could have. I pray that you are not disappointed with me and what I have done... what John and I have done.

• • •

Angela wanted to contact her sister in Rhode Island and her brother in Maryland. She had not talked to them for almost eight years. What must they think of her? However, if she contacted them, their lives might be in danger.

Danger.

It was everywhere. Look at what just happened in Anguilla.

"Holly has protected me, thus far, and for that I am very grateful—not only to Holly but to Dominic for arranging it," Angela thought. "But how long can I stay with her? What if something happens to Holly? What if I cause her harm?"

Angela realized how much she wanted to go to a church to pray. During her time at the ACLU, she found herself in church often. It was more than just a Sunday obligation. Inside one of the Catholic churches on Staten Island or in Manhattan, she felt safe. She had found comfort in the smells, the statues, the candles, and the dim lights, all familiar memories to an Italian Catholic girl growing up in Providence, Rhode Island.

She prayed for her husband, her family, Holly, and everyone involved in protecting her. She prayed for herself to be strong and patient.

69

THE UNITED STATES Conference of Catholic Bishops held its annual meeting at Catholic University of America in the northeast quadrant of Washington, DC. Today was the last day of the two-week meeting. The president of the conference would be releasing the bishops' joint report and a proposed new policy addressing sexual abuse by priests and bishops. Archbishop Baccari, the papal nuncio, would be present to receive the report and proposed policy change on behalf of Pope Benedict, after which Baccari would say a few words to express his gratitude and that of the Holy Father.

Catholic University had campus police and volunteers providing crowd control in anticipation of disruptive protestors. As a backup, the District of Columbia Police arranged a squad to be available to assist, if needed.

When the president of the conference began his prepared comments inside the auditorium, hundreds of protestors shouted as loud as they could outside the building. It was quite the show for the media who were covering the conference.

At the end of the program, Archbishop Baccari thanked the bishops for their hard work. On behalf of the Pope, he officially accepted the report and the new policy proposal. Next, he gave a short speech in which he apologized to all the victims of the horrible sex crimes inflicted on them by priests and bishops. He said this sad chapter in the church's history was closed.

Campus police tried to keep protestors away from the departing bishops, but a few broke through the police barricade. They were tackled before they could reach any bishop and taken into custody.

Baccari sat inside, waiting until the auditorium was almost empty. Only maintenance workers and those responsible for sound and lighting remained. He waited because he wished to avoid all the protestors and reporters so he did not further burden the police.

After a while, the protestors faded away. Campus security followed the protestors, and the media was off covering something else. At last the time came for him to leave. His assistants helped Baccari to his feet and walked with him toward the front door.

Two maintenance men pushing plastic trash cans on wheels were working between the front of the auditorium and the archbishop. Baccari glanced at them. He thought they were the biggest maintenance workers he had ever seen. Suddenly, they converged in front of Baccari and pulled handguns with attached silencers from their trash cans. Before they could raise their guns, their heads exploded.

Their heads exploded!

Baccari could not believe it. He had never seen anything like it.

When he saw their guns lying on the floor next to their bodies, he took a breath to calm himself. Baccari then knelt down to administer the last rites to the two men, knowing he could not make the sign of the cross on either man's forehead.

They had no foreheads.

Above the main floor, in the dark, hidden area where the sound-and-lighting people worked their magic, two men removed their sniper scopes, unscrewed their sound suppressors, disassembled their rifles, and packed everything away in less than one minute. While they worked, another man with a stubby machine gun stood guard until all three of them left the building.

Two more men from RavenRock silently escorted the papal nuncio to his car. He had no idea who these people were, but he quickly understood that they had stopped an assassination attempt on his life. He trusted them. What else could he do?

When Baccari and his assistant reached their car they found a man lying beside it.

Another dead assassin.

The papal nuncio's vehicle was escorted by two vehicles all the way to his residence.

Baccari realized how lucky he was to have had these men as his guardian angels today.

He did not know who had arranged this secret security.

He did not know Holly Waters.

70

US AIRWAYS FLIGHT number forty-eight was on approach to Las Vegas McCarran Airport when Roist opened his eyes. From his window seat he looked out at the desert and the crazy-looking buildings. He remembered the last time he was here. It was for pleasure. Since that last trip, he believed many new hotels and casinos had been built on the Las Vegas Strip. "An ugly city by day," Roist thought, "less ugly at night."

He picked up his rental car, checked the map provided him in Anguilla, and followed the directions to Desert Oasis Storage in Henderson, Nevada. After he punched in a four-digit code, the gate opened. Once inside the fenced storage yard, he found the numbered storage bay. With the key provided him, he unlocked and opened the small garage door. The late-morning sun helped Roist see inside the space. There, among boxes of household goods and other items, was an aluminum briefcase and a garment bag hanging on a clothes pole.

Roist picked up the briefcase and put it in the trunk of his car, next to his small rolling bag. He hung the garment bag inside the car, and then he drove back to the Strip to Mandalay Bay Resort and Casino where he parked his car on the second level of the parking structure. Check in was simple at the registration desk, using the prepaid reservation Holly's people had made for him.

Once in his room, Roist unpacked the few articles of clothing he had brought, shoved the briefcase under the bed, washed his face, brushed his teeth, combed his hair, and went back down to the main floor. He walked around the casino to get his bearings. Next, he followed the signs to the events center, which turned out to be a considerable distance from the casino area.

When he arrived at the events center, there were velvet ropes set up across the entire entrance approach, with more than ten uniformed security guards standing on the other side of the velvet ropes, facing out. Roist took in the scene and then returned to the casino where he played slot machines for an hour, grabbed a sandwich, and retired to his room for a nap.

At approximately nine o'clock that evening, Roist showered and put on the tuxedo that was in the garment bag from the storage facility. He opened and examined the contents of the packet Holly had given him in Anguilla before putting it in the pocket of his tuxedo jacket. Next, he opened the briefcase and read the directions taped on the inside of the cover. When he was finished, he closed the briefcase. He pinned the VIP attendee badge to his jacket lapel, tucked the ticket into a pocket, grabbed the briefcase and left the room.

The aroma of gardenias and tropical flowers filled the air on the main floor of the hotel, which he walked through on his way to the events center. Many other people were walking in the same direction. Most of them were young, good-looking men and women, all fashionably dressed. He assumed they were all going to the events center for the same reason: to attend the Annual MAXXX Adult Entertainment Expo, the biggest adult-entertainment convention in the world, sponsored by *MAXXX Magazine, the* magazine of the pornography industry.

After showing his badge at the security checkpoint, Roist walked into the main exhibit hall and picked up a map of the exhibitors and a glossy red plastic bag with the word "MAXXX" on both sides. He put his briefcase inside it and then he walked around the floor. According to the schedule, today was the third day of the convention but the first day it was open to the general public. Real business had already been transacted during the past two days when the convention was closed to the general public.

Roist stopped for a soft drink, sat at a table and read through some of the information he had picked up at the entrance. There were over three hundred vendors of porn-related material: magazines, DVDs, sex toys, and other paraphernalia—including condoms, health information regarding sexually transmitted diseases and a wide variety of other items offered for sale by producers, manufacturers, and distributors. One brochure stated that forty thousand attendees were anticipated at the three-day event.

Holly knew that The Fat Man would be here. After all, The Fat Man was the owner of *MAXXX Magazine*, the principal sponsor of this convention. "Where did she get this information?" Roist wondered. Holly told him The Fat Man rarely showed himself on the convention floor. He conducted all his business in the grandest two-story penthouse suite at Mandalay Bay—a suite reserved for the highest of high rollers, the biggest whales from all over the globe. Holly said there was going to be a live interview of The Fat Man on the convention floor during the eleven o'clock news program of a Las Vegas television channel.

The ticket and the badge gave Roist admission to the MAXXX Adult Entertainment Expo VIP Party located in a reserved section inside the main exhibition floor. Security guards checked his ticket and badge carefully before letting him into the privileged area. Upon entering, he was immediately wet-kissed by scantily clad hostesses with Grand Canyon cleavage, young actresses in the adult-entertainment business on hand to ensure that this was a press-the-flesh memorable moment for those at this VIP party. He declined having his photo taken with the nubile hostesses.

Roist plucked a glass of champagne off an attractive waitress's tray and moved farther into the room. He figured there were about one hundred people or more at this private party, all drinking and eating and mingling. Adult films were playing around the room on huge screens that were at least twenty feet high. Hardly anyone looked at the films. He surmised that the people enjoying themselves in this room were in the business of making and distributing pornography—not watching it.

Roist spotted The Fat Man. He was standing at a long bar in the rear of the party space. Above the bar were neon lights spelling out "MAXXX." The bar was crowded with adult-entertainment celebrities. Roist worked his way to the bar to check out The Fat Man's bodyguards. He then slowly walked back to the entrance and out of the VIP private party.

As he walked around the exhibition hall, he took note of the many security cameras that were visible—similar to those in the casino, although not nearly as numerous. "So what?" he thought. He would be one of thousands of people walking around with a MAXXX bag. Nothing criminal in that.

He finished his champagne and focused his attention on the booths and displays located in the center of the exhibit hall. Finding what he wanted, Roist moved to an exhibitor's display booth that had a Victorian-inspired velvet fainting couch as a prop for the vendor's naughty lingerie on display. "Fashion for Passion" was the label. The vendor was busy talking with a prospect, and he didn't notice Roist place his MAXXX bag containing the briefcase behind the couch.

Roist walked back into the VIP private party, noting that The Fat Man was holding court with a number of middle-aged Indonesian-looking men. Roist helped himself to the exquisite buffet and had another glass of champagne.

He meandered through the VIP crowd, gradually making his way closer to the group of people encircling The Fat Man. By now there were at least another hundred people inside the VIP section. It was standing room only. Roist put down the glass of champagne and reached into the inside breast pocket of his tuxedo jacket. Suddenly, a loud explosion echoed inside the exhibition space. White smoke snaked upward from the center of the spacious exhibit hall.

For a split second, everyone inside the hall seemed stunned by the noise and the visible pillar of smoke climbing to the ceiling, but then they started to rush toward the entrance and every other available exit. Emergency-door alarms screeched in various parts of the hall competing with fire alarms. Exhibitors and guests trampled trade booths and pushed and shoved each other in their haste to find safety away from the smoke-filled exhibit hall. It was mass chaos.

People yelled and screamed as they ran through the massive events center. In sections of the vast hall fire sprinklers sprayed water in overlapping radius patterns, soaking everyone and everything below. Red emergency lights overhead painted the water crimson.

Roist pushed through the Indonesians who were running past him to find an exit. He moved quickly, taking two needles from the packet in his jacket and sinking them into The Fat Man's neck. He rapidly pushed the small plungers to release the lethal contents into the man's overfed body. Then he pulled out the needles and put them back in his pocket. Roist worked so deftly and so quickly that no one noticed: not the security guards and not even The Fat Man himself, who felt nothing until his eyes locked in place, his heart stopped beating, and he fell to his knees and then sideways to the floor.

Roist bent down to perform CPR on The Fat Man. He yelled for help, shouting to the security guards that this man must have had a heart attack. He directed them to call 911, as he continued to press on The Fat Man's body. After a short while, he asked one of The Fat Man's security guards to take over. He waited until emergency medical technicians arrived, and then he slowly moved away and joined people hurrying from the events center.

He returned to his room where he changed into comfortable clothing. He packed the tuxedo, shirt, and shoes into his bags and took the elevator to the parking ramp. He threw the bags in the trunk of his car and drove out into the Las Vegas night. He headed south on Interstate 15 toward the City of Angels, with Sin City in his rearview mirror.

71

SABINO ARANA WALKED along Via Dolorosa in the early evening. The light drizzle that fell during the afternoon had pushed on to another part of Italy, leaving the night air fresh and clear, with visibility limited only by one's eyesight.

He wondered where all this was leading. Worse, he wondered whether they had made a mistake years ago. Perhaps they should have pushed back more or developed an end-game strategy for a worst-case scenario. Isn't that where they were now? Five hundred people dead!

"Actually, as bad as it is, this might not be the worst case," thought the superior general. "This is just the reality of war, complete with skirmishes, battles, tactics and strategy, victories, losses, and casualties—and, of course, diplomacy. How could I forget diplomacy? Diplomacy that solved nothing.

"After all, wasn't it diplomacy that started it all—with Carson Elliott the first casualty?"

His thoughts transitioned to the late Pope John Paul. Now there was a man who knew the intricacies of diplomacy. Had he not died, maybe things would now be different. His idea of diplomacy was to take action.

"Now we have Pope Benedict," he continued thinking, "decid-edly not a man of action, but a man of deep thought. He could do more with words than others could do with swords."

As he continued walking, he wondered whether he should have declined John Paul's request to become superior general of the Society of Jesus. "He knew I would obey his orders, unlike the previous superior general. Here I am: older, but am I wiser?"

Arana entered the family-owned restaurant. The proprietor greeted the superior general warmly and led him to the private room in the back, opposite the small kitchen. Waiting for him was a man dressed in casual street clothing, all black.

"Ah, he lives," Arana said, embracing the man. "I am so happy that you are still with us."

"I do not think I am martyr material," responded Monsignor Pacelli. "John Palmer is the martyr and my poor brother, Leo—a martyr by chance. I am saddened that my brother died in my place. I am sorry to have put him in danger. Surely John and Leo are together in heaven."

"Dominic, we can only do our best with what we know. You have done your best. Your family has given more than we could ask of a family. Your brother—surely with God—your sister…the fact that she is alive is proof of God's love at work," said Father Arana. "As for John, whether we think it good or bad, nothing would have happened without him…and Carson, another martyr."

"You know they tried to kill Baccari?"

"Yes, I heard that. It would have made life difficult for Benedict."

"Yes."

Arana said, "We must speak to Benedict."

"How much does he know? He never agreed to any of this," the monsignor observed. "It would be such a burden on him."

"Benedict is far too smart. He may not have the details, but he isn't totally in the dark," Arana commented, with a hint of resignation in his voice.

72

THE LAW PROFESSOR walked in and sat down. Farrell turned away from the window to look at the imperially slim man in his tailored tweed coat, suede vest, wool slacks, button-down blue shirt, and patterned bow tie, looking more Brooks Brothers than seemed possible. Farrell smiled, not because he was pleased to see the man but because the man seemed like a caricature of people Farrell disliked: the elite. They were the elite only because they acted that way, thought Farrell.

"How did it go wrong?" asked The Law Professor. "How did the papal nuncio anticipate an attempt on his life? That is beyond miraculous, if you ask me. We have a major problem. We must have a leak, a mole."

Farrell had nothing to say. This time he tended to agree with The Law Professor. "If there's a leak, it must be on your side. Have you checked all your colleagues? Some of them are kind of squishy, if you ask me."

"This was not a botched assignment, like the ones before," The Law Professor continued, ignoring Farrell. "This was an ambush. There are three dead bodies for the police to investigate. And the papal nuncio now has added layers of security. I wish The Fat Man were here to discuss what happened."

Farrell said nothing.

"Do you believe The Fat Man died of a heart attack?"

"Who knows? The man was a fuckin' blimp. Maybe his tiny heart couldn't handle it anymore, trying to push his chunky blood through layers of plaque. Who knows? Look at it this way, other people got hurt trying to get out of that place, but only one died. The fattest one.

"There are no autopsy results yet, although I don't think his associates wanted an autopsy because they probably have no idea what junk he had in his body. Hell, he could have overdosed, for that matter," responded Farrell, not caring one bit about The Fat Man's passing and wishing the man in front of him would die soon, too.

"Well, the circumstances of his death are strange. I would like to know if he was murdered. That is an important question that needs an answer," stated The Law Professor.

"Maybe, just maybe, his death was a message, telling us that we can be killed anywhere, anytime," continued The Law Professor. "Don't you think it odd that the only death caused by that little smoke bomb in Las Vegas was our Fat Man? Maybe it was in retaliation for the failed papal nuncio attempt."

Farrell turned away, slightly shaking his head. He looked out the window. How important a question was it? Any number of people may have wanted The Fat Man dead. After all, he had many enemies brought on by his porno business. Plus, he was an arrogant pig.

"I don't wish to talk to your back," said The Law Professor, tired of dealing with this lowlife.

Farrell turned to face him. "What do you want from me?"

"Well, at the least, I want your attention," scolded The Law Professor, sounding very much like the academic he was. "I do not, for one minute, believe the man had a heart attack."

Farrell smiled broadly and sat down at the table. "Okay, you've got my attention. Now what? Are we arranging a memorial for The Fat Man?" asked Farrell, sarcastically. "Look, anyone could have killed him. And, besides, if they wanted to send you a message, why not just kill The Fat Man in his home in Los Angeles? Why go to all the trouble of doing it in Las Vegas, with so many people around?"

"Because"—The Law Professor wanted to say *you idiot*, but refrained—"that is the genius of it. Unlike the blast in San Francisco that indiscriminately killed everyone in and around the restaurant, this was pinpoint, precise, and quite personal. And it has us guessing."

Farrell responded, "I think you're lost in your own make-believe. What do you call them? *Hypotheticals?* Most of us live in the real world. We don't have time to play around with hypotheticals."

Ignoring Farrell, The Law Professor stood and responded, "I have been thinking. We need bold action. Something aggressive. Something daring. That's what we need." The Law Professor seemed to be channeling his friend, Ruth. This was what she had said about killing the papal nuncio.

Farrell didn't make eye contact with the man standing over him. Instead, he looked at the wood grain in the tabletop. He waited and thought, "What a putz."

"Yes, well, judging from your nonresponse, I suspect you feel the same way," observed The Law Professor, injecting his own brand of sarcasm.

"Here it is." With that statement, The Law Professor reached into his tweed jacket and took out a folded note card. He placed it on the table and pushed it a few inches in the Farrell's direction.

Farrell hated The Law Professor's theatrics. He reached for the note card.

"What is this? An invitation to a cocktail party?"

"Open it."

Farrell opened the note card and read the contents: *Kill the Pope*.

This time Farrell looked up at The Law Professor in disbelief. "You can't be serious," he said. "If you haven't noticed, there is an ocean between us and the Pope. You've come to the wrong man. You need the Mafia."

"Listen, you idiot," The Law Professor raised his voice. "The Pope will be in Washington the week after the inauguration. Make it happen."

"Don't ever call me an idiot again," Farrell threatened.

73

SHE LOOKED LESS attractive now than at any time in her life. She had never been a beauty or even qualified as a cutie. She barely scraped the "strong-looking woman" bottom-of-the-barrel description, but she was, nevertheless, one of the most powerful women in America. At age seventy-three, she was two inches shorter than she was thirty-five years ago. Looking out the high windows of her office, Justice Ruth Adler Bergman of the United States Supreme Court wondered how tall she would be if she lived another thirty years.

Wearing a long-sleeved cashmere sweater under her business suit, Justice Bergman bent over to turn up the electric heater she had under her large desk. Her feet and ankles were warm because she was wearing sheepskin-lined boots from Australia, but her knees and thighs were cold. "Where did I put that fleece blanket I had last winter? Imagine how much more comfortable this office would be if it did not have twenty-five foot ceilings," she thought. "All the warm air is up there, and I am freezing down here. Thank you, Cass Gilbert," she muttered to herself, blaming the architect of the Supreme Court Building for her immediate discomfort.

She was the only justice whose office was on the third floor of the building. All other associate justices, and the chief justice, had their offices on the second floor. She liked being special in every way possible. How else could she have gotten here? No one had ever offered her a helping hand her entire life. She had achieved everything by herself.

The medical report lay on her desk. She had already read it: her husband was dying. "How unfortunate," she thought, "but inevitable." His health had never been very good. He would die, and she would live. That was it. Then, sometime later, she would die, and after a few years, no one would care. Not their children. They didn't care now whether their parents lived or died.

"What an odd day," she thought. "On the one hand, I have the news of my husband's impending death, a death I cannot stop. On the other hand, there is a prospective death that I can stop, except I will not. *I will be the Pope's executioner.*"

Her thoughts segued to the number of times, in her official capacity as associate justice, she was asked *to stay* a prisoner's execution. In every instance, she ordered a stop to the execution. Her legal philosophy and temperament abhorred the notion of the state taking a person's life.

"Now here I am, planning a private execution.

"We kill them, or they kill us. How existential.

"We failed to kill the papal nuncio, but now we will kill his superior. This time we will be successful. I know it."

74

"LOOK AT THIS!" Sapphire said. "We have a report that four nuclear scientists in Eastern Europe died of natural causes within days of one another. One died in Estonia, one in Romania, one in Croatia, and one in the Czech Republic. Is this just another coincidence?" asked Sapphire, in disbelief.

"We don't believe in coincidence. How old were they?" asked Samantha, happy to be back at work. Happy to be alive.

"They were all about the same age, eighty-eight to ninety-one."

"Maybe it is a coincidence. There is old age, after all."

"What else do we know about them?" asked Blake.

"They were experts in designing and building nuclear weapons for the Russians. They knew where to find enriched uranium. A lot of nuclear material conveniently disappeared after the Soviet Union disintegrated," Sapphire said.

"I think the term is *glasnost*," Leon observed, "not *disintegrate*. Remember the balding man with a Texas-shaped birthmark on his head? Mikhail Gorbachev?"

Sapphire shot him a look that married people understand.

"Or was it *perestroika*?" Samantha added.

"Anything else?" Blake asked.

"Yes, how about this for another coincidence: they were classmates at the University of Krakow in Poland," Sapphire said.

Leon added, "I am starting to believe in the power of coincidence."

"There is even more. We also have information on something that might qualify as a major breakthrough," Sapphire continued.

"Yes?"

"Remember when we were just starting to investigate the explosion in San Francisco? We watched that live video feed from the local news channel that covered the ACLU fund raiser. Remember that?"

"Yes."

"The pudgy, nerdy-looking guy who was standing next to the mayor of San Francisco—the billionaire geek who picked up the tab for the fund raiser, Lawrence Perry—well, we just received information from Interpol that two of the dead Polish scientists had letters from Perry in which he personally thanked them for their assistance and gave each of them payment of some kind.

"We don't know yet whether they were paid in cash or what form the payment took or why he was giving it to them. The letters don't describe what work the professors did for Perry. We are trying to find out more but we have to go through international police channels. The letters were dated about two weeks before the ACLU fund raiser. *Two weeks before the explosion,*" Sapphire emphasized.

Blake said, "So, we have four dead nuclear scientists living in different countries and dying within a few days of one another. They worked in the Soviet Union military until it collapsed. After that, they went their separate ways. They are Polish. They went to the University of Krakow together. Two of them recently received thank-you notes and some remuneration from the late Lawrence Perry. Is that about it?"

Sapphire said, "Yes. That's about it."

"Where do you see this leading?" Blake asked everyone.

Samantha said, "This is fascinating information. What can we make of it? How do we find evidence to connect any of it to the explosion in San Francisco? Clearly, the fact that they were nuclear physicists familiar with manufacturing nuclear weapons points us in the direction of the nuclear device used in San Francisco."

"Leon, can you put together a dossier on Mr. Lawrence Perry?" said Blake. "Sapphire, we need a chronological chart with biographical information on the scientists. The Department of Defense or the CIA or some other agency must have dossiers on the scientists who worked for the Soviets, including where they went and what they did after they no longer had any Soviet bosses. It shouldn't be hard to find.

"I thought we had people in our defense department keeping track of enriched uranium needed to make a nuclear weapon. Maybe there's some information that these dead scientists had access to weapons-grade plutonium, or whatever triggers neutrons. Were any of these scientists on the short list of likely suspects for making the bomb that exploded in San Francisco?"

"Nope, none of them was on the short list," answered Sapphire. "I already checked. But why weren't they? I think we need to find out. Don't you agree?"

"I do," answered Blake. "Sapphire, will you do that for us?"

"Absolutely."

"I wonder if John Palmer knew them. He worked with universities all over the world, buying—or trying to license—their technology. We have John's travel information for the last five years, I think, but we were focusing mainly on Italy and cross-referencing travel with Blake's father, Holly Waters and the monsignor. Maybe John had business in the cities and countries where the scientists lived," Samantha said. "We should find out."

Sapphire added, "We never had any reason to look into Lawrence Perry's travels or his background vis-à-vis the dead scientists. Such information could be extremely helpful. He's already been investigated but not from this perspective. Maybe we'll find something."

75

ANGELA FLOATED IN the pool on the aft deck of the seventy-meter yacht Holly had borrowed from a friend, complete with captain, crew and full-time chef, with enough room for Holly's security people.

This luxury yacht was built in Germany by the same ship builder that built custom yachts for billionaires. Named *Rhine Wine*, it was only three years old. There was a modern business center on board that offered redundant satellite feeds to ensure uninterrupted global communication around the clock. In addition, the yacht had a helicopter. This was the feature that sold Holly on the idea of staying at sea in the Bahamas. Since it was yachting season, *Rhine Wine* would just be one of thousands of watercraft motoring around the islands of the Bahamas.

Angela got out of the pool and sat next to Holly. "I can't do this anymore, Holly. I need to get involved again. I need to do something to help Dominic."

Holly didn't answer right away, but Angela didn't seem to mind. Holly was working through her own feelings. "Maybe the time is right to come out of hiding," Holly considered. "Maybe the time is right to contact Blake to steer him in the direction most advantageous and safest for him. Maybe the time is right to tell him how his father died and the reason why."

She finally said, "I know it is difficult for you; however, I think it is still too dangerous for us. Believe me, Angela, I know how you feel. I felt the same way after Carson died. So much was going on and then, all at once, everything stopped. Worse, the most important person in my life was gone. And I could not even call Carson's death what it was: *an assassination.*"

Holly paused, worried she was saying too much. Yet, she felt the need to tell someone. Who better than Angela, who had lost her husband?

"Carson frequently commented on your bravery, Angela. I know he prayed for you and worried about you—as did John, who also prayed for you every day. Your courage and your intelligence gave us all a tremendous boost. You provided the critical information we needed to expose them…or at least to try."

Holly's eyes narrowed. She realized she wanted to kill some of them herself. What an exhilarating feeling to finally admit what she had suppressed for years. Now it was so clear: kill them. What surer way to end this madness?

Holly continued, "Now is not the time to make ourselves known. Right now we need to remain vigilant. We will pick the right time."

76

TARYN MCNEILL, ONE of the two legal assistants Tom Owens had brought with him from his law practice when he became attorney general, had grown up in a family of police officers. Her father, her brother, and her sister were cops. Her father had been a detective for more than twenty-five years, her sister had just become a detective and her brother worked as a vice cop.

Taryn had learned to be suspicious of people since her childhood. This trait became part of the fabric of her very being. Unfortunately, she lost a number of boyfriends and some girlfriends because they thought she was too suspicious. It was in her DNA.

Taryn and Barbara Dodge, the other assistant, had become close friends over the years they worked together for Tom. They believed no one knew him as well as they knew him. They lived to serve him and to protect him, and they fervently believed they were the two doting sisters he never had. Taryn and Barbara trusted each other completely, but neither of them trusted Tom's administrative assistant, Mrs. Arnison.

Mrs. Arnison moved slowly around the attorney general's office, putting down papers, picking up papers, taking papers away, and filing papers in cabinets that contained highly sensitive material. The cabinets were built into the wall to the right of the general's desk. Access to the cabinets was limited to a select number who used their identification badges to open the drawers.

Taryn wondered why Mrs. Arnison spent so much time in the general's office when he was gone. She told Barbara about her suspicions, thinking Barbara would laugh at her suspicious nature. But instead of laughing at her, Barbara agreed with her. She thought Mrs. Arnison's work methods were unusual. Barbara also didn't think Mrs. Arnison was very good at her job. But that wasn't really the issue, was it? Something about her was not right.

One night Taryn and Barbara ate at Old Ebbitt Grill and shared what they knew about Mrs. Arnison. Most of the information came from Mrs. Arnison herself, during times of idle chitchat. She told them she was a widow with no children and that her husband had died six or seven years ago. For the past thirty-two years, she had worked in the Department of Justice as an administrative assistant in a variety of areas, including the criminal division, Obscenity Prosecution Task Force, and then the leadership offices within the department.

When the administrative assistant to a previous attorney general was mugged and permanently disabled, Mrs. Arnison, who was next in order of seniority, became the administrative assistant to the attorney general. That was four attorneys general ago. Tom Owens was number five for Mrs. Arnison. While attorneys general moved in and out of the Justice Department with regularity, Mrs. Arnison stayed put.

Few people knew as much about the day-to-day operation of the Justice Department as Mrs. Arnison. Barbara told Taryn about her conversation with another administrative assistant named Shondell White who had almost as much seniority as Mrs. Arnison.

Shondell worked in the criminal division. She told Barbara that it wasn't just seniority and the previous administrative assistant's accident that put Mrs. Arnison in the outer office of the attorney general. According to Shondell, Mrs. Arnison's deceased husband had been an influential union official for AFSCME, the Association of Federal, State, County, and Municipal Employees: a union with over one million members, all civil servants. Shondell said that because of his high-level union position, it was he who finagled his wife into the office outside the attorney general.

After Shondell told Barbara this tidbit, she smiled broadly, winked, and asked, "Do you want to know the rest of the story?"

Before Barbara could respond, Shondell said that Mr. Arnison wanted his wife at a *listening post*, as he called it, so she could tell him what was going on in the Department of Justice from the attorney general himself.

Barbara asked Shondell about Mrs. Arnison's husband. "He was a jerk, even before he became a big shot in the union. Then he became even a bigger jerk, if you ask me," Shondell said. "Plus, he thought he was quite the ladies' man. What a joke. He was always hitting on me."

Shondell acknowledged that she really didn't care for Mrs. Arnison because she became arrogant after she landed in the office outside the general. As a result, according to Shondell, Mrs. Arnison had no friends in the department.

"Do you believe her story?" Taryn asked Barbara.

"Yes, I do, although Shondell has issues," laughed Barbara in response. "But I'd like to know more about Mr. Arnison. Maybe we can find someone to fill us in, so we can make our own assessment."

77

MONSIGNOR PACELLI WAITED. He was alone in a room with enough chairs and seating for a hundred people, and he did not know what to expect. He prayed. He always prayed when he didn't know what else to do. "So simple," he often thought. He never prayed for himself. He prayed for his sister's safety. He prayed for the soul of his brother Leo. He prayed for his remaining siblings. He prayed for his religious order, and his friend, Sabino Arana. He just prayed to glorify God.

His head was bent and his eyes were looking at his shoes when another pair of shoes suddenly appeared in his vision. Standing in front of him was Cardinal Derek Luantanda from Senegal. He stood up and greeted the cardinal, apologizing for being lost in prayer.

"We are never lost in prayer, Monsignor," said Cardinal Luantanda, smiling as he embraced Monsignor Pacelli. "We are only found."

"Thank you, Your Eminence," answered Pacelli.

"You may be wondering why you are the only person sitting in this enormous room painted by Michelangelo?"

Pacelli felt the personal warmth of this cardinal, well-known for his humble demeanor and keen intellect. "Here is a holy man," Pacelli thought. He said, "I am at your service, Your Eminence."

"You have been in God's service for a long time, Monsignor. We do not know where all of this will lead, but we know it started with your desire to please God and for no other reason. We pray that God will guide us."

Pacelli did not understand what the cardinal was saying.

"Please come with me, Monsignor," said Cardinal Luantanda, leading Monsignor Pacelli through a door that was hidden within the artwork on the walls.

They walked through a short, narrow hallway that opened into a much smaller room than the one where Pacelli had been waiting. There, against the far wall, sat Pope Benedict in an ornate chair on a red-carpeted platform elevated six inches above the floor. Cardinal Luantanda took the monsignor's elbow and directed him to a place in front of the Pope. Then the cardinal moved away.

Pacelli stood there, momentarily forgetting protocol. Recovering quickly, he knelt on one knee in front of Pope Benedict and kissed his papal ring. "Your Holiness," he said, standing up.

Benedict smiled warmly as he stepped forward to embrace Monsignor Pacelli.

Pacelli wondered why he was so *embraceable* all of a sudden.

Benedict looked over Pacelli's shoulder. Two priests appeared. One of them carried a silver tray upon which were a scarlet zucchetto, or skullcap, and a ring. The other carried a large, open leather-bound book.

Pope Benedict looked at Pacelli and said, "Dominic, you have been a man of God for many years. You have served him faithfully—not only in working tirelessly to produce our new catechism, but also putting yourself and your family in danger in order to do his work in America. His Holiness Pope John Paul loved you greatly. He worried about your sister's personal safety, as well as your own. What could we do to thank you for your sacrifice, for giving us the knowledge and the fortitude to take action in the name of God?"

Pacelli wanted none of this.

He was unworthy.

The honor of having been named a monsignor was more than enough; he had never wanted even that.

Pacelli stood still.

"Dominic, before he died, Pope John Paul appointed you a cardinal. He chose not to name you in public at that time, for obvious reasons, but to keep you secretly in his heart, in pectore. We did not want your secret appointment to go to the grave with him. It was his wish, *and now it is our wish*, to make you a Prince of the Church."

"*For obvious reasons*...Benedict knows," Pacelli thought. Stunned, but ever obedient, Pacelli knelt down as Pope Benedict said the words in Latin that made him one of only two hundred cardinals in the Roman Catholic Church.

Benedict, sensing Pacelli's uneasiness, stopped reading in Latin and spoke to him in English: "Dominic, please do not refuse this honor. The Holy Spirit has been working through you for many years. The church is filled with hope, even though the times are perilous for you and for America." The Pope resumed reading in Latin.

The Pope presented the red zucchetto to Pacelli, putting it on his head and praying over him. Next, he presented a gold ring to Pacelli. He blessed the ring and gave it to Pacelli.

After the brief ceremony, Benedict said he would like to talk with Cardinal Pacelli in a few days. His secretary would make the arrangements, but now he had to leave to perform other official duties. Before he left, he grasped Pacelli's forearm and said, "You have a unique position, Dominic. You are the only cardinal to have been appointed by not one, but *two* popes." Benedict had a twinkle in his eyes and a kindly smile. With the sign of the cross, he blessed the newest cardinal of the church and then he left the room.

Pacelli slowly turned around. Sabino Arana and Cardinal Luantanda were standing behind him. He walked to them. He was about to remove the red skullcap when Cardinal Luantanda stopped him.

"You are a cardinal, now, Dominic; accept it. It is an honor *and* a duty," the cardinal from Senegal said quietly.

78

"LAWRENCE PERRY IS quite the story," Leon said. "Here are copies of his biography from his company and other business news sources. We also have background information about him that he submitted in order to do business with the federal government, including Office of Personnel Management, Health and Human Services, General Administrative Services, the Defense Department, the Nuclear Regulatory Commission, and many, many others.

"They all had to vet him, although not all of the information is current. His company, DataBasic Systems, is a big government contractor for systems software."

They read the information Leon passed out. Perry was like many of the dot-com billionaires who survived the tech wreck. He started out at Stanford but didn't graduate. He and a few other fellow students began developing business software, tinkering with computer hardware, and providing services where none existed before. They found a niche. They parlayed their ingenuity into various businesses—chief of which was developing software for complex organizational and enterprise applications, as well as software to transition data inside a laptop, mobile phone and other personal tech devices.

Perry never married. Most of his friends never married, either. Some drifted away completely, never to be heard from again. Some cashed in, took their money, and moved on to totally unrelated ventures. Others continued in related fields, making even more money. Perry was the most successful of them all, based on the market value of the companies he created and his personal wealth, which put him somewhere on the one-hundred-wealthiest-people-in-the-world list.

At age thirty-seven, Perry dropped out of the business world completely. He no longer wanted day-to-day involvement with any of his companies. Instead, he started a nonprofit foundation into which he poured most of his considerable wealth—in the billions of dollars. He hired the best foundation president available and let that person take over grant making, with one exception: the ACLU of Northern California. The Lawrence Perry Foundation directed money to this ACLU chapter for one express purpose: to litigate First Amendment issues relating to adult entertainment.

There were blogs about Perry suggesting he had an enormous collection of pornographic films—large enough to warrant having a part-time librarian to catalogue his collection of early films, international films, and the many subcategories of hard-core porn, including kiddie porn and bestiality. It was a lending library, a busy one, utilized by Silicon Valley executives for parties and private viewing. Pornography was Perry's passion. He wanted everyone to enjoy it.

After Perry set up his foundation and began giving money to the local chapter of the ACLU, he asked to be introduced to Sylvia Roberts, the president of the National ACLU. She lived in New York where she was a First Amendment lawyer in private practice and an adjunct law professor at Columbia University Law School. If the pornography industry in the United States had a guardian angel, as perverse as that thought might be, it was Sylvia Roberts. Her legal arguments for freedom of expression, and her extreme legal positions regarding what constituted art, brought her to prominence; and her prominence in this area brought the ACLU large sums of money from the adult-entertainment industry and Hollywood.

Perry became her personal benefactor. She was a frequent guest at his mansion in California. Although she defended the most bizarre and outrageous hard-core pornography practices, she herself didn't care for it, which disappointed Perry. Her interest was intellectual, from a First Amendment viewpoint, while Perry's was true prurient interest.

"Okay, well, that is interesting reading, but what else is there?" asked Blake.

"I found something else about Perry that is possibly more interesting, or equally as interesting," Leon answered. "Here are some of his medical records."

A minute of silence passed as they read the pages Leon gave them.

"He had AIDS," Samantha exclaimed.

"Full-blown AIDS," added Leon.

"He was already living on borrowed time when he died in the explosion," Leon said. "Maybe he wanted to go out in a big way."

Samantha asked, "What are you suggesting? Are you suggesting that he might have been suicidal? Are you saying he may have had this tactical nuclear weapon developed to kill him and others, including his precious Sylvia Roberts? What would be the point?"

"Wait, wait," said Blake. "We're getting ahead of ourselves. Let's look at all the information."

"He was the only one sweating and looking disturbed on the news clip," Sapphire observed, referring to the San Francisco television channel footage where Perry vomited on the reporter's shoes.

"Remember? Mayor Billy Brown looked spiffy, cool and collected, but Perry looked disheveled and sickly. He was paying for the party. He should have had a smile on his face," Sapphire said. "Maybe he had a sour stomach."

Leon continued, "Look, Perry had enough money to raise an army, why not build a nuke? Or have one built?"

"Why build a nuke? For what purpose? To commit suicide and take four hundred of his friends with him? Does that make any sense?" Blake said.

"Unless they were not his friends," Samantha said. "None of this has to make sense, does it? After all, it could be that Mr. Perry was mentally deranged—maybe deranged enough to have a nuclear device created, assuming he had the wherewithal to find people to develop such a weapon."

Leon added, "He had the money and the contacts to have a bomb built. It would have meant breaking laws in many countries, but so what? If you aren't caught, what's the problem? Private guilt? What about those notes to the scientists? Apparently, he paid them for something. Maybe it was to build the explosive device used in San Francisco."

"We don't know enough at the moment to make informed guesses about those notes or Mr. Perry's medical condition," said Blake. "What more do we have?"

"I'm waiting for some information regarding John Palmer and Perry to determine if Palmer worked for any of Perry's companies and whether Palmer ever met, or had any dealings with, any of the four nuclear physicists," answered Sapphire.

They discussed Larry Perry some more, noting that his wealth made many things possible. The topic of wealth brought them to Holly Waters once again.

"What about Holly Waters? Can we find her…again?" Blake asked Leon.

"I don't have anything," said Leon. "All the methods you might use to find people do not apply in her case. Apparently, money trumps everything."

Sapphire observed, "Larry Perry had gobs of money. Holly has gobs of money. I am feeling a little stretched monetarily."

"One is dead—a possible suicide. The other is in hiding to avoid being killed. Maybe being a little stretched monetarily is not a bad thing," Blake observed.

79

"**HE WAS A** vice-president," said Barbara, entering their cramped office. "Shondell was correct."

"Who was a vice-president?" asked Taryn, not taking her eyes from her computer screen, and not quite tracking Barbara's statement.

"Arnison. Mrs. Arnison's husband. He was VP in a system of multiple unions. AFSCME—the Association of Federal, State, County and Municipal Employees—is part of the AFL-CIO, I just found out."

"I've never belonged to a union. Not even marriage. Tell me again, what does AFL-CIO stand for?"

"American Federation of Labor and Congress of Industrial Organizations."

"Are we in the Soviet Union?" Taryn asked, facetiously, still looking at her computer.

"Should I come back?" snapped Barbara, irritated that Taryn was not paying proper attention.

"I'm sorry. I just want to finish this one thought. There. Okay, I am all ears. Congress of Industrial Organizations? What a funny name. I would be embarrassed to be a member."

"We don't have a way to discover what Mr. and Mrs. Arnison did in the past, but I have an idea for now," said Barbara.

"Okay, what is it?"

Barbara explained her idea to Taryn. She wanted to examine Mrs. Arnison's time records to identify the days when she came in early and cross-reference those days with the days that meetings and events took the attorney general out of the office.

"How do we get that information?"

Barbara answered Taryn, "I have a new friend who can help us get Mrs. Arnison's time records."

"New friend? You don't mean that guy in the office of personnel management, do you?"

"Maybe."

80

"WHY NOT KILL the president? He's much closer."

The people in the conference room at Parton and Crownell did not appreciate DuPont's sense of humor, bordering always on the bizarre; but how bizarre was his statement compared to killing the Pope? Both were outlandish. This was the surreal existence in which they found themselves.

Holder, the university president, looked as if her stomach were eating itself, which it was. "We are in a private war. Who would ever believe this? How many people do you think even know we are at war?"

They recognized a rhetorical question when they heard it.

Silence.

"We believe it is Pope Benedict, but we are not certain. I mean, this pope—as far as we know—was never involved. If we do him harm, the consequences surely will be far worse than what we think is happening to us today."

She continued, obviously having given the situation some thought, "It was a big bang that got our attention: five hundred people killed. Then The Fat Man killed John Palmer but missed Monsignor Pacelli. He missed killing Blake Elliott and Holly Waters in Anguilla. Then, he totally botched the assassination of the papal nuncio. Now the police here and in Anguilla have dead bodies that might be traceable to The Fat Man…and maybe to us."

Silence.

"I mean, The Fat Man was surely expendable, if you ask me. We should have had him killed," she concluded.

The Law Professor knew, as they all knew, that she was directing her statement at him. "She is frightened," he thought, "like so many of them. They are only invested in success—not hard work, not tactical issues, not fighting, that is for certain. But she is correct, nonetheless. If they could not kill the papal nuncio, what chance would they have in killing the Pope…especially now that The Fat Man was dead?

"All they think about is what they might lose," The Law Professor thought. "None of them thinks about what they might gain. Well, to be fair, a few do." He could rely on his old friend sitting in Washington, but he would not trust the rest of them.

He realized now that all eyes were on him, as if he had to respond to the woman's preposterous statements. "Say it *with feeling*," he tutored himself, "and half the listeners will believe it. That's what she did.

"I have nothing to say," he started, meaning the exact opposite. Pausing for affect, he continued, "Except this. Now that The Fat Man is dead—no matter how he died"—he looked at Holder, dismissing her with his highly sophisticated inflection and body language—"we have no one doing the work he did. None of us has his contacts. Yet the work must continue. If, indeed, we are in a private war, then we need artillery and foot soldiers."

Holder responded, knowing she was speaking for the others, as well: "What if we choose not to fight? What if we choose diplomacy instead of bullets and bombs or, as you say, 'artillery and foot soldiers'? What if we go back three years and revisit that scenario?"

DuPont looked at her, "Are you serious? We can't go back," he said, dismissively.

"Why not?" demanded the foundation president, siding with Holder and thinking DuPont foolish for making unequivocal statements. "It may be a prudent thing to do. Call it an overture to a truce."

"Truce?" scoffed The Law Professor. "Are you insane? Do you really think the other side would agree to such a thing? Don't confuse a truce with complete surrender."

Farrell loved watching these morons go at one another. He wondered how they could be in charge of anything. But, then again, they really weren't in charge of anything. They were busy patting each other on the back for something none of them did. "It was only because Carson Elliott focused on them that they became important. Otherwise, they were just country club buffoons," he thought. Then he went one thought further: "What in the hell am I doing here?"

Too late.

"Mr. Farrell," asked the foundation president, "what do you think? How do we extricate ourselves from the mess *your* Fat Man put us in?"

"*My* Fat Man? I think you need to find out what is going on. You need to grab someone in the know and get information out of them. Torture them, if need be."

The foundation president looked at Farrell and burst out: "Torture? Torture whom? How stupid can you be? What an idiotic thing to say. No wonder our situation is so dire."

Farrell flew into a rage. "You bastards were losers from the very beginning. I sure as hell don't need any crap from you, *pussies galore*. That's what you are." Farrell stormed out of the room, not even closing the door behind him.

After a second or two, The Law Professor said, "Good riddance."

"Listen, we can do this ourselves. We have many contacts in unions, not just the AFL-CIO. Farrell was a jerk, anyway. It was a mistake to have him at the table, but now we can rectify it," Holder said. "Maybe the Teamsters or SEIU…or the Teachers Union."

81

FARRELL WAS PLEASED with himself for walking out of the meeting. "Nice move," he congratulated himself. "Pompous asses, all of them. Someone else can take my place. I've been listening to these phonies for over nine years. Or was it a lifetime? It seems like a lifetime." Farrell smiled. "Now I am free. Free at last," he chuckled to himself.

He took a short cab ride to Penn Station for the train back to Washington. "Better than flying—faster, too, what with those stupid perverts in TSA groping everyone," he thought. He might be home before those *elite* fools figured out they had nothing to talk about, not that they would ever stop talking. Pontificating blowhards, all of them.

Farrell knew Carson Elliott could have run circles around these fools, but instead he played it straight, helping these idiots think their way through a little complexity. And that Holly Waters, the woman who came with Elliott, whenever she spoke she had something smart to say. She was smart and good-looking, too.

For a second Farrell felt like a traitor.

A traitor to what? To whom?

"Someone else can drop off the money," he thought. "Someone else can find the muscle."

On the train Farrell closed his eyes thinking about the day's events and where all this would lead. Kill the Pope? What nut jobs. This pope might not even be involved. If they killed him—and those stumblebums might actually figure out a way to do it—what would they gain? They would all be dead, probably in forty-eight hours.

At best, Farrell was a fallen-away Catholic; at worst, he had fallen too far already, beyond redemption. Still, he could never endorse killing the Pope. The Pope was Christ on earth…or something like that.

He had heard from many sources that the ACLU's global partners had put out a contract on Pope John Paul. Three times they tried to kill him. Two times their hired assassins were killed by the Pope's bodyguard before they could pull a trigger. The third time was unsuccessful. The first two assassination attempts were never reported. John Paul beat the assassin's bullets the third time.

Farrell reached inside his jacket and pulled out a silver flask. He opened it, sipped some of the contents, closed it, and put it back in his pocket. The Redbreast twenty-one-year-old Irish Whiskey warmed his throat all the way to his stomach. It was well worth the price. Yes, definitely worth the price.

82

"HE HAS NEVER met me. He may have an old photo of me, but he couldn't recognize me now," said Angela. "My hair is a different color, styled differently, and I have different-colored eyes, thanks to cosmetic contact lenses."

Holly listened closely. She empathized with what Angela was experiencing. Still, she did not think that now was the time to become involved.

"I have to do this. It makes sense, doesn't it? We know so much. His life is in danger. He needs to know why. He needs to know who they are."

Holly agreed Blake needed to know, but once Angela made contact, everything would change. How could it not? Was this the wisest course? There were killers after them.

"How much more sun and warm water can I handle?" Angela asked, sitting on the deck in her swimsuit, pleading with Holly.

The two of them talked for a while longer until they talked themselves into returning to the United States and to Washington, DC.

Should they stay together? It made sense to stay together because security would be easier to manage. However, some things they needed to do separately.

"I should tell him," said Holly. "Not you. He knows me."

"That would be dangerous for you."

"I understand."

"Worse than that, the ACLU is looking for you. What if they spot you and try to kill you? They can do that from a distance. I don't think Blake's security, or ours, can stop a sniper."

Holly looked out over the calm sea, thinking about the last three years of her life. How it had changed so dramatically. "Three years ago, what were my dreams?" she mused, making a mental list. "To outlive Carson's wife. To marry the man I have loved all of my life. To live the life we often talked about. Those were my modest dreams. Look at my life now, three years later: Carson dead. John dead. Dominic in hiding. Angela in hiding. I am in hiding."

She recalled her last day with Carson and how passionate he was about their future together. Then, in a seeming instant, he was gone.

Carson always told her that no matter what life throws at you, you must keep moving forward. No matter what the circumstances, you must maintain forward momentum. Create a goal and pursue it.

Holly did that. With John's help, she achieved her goal. Carson would not have approved, but it was *her* goal, after all.

Now she must create a new goal: one tailored to these circumstances. "Turn it around," she admonished herself. "They want to find me so they can kill me. Turn it around, Carson would say. Find them first. Kill them?"

83

"**THIS IS TOO** much," he thought. "Look at what has happened: My brother murdered in my place, and I could not even attend his funeral. John killed, and I could not attend his funeral, either. My sister, Angela, is in hiding and will likely be in danger for the rest of her life. I am in hiding, too, in a Roman palace.

"All of this is my fault. *Mea culpa. Mea culpa. Mea maxima culpa.*"

Many thoughts rambled about inside Pacelli's brain. "My dear brother, Leo. No doubt he died more painlessly than would have been the case had his cancer continually poisoned his body over time...still...but for me..."

Leo had made the better choice, becoming a monk and leaving the world for a simple life of work and prayer. God Alone. That was the sign over the entrance to Leo's monastery, his home.

God Alone. What else do you need? Not much of the real world penetrated the monastery because the monks assiduously worked to keep it out.

It was so simple. Your head bowed in prayer many times a day at the same time every day, day after day after day. It was a much better life, indeed. Pacelli's anguished thoughts continued: "My brother could do it. I could not. What happened to me?

"I never had a place to anchor my life. I moved from city to city, country to country. I saw too much, and I couldn't keep my mouth shut. So, here I am: no longer a free man…a captive of the Vatican.

"But was I ever really free? My vows, most importantly my Fourth Vow to the Pope, trumped any freedom I may have thought I had. The work I did on the new catechism should have been enough. Except it wasn't. The truth is, I volunteered for the life I am now leading. I did it willingly. I have no reason to complain.

"Do I have regrets? Yes, I have many. With more to come, I am afraid. I am imperfect."

Pacelli continued thinking about the recent past and how all the tragic events had sprung from innocent intellectual discourse over a glass or two of red wine. At that time, decades ago, Cardinal Joseph Ratzinger—now Pope Benedict—hosted some of his students and assistants in his modest apartment in the Vatican. Cardinal Ratzinger, conservative to his bone marrow, loved discussing theology and liturgy and the craziness of the *misdirected* modern Catholic Church, as he characterized it.

"I agreed with him. Because I was often the sole American in these discussions, I related what the decade of the sixties did to the United States, in my view: the sexual revolution, political anarchy, protests, and disdain for authority.

"Cardinal Ratzinger agreed with me. The Roman Catholic Church and America were equally devastated by the sixties. Worse, the people of the sixties are still alive and still destroying."

Ratzinger and Pope John Paul believed that the downfall of the Roman Catholic Church in America started as a result of the ambiguous pronouncements of the Second Vatican Council in 1965. They believed, as did Pacelli, that Christianity was under attack in America, particularly Catholicism.

The damage done to the church in America over the last four decades was incalculable. They saw the ACLU as the principal, unrelenting antagonist against Christianity in the United States. It was the spearhead of a plot to change American society, they believed. They also witnessed the church devour itself by allowing predator priests to destroy the lives of young men, only to hide the priests, not caring one bit about the damage done.

"We were very much alone in our thinking," thought Pacelli. "No one wanted to hear this. There was so much euphoria and excitement in planning how to modernize the Catholic Church...how to make it more *relevant*, as if saving souls for eternity wasn't sufficiently relevant enough as the church's mission..."

"Your Eminence, excuse me," said the young priest standing next to Pacelli, looking down at him. "Your Eminence, would you please follow me?"

Pacelli looked up at the voice, realizing the priest was talking to him.

Your Eminence.

"Is that the sound of laughter in heaven?" he wondered. "Is Leo laughing at me?" Cardinal Pacelli stood and followed the priest into Pope Benedict's private study.

84

"**WHAT BOWL GAME** is Maryland playing in this year?" asked the attorney general of the United States, smiling at Leon, although he knew the answer: none. But he loved tweaking Leon.

In response Leon said, "Maryland is an academic institution of higher learning. Football is a club sport, just as football is a women's sport at Virginia, your alma mater."

"The ACC is a basketball conference, gentlemen," Sapphire observed, putting an end to the boys-will-be-boys banter.

"Thanks, Sapphire, for getting us back on track," Tom said. "What do you have for me that a thousand other investigators do not?"

Blake gave Tom a memo that summarized their investigation to date. He then said, "We don't have much more information about my father, John, and Holly and their involvement with the ACLU. Since the abrupt end to our trip to Anguilla, we cannot find Holly. Her place in Anguilla was abandoned, except for seven dead men who have yet to be identified plus our own agents.

"Investigators working for the Department of Defense reported that four nuclear scientists died of apparent natural causes in the same week. They had been friends since they were students at the University of Krakow. In addition to being friends and classmates, they were also good friends with another student: Karol Wojtyla. The world knows him as Pope John Paul II.

"There is more. When two of the scientists' bodies were discovered, the police found notes from Lawrence Perry on their desks. The two notes said basically the same thing. Perry thanked the recipient for his work and referred to some sort of payment made to each scientist. We are trying to find out what type of payments were made, why, and for how much."

"Refresh my recollection: who is Lawrence Perry?" Tom asked. "His name is familiar, but why is it familiar?"

"He is the founder of DataBasic Systems. He bankrolled the ACLU fund raiser in San Francisco. He was a big, big donor to the ACLU. Perry is on the television video we have from the local news station the night of the explosion—in fact, at the moment of the explosion," answered Blake.

"We found a link between John Palmer and Lawrence Perry, and John Palmer and all four scientists. By link I mean this: John worked as a consultant for Perry's companies for years, up to the time of his death. We do not know exactly what John did for those companies—whether he worked for Perry himself or if he had any contact with the scientists while working for Perry or Perry's companies," said Blake. "But we do have information that John met with the universities and companies that employed these dead scientists. This is based on John's travel records and files.

"John's notes simply reflect who attended some of the meetings but not much else. Interpol and other agencies in Europe are helping us secure the four scientists' available travel records. We will cross reference their travel with John's travel to see if they intersect.

"Sapphire and Leon have contacted DataBasic Systems regarding the work John did for them. We should have a response soon.

"One more thing: Lawrence Perry had AIDS. At the time of the explosion, he was dying. We studied the video feed from the San

Francisco television station when the mayor was interviewed. Perry was at his side, sweating and looking like he was a dead man walking. In the video, he seemed to have a difficult time focusing before it was his turn to be interviewed. Then he vomited on camera. None of this seemed particularly important when we watched the video. We all thought he was just a big man who perspired a lot or drank too much or ate bad oysters."

Tom looked at the people around the table. "Did I miss something?" he asked. "Did someone connect the dots and not tell me?"

Blake responded, "We wanted to give you a summary of where we are at this time. Any one of these scientists could have produced a device similar to the one that exploded in San Francisco, provided he had the proper equipment and material…and money.

"Was Perry involved? We can only speculate at this time, given the notes found in those two offices: thank-you notes with payment of some sort, from Perry himself, dated two weeks before the explosion. As much as I hate to say it, John Palmer could have been Perry's intermediary.

"If Perry was involved, then these two scientists didn't take much care in keeping it secret. We do not know if the other two scientists received notes and payment from Perry. We may never know.

"Finally, if John Palmer was not involved, but found out about it, Perry might have wanted to keep him quiet. Maybe that's why John was killed."

"Wait. Wait. Why kill John *after* the explosion? Perry was already dead," Tom asked.

"Possibly other people were involved who did not die in the explosion," said Blake.

"If John had any knowledge of this, why didn't he come to us? Why wait? He must have known that he was in danger. It makes no sense to me," Tom said.

There was a knock on the door. Mrs. Arnison opened it and told the attorney general that the White House was on the phone.

Tom stood up, thanking them for the update. He took his memo with him and left the room with Mrs. Arnison.

85

THE FUNERAL SERVICE was a private family affair. It was held in the funeral home since neither the deceased nor his wife believed in God. Burial took place in the Jewish cemetery in Chevy Chase, Maryland. Only a few words were spoken at the cemetery. There really wasn't much to say. The dead man's children robotically comforted their mother. They then left her to return to their busy worlds, not caring about her anymore, only about themselves—something they had learned from her.

Later in the afternoon, the new widow received a guest. She opened the door to The Law Professor. He held flowers in a gloved hand. He looked twice his size, bundled up in a hat, scarf, overcoat and gloves.

"Madame Justice," he said to his old friend and colleague, bowing ever so slightly.

"Please come in, Justin," she replied, taking the flowers from him. "Thank you for your thoughtfulness."

After he peeled off his layers of warmth, he sat in the small living room waiting for her to return. He looked around the room, crowded with furniture and with framed photos everywhere. There was not one piece of artwork, only photos capturing her lifetime; a few photos were of the recently deceased, but the vast majority were of her. *After all, it was always about her.*

She returned with tea for both of them. As she settled in, The Law Professor expressed his condolences, although he hardly knew the man whose funeral had been that morning. Not that it made any difference. After all, condolences go to the living.

They discussed many things, not one of them having to do with her freshly buried husband. Together, they reminded each other of their points of view relating to the events that had transpired during the past three years.

One memory was vivid: the day Justice Bergman was visited in her chambers by Carson Elliott, a lawyer she knew personally and professionally because they had been adversaries so often before she was appointed to the Supreme Court. Elliott told her he was there on a private matter on behalf of a client. She demurred, telling him she was not interested, unless it was a matter involving the Court. He then mentioned things that only a few people knew—very, very few—she being one of them. She was shocked but tried to maintain a blank expression; however, she knew Elliott could see right through her facade.

His opening statement—that was how she viewed it—was simple, clear, and to the point, something for which Carson Elliott was well known. No wasted time. No wasted motion. No unnecessary words. Straight to the point. Disarming in its precision. That was how it began.

Bergman got up to refresh their tea and to get some cookies for them both. In the corner of the room, a grandfather clock ticktocked, ticktocked, in sync with a pendulum devouring time, second after second, until day is done…gone forever.

Bergman returned with more tea and the cookies. The Law Professor told her how much he had detested Carson Elliott from the very beginning. He hated him still, even though Elliott was in his grave. He hated him now because of what Elliott had set in motion.

"Elliott believed in what he was doing. That is what gave him such strength and sense of purpose. I think he saw that in me, but he was so judgmental he could not see any virtue in my beliefs. But he understood us and our organization better than anyone else," Bergman said, sensing that The Law Professor might lapse into a tirade against the dead man. "For what purpose now?" she thought.

"What I found startling was how much Elliott knew...how accurate his information was. Remember those early meetings we had? We were trying to figure out how he managed to get such information. A mole, of course! That had to be it. But we never found out who it was. Remember that, Justin? All moot points now, I guess."

She drank some tea.

"We had to kill him. We had no choice. He was a bulldog. Once he got his teeth into you, he would never let go," she said, convincing herself again of the merits of their actions. She, more than anyone else, had wanted him dead.

"Well, that may be so," said The Law Professor. "But the situation now is far more serious than it was when Elliott was our only known adversary. Somebody has killed five hundred people. Surely they will want to kill us, as well."

Bergman looked at her old friend. "The attacks have only been on the ACLU itself and its donors—no one else, no select trustee," she said. "Therefore, it may be that whoever did this does not have the same level of knowledge that Elliott had. For example, no one has contacted us like Elliott did." She wondered if they were all misreading the situation.

"The Fat Man is the only person close to us who has died or been killed," she continued, "and, if he died of natural causes, then maybe we are secure. If that is the case, why would we think of anything as crazy as killing the Pope?"

"Ruth, it was *your* idea. You are not thinking clearly," The Law Professor said, both concerned about her mental health and knowing he was now irritating her by challenging her reasoning. "So be it," he thought.

"The point is: we need a plan," he continued. "If someone starts killing us, then we must be prepared to strike back. I agree that the idea of killing the Pope at this time is outlandish. However, it may become necessary. His visit to Washington is weeks away. A lot could happen during that interval, but we must be prepared for the worst."

"No, Justin. You may not have understood what I just said. Elliott knew everything. *Everything*. Wherever he got that information, it was accurate down to the minutest detail. When we refused to negotiate with him, we were trying to buy time to find the mole, but we had no success. Then we had Elliott killed. That seemed to end it, until a few weeks ago. But, as I said, the attack was on the ACLU only and not on any one of us. This leads me to believe that whoever attacked the ACLU does not have the same information that Elliott had. Therefore, it may not be this new pope—or anyone else in Rome, anymore," Bergman said. "Maybe Elliott gave all his information to someone else? John Palmer may have started this. We just do not know at this point."

"Our colleagues now question the decision to have had Elliott killed, even though at the time they all agreed. I still believe it was the correct course of action. He alone could have destroyed all of us. He had that much devastating information and influence," said The Law Professor. "If it is someone else, then we will find out soon. But I strongly believe this new pope knows everything. He has been an ally of John Paul for thirty years or more. He must be behind all of this."

Justice Bergman poured more tea for her friend and for herself. "I don't know. But to kill him now, I believe, would be a grave mistake. We may need him to put an end to this."

The Law Professor wondered about her mental faculties. But he kept this thought to himself.

86

SNOW ACCUMULATED TO three inches overnight, enough to paralyze the federal government in the Washington metro area. Today the federal government would be limited to essential employees, which made the radio weatherman snicker and wonder why nonessential employees were not laid off immediately.

The Wilsons, Samantha and Blake entered the conference room together. After a few minutes, Blake asked, "Did anyone use these files last night?" referring to the stack in front of him.

None of them had used the files.

"Someone did," exclaimed Blake. "I left these tabbed in a certain way, with loose notes on top. Someone looked at these files; I am certain. They're not the way I left them."

"So much for security in the Justice Department," said Sapphire.

Samantha offered, "Maybe the cleaning people bumped the files, or they moved them while dusting."

"No, that would be different. This was done skillfully, but they made a mistake."

Sapphire said, "Who would want this information and why? There are investigators all over this country working on this explosion, including a lot of people across the street in the FBI Building. Why would someone choose files from this room?"

Samantha responded, "Here is one reason: only our files include information about John Palmer, the monsignor, Holly Waters, Angela Carr, and Carson Elliott. No one else has this information."

Sapphire said, "Here are my thoughts on this: the explosion, the fires and killings, and even John Palmer's murder, have been professional—possibly even special-operations type professional. So, if professionals broke into this room to look at or to copy some files, wouldn't you think they would put the files back exactly the way they found them? That's their expertise, right?"

"I agree," offered Leon. "What is this? Amateur hour?"

"Thank you, honey," commented Sapphire, smiling at Leon.

"I agree with you both," Blake said. "But what does it mean?"

"It means it was someone in this building," answered Samantha, Sapphire and Leon, all at the same time.

• • •

It was almost midnight in the District of Columbia. They waited until the cleaning crews were finished working on their floor, and then Taryn opened Tom's office door and turned on the light. Wearing latex gloves, she carefully put three memos in a row on Tom's desk pad. Nothing else was on the desk.

While Taryn was in the office, Barbara stood lookout at the door to the hallway.

Taryn used her digital camera to snap a number of photos of the desk top. Once satisfied with the camera shots, she turned off the office light to save the government some money, locked the door and left.

"Okay. Let's see what happens," she said.

Barbara performed one last check of the hallway before they left the office.

• • •

The next morning the attorney general had a meeting on Capitol Hill that kept him out of the office until ten o'clock. When he arrived at his office, the door was already open. Mrs. Arnison had a key to all the offices on the floor, and she generally opened Tom's door upon her arrival.

Tom stopped at Mrs. Arnison's desk to greet her and to ask her if he had any messages. She gave him his call slips. She also told him Taryn and Barbara were waiting in his office.

"Good morning," he said to his assistants. "Are we having coffee and doughnuts?" he humorously inquired.

Barbara stood up and closed the door. When she sat down, she reminded Tom that his office should have no listening devices. It was swept routinely by the FBI. The most recent sweep was late yesterday afternoon, before Mrs. Arnison left for the day. The sweep did not find anything.

Taryn called an internal number. "Okay," she said, and hung up.

Tom looked at them curiously and asked, "What is going on? Does this mean we're not having coffee and doughnuts?"

He realized what they were doing, but it was too late to stop them.

"We think your office may be bugged. So we thought we'd set a trap," Barbara answered.

After a few minutes, there was a knock on the door. "Come in," said Taryn. The door opened, and three men walked in, all carrying electronic sweeping devices.

"Should we do this now?" the lead man asked.

"Please," Taryn replied.

Barbara asked Tom to stand by the door with them. They watched the men sweep the office. After approximately three minutes, the men found a listening device attached to the potted plant Mrs. Arnison watered every day. The man who found it put the device on the table. They left the room after they were certain there were no more bugs.

Taryn made another phone call.

Barbara walked out and asked Mrs. Arnison to join them.

When Mrs. Arnison came in, a man walked in behind her. He had obviously been waiting nearby. In his hand he held something that looked like a flashlight.

Turning to the senior civil servant, Barbara said, "Mrs. Arnison, would you mind holding out your hands?"

Mrs. Arnison stared at Barbara and then at Taryn. She avoided looking at Tom. "Just what do you girls think you are doing?" she asked, using a voice that suggested she would not be agreeing to anything they demanded.

The man walked over to Mrs. Arnison while she was talking and turned on the device he was holding. Immediately all conversation stopped. Mrs. Arnison tried to quickly move her hands from the tabletop to her lap, where the light could not reach, but she wasn't fast enough. Everyone, including Mrs. Arnison, saw the deep-purple coloring that covered much of her hands, especially her fingertips.

Mrs. Arnison watched, along with the others, as the man moved to the attorney general's desktop and pointed the light at the three memos on the desk pad. The paper showed deep-purple fingerprints. Without realizing it, Mrs. Arnison looked down at her hands.

Taryn, who was sitting next to Mrs. Arnison, asked her, "Did you make copies of those memos?"

"No," said Mrs. Arnison, emphatically—adding, "I am going to report you."

"Mrs. Arnison, please come with us," Taryn requested, as she walked out of the office and into Mrs. Arnison's work area.

The man with the light followed her. When he saw the copy machine, he went to it and scanned it with his device. A number of deep-purple finger prints popped up near the on-off switch, the number-of-copies switch, and the cover on top of the machine. He opened the top cover and the light on his device highlighted deep-purple markings on the glass area where papers would have been placed.

While the others, including Mrs. Arnison, focused their attention on the fingerprints and markings, Barbara stepped into the hallway and to get two security guards who were waiting there.

Mrs. Arnison now claimed she had made copies of the memos for the attorney general's files. When asked to find those copies, she refused. When asked where the files were that contained the copies, she did not respond. She refused to answer any more questions. She asked for her union representative.

The security guards took her away.

"Nice work," Tom said to Taryn and Barbara. "I want you both here when they search her desk and everything else out here."

Tom started for his office. Turning back to Taryn and Barbara, he asked, "Who knows how long this has been going on?"

He knew the answer to his question.

Taryn and Barbara looked at each other. Barbara answered, "We have a pretty good idea."

But they were wrong.

87

"**IT WAS THROUGH** God's divine intercession that I am still alive," declared the Reverend Peterson, sitting in an ornate, leather-padded wheelchair with a high, tufted back. His wheelchair was next to the end of the couch that he normally shared with his wife. She now occupied the end place, closest to her husband. They held hands as the Reverend Peterson continued.

"Thank you for your prayers, your cards, and, especially, your generous donations. Without the love of my family and our extended television family, I never would have survived.

"Please bow your heads and join me in prayer for the children we lost, for our friends and family we lost in the heinous attack in our studio. We pray that our Heavenly Father will welcome them to their joyous safe place. We pray for the recovery of those who have been physically and emotionally injured by that sad event.

"I wish to extend my deepest gratitude to those men and women of God who so ably filled in for me during my recovery. Please thank them by praying for them.

"You know, my brothers and sisters, I came very close to meeting our Heavenly Father as I lay dying on the floor of this very studio auditorium. I saw his concern, and I felt his love for me…for all that I have done in his name."

Ruth Peterson started to cry.

"God whispered to me, telling me he wanted me to live so I could do even more in his name."

Tears rolled down Ruth's well-nourished cheeks.

"And so, brothers and sisters, my God—our God—wanted me to return to this stage so Ruth and I can continue spreading the Good Word to God's people and those yearning to be God's people."

Ruth squeezed her husband's hand. He turned to her and tried to kiss her; however, the large wheelchair prohibited any lateral movement.

"In God's name, and for his glory, we have started a campaign to raise one hundred and forty-five million dollars in donations and pledges over the next three months. We will use that money to build a day-care center and preschool on our campus. Plus, we need to redesign our buildings for the installation of metal detectors to keep us safe. Sadly, it has come to this. God's children are under attack!"

Ruth's large head nodded affirmatively, but her hair did not move one bit, attesting to the holding power of her hair spray.

The Reverend Peterson never mentioned Rudy Smith, the man he killed with his bare hands.

88

THE PANEL WAS diverse: men and women, black, Hispanic, white, and even an Asian from somewhere. However, they were all Democrats; diversity only went so far. They were live in prime time on a rarely watched cable network discussing the lack of progress in the ACLU investigation.

"The deputy mayor of San Francisco is disgusted with the lack of progress in the investigation of the terrible bombing in her city. She wants nothing to do with press conferences where there is nothing to report. Why is it taking so long to come up with leads? Is it for lack of trying? Is that it?" suggested Devon Cummings, a long-time reporter for the *Washington Post*.

"I agree. This administration should be ashamed of itself for the way it is handling this matter. Think of all the grieving people who have suffered by losing loved ones in the explosion; they desperately need closure to get on with their lives," added Jasmine Wang, chief political reporter for the cable network. "How long has it been? Two weeks? Someone or some group kills five hundred people and there is no evidence? Who would believe this?"

The moderator offered this: "The evidence, whatever it may have been, was likely destroyed by the bomb blast. If there had been fingerprints on the explosive device before it was triggered, there was nothing remaining after the explosion.

"Patrick, you are a former homicide detective for the District of Columbia; what are your thoughts?"

"This is either a massive investigation or a small one. Why do I say this? If the investigators cannot readily find the perpetrator from the standpoint of the manufacture of the explosive device, then they will have to go into the backgrounds of all the people inside the building who were killed—one by one, a tedious and time-consuming task. The investigators may wish to say it was the ACLU that was targeted, but what will that get them?"

Everyone on the panel nodded their heads, but no one knew what he meant.

Lily Yankton, a writer for the *New York Times*, added, "Call me crazy, but I believe this administration already knows who did it and is dragging its feet until the new guy comes in. I think the people behind this horrible crime are right-wingers, far-out right-wingers, pro-lifers, gun nuts, Evangelicals, you name it...the same type of people who voted in this administration in the first place."

89

SAMANTHA STUDIED THE file on Lawrence Perry. She reviewed his biographical information. She read hundreds of press releases from Perry's companies that mentioned him and all the print-media coverage he received over the past ten years, including every reference of his involvement with the ACLU. Nothing in the material she reviewed identified any of the four dead nuclear scientists or any technology with which they were associated. Nothing in the material mentioned their universities or any scientific institutes sponsored by their universities. Nothing mentioned John Palmer either.

She looked for patterns or links that might provide clues into Perry's mind-set, motives, and thought processes. However, the variables regarding Perry were so considerable that any chance of hypothesizing scenarios would be worthless, she acknowledged to herself. Maybe Perry was just a sick man. Sick in many ways. End of story.

Her focus right now was when Perry met Sylvia Roberts, the president of the National ACLU. She was an intelligent woman who did not disapprove of his penchant for pornography. Before Perry met Roberts, he was already donating time and money to the Northern California chapter of the ACLU. He was asked by them to join a panel to identify pressing issues affecting Silicon Valley enterprises. It was widely known among the dot-com businesses in the area that the real purpose of this panel was a gentle shake-down for a contribution to the ACLU's coffers. Perry made a large donation.

Soon, he was asked to help them strategize and prioritize their future activities. This occurred during the time Perry was involved in establishing his foundation and recruiting a foundation president. The next year Perry began devoting more time to ACLU chapter activities. As a result, money started to flow from Perry's foundation to the ACLU of Northern California. Perry's largesse soon drew the attention of the executive director of the national ACLU, Miguel Torres, who invited Perry to the New York headquarters to serve on an ad hoc committee.

It was in New York where Perry had met Roberts. After that meeting, he spent more and more time with her there and also attended many of her many speaking engagements around the country. She introduced him to a spider web of pornography and related perversions, all expressions of free speech, in her intellectualized legal opinion.

Did Perry have a platonic love affair with Sylvia Roberts? Samantha wondered. Perry had spent a great deal of time with her, donated huge amounts of money on her behalf, and showered her with gifts. Or could it have been a physical love affair and not a platonic one? That possibility was dismissed immediately as she looked at a photo of Perry.

A number of photos of Perry were in the file: photos from his childhood, his college days, his foray into entrepreneurial wealth, and then photos after he became involved with the ACLU—including photos a month or two before the explosion in San Francisco. Samantha noted the physical changes in Perry: the sad trajectory of a man's life in photos. It was *Dorian Gray* in the worst, visible way.

Samantha reviewed Perry's medical records. For a relatively young man, Perry's medical file was huge. He had numerous doctor visits, often on a weekly basis, for ailments Perry described but most of his doctors could not find or confirm. However, his many doctors wrote prescriptions for him, even though they were medically unnecessary. He was taking twenty-three or more pills a day for management of unknown medical conditions. That explained the abundance of medical records, Samantha realized. He was a hypochondriac.

What intrigued her, in particular, was the fact that Perry's doctors' visits stopped entirely during the last two years of his life. At least, there were no medical records the FBI could find during that time frame. She wondered whether Perry actually stopped going to doctors, which seemed highly unlikely, or whether the medical records for that period simply could not be found. That was more likely. Most likely of all was that they were shredded after the explosion in San Francisco.

Samantha watched the video of the television interview with the mayor of San Francisco the night of the explosion. Perry stood next to the mayor during the interview, waiting for his turn to be interviewed by the television reporter. Samantha played the video segment over and over again in slow motion, each time looking carefully at Perry's face. When she enlarged the video to see Perry's face better, the picture quality deteriorated, but she could see huge drops of sweat pouring down from Perry's hairline, over his forehead, and into his eyes. She watched him wipe his forehead with a wrinkled handkerchief that, on closer inspection, already looked saturated with sweat.

When she zoomed in even more, Samantha could faintly see multiple smudge marks on Perry's eyeglasses—so many that it was difficult to look into his eyes through the lenses. Fortuitously, his glasses continually slid down his nose, revealing milky-looking eyes.

Samantha turned off the video. She sat back in her chair and looked up at the ceiling. "Could he have done this?" she wondered. "Did Perry know he was about to die—not from AIDS but from a bomb blast seconds away? Is that why he was sweating so much?"

90

ICY WIND RUSHED over the Seven Hills of Rome in advance of a sizable winter storm. In the Vatican, Pope Benedict sat at his desk in his private residence. He had just completed the last pages of his first encyclical, his first official letter to the faithful as the supreme pontiff of the Roman Catholic Church. Already he feared what the global response would be to it. Worse, he feared what the response would be from the cardinals and bishops inside the Vatican walls. It could be his undoing.

"I firmly believe what I wrote," he thought. "Whether it is from pragmatism or guilt, I believe it. Our whole notion of *social justice* must change. It is folly to keep repeating the same stock phrases over and over again, as if something different will happen. We are tethered to something that was written and manipulated over centuries, but we will never admit it."

He looked at the handwritten pages on his desk, thinking about how the words had come so effortlessly, as if his hand and thoughts were guided by the Holy Spirit. If that were the case, then why was his soul so restless? "Why do I not have peace in my heart and mind?" he thought. "How ironic that here, at this stage of my life, I am not finding solace in prayer when I need it so desperately. Why, I wonder?"

On his desk was a tiny insulated teapot. He poured some tea into a cup and sipped it slowly, feeling the tingle of citrus on his tongue and the warmth of the tea in his throat. A strong gust of wind attacked the windows on one side of his office, rattling them. He looked out through the windows at dark-gray, threatening clouds moving quickly across his line of sight, changing shape as they passed the windows. "Is it going to snow?" he wondered.

As Benedict sipped his tea, his thoughts were of his predecessor, John Paul. They were friends but not close friends. They were more like colleagues who independently arrived at the same conclusions on matters respecting ideology and governance of the church. They had tried to assassinate John Paul. "Thus far, there have been no assassination attempts on me," he thought, "but that might change. Who knows? God? Maybe God will be sending the assassins because I am not doing a good job." He laughed to himself.

But Benedict knew it would not be God sending the assassins.

91

BERGMAN PUT DOWN the morning paper and called The Law Professor. "Did you read it?" she asked, referring to the article about the autopsy results of the CEO of MAXXX Enterprises. "He was poisoned."

"Yes," The Law Professor replied, knowing immediately that she was referring to The Fat Man.

"I think this removes any doubt about what is happening here," she observed.

"I agree."

"Have we been sent a message?"

"That would be my conclusion," The Law Professor responded. "We are all much more vulnerable than The Fat Man. He had his own bodyguards, and they still killed him. The message could not be clearer than if they put it in neon lighting."

"Do you think they will try to kill us?" she asked.

"I don't know. But you are safe, of course," he responded.

"Well, during the day I have the Supreme Court Police, but when I leave the building, I have no one protecting me."

"I will get security for you and for all of us," he said, wondering who he could turn to for help. They had no backup to The Fat Man, and Farrell was gone.

For the first time in recent memory, they were concerned for their safety. Neither of them had anticipated this type of delayed action. After they had Carson Elliott killed, they surrounded themselves with security, waiting for retaliation. But none came. Now, almost three years later, was this retaliation? Revenge? *Revenge served cold?* Or was it something different? Something else?

"I have to find someone to help us, now that The Fat Man is no more. Fortunately, The Fat Man wasn't one of us," observed The Law Professor. "Maybe they killed him knowing that it was he who arranged to have Elliott and Palmer killed, and it was he who tried to kill the papal nuncio. Maybe that is enough for them."

"I wouldn't think so. The Fat Man only arranged it. He didn't order it. We did. They clearly know that."

"Yes, I see your point."

"We need the best personal protection we can find. And lots of it. I think two or more guards for each of us," Bergman said, trying to control her voice to keep it from quivering. She did not want the fear she now felt to seep into her voice, to be noticeable.

"Why not go back to Farrell?" continued Bergman. "He is a low-life, to be sure, but he has access to the type of security we need. And, equally as important, Justin, he knows why we need the security. He is probably getting security for himself right now."

"I refuse to deal with that man," The Law Professor declared. "You haven't had to deal with him, Ruth. I, more than any of the others, have been tasked with working with that imbecile."

"Okay, Justin, then have someone else work with him. In fact, that might be beneficial for both you and Farrell," stated Bergman. "The sad reality of our situation is that we need Farrell—at least, for the short term."

"I still think it would be a mistake," The Law Professor shot back.

"The big mistake, Justin, was having Carson Elliott killed. I take responsibility for that. I doubt that any of this would have happened had he been alive. He could have controlled the mayhem, I am certain. Now we have no connection to the people who are doing this. If Elliott were alive today, he would have been our contact."

"That may be wishful thinking, Ruth. In fact, all of what you say may be entirely wrong. For all we know, Carson Elliott could have planned all of this. What we should have done, in retrospect, is this: we should have killed Palmer and that Waters woman when we killed Elliott. *A trifecta*. Then none of this would be happening now," The Law Professor argued. "If I recall correctly, you did not want us to get rid of Palmer and Waters at that time. Maybe that mistake is yours, too, Ruth."

Bergman sighed heavily, "That may be true, Justin. I am certain there are enough mistakes to go around. I still believe that it was Pope John Paul who set this in motion. It just took a while."

"Do you really think that grand holy man from Poland would do such a thing? Kill hundreds of people?" The Law Professor asked, facetiously.

"Four or five hundred people are a mere drop in the bucket for the Catholic Church. How many hundreds of thousands of people have been killed in the name of Jesus Christ over the last two thousand years? Jews, Muslims, native people, and so on—other Christians, too. Everything points to Rome, if you ask me…even the timing, during the Christmas season," Bergman responded. "It all fits."

"Ruth," The Law Professor reminded her, "we were the ones who had the fund raiser in December. Don't forget that. We were all delighted at the timing and the notoriety of the Annual Separation of Church and State Gala, as it came to be called."

"Elliott never told us the identity of his client. Perhaps he had no client. It could be that he figured it out himself, maybe with some inside help. He was that smart. I just don't know," considered Bergman, acknowledging her uncertainty.

"That's right, Ruth. You don't know. And I don't know, either. None of us knows for certain," The Law Professor added.

92

"I CAN UNDERSTAND Holly Waters easily disappearing because she has a ton of money, but the monsignor has zero money, and we can't find him," Leon said.

Samantha observed, "I think the answer is obvious. Holly must have helped the monsignor. I bet she helped the monsignor's sister, too."

Sapphire remarked, "Well, at least we know where to find four dead nuclear scientists, although our colleagues in the Defense Department and the National Security Agency still cannot determine where the nuclear device came from or who was responsible for manufacturing it. I think these four scientists, or some of them, made the bomb.

"Lawrence Perry may be all we have at the moment," Sapphire resumed. "Maybe he *is* our guy. Remember, the general asked us to think *outside the box*; well, Perry definitely fits that requirement."

"Perry certainly had the means to pay for the talent needed to manufacture this type of nuclear device, as well as to torch the three ACLU offices. But why would he do it?" asked Leon.

Sapphire had traced Lawrence Perry around the world for the last three years of his life using all available travel and credit-card information and customs information she could find to establish his itinerary. Fortunately, he did not do that much traveling. Perry spent a great deal of time at the ACLU offices in New York, San Francisco, and Washington, and—with the exception of a few trips to Thailand and to Holland—Perry never left the United States after he hooked up with the ACLU and with Sylvia Roberts, especially.

One place where Perry also spent time was Southern California. Sapphire discovered that Lawrence Perry stayed a month or more of every year in Los Angeles visiting the adult-entertainment industry and watching them make porn flicks. In fact, Perry bankrolled a number of gay and lesbian films and child pornography films. So enraptured was Perry by the pornography industry and the burgeoning X-rated porn website business, that he invested in MAXXX Enterprises as a minority partner of The Fat Man. Sapphire found photos of Lawrence Perry and Moshe Freedman—aka The Fat Man—in various MAXXX publications. One of them identified Perry as a new capital partner in MAXXX.

Leon had information from the FBI linking The Fat Man to an array of criminal activities. The Fat Man maintained his own stable of street thugs to muscle out competitors and to control wayward producers and troublesome porn actors and actresses.

In addition to capital contributions from people like Lawrence Perry, The Fat Man received financing for his diverse adult-entertainment ventures from union pension-fund money—especially the AFL-CIO and Teamsters and, to Leon's surprise, the National Education Association, Teachers. The return on their capital investment was much better than the stock market and virtually recession proof.

Sapphire discussed the autopsy results that had emerged following The Fat Man's death in Las Vegas the week before during the MAXXX Adult Entertainment Expo. "It had to be enough poison to kill a Budweiser horse."

"I don't think so. Some poisons are incredibly lethal in small doses, without any consideration of the size of the intended victim,"

Leon responded. "Even someone as obese as this guy would drop dead in no time from some of these poisons."

"What if Perry had him killed?" asked Samantha. "I don't know the reason why, but the question has validity; don't you think?"

The more they looked into Lawrence Perry, the more interesting the man became. But did he mastermind the nuclear explosion? Could he? Did he arrange for the fires and the murders at the ACLU offices *after* his death? And did he have John Palmer and The Fat Man killed?

"Maybe there were two people, one being Lawrence Perry... maybe more than two. But who could they be? All the information about Perry indicates he had no friends. His sad existence meant buying companionship," offered Sapphire. "Perhaps he bought some killers."

"Maybe Perry arranged for the explosion that took his own life, and someone else arranged the fires and murders in the ACLU offices," said Samantha.

"If so, why these particular offices and not others? Why kill innocent people? Unless the killers did not view them as innocent," Sapphire added. "Or they were collateral damage."

"One interesting fact that I took from the arson reports was that each of these offices had a wall safe. Generally speaking, wall safes are used to store documents, expensive trinkets, watches, football trophies, and the like," Leon said, smiling when he mentioned football trophies. "The safes in all three offices were open. The arson investigators found nothing in them. What's wrong with this picture? What is the likelihood that all three wall safes would be left open at the end of a work day? Doesn't that seem odd? Why have wall safes in the first place, if you are going to leave them open?"

Blake agreed. He had read the reports, and he thought that odd, as well. There was no way to tell whether the safes were burglarized or whether they were opened and the contents spread onto the floor so they could burn.

He sat listening to his colleagues, and he worried that there was a rush to judge Perry as the principal suspect.

And why not? The FBI had determined, through expert analysis, that it was Perry's handwriting on the notes found on the desks of two dead nuclear scientists.

93

WHEN THE PHONE rang he pressed the mute button on the remote to turn off the audio of the football game he was watching on television. When he eventually terminated the phone call, he did not turn on the audio right away. Instead, he stared at the screen without focusing on the game. He surprised himself by his reaction to the news. After so many years they were now losing their listening post outside the attorney general's office. Worse, the Department of Justice would now be investigating and monitoring everyone in its employment, especially the administrative staff.

How many years had it been? Fifteen? Twenty? For so long the government had been keenly invested in chasing after terrorists, scrutinizing everyone in sight, except the most obvious people sitting outside the offices of policymakers and administration leaders—not that they were terrorists, mind you.

"How funny," he thought, "the government cannot help but be the government. These long-time administrative civil servants were invisible to their higher echelon bosses, but they were very important to us, since they had access to everything important.

"It was probably closer to twenty years," he thought. Twenty years of information from the attorney general's office. He was convinced that he and his union colleagues had more actionable intelligence about the federal government than Russia or China or any other country…or even WikiLeaks.

Mrs. Arnison would go to jail. She would not be able to cooperate with her interrogators regarding contact information because she knew nothing. Farrell had kept her in the dark after her husband died. She could only talk about the many years she provided information to her husband, who passed it on. After his death, she called the information into a voice-mail system—never to anyone she could name or identify. He sent her gift cards in payment. So simple.

Farrell swallowed a generous portion of Redbreast, loving the excellent, sweet burn all the way to his toes. Simple pleasures for him: good Irish whiskey…warm, cozy apartment…food in the refrigerator…college bowl games on many television channels.

Mrs. Arnison? She didn't know anything.

No worries.

The phone rang again. It was the Law Professor. Farrell unmuted the television and started listening to the play-by-play, ignoring the ringing of his phone.

"Go to voice mail, you bastard," thought Farrell. "Better yet, go to hell."

94

A BISHOP ESCORTED Cardinal Pacelli into the Pope's office. Benedict was standing in front of a window looking out over St. Peter's Square.

"Your Holiness," said Cardinal Pacelli.

Benedict did not turn to face him. "Dominic, it is good to have you back with us," the Pope said, adding, "I have a special favor to ask of you."

Without any thought, Cardinal Pacelli answered, "Whatever you wish me to do, I will do."

Benedict turned to look at him. "You are a faithful servant of God, Dominic. I know that more than almost anyone. What I am asking of you is fairly simple and without risk for you. For me, however, it has great risk.

"I would like you to read what I have written. This is a draft of my first encyclical, my first letter to the Universal Church. To be honest, Dominic, I am not certain I even wrote it. I think the hand of God came over mine and scribbled the words onto the paper," Benedict said, looking down at the pages on his desk.

Pacelli stood listening to Benedict, a man he respected and loved. Throughout his long friendship with this man who became pope, Pacelli had often thought of him as an incredibly self-contained person—a modest man, happy within himself, seeking nothing more than to be of service to the church. So it was surprising to hear these words. The man Pacelli knew would never have presumed that God, or any member of the Holy Trinity, was speaking to him or through him. Benedict was too humble to even formulate such a presumption, unless he believed it had actually happened.

Benedict continued, "You may find this document surprising. I myself find it surprising and alarming. But, as I said, the words just spilled out onto the paper. I have never written anything as fast. The process was a blur."

"Yes, Holy Father, I will read it immediately. Do you want me to mark it up in any way?"

"No, Dominic, please do not mark it at all. Whatever comments you may have, please put them on separate pieces of paper referencing the part where you have a comment," said the Pope very clearly.

Cardinal Pacelli approached Benedict's desk to pick up the document he was to read. Benedict looked at him from head to toe, observing Pacelli's black suit. "Dominic, what must I do to make you look like the Prince of the Church you are? Please dress the part. As I said earlier, it is an honor that two popes have bestowed on you."

Pacelli bowed, kissed the papal ring, and told Pope Benedict he would dress the part.

Benedict smiled at his former student and raised his right hand to bless him with the sign of the cross.

• • •

Pacelli carried the document to his apartment in the residential complex within the walls of the Vatican. He shielded the document inside his wool coat. Once in his apartment, he sat down in his only easy chair, put on his reading glasses, and began to read this papal letter from Benedict to all the Catholics in the world.

ENCYCLICAL LETTER
Dies Irae, Dies Illa
OF THE SUPREME PONTIFF
BENEDICT XVI
TO THE BISHOPS
PRIESTS AND DEACONS
MEN AND WOMEN RELIGIOUS
AND ALL THE LAY FAITHFUL
ON GOD'S JUDGMENT

Introduction.
Dies iræ! dies illa
Solvet sæclum in favilla
Teste David cum Sibylla!

1. "Day of Wrath, Day of Mourning, turning the world into ashes and the people weeping in fear of God's judgment." This famous Latin poem by Friar Thomas of Celano composed in the thirteenth century, and used in the Requiem Mass for the Dead for centuries, told of the terrible Judgment Day when God would no longer grant mercy to sinners and the wicked. The day of wrath is the day when God judges all of mankind, condemning many to eternal fire and damnation and others to eternal bliss with him.

Pacelli took off his reading glasses and closed his eyes. In his mind he sang this great Latin hymn in the somber Gregorian chant he had sung, or heard sung, countless times as an altar boy, college student, seminarian and priest. "Dies Irae" was one of the most famous Gregorian-chant melodies in the church. It set the tone for the Mass for the Dead, where black vestments were worn by the celebrant. There was nothing joyful in this liturgy, Pacelli remembered. The casket was sprinkled with holy water as the celebrant of the Mass asked God's forgiveness and mercy on the departed soul of *so and so* lying inside the casket. Rest in peace, so and so. *Requiescat in pace.* That was the hope, at least. Benedict was off to a very interesting start, Pacelli thought, as he put his glasses back on and continued reading.

2. We live our lives as if there will never be a final judgment. We live our lives without daily reference to the Word of God, without realization that Satan is always hunting for our soul.
3. Our Savior suffered torment and death, so we could be set free of sin. More than that, he redeemed us from the path that would ultimately lead to our eternal destruction. His love and mercy is boundless, timeless, unconditional, that is, until the Final Day of Judgment when there will be no mercy, no forgiveness. The world will melt away in fire and ashes.
4. The mercy that Christ bestowed upon us, we, in turn, bestow upon each other. Christ tells us to forgive others just as he has forgiven us. This is the Great Christian Imperative from Jesus Christ: love one another as I have loved you; forgive one another as I have forgiven you.
5. My brothers and sisters in Christ, I fear we have gone beyond that Imperative. We have gone too far in loving and forgiving one another. As a result, God's church on earth is suffering terribly because Lucifer, the angel of darkness and dread, gloats in anticipation of our ultimate destruction as a result of our abundant love and forgiveness. Over time, we, the people of God, have become passive in the face of evil in our daily lives; so much so, that we have lost sight of the Absolute Values that are at the heart of our Catholic faith. The sad truth, but the truth, nevertheless, is that we human beings cannot stand up to evil without God's help, yet we have been trying to do it alone.

6. We have witnessed the collapse of the church in Europe. We have seen the decay of Christianity all over the globe. We have seen our Catholic faith being transformed into something never intended by Christ and his apostles. Christianity is relentlessly under attack by forces of evil.

Pacelli looked at the crucifix on the opposite wall. Jesus in agony for our sins...because his Father asked him to redeem us in this way...the agonizing way of the cross. Taking off his glasses again, Pacelli rubbed the bridge of his nose, and then he rubbed his forehead. He continued reading.

7. Now is not the time for Christians to remain passive and forgiving. We Christians must stand together and take immediate, informed action against the multitude of evils in this world, at every level and in every place.
8. We are mindful of previous letters from Rome in which we promoted the concept of social justice in all countries, especially those countries where we believed capitalism caused inequities in the conditions of the faithful. Historically, we looked at the disparity of wealth between countries of the world and within countries themselves. In the past, our response was to blame the economic success of capitalism for many of the impoverished conditions without fair consideration of the immense good capitalism does and, in particular, the good the United States of America, a magnanimous country of capitalism, does throughout the world.
9. It is now our belief, considered very carefully, that the church in Rome has treated America unfairly. We have reached a new, profound understanding that America is a country blessed by God, with its Christian citizens displaying a loving sense of fairness and generosity unlike anything previously seen throughout the long, painful history of humankind.

"This is incredible," Pacelli thought. "It's not like anything written by previous popes in the modern era. Benedict is not only apologizing for the way the church has viewed and treated capitalism and America, but he is also declaring the United States as the greatest Christian nation in history. It's a new twist on what *social justice* really means."

10. For so long we, the people of God, have taken no action in the face of evil in this world, other than to pray for its destruction. By doing so, we chose to coexist with evil, praying it would be overwhelmed by our goodness and love.
11. Today I say to you, as your Holy Father, that we should do otherwise. We now believe that the principal problem facing our church is inaction on the part of the faithful. Now is the time for all those who follow Christ to revolt spiritually, mentally, and physically against evil in all its guises and disguises, in all its machinations and manipulations.
12. Of all the nations on God's earth, we believe that none is now more important to humankind than the United States. For this reason, our principal concern is for America's well-being. We pray for America, not solely because American capitalism assists other countries in generous ways that redefine the concept of social justice; and not because America is the most influential, militarily powerful, and wealthiest country on earth; no, we pray for America because we have come to appreciate this great country for all the good it does in the world. And now it is under attack by the forces of evil precisely because it is a magnificent Christian nation.
13. We recognize and honor the United States as the most exceptional nation on earth; however, America is now the principal battlefield in the war of good versus evil. Sadly, few people comprehend this. We believe America is a great

> country for one reason: it was founded on a belief in God and trust in God. And God has blessed America and its people, in return. We fear, however, that Satan and the angel of darkness, Lucifer, and his legions of hell, are systemically and systematically eroding America's greatness by destroying America's faith in God and in God's Word.

Cardinal Pacelli got up to stretch. He walked to a small pantry and poured himself a glass of red wine. His heart raced in his chest and his breathing was quick and shallow; Benedict's words were affecting him physically. What he was reading enlightened him and scared him at the same time. He believed what Benedict was saying; he had believed it *even before* Benedict wrote it. It was something they had discussed numerous times decades ago.

How would Benedict ever get this published and circulated to Catholics all over the world? The sluggishly cautious bureaucracy in the Vatican would rally against Benedict and advise him not to publish this document. "Too inflammatory," they would say. And they might be correct. But Benedict's writing was brilliantly powerful in its clarity of purpose.

Pacelli understood why his heart was beating so hard and his breathing labored: he was concerned for Benedict, whom he visualized standing precariously on a cliff of his own making.

Walking back to his chair, carrying his glass of wine, Pacelli stopped in front of the crucifix and said a prayer for Benedict. He sat down again and read:

> 14. To our beloved of Christ living in the United States, we implore you to take aggressive action to battle the evils in your country that seek to diminish the Word of God. Your nation proudly proclaims as its national statement "In God We Trust." Yet, we see every vestige of Christianity and God's love being removed from public buildings, public squares,

public education, and public gatherings by legal activism, judicial fiat, or legislative indifference. We believe that Lucifer, in his many forms and through his many disciples, is responsible. His legions are sophisticated and active. Christ's Faithful are passive and needlessly forgiving. That must change. That must change immediately. Return to public buildings in the United States the commandments God gave Moses, just as the founders of America approved. Allow the recognition of Christ's Nativity to be in every public place where the people wish it. Reflect on the words of God, and weigh them against the words of judges who ignorantly try to separate church from state in a way the Founding Fathers of America never intended. We understand this. Why do the courts in America not understand?

15. We urge Christian parents in America to protect their children against the daily onslaught of creeping moral relativism. It is vital that parents show their children a value system that is absolute: one rooted in the love of God and God's love for them. To that end, it is crucial that every Christian identify evil and destroy it. Ignoring it is not destroying it.
16. Destroy all aspects of pornography, including the promotion of casual sex in all its forms and formats. Revisit the manner in which women and children dress. Decry sexual violence in its many forms. Remember that the bodies God gave us are earthen vessels of the Holy Spirit in thought, word and deed. Honor yourselves by honoring God, first and foremost.
17. We are at war, beloved of Christ. We are at war with Satan, the devil, Lucifer, the angel of darkness, and his minions. Be proactive in attacking evil. Be merciless in dealing with those who foment evil. Be unforgiving of those who are evil. At every hour of every day the people of God must take action. If a revolution is necessary, then may God judge

our motives, our actions and our faithfulness to His Word. Remember, our judgment day is every day.

Quantus tremor est futurus,
quando iudex est venturus,
cuncta stricte discussurus!
What horror must invade the mind
when the approaching Judge shall find
and sift the deeds of all mankind!
Lacrimosa dies illa,
qua resurget ex favilla.
iudicandus homo reus:
huic ergo parce Deus.
Full of tears and full of dread
is that day that wakes the dead,
calling all, with solemn trumpet blast
to be judged for all their past.

"This encyclical," Pacelli thought, "must be Benedict's shortest written work in his long life." Of all the books and articles and commentaries and declarations that Benedict had ever written, nothing came to Pacelli's mind that was as succinct and to the point as this.

Pacelli, who was a student of religious history, thought that this must be the first time since the Crusades that a pope had ordered Christians to take the offensive—this time not reclaiming Jerusalem from the Turks but reclaiming humankind from the devil. In particular, Benedict identified America as an exceptional country. Pacelli thought it had once been extraordinary, but it was now in need of immediate help to thwart evil in its midst.

The reaction to this papal encyclical would be...would be... Pacelli could not fathom what it would be. *Explosive* came to mind.

The encyclical was more than thought-provoking; it was a clarion call to action. It was a declaration of war against evil in its myriad disguises, with the main battlefield being the United States of America. In this letter, Benedict brought forward the conflicting thoughts John Paul held as a belief in the waning moments of his life:

> Evil in America.
> America, the last, best hope of Christianity.

95

THE NEXT MORNING Sapphire carried a new file into the conference room where they were all working. "This is revolting," she announced, sitting down at the table. "But I think we have our motive."

"What?" Blake asked.

Samantha and Leon looked at Sapphire.

"I found out how Lawrence Perry got AIDS. He was infected with HIV-contaminated blood…*intentionally pumped into his body*." Sapphire had the attention of everyone. "Interpol sent us reports of unbelievable criminal activity in Holland involving Lawrence Perry."

"What did he do?" asked Samantha.

"It's not what did he do but, rather, what was done to him," answered Sapphire. "About fifteen months before the ACLU fund raiser in California, Perry and some gay guy pals spent a week in Amsterdam partying. According to the police report, Perry and his friends spent almost the entire week at sex orgies there."

"Gay men?" asked Leon, just confirming what he thought he heard.

"Right. Gay men. Many of these men were still in the closet. The orgies, or sex parties, were arranged over the Internet. Perry and his friends paid for the parties, which were held in the private homes of porn stars and porn producers in Amsterdam or places close by. Much of the activity was filmed for private collections, including Perry's. He planned to show the film back home in California. And guess what? Some of the Catholic priests who died in the explosion in San Francisco? They were with Perry in Holland at the sex orgies."

Samantha cleared her throat.

Sapphire looked at her and said, "It gets worse. We have copies of Dutch police reports spanning a nine-month investigation following the dates of the sex orgies.

"By the way," Sapphire clarified, "The term 'sex orgies' is not my terminology. This little descriptive phrase is used extensively throughout the investigative reports from Interpol and Dutch police. I am only using the term they used in their reports.

"Some of the men at these parties were married but led a secret, promiscuous gay life. Apparently some were bisexual. In some cases, guys were cheating on their gay partners."

"Sex orgies," Leon said. "What does that even mean these days?"

"For you, honey, it means *under penalty of death*," Sapphire said. "But for those gay guys in Holland, it meant there was a lot of kinky sex acts with people who met each other at these parties. Free alcohol. Free drugs. Lots of porno movies. Single sex acts. Group sex acts." Sapphire stopped for a moment to sip some coffee. "But it gets even worse," she continued.

"Worse?" asked Samantha.

"Worse," answered Sapphire. "Over the course of this kinky, sex-saturated week, a small group of gay men at the parties drugged and raped some of the other men.

"Now it gets really weird," Sapphire said.

"You mean this isn't weird enough?" asked Leon.

"It gets worse. Weird-worse. This 'gay gang,' and that's the term the Dutch police report used, injected their victims with HIV-contaminated blood while the victims were passed out. The report uses the term 'victims' because none of the people injected were

HIV-positive prior to attending these orgies, including Perry. The gay-gang members—only three people, by the way—were already HIV-positive, and one had full-blown AIDS."

Leon visibly shivered.

"One report states that 'the victims were sedated with a combination of the drug Ecstasy, alcohol, and the date-rape drug GHB. These drugs, in combination, leave victims helpless and often with no memory of what happened.' Their victims were then raped and injected with HIV-positive blood. One of the gay-gang members was a nurse. He was the one who drugged the victims. He drew blood from the gay-gang member who had AIDS and injected this contaminated blood into those who were passed out," said Sapphire.

"I don't understand how these people were raped. I mean, they were already at a sex orgy. What am I missing?" Samantha asked.

"I can only assume that they called it *rape* because the victims were passed out and unable to give their consent. That must be it," said Blake. "Perry was a victim."

"Yes, Perry was infected. So were the Catholic priests. The police reports identified twenty-two men who were infected this way. These men, not knowing they were HIV-positive, continued having sex with other guys and ended up infecting at least another forty-six men, at last count. One guy infected his girlfriend. Another one infected his wife," said Sapphire.

"That's seventy people, counting the women! Why are we just hearing about this? It happened almost two years ago," asked Blake, in disbelief.

"The investigation took a long time because the police knew nothing about the sex parties. It was not until a few of the victims became HIV-positive and contacted the Dutch police that the authorities learned what had happened. Even then, information identifying the partygoers came in very slowly. Once the police identified more of the partygoers, they were able to accelerate their investigation to discover all the sex partners."

"What happened to the three guys who did this?" asked Leon.

"They go to trial next spring. The maximum sentence is fifteen years, but there are multiple counts. If they are convicted, these guys may never get out of prison. But, hey, the trial is in Holland," Sapphire said. "Who knows? They're pretty lenient over there."

"Was this the first time Perry did this orgy thing, or was he an old pro?" asked Leon.

"Perry never traveled very much outside the country. However, he had been to Thailand a few times for child-sex in a controlled environment. *A controlled environment*. Can you believe this stuff?" Sapphire exclaimed, adding, "Interpol says it was his first time doing the secret, adult, sex-orgy Internet thing in Holland."

"Poor Larry Perry," observed Leon.

"Do you want to know the kicker?" Sapphire said. "It was Miguel Torres, the executive director of the national ACLU, who arranged the trip for Perry and his priest friends. That information came out during the investigation. Torres supposedly planned to be there with them but something came up at the last minute, and he couldn't attend."

"Let me guess, Perry blamed Torres for his AIDS?" said Leon. "To me, that spells motive: *m-o-t-i-v-e*."

"That's right. We have bits and pieces of Perry's story after he found out what happened to him. We just located his mental-health records. They were not part of the medical records we already have.

"He went to a psychiatrist in San Jose after he found out he was infected with HIV-contaminated blood from his trip to Holland. The psychiatrist said Perry had a *meltdown*. That's clearly not a medical diagnosis, and probably not even a psychiatric term, but we all know what it means. According to these mental-health notes, Perry blamed Torres for what happened to him in Holland. He believed he was set up by Torres. Why? Because he thought Torres was jealous of his relationship with Sylvia Roberts."

"A reason to kill?" Blake asked.

"Possibly," Samantha replied.

"Why not just kill Torres instead of five hundred other people—including Sylvia Roberts, the porno-platonic love of his life?" Leon wondered out loud.

"I don't know. But if Perry is the guy, that question will be debated ad nauseam," Blake said.

"Maybe he had an *irrational* reason," Samantha observed.

96

THE EARLY AFTERNOON overcast dissolved into a drizzly dusk—another winter's day in the District of Columbia—as Blake walked into the office of the attorney general of the United States to give him the most recent information his team had worked up on Lawrence Perry.

"So, Perry is our guy?" Tom asked.

"I am telling you what the evidence suggests—well, more than suggests. This is where the trail of evidence has led us. I know there are gaps. I know there are assumptions without the ability to verify, at this point. We have taken what was given to us in the way of factual information, and this is our conclusion."

"What about John and your father? How are they tied into this?" Tom asked. "Who attacked Samantha? Who killed John? Who killed our FBI agents in Anguilla? And why were you, Samantha, and Holly attacked in Anguilla?"

Tom's questions were the same as Blake's. And they needed resolution. But now the focus was on the ACLU investigation and, possibly, its resolution.

"I need to clue in a number of people and let them take a look at this Lawrence Perry suspect before I tell the White House. Please ask Leon and Sapphire for all the information I need to make the case that Perry is the sole perpetrator of the first nuclear explosion on American soil, killing five hundred citizens," Tom said.

"We'll get everything you need," Blake replied.

"One more thing, do not share this with anyone else until I tell you. Please convey this to Sapphire and Leon and Samantha: not a word.

"By the way, I'm asking the federal prosecutor to turn the heat up on Mrs. Arnison. We have two dead FBI agents, and I believe it is because of her. I suspect she gave out the information about your trip to Anguilla."

97

THE MIDDAY WINTER sun radiated off the facade of the abbey, creating a lopsided halo effect on the wall. "How long has it been?" Angela thought, as she waited in the parking lot. When was the last time she had seen her brother, Leo? Now she was here, and he was not. Well, he was not here in the physical sense. Still, this was the place where Leo had lived and prayed and filled his soul and heart with joy.

Leo never left the confines of this peaceful place until he went to Washington, where he gave his life for Dominic. "Wasn't that miraculous?" she thought. It had to be the hand of God directing Leo to that certain place and time so that Dominic might live. Even though Leo had no inkling, he would have understood, she believed. He would have given his life gladly.

Another car came into the parking lot and parked next to her. She looked over at the car but could not see inside the dark, tinted windows. Emerging from the backseat of the car was a man she had not seen for years. He looked thinner than she remembered, and his great volume of hair, once as black as hers, now had streaks of silver in it. He was dressed in a black suit, white shirt. and black tie.

She watched him stand up. "Ever the athlete," she thought and smiled as she watched his fluid movements. He was handsome beyond what a priest should probably be: as handsome as Leo the monk was the family joke about the twins.

She opened her car door. Dominic was already standing there, arms open wide. She moved into the comfort of his embrace, and they stood holding each other, lost in the moment.

"Look at you," said Pacelli. "The years have been good to you, Maria: only a wrinkle or two…mostly laugh lines, I am certain," he said, smiling at her. "Or maybe I should be calling you, Angela, my angel."

She laughed with him in the easy way that siblings can. "You have grown more distinguished looking, Dom. Is that what happens when you spend so much time in Rome?"

"Ah, so you noticed! Nothing escapes Angie's scrutiny," Pacelli laughed. "Let's go in and congratulate our brother, Leo, on a life well-lived. I know Leo is with God—no more earthly woes."

"He saved your life," she remarked. "I sat here waiting for you, thinking that it was a miracle, thinking that Leo was sent to Washington to protect you and to give his life for you, Dom. Don't you believe that is miraculous?"

"Please, let us go in. The abbot is waiting for us, I am sure," answered Pacelli, not wanting to discuss the matter. "We can talk more inside. We must not stay out here much longer; otherwise, our security people will be unhappy with us."

Arm in arm they strode toward the front archway of the abbey, above which was the inscription *God Alone*. Pacelli and his sister slowed their pace as they looked up at the words. He said to his sister, "That says it all, doesn't it, Angie?"

"Yes it does."

The abbot greeted them warmly. "Monsignor Pacelli, we are very pleased to have you with us. And you must be Father Leo's sister, Maria. He spoke often of you." The abbot expressed his sympathy for their loss. While telling his visitors how sorry he was for Father Leo's death, the abbot seemed very cheerful. He, too, believed that Father Leo was with God.

When Pacelli had made the appointment with the abbot, he did not—could not—tell him he was now *Cardinal* Pacelli.

In the background a choir sang in Latin:

Venite adoremus.
Venite adoremus.
Venite adoremus Dominum.

The Abbot introduced the monks who were standing with him. Pacelli figured they were present to see for themselves that Father Leo, indeed, had a twin brother. Abbot Thaddeus Malone led them to his office.

"Father Abbot, thank you for allowing us to visit Leo's home," Pacelli said. "For reasons that are very private and personal, neither one of us was able to attend Leo's funeral Mass. That is our deep regret. Thank you for allowing us to see Leo's room and to pray at his grave."

The three of them sat in the abbot's office talking about Father Leo and his life in the abbey. The abbot was a man who knew their brother Leo better than they did. Father Leo had spent his entire adult life here, following the strict Trappist routine: up at three-thirty in the morning, prayer, breakfast, work, and then more prayer, work, food, prayer, and so on—regimented, quiet, contemplative.

The abbot informed them that Father Leo had become a cheese maker of local renown. In fact, he alone was responsible for more than 50 percent of the revenue generated from products the monks made and sold at the abbey gift shop.

Pacelli and Angela were amused, thinking of their brother as a cheese maker. Personal memories of Leo filled their minds; none of the memories, however, suggested a future cheese maker.

The Abbey of Gethsemani owned two thousand acres of land. On this land the monks grew, or raised, all the essentials of their simple existence, including sufficient excess to make products to sell, such as cheese, sausage, bread, and honey. The monks relied on their own husbandry, the sale of their wares to a retail market, and donations to the abbey to sustain themselves—just as they had for hundreds and hundreds of years in Europe and, recently, in America.

Angela was quiet. This was not her world. What the abbot and Dominic shared was unfamiliar to her. They were men of God. For her part, she was pleased that her brother Leo lived the life he wanted. It was Leo's choice to remove himself from the world: to pray and to work every day for all the days of his life.

So simple.

Or was it?

The abbot walked them to Father Leo's cell. This was the place where he lived his life. There were no creature comforts at all, only a single bed and thin mattress, a dresser, a small table, one chair, and one lamp—no bathroom, even. Leo shared a communal bathroom and shower area.

Brother and sister paused to say silent prayers. Praying in Leo's room without him present seemed strange, but life was strange, Angela thought.

The abbot took them outside to the cemetery. There, at Leo's graveside, Dominic and Angela prayed for the soul of their departed brother.

On their way out, Father Abbot took them past his office where he asked them to step in for a moment. He gave them a small box of personal items that belonged to Father Leo. It was not much. The abbot also gave them each a brick of cheese that Leo had made.

Brother and sister walked out into the brisk afternoon sunshine in the hill country of Kentucky. They walked arm in arm to their cars.

Pacelli told Angela they would meet in Rome soon, where she would be safe. In the meantime, he entrusted her security to Holly Waters, a woman in whom he had enormous confidence.

98

THE TRANSITION FROM one administration to another can be handled with dignity and respect like the Bush administration, or it can be handled poorly, as was the outgoing Clinton administration before him. In the current situation, this peaceful transition of power from one administration to another was a model of dignity and respect for the office of the president—admittedly quite helpful to the incoming administration. It was a gracious act of the outgoing president and his conservative administration.

Pursuant to the president's directives to all cabinet-level officials and the heads of all other agencies of the executive branch of government, they were to ensure that their agencies were in order, all information up-to-date, and all activities clearly documented and calendared so the incoming administration could start work immediately.

For Tom Owens, though, his situation at the Department of Justice wasn't as rosy as the other members of the president's cabinet. While the incoming administration had already named its appointees to most cabinet-level positions, the president-elect had not yet identified his attorney-general nominee. Well, actually, he did nominate someone; however, that person voluntarily withdrew, under pressure, once it became known he was a tax cheat.

What this meant for Tom Owens was that he now had to deal with a *committee*. This was unfortunate in personal terms, since he trusted only one person on the Department of Justice Transition Committee, as it was called. As for all the other members on that transition committee, he thought he would love to feed them week-old sushi. Not surprisingly, the status of the investigation into the ACLU bombing was one of the main topics to be discussed by this transition committee. They wanted the investigation wrapped up by Inauguration Day.

"So the best suspect you have is Lawrence Perry? Are you serious?" questioned Lester Zepester, the man Tom disliked most on the transition committee. Tom tagged him *Led Zeppelin*.

"What a *schmuck*," Tom thought, while answering politely, "All the evidence we have points to Lawrence Perry. We follow the trail of evidence wherever it leads us. Here is a summary of what we have."

Taryn and Barbara passed out a three-page summary of the investigation details to each person. It had SECRET AND CONFIDENTIAL boldly stamped in red on the top and bottom of each numbered page. Tom asked the members of the transition committee to quickly review the summary.

"We don't have time now," said Led Zeppelin. "We will take it with us."

"Sorry, but you cannot take it with you. This summary is confidential and cannot leave this office. I am sharing this with you as a courtesy, and I am asking all of you to give me your word that none of this will be leaked to the media."

The person he trusted, the senior member of the transition committee, interceded, "Of course we will agree not to disclose this information, Tom. We want you to finish this investigation on your own terms and with the strictest confidentiality."

"Thanks, Burton. Getting back to the investigation, we drilled down into the details surrounding this explosion, and we found a sick billionaire, Lawrence Perry. We believe he was mentally unstable prior to the date of the fund raiser. We know this from his medical records. We also know that he had AIDS and had only a very short time left to live.

"As you will note, there is sufficient circumstantial evidence and some demonstrative evidence to point the finger at Perry as the one who arranged to have the explosive device made by Eastern European nuclear scientists who had once worked with tactical nuclear weaponry for the Soviet Union. We believe Perry had motive because of his horrible homosexual ordeal in Holland and his belief that his situation was directly caused by Miguel Torres, the executive director of the ACLU.

"We believe Perry had the means to make this happen. He was a billionaire for a running start, plus he had connections to the nuclear scientists, his own fleet of planes, and easy access to the restaurant where the fund raiser was being held. After all, he was footing the bill.

"As far as opportunity, we have to assume he was able to bring the explosive device into the United States and place it in the restaurant. Perry's companies have private planes flying around the globe twenty-four hours every day, almost all of them flying in and out of the Bay Area.

"In the end, we believe there is sufficient evidence to indict him, if he were alive, and to convict him of premeditated murder on a grand scale."

"How convenient that everyone involved is dead, including the four nuclear scientists," observed Zoe Levin, the sole woman member of the transition committee. Tom knew she was under consideration to be the next attorney general. He looked at her and thought, "Yale Law School, no moral compass, political sycophant. In short, perfect for the incoming administration but bad news for the country."

"Well, it is what it is. We're not fabricating facts, only reporting them based on the results of an extensive investigation," Tom said, in a neutral tone of voice, which he hoped would set her off into a screeching tiff.

"I do not know what my colleagues think," Zoe Levin screamed, "but as for me, I find this very, very suspicious. So will the media, I am sure."

The senior member of the transition committee said to her, and to all present, "We are not in a position to dispute the findings of an exhaustive investigation. Tom is giving us the result of thousands of hours of work by investigators in this country, and around the world, who have been trying to figure out what happened, how it happened, and the people involved.

"Remember, Zoe, we do not have to endorse the investigation results. We need to keep an open mind about the findings. Certainly, it would benefit all of us if this investigation were concluded by the time we have a new attorney general. Otherwise, the new attorney general will be picking up the pieces. That would be an unfortunate diversion," Burton Greenfield said.

Another transition-committee member commented, "I agree with Burton. You should, too, Zoe. We want this investigation closed before the new attorney general is sworn in. Plus, we have agreed not to take this to the media. It is up to Tom to do that."

Zoe Levin looked at him and then at Burton—but not at Tom, ignoring him as if he had pustules covering his face. "That may be so, but what about the fires and the murders that happened *after* the explosion? Were those deeds done by a dead man, too?"

She slowly gathered her things, stood up, threw the summary down on the table, and walked out of the room. She was quickly followed by Led Zeppelin. He, too, stood up and threw the summary down before walking out.

Greenfield looked at Tom and shook his head. The other transition-committee members looked at Greenfield. Some smiled, and some did not. Greenfield said to Tom, "We were appointed to this transition committee, Tom. We did not have a vote regarding all of our members," obviously referring to the two people who had just stormed out of the room. "I think I am speaking for the rest of us when I say that we are accepting the work your investigators and the FBI have done.

"Zoe made a good point, though. What is the status of the investigation involving the fires and additional murders? It would be helpful to the new administration, Tom, if your team could wrap up that part of the investigation so that it is airtight and doesn't embarrass the outgoing administration."

99

HE LOOKED AROUND his office trying to think of some fond memories. Maybe some merry ghosts of Christmas past? Unfortunately, his memory bank registered empty at the moment. "What a pity," he thought. "So many years here and now I cannot even recall one pleasant memory."

When he considered his previous life in private practice and private equity, he could instantly rattle off great memories.

"This is what Washington does to you." He sighed. "All these years invested and no emotional return on that investment."

In the background a Christmas carol played on his small audio equipment:

It came upon the midnight clear,
That glorious song of old,
From angels bending near the earth,
To touch their harps of gold
Peace on the earth, goodwill to men
From heavens all gracious King!
The world in solemn stillness lay
To hear the angels sing.

Tom got up from his desk and walked to the window. Reflection from his office lights made it difficult to see down into the snowy courtyard. However, he thought he saw the silhouette of a lone smoker poisoning herself with each nicotine-laden inhalation.

Ah, freedom to piss on the government, in a manner of speaking, by choosing to ignore the warning label. Good for her. Tom chuckled. God Bless America.

Those pesky staffers at the White House must be worried about something else since their frequent calls about the ACLU investigation had stopped. Maybe they were satisfied with Lawrence Perry as the single suspect. Or maybe they were out looking for jobs. Perhaps they just didn't care anymore. After all, they could divert any suggestion of a scapegoat resolution back to the Justice Department. Back to him.

"No wonder there are no fond memories," he laughed to himself. Play the game or it plays you. That was the principal survival tactic of this job: gamesmanship.

In perverse Washington logic, politics here was a team sport—but with every team member looking out for him or herself. "This is the place where you put an *I* in 'team,'" he thought. And, then, of course, there was always the media-hyped notion of *legacy*, as if anyone outside the beltway cared.

He continued walking around the room, looking at the obligatory framed photo ops with dignitaries, most of whom he would not trust with his junk mail. "What will I do with all of these photos when I leave?" Tom pondered. "Put them up in my next office? No, not a chance. More likely, I will stack them in my garage and let the spiders have their way with them."

Tom stood in front of his framed law degree from the University of Virginia. Of all the items in his office and on his walls, this was what he cherished most. This was real—the result of hard work. It was the beginning of everything in his adult life. The key to his success.

"Soon, it will be over," he thought, sitting back down at his desk. He wondered, ruefully, whether he would have *safe passage* to the other side of the beltway. If any investigations were to begin against him, it would not be for a number of months, and by then he would be living in Barbados, he laughed to himself. He wondered if the United States had an extradition treaty with Barbados.

"I documented everything. I covered myself as best I could from every side—more gamesmanship. And what would they find if they did investigate me? Nothing."

For a second, he thought he heard Mrs. Arnison walk into his office without invitation, eyeing everything on his desk. He wondered if it was a phantom memory, like having your finger cut off but still believing it was attached.

In a way, it was too bad Taryn and Barbara had discovered Mrs. Arnison's secret activity. He had enjoyed feeding her misinformation, just as his predecessors had. That was part of the game. That was gamesmanship.

100

FROM THE CHRISTMAS playlist on her cell phone, Jordan selected one of her favorite Christmas carols:

> Hark the herald angels sing
> Glory to the newborn King
> Peace on earth and mercy mild
> God and sinners reconciled
> Joyful, all ye nations, rise
> Join the triumph of the skies
> With the angelic host proclaim
> Christ is born in Bethlehem
> Hark! The herald angels sing
> Glory to the newborn King

Jordan walked to the metro station near the Navy Yard in the southeast quadrant of the District of Columbia, a block from her office. It was five o'clock. The city lights, traffic lights, decorations, and taillights on passing vehicles made the world sparkle in a wintry, urban way.

As she stood on the platform inside the subway station, her thoughts flew in many directions: planning dinner, thinking about work, wondering what her brother was doing, curiosity about Samantha, thinking of her children's activities, wondering how David was doing on his business trip. When the train came, she moved with the masses and found a place to stand. At her stop, she walked off the train, up the stairs, and into the frigid night. She adjusted her coat and scarf, this time pulling the scarf over her chin, mouth, and nose to stay warm.

After a block, the neighborhood became completely residential. Old streetlights, charming in a historic way, but barely illuminating the night and the irregularly cobbled sidewalk. Jordan strolled with her eyes cast down to inspect the sidewalk so she wouldn't stumble and fall. Three more blocks to her house. Her glasses started to fog because some warm breath leaked out of her scarf. She stopped, reluctantly pulled off her gloves, and cleaned her glasses with the end of her scarf.

Sensing someone behind her, Jordan turned.

No one.

She thought of Blake and Samantha being attacked in Anguilla and Samantha being mugged downtown...and her father being mugged and murdered.

Would anyone want to harm her?

She turned off the music, pulled the earbuds from her ears, and put them in her coat pocket. She picked up her pace. She turned again, checking behind her.

No one.

"I am driving myself crazy," she thought.

Driving.

"That's it. A car is following me!

"Only a half block left to go," she said to herself, almost audibly.

And then she was home. She opened the door, hurried in, and locked it. "Should I call 911?" she wondered. "What would I say?" Her situation spawned scattered thoughts: "David is out of town on business. Where is Paul? Where is Jennifer?"

The house welcomed her with familiarity and warmth…and the smell of cookies baking. Cookies baking? Jennifer must be home. Where was Paul? She remembered that he had basketball practice. Jordan went back to the window to look outside. Nothing. She felt relief, but as she turned away from the window, her peripheral vision spied a car crawling by on the other side of the road.

Was it the same car?

"They all drive slowly around here," she reminded herself.

Jordan removed her coat and scarf, hanging them in the front hall closet. She took off her boots and put on slippers.

"Nothing is wrong," she told herself. "Nothing is wrong."

"Hello? Hello?" she called out, moving down the hallway to the kitchen.

"Hi, Mom," responded Jennifer. "I'm baking cookies."

Before Jordan could reply, she was startled by the doorbell ringing.

"Jennifer, I want you to grab the phone and be ready to dial 911," she yelled out, scaring her daughter.

Through the peephole in the front door, Jordan could see that it was a woman standing there, but the dim lighting made it difficult to see her face. Jordan saw a car at the curb! Was it the same car? Did this woman get out of that car?

Jordan shouted to Jennifer, telling her to check the back door to make sure it was locked and to come to the front hallway with the phone in her hand. Then she cracked open the front door.

"Jordan," said the figure standing before her. "It has been too long."

101

BLAKE STEPPED OUT of the conference room to take the call from his sister.

"Blake, I need you here right away," Jordan said, urgently.

"Are you okay?"

"Yes, I am."

"Where are you?"

"I'm at home."

"Samantha is with me. Do you want her to come, too?"

"Yes, bring her. Please hurry."

• • •

Their new FBI security detail kept Samantha and Blake in the car until they checked inside the house and the perimeter outside. After that, they allowed them to enter. One agent went ahead of them. He stayed in the living room. The other stayed in the car, watching the area.

Blake and Samantha hugged Jordan. She took their coats and then led them to the kitchen. Sitting with Jennifer at the table, eating cranberry-oatmeal cookies and drinking hot chocolate, was Holly Waters. She stood up to embrace a surprised Blake and Samantha.

"Please sit down, we have more than enough cookies to go around and spoil our dinner," Jordan said, winking at her daughter. "Holly followed me home. She has something important to tell us, Blake."

Feeling like an interloper, Samantha tried to excuse herself from the table.

"No, please," said Holly, "Samantha, you should hear this, too."

Since Jordan had no idea what was coming, she asked her daughter to go upstairs to her room and finish her homework.

"Would you like to move into the living room?" she asked, thinking everyone would be more comfortable there.

Blake answered for the group, "Let's stay here, close to the cookies."

"Blake and Samantha, I apologize for our brief encounter in Anguilla. I suspect someone in the Justice Department must have disclosed your whereabouts. Thankfully, you both are well. It is a dangerous time. I was concerned for your safety when I saw you," said Holly. "I am thankful that you both were not badly hurt, but I am very sorry your FBI agents died."

"I am, too," Blake answered, flashing some anger. "Two families are devastated right before Christmas."

Holly calmly continued, "Your safety is still my concern. That is why I am here. I have information that will answer the questions you have regarding your father's trips to Italy.

"It was because of Italy that John was murdered and Monsignor Pacelli's poor brother was murdered by mistake. It was because of Italy that we were attacked in Anguilla."

Before anyone could respond, Holly continued: "It all started more than five years ago with John's growing friendship with a colleague at Georgetown University named Monsignor Dominic Pacelli, a Jesuit priest. After a while, John introduced Monsignor Pacelli to your father. The three of them frequently had dinner together here in Washington. Sometimes I was invited, as well.

"About four years ago, when John and the monsignor were in Rome, John met Father Sabino Arana, the superior general of the Society of Jesus. They spent a day with Father Arana, touring the Vatican, discussing world politics, and enjoying meals together. I later learned from John how impressed he was by Father Arana's knowledge of American life and his concern for America's future.

"At some point, John mentioned your father's name and the law firm to Father Arana. He recounted numerous stories about Carson's…your father's…high stakes, bet-the-company litigation successes around the United States, as well as his pro bono work against the ACLU.

"The next day, John called me from Rome to tell me to get your father there immediately for a meeting with a prospective client, an extraordinarily important prospective client. John said he could not reveal the identity of the client. He also said this was confidential.

"I believed in John. I adored John. He was a great, great lawyer and a magnificent human being. If he felt so strongly about a client meeting, so be it. I spoke to your father as persuasively as I could and managed to get him on a plane to fly to Italy for the client meeting.

"I accompanied your father to Rome. We flew first class on the biggest plane I could find," Holly smiled. "John met us at the airport with a car and driver. We went to our hotel to freshen up while John waited. Our next stop was Jesuit headquarters, where Monsignor Pacelli was waiting for us. He introduced us to Father Arana, who thanked us for coming to Rome on such short notice.

"We spent only a short time in the library. Soon we were outside, the five of us walking the neighborhood, stopping for lunch along the way. Father Arana understood we needed to stretch our legs after our long flight.

"During the time we were together, Father Arana kept up a continuous conversation with your father. The topics were many and varied, including their respective childhoods, families, schooling, and thoughts about politics and religion. Occasionally, John or the monsignor or I would join in the conversation, but mostly it was a dialogue between your father and Father Arana. After the walk we went back to our hotel.

"The next morning we went back to the Jesuit headquarters to meet with Father Arana and the monsignor. This time, they were with three other priests, all of whom were lawyers. This meeting quickly became more serious and more focused. One of the discussion topics pertained to the legal battles your father had with the ACLU.

"One priest from New Jersey, who graduated from Seton Hall Law School, remarked that the ACLU's apparent strategy regarding religious symbols in the United States was to file endless lawsuits in order to wear down their targeted opponents, like small cities. Because of the cost of litigation, most cities chose not to defend themselves in court or, due to budgetary restraints, simply could not afford to defend themselves. Either way, it was a victory for the ACLU, which used litigation as its weapon. He pointed out that the ACLU had the benefit of free legal talent: pro bono lawyers. What he admired about our firm was our commitment to provide pro bono lawyers to defend those cities who chose to fight the ACLU.

"We spent the entire day there. We understood that every moment spent with Father Arana and the monsignor, as well as these other three priests, was a vetting process. All the questions were directed to your father and, based on the specificity of some of the questions, it was clear the three priests had a great deal of information about our law firm, our practice, and your father.

"During this time, no one mentioned the nature of the legal work we might be doing or the identity of the client we would be doing it for. John hardly said a word, causing your father to suspect that John knew something but did not choose to share it.

"The next day, John and his driver took us around Rome and the Vatican for some sightseeing. Father Arana arranged to have a guide take us on a private tour of the Sistine Chapel, private areas within St. Peter's Basilica, and the famous Vatican library. We very much enjoyed this downtime—but it was downtime. Your father, however, decided *not* to be impatient.

"John had chosen a quaint, family-owned-and-operated restaurant for dinner. During all this time, your father never once asked John what he knew. I think John was as surprised by this as I was. Your father could be such a devil sometimes, even in Rome," laughed Holly.

"Normally, your father would have been ready to go home; however, he seemed to be enjoying himself. Apparently, he had decided to wait for whatever John had in mind.

"Later that evening, at our hotel, Father Arana and Monsignor Pacelli joined us for a nightcap. Father Arana told us he had arranged a meeting the next morning with Pope John Paul.

"So, this was the reason we were in Rome!

"The next morning a car was sent to our hotel for the three of us. We were taken inside the Vatican walls to a tiny parking area behind one of the buildings next to the Basilica. Uniformed Swiss Guards opened the doors for us. Monsignor Pacelli was waiting inside, and he asked us to follow him. He took us to a small room on the third level where we waited. After a few minutes, another priest took us down a hallway. We walked about a minute before he opened a door and ushered us into a small room where Pope John Paul was sitting in a chair.

"The moment took my breath away. I remember the Pope wore a white cassock and had on a white skull cap. He was magnetic. I worried that, because of his advanced Parkinson's disease, he might not make it through our meeting. But then, when I looked into his eyes—so incredibly blue, vibrant, and intelligent—I changed my thinking immediately. In front of us was a man fiercely fighting to stay alive within his failing body.

"We stood until he asked us all to sit. He spoke in English. He thanked us for coming, and he talked about the two-thousand-year history of the church, during which time it had seen every type of government, kingdom, and empire imaginable. It had witnessed atrocities beyond human comprehension. 'Evil walks everywhere,' he said. He admitted, sadly, that Christians were part of the human fabric who committed inhumane atrocities, as well.

"What he said next took us by surprise. He said no country was more important to the world than America. However, with visible sadness, he declared that America was under attack and was rotting from within due to the seductive evils it enjoyed and the evils it chose to ignore. If nothing was done, America would fail as the last beacon of hope for the rest of the world—and for all of Christianity.

"When the Pope spoke next, he talked about something your father and I did not understand at the time. He referred to a Catholic miracle called Our Lady of Fatima. Of course, John, a devout Roman Catholic, understood the Pope's reference, but we did not.

"The Pope focused on what he called the Third Secret of Fatima. He said that the Third Secret of Fatima predicted an assassination attempt would be made on the Pope on May 13, 1981. He said *that* assassination attempt was made on him on that date, and, but for the grace of God and the intercession of the Lady of Fatima, he would have died.

"He then said that the remainder of the Third Secret was more devastating. It identified the year 1960 as the beginning of the end of Christianity in America—the year when Satan would gain his foothold, with evil growing so slyly and incrementally that Americans would, at first, not recognize it. As time went on, however, they would accept the evil, but they would call it *freedom*.

"He looked at us a long time, as if he had difficulty focusing his vision. He said we might not believe the story of Fatima, and he could understand that, but he assured us it was true. He clearly believed it to be true."

Holly paused for a minute. When she picked up her story, she said none of them had any idea where the Pope's conversation was leading. They wondered if he had lost his train of thought. They waited.

"The Pope said the universal symbol of Christianity is the cross. And the universal symbol of America is its flag, the flag of a Christian nation that trusted in God. He said when people around the world saw that flag, they knew it represented an exceptional country, one unlike any other. He went on to say that the evil flourishing in America had become quite evident by the way Americans have come to treat their flag. They burn it. They spit on it. They rip it. They drag it in the dirt. All of these actions are permitted by law enforcement and judicial decisions in America, as *freedom of speech*.

"He said that the same is true for the cross in America. Even though the entire world knows America was founded as a Christian country, now the American people spit on the cross, urinate on it, defile it, and remove it from public places and historical monuments and, ultimately, from their memory. Christians have allowed this to happen in their midst. Where is the outrage? Where is the anger? He said people were too passive in America—that they must recognize evil and destroy it, before it was too late.

"The Pope motioned us to come closer. He offered his left hand to your father to hold while, with his right hand, he blessed him with the sign of the cross."

Holly paused. She looked tired. Blake asked her if she wanted to take a break, and they decided to stand up and move around to restore circulation and to loosen muscles that had become tense during Holly's story. Jordan put her arm over Holly's shoulders and held her, neither one of them saying a word. After a short while, Holly continued.

"Monsignor Pacelli escorted us out the door and back down the hallway to another room. We talked for a while until Father Arana walked in. He said the Pope would like to retain us on behalf of the church, if we were willing. Father Arana thanked us, again, for coming to Rome on such short notice. He told us the monsignor would fill in the details of our engagement. We said our good-byes, and then he excused himself.

"That was the first time, and the last time, we saw the Pope. Months later, he died."

Holly stopped, took a deep breath, and said, as if to herself, "I believe Fatima's Third Secret is true. Satan has more than a foot-hold in America.

"The monsignor acted as the proxy client for Pope John Paul and the church. And what did he want us to do? That is the reason why I am here. I want you, Jordan, and you, Blake, to know what your father did and what it cost him. What it has cost all of us.

"Dominic told us about his sister who worked for the ACLU National Office in New York City. She had been there a few years, and during that time she had become the chief administrative officer."

"Angela Carr?" Blake asked.

"Yes, his magnificent, brave sister. He told us his sister had discovered documents containing highly sensitive coordinated plans dating back to the 1960s and updated every five years since. The documents laid out a strategy involving a network of organizations to bloodlessly transform the United States by destroying its belief in God and patriotism. The documents identified law schools, philanthropic foundations, universities, media outlets, government organizations, the entertainment industry, teacher unions, and other organizations as part of the network.

"What almost caused the monsignor to have a heart attack was information that the ACLU and a handful of Catholic priests, including some in his own religious order, worked together to recruit homosexual men to enter Catholic seminaries to become priests. The strategic bet by the ACLU was that gay priests would one day weaken the conservative underpinnings of Catholic clergy and, ultimately, lead to distrust of the church and its priests in the eyes of the faithful—hence, the predator-priest problem and cover-up attempts. Unbelievable! But the strategy worked.

"After the monsignor analyzed the information, he went to Rome."

"Why go to Rome, if the problem was here?" asked Jordan.

"He did not think he could trust anyone here with that information; whereas, he knew he could trust Father Arana because he had been appointed superior general by Pope John Paul.

"Father Arana kept the monsignor's analysis for about three months, during which time he used his own reliable resources to review it. He told the monsignor to do nothing in the interim.

"During the time Father Arana had the information, he must have conferred with John Paul because the Pope asked the monsignor to formulate a plan to address the situation in America."

Blake asked, "And that is where you, Dad, and John came in?"

"Yes. It was about three years ago that we started working on what we called a *confrontation and cease-and-desist strategy*, for lack of a better term. We had to determine the optimal way to approach the ACLU in order to negotiate a cease and desist. Our goal was for the ACLU to stop attacking Christianity. If they chose not to do what we were asking, we would expose them with the information we had. In short, we had to create leverage that would pressure the ACLU into capitulation.

"But how could we do that without jeopardizing the monsignor's sister? The ACLU would quickly determine there was a mole who revealed the documents; however, we wanted her working at the ACLU while we were talking to them, in case she could provide helpful information to us about their side of the negotiation."

Jordan stood up. "I need a drink. Can I pour anyone else an adult beverage?"

This comment eased the tension that had been building in the kitchen. Jordan tried to remember the last time Holly had been in her house. She couldn't remember; yet, Holly had always been part of her life because Holly and John were such close friends of her father. When her father died, Jordan's grief seemed bottomless. Holly was there to help her get through that sad time. Now she wondered who had consoled Holly. How horrible it must have been for her. Jordan poured a robust red wine for all of them.

"Was Dad in any way responsible for what happened in San Francisco?" asked Jordan, not managing to delay asking this question any longer.

"No, your father had no knowledge of any future attack on the ACLU. Had he known, he never would have allowed it."

"Holly, do you have any idea who might be responsible for what happened in San Francisco?" Blake asked. "Could it have been Pope John Paul? He was terrifically clever. Could he have used all of you as cover while he was planning an attack on the ACLU?"

"What do you mean?"

"Could Pope John Paul have set up a cover for his intentions to destroy the ACLU in San Francisco, New York, and Washington? Even though these things happened years after his death, he could have set the whole thing in motion," Blake replied.

Holly continued looking at Blake, even after he finished speaking. She thought to herself, "This is Carson's son, indeed. Just as Carson was a skeptical presence—an important attribute in a litigator—so, too, is his son. He is challenging without being irritating."

Aloud, she said, "Your father had the highest admiration for Pope John Paul. After all, he helped destroy the Soviet Union. Even though he was fighting Parkinson's disease when we met him, he still had a plan for us to execute in America. He saw the evil. He wanted to protect the faithful in America, especially children and young people. However, at no time while we were with him in Rome did he or anyone else advocate violence," answered Holly.

Blake pressed, "But, Holly, how many times have clients lied to their lawyers? Surely there is the possibility that the Pope and others may have lied to you about planned violence, knowing that none of you would agree to represent him if there was the prospect of such violence."

"We believed him, Blake. Who wouldn't? We were talking to the Pope."

"Presidents lie. We know that for a fact. Why not Popes? Wouldn't the Pope be a logical suspect in this?" Blake pressed. "We have information about four scientists in Eastern Europe, all of them experts in nuclear weaponry. They went to the University of Krakow at the same time and were close friends with another student who ultimately became Pope John Paul. How do we ignore these facts?"

"Do you have evidence connecting them to the explosion in California?" Holly asked.

"No, no, we don't have anything like that. Just suspicions raised by the facts that I just gave you. Circumstantial evidence," Blake said, not mentioning the notes from Perry.

Samantha listened to the conversation between Holly and Blake. She wondered if Blake had forgotten that Holly didn't know about the incriminating notes from Larry Perry. Then she dismissed her thought, deciding that Blake did not forget anything. He had simply decided not to tell Holly.

"Have you contacted the scientists?" asked Holly. "What do they say?"

"They are all dead," Blake answered.

Holly looked at Blake and said, "I don't have the information that you have, Blake, so I am at a loss to comment on any scientists or their relationship to Pope John Paul. All I can say is that your father would never have condoned violence. If you think we were played for fools, then so be it. *But your father was no fool,*" Holly said, with a flash of anger.

Jordan stood up to offer wine refills. When she stood, everyone else moved too, either standing and stretching or walking around.

Holly seemed more relaxed now when she spoke. "Your point, Blake, is a good one. I can only say that we never believed, for a moment, that Pope John Paul or anyone working on his behalf would have killed anyone."

"Father Arana? The monsignor? The Jesuits?" Blake asked.

Holly answered, "There is no doubt in my mind that the Jesuits are smart enough and powerful enough to have had a nuclear device made and planted in San Francisco. These are extraordinary people. Look at their history. But, again, I do not believe that is what happened."

"We found a postcard of the Bay View Brewery and Pub in John's apartment," Samantha said.

"Is that where the explosion took place?" Holly asked.

"Yes, it is. Would you have any idea why he had the postcard?"

"I have no idea. John traveled a lot; maybe he ate there," Holly said.

Blake did not look satisfied. He continued, "Is there anything you can tell us that might help in this investigation?"

Holly appeared to be thinking hard. She said, "I don't know if this is of any relevance, but there was one odd thing your father noted when we were doing our due diligence on the inner workings of the ACLU. Well, it wasn't so much an odd thing as it was an odd person."

Blake waited.

"You know your father. He over-prepared for everything. We needed to know the influential people in the ACLU so we could develop our confrontation strategy," Holly explained. "When we looked at the executive staff of the ACLU and tracked their activities for a short while, this odd fellow kept popping up. We later found out he was not an employee or a volunteer. Well, I suppose you could say he was a volunteer, but he was more like a groupie—a very wealthy groupie, in fact. He gave the ACLU millions of dollars and seemed content just to hang out with them, especially with their president, Sylvia Roberts."

Samantha and Blake exchanged quick looks. Blake asked Holly, "Do you remember this person's name?"

"That's easy. Once we found out his identity, we realized we saw his name many times a day on the computer-operating system and software his company developed. His name was Lawrence Perry, founder of DataBasic Systems. He was a client of John's."

102

JORDAN MADE PROSCIUTTO sandwiches with provolone cheese, EVO, tomato, and basil, while Samantha put together a green salad. Blake poured more wine and water for everyone.

After they were all reseated with their food, Holly continued her story. "We decided against contacting the executive staff of the ACLU because we felt they would reflexively push back, without any discussion. Most of the ACLU executive staff had no knowledge of the information we had anyway. They were not in the loop. We thought they would deny, obstruct, and lash out at us, creating communication issues right away. So, we decided to make our contact at the highly secretive select board-of-trustees level. Again, we researched each one of the trustees. The select board of trustees managed a number of funding entities and higher-education incubator systems promoting their ideology. Most importantly, they gave marching orders to the executive director of the ACLU.

"Your father had a hunch that proved to be correct. His hunch was that Ruth Adler Bergman, the associate justice of the Supreme Court, was the de facto head of this group—even though this would be expressly prohibited by the Supreme Court conflict-of-interest policies. Your father managed to validate his hunch. He did not tell us how he did it, but in short order he was completely satisfied that she was their leader," Holly said.

Blake interrupted with a question, "My father battled Bergman in court many times before she went on the Supreme Court, didn't he?"

"Yes, many times, Blake. He beat her every time, everywhere. And when she was general counsel of the ACLU, he beat all the pro bono lawyers she sent out to harass local governments. To say that your father was a thorn in her side wouldn't be accurate. He was like a *rhino* in her side," Holly said, relishing the memory.

They sat in silence for a few moments, thinking of Carson Elliott's brilliance in court and his great qualities as a human being.

Samantha asked, "Have you met Angela Carr?"

Holly looked at Samantha. "Yes. I have met her. As I said earlier, she is a courageous woman. During our discussions with the ACLU, she continued providing us with information."

Samantha continued, "Do you know where to find her?"

Holly slowly answered, "Yes, I know where to find her."

"Will you tell us?"

"Samantha, Angela's life is in danger. I cannot tell anyone where she is. It would not be fair to her."

"What about the monsignor? Is he alive? If so, do you know where he is?"

"He is alive. As for his whereabouts, I do not know where he is."

"What did John tell you when he called the night before he was killed?" Blake asked.

"He told me he had run into you. We often talked about you, Blake. He worried about you. *We* worried about you. He told me you were back in Washington and looking well. He also told me about Samantha and the wonderful time he had working with her in Korea."

"Anything else?"

Holly understood his persistence. "He told me about your involvement in the ACLU investigation. He feared you might unknowingly trigger a response from the select trustees."

"Why?" Blake asked.

"Blake, they *murdered* your father; I know that *for certain*," Holly said, with rage and defiance in her voice. "He was murdered because of what he was doing for the Pope and because of what he knew and, most probably, because of who he was."

Jordan let out a loud cry. They turned to her and saw that she already had tears streaming down her cheeks. She excused herself from the table, got up, and grabbed a tissue to blow her nose. She stood against the kitchen counter—head down and her arms crossed over her chest as if to protect herself.

Blake looked from Holly to Samantha, and then went to his sister and held her in his arms. Tears welled up in Holly's eyes as she watched them. Samantha reached out and held Holly's hand on the tabletop.

Jordan cried out, "We never knew. We thought it was a random act of violence. I mean, my God, that was bad enough. But this…this is pure evil. What kind of people are they?"

"Evil, just as you said," Holly responded, squeezing Samantha's hand as she did so. "This is why John was so concerned when he found out that you, Blake, were hired to help in the ACLU investigation. He worried about your safety. He was going to tell you all of this, but he did not have the chance. They killed him first."

Blake asked, "How do you know that our father's death wasn't just a random act of violence?"

Holly turned in her chair to face Blake and Jordan more completely. "Killing your father was the quickest way they could rid themselves of their greatest fear that he—so skillful and so smart—would destroy them. They did not want to deal with him. *I know all of this for a fact.*

"Blake, your father dealt with only two people on the ACLU Select Board of Trustees: Bergman and Justin Lowell, her second in command. We know Bergman hated your father and had for years. As for Lowell, he was an intellectual—an academic lifer—certainly not a litigator. He feared your father because your father was just as intellectual but was also a man of action and a fierce trial lawyer. Both of them knew they could neither contain nor dissuade your father from doing what he intended. They feared him. They hated him. That is why they killed him."

"What happened to you and John after they killed Dad? Did they try to harm you or John? Or the monsignor?"

"After your father's death, we hired security for ourselves, but nothing ever happened. Everything just stopped. John wanted to pick up where your father left off, but we felt we could not do so without first talking to our client. We asked the monsignor how to proceed. He was concerned for our lives. Because of the secrecy involved and the extreme confidentiality required to deal with the information we had, we could not proceed without Pope John Paul's permission. That proved to be a moot point anyway since John Paul was dead.

"The monsignor spoke with Father Arana who told him to have us stop what we were doing. The monsignor no longer received any direction from Rome. He did not want to proceed on his own. So, our engagement ended. It just ended."

103

"THIS IS FARRELL."

"Mr. Farrell, this is Andrew DuPont. We do not want you to think we are not appreciative of all you and your organization have done for us over the years. We are not ungrateful. We apologize if we have offended you."

"They want something," Farrell thought, otherwise he would not have heard from them again. "The Fat Man is dead, and they don't know what to do. They are running scared. How predictable. Masters of the Universe, my ass."

DuPont, believing Farrell was pleased to hear from him, continued, "I will be in Washington tomorrow on business. I know it is short notice; however, I was wondering if you would be available for dinner?"

Farrell smiled, but it was not a happy smile. "What does he want?" he thought. "I bet he wants me to do their dirty work for them, all because The Fat Man is dead." Farrell did not respond immediately.

DuPont continued, "Ah...well, let me see, I will be available any time after six o'clock. My business is close to your downtown office. Could we meet in the bar at The Prime Rib at six-thirty?"

Farrell did not respond.

Thinking that Farrell had not heard him, DuPont repeated himself.

"I tell you what," Farrell responded slowly, taking his time, "we can meet for a drink at six-thirty. I am not available for dinner," Farrell lied.

DuPont waited. He did not want to interrupt Farrell.

"I suggest we meet at Brady O'Brien's," Farrell continued, knowing that—even on his knees begging—DuPont would never have considered Brady O'Brien's as a meeting place. It was too pedestrian for his type.

"Sure," DuPont answered, too quickly, showing his eager compliance. "Six-thirty it is at—I forgot where..."

"Brady O'Brien's," said Farrell, smiling a happy smile this time.

"Brady O'Brien's," repeated DuPont, not smiling at all.

• • •

Brady O'Brien's sat at the tip of one of the commercial peninsulas surrounding Dupont Circle in the northwest quadrant of the District of Columbia. Although it sounds oxymoronic, the sobriquet "sophisticated Irish pub" had attached itself to Brady O'Brien's over the years.

It was not a raucous haven for drunken Irishmen, no matter their real nationalities; instead, it was a neighborhood pub with excellent food and copious amounts of beer and liquor in a nice environment. The restaurant ambience was very comfortable—with leather-padded chairs and barstools with padded backs, rich wood paneling, wrought-iron trim, and a meandering bar for Irish-whiskey pours and pints of Guinness, Harp, Kilkenny, and other ales and beers. It was reminiscent of the upscale pubs one might find in Dublin—as it should be, since the pub itself was actually built in Dublin and then completely disassembled and shipped to the United States to be reassembled and, finally, blessed with spilled Guinness and Jameson in the District of Columbia.

Farrell was one of the locals who patronized Brady O'Brien's on a twice, thrice, or more times a week basis, depending upon his travel schedule. Often he would eat there two times in one day when he was in Washington. Since he lived alone and did not like to cook, he ate at restaurants for almost every meal. In return for his loyal patronage, the management at Brady O'Brien's set aside a special table for Farrell where he could eat, conduct business, drink, or just sit and stare out the window.

Tonight, Farrell sat at his special table looking out at the cars moving around Dupont Circle. Instead of beer or ale, Farrell sipped Irish whiskey. In the background Celtic Christmas music played, although most Americans would never recognize it as Christmas music.

Andrew DuPont was late.

Farrell smiled, thinking this would be fun tonight. The whiskey he ordered was fifteen dollars a pour. No problem, Andrew DuPont would be picking up the tab. Farrell knew DuPont's team well enough to know that their circle was small. They were afraid to make their circle larger because they did not know who to trust. Even though Farrell had walked out on them, he predicted that tonight DuPont would be begging him to help them find some muscle to do the things The Fat Man had previously arranged for them.

As Farrell sipped his whiskey, wincing slightly as it sweetly seared his throat on the way to destroying his liver, he wondered why that snobby law professor wasn't along for the ride. Oh, wait, that's right, that arrogant jerk didn't like him.

He looked at his watch. The idiot was fifteen minutes late. "Am I being disrespected, or is DuPont lost? Maybe DuPont can't find Dupont Circle," he chuckled. "So what? Let him be late. His punishment will be drinking here with me."

Farrell knew that DuPont wanted to eat and drink at a better restaurant, one where beer wasn't on tap or even on the menu…

one where the least expensive bottle of domestic red wine started at one hundred dollars and the menu needed English subtitles. "Fuck him," growled Farrell, staring at his watch. Now the little bastard was twenty minutes late.

Looking around him, Farrell nodded to the regulars who were obliquely glancing in his direction. He knew they were always interested in the people he was meeting. He saw some new faces in the bar—lawyers, probably. They were too well dressed to be tourists. Almost all the barstools were taken, he noticed. "Business is good," he thought. "What recession?"

And business just got better.

"Mr. Farrell," announced Andrew DuPont, who had quietly approached Farrell's table. "Sorry I'm late. Traffic," he said, as he sat down at the table.

"I'm not accustomed to waiting for anyone, especially anyone who might be asking me for a favor," replied Farrell icily, letting the young snob know his place, as well as Farrell's state of mind.

DuPont apologized again, displaying gentlemanly manners born and bred over three hundred years, as he was descended from one of the first families of the Delaware Colony before the Revolutionary War. Even though he held Farrell in contempt as blue-collar, union lowlife, DuPont was here on a mission. Therefore, he would remain civil until he got what he needed: around the clock security for the trustees and assassins to kill the Pope.

• • •

Roist enjoyed his Black and Tan, served at the perfect Irish-pub temperature. When in an Irish pub, do as the Irish do.

He found his barstool to be quite comfortable, more so than most of the pubs he frequented. Plus, his location along the ambling bar gave him a good view of the two men at the table.

Roist waited.

He watched the younger man leave.

• • •

Over a meal of roast beef, brown gravy, mashed potatoes, Yorkshire pudding, and two pints of Guinness, Farrell contemplated the requests made by that trust-fund baby, Andrew DuPont. They wanted security night and day for themselves and their families.

Farrell had people he could recommend or provide for a nice markup, but he didn't want any involvement with these loons anymore. He knew they had tons of money. "The more they spend, the safer they feel," Farrell thought. "How stupid are these people?" He would call tomorrow and tell them to use RavenRock, the very best and the most expensive. Let those bastards pay through the nose.

Kill the Pope?

"No way am I helping with that."

104

THE ELEVATOR DOOR opened and closed, followed by the sound of muffled footsteps along the carpeted hallway, stopping in front of the apartment door. Keys clanged and made a slight scratchy sound, the noise made by a key clumsily inserted into a lock.

Farrell walked into his apartment. He took off his gloves, coat, and hat, slipped off his shoes, and put on the slippers waiting on the floor by the hall closet. Since he lived alone, he did not anticipate anyone waiting up for him. Farrell walked down the hallway to the bathroom to relieve himself. Water turned on and then off.

Roist could hear Farrell brushing his teeth.

Farrell finished in the bathroom. He walked into his bedroom, pulling his shirt out of his pants. It was then that he saw Roist sitting in the armchair in the corner of the room.

"Wha...what...who the fuck are you?" demanded Farrell, not showing any fear. "What the fuck do you think you're doing here, asshole?" Farrell shouted, but he didn't step toward Roist. It was the gun in Roist's hand, pointed at him, that kept Farrell's feet glued to the floor. Farrell stopped talking. He looked at the gun; it had a silencer.

Roist tossed a role of gray duct tape to Farrell. "Here, tape your mouth."

"Fuck you," Farrell shot back. "You're messing with the wrong man, punk."

"Tape your mouth," Roist calmly reiterated, shaking the barrel of the Glock .45 caliber handgun ever so slightly.

Farrell waited a few seconds to showcase his bravado, and then he tore off a length of tape from the roll and spread it over his mouth.

"Now pull a long piece of tape off the roll and wrap it around your left wrist. Do it four times, and do not tear the tape from the roll."

Farrell stared daggers at Roist but complied with his demand.

"Put your left hand on your right knee. Bend over. Tape your hand to your knee. Do it six times around."

Farrell hesitated, instantly realizing that by doing so he would hobble himself, like a crippled horse. But if this guy wanted to kill him, he would have done it by now.

"Do it!" shouted Roist, gun in hand.

Farrell put his left hand on his right knee. He wrapped the tape around his knee and over his hand six times. When he finished, Farrell could no longer stand up straight.

Roist got up from his chair and walked over to Farrell. He tore the tape and put the roll back into his jacket pocket. "Good, now come with me." He shoved Farrell into the hallway. Farrell fell down but managed to get back to his feet, struggling awkwardly.

"Into your office."

They moved into Farrell's office.

"Sit down at the desk," Roist said, watching Farrell stumble into his office chair, his left shoulder and upper body imprisoned by the duct tape, forcing his head inches from the desktop.

Roist shoved three separate pieces of note paper in front of Farrell and put a pen in Farrell's right hand. He told Farrell what he wanted him to write on each piece of paper: "LP thinks this should help. Kill anyone inside. Open the safe, and dump the contents."

Farrell grunted in painful discomfort from the duct tape and from his severely torqued position. Roist could see that Farrell's eyes were watering and that he was trying to say something. Roist lifted a corner of the tape covering Farrell's mouth.

"I write with my left hand," Farrell managed to say.

Roist looked down at Farrell, smiled, and said, "No you don't. I've been watching you. You are right-handed." He pushed the tape back in place.

Watching you? Farrell's eyes registered alarm. He looked up as far as his head would go, trying to see the face of the man talking to him.

Farrell wrote what he was told to write. When he finished, Roist ordered him to move into the living room. Once there, he pointed to the couch and pushed Farrell toward it. He fell into the couch and then tried to straighten himself into a better sitting position, but the duct tape handicapped his normal movements and painfully contorted his body. All he could manage was to perch sideways on the couch.

Roist told him, "I was sent here by Holly Waters."

Holly Waters? Carson Elliott!

Farrell now realized he was going to die. He started to gag, cough, and wheeze.

Roist moved to help him.

Unexpectedly, Farrell kicked out his unfettered left leg, desperately trying to hit the back of Roist's knees. With split-second reactions, Roist jumped out of the way. He fired once into Farrell's left knee, shattering it into bloody fragments, large and small.

Farrell screamed into the duct tape. He gasped desperately for air through his nostrils, as if he were drowning. Roist stood still to avoid leaving footprints in the bloody carpet, stained messy-red from Farrell's destroyed knee.

Farrell's face turned the color of Irish oatmeal. He heard nothing that Roist said. The pain in his blown-out knee cut off his ability to hear anything except his silent screams. Roist noticed Farrell fading into unconsciousness. He aimed the gun at Farrell's right shoulder and pulled the trigger. The blast blew Farrell back into the cushioned couch, causing him to bounce forward and onto the floor. Blood and bone fragments splattered everywhere.

Roist looked at Farrell's knee and shoulder, calculating the amount of blood lost and the amount streaming from both gun-blast wounds. Reaching down, he ripped the duct tape from Farrell's mouth. Farrell gasped desperately for air. He was too weak to scream. He just wanted to breathe.

Roist shot the other knee, through the hand that was taped on it.

Pain from this blasted tissue and bone did not register on Farrell's face. He was in severe shock already, insulated from the effects of any more pain.

Roist aimed the gun at Farrell's head and pulled the trigger, putting Farrell out of his misery…and on his way to hell.

105

THE LAW PROFESSOR awoke before dawn. He had a poached egg, a piece of rye toast, and tea. It was his usual breakfast, but this morning his enjoyment of the meal was spoiled by thoughts of that bastard Farrell and the inept Andrew DuPont. He thought it had been a mistake to send someone so inexperienced to deal with a professional liar like Farrell. Maybe one of the others should have contributed something, for a change.

"Yes," DuPont answered after The Law Professor dialed his number.

"Well...what did Farrell say?" The Law Professor asked.

"Are you serious? It is only nine in the morning. I haven't had my breakfast yet."

"I do not care about your eating habits. I want to know about Farrell."

DuPont hated old men. Didn't they sleep? Did they expect people to conduct business before breakfast?

"I told you last night. Farrell said he would contact me today. In case you have not noticed, the day is quite young," DuPont responded.

Undeterred, The Law Professor continued, "Listen to me. We all need security guards. We need Farrell's help now. This minute. Do you understand?"

"I understand," DuPont answered, looking over the room-service breakfast offerings. "I understand. But what can I do? He said he would contact me today. It is only nine o'clock in the morning."

"Yes. Yes, it is."

"Okay, okay. I will call Farrell, and, when I have something to report, I will call you." DuPont rang off. Then he placed his breakfast order. He would call Farrell after he ate breakfast.

• • •

The Law Professor hated his life at the moment. He was not convinced that Andrew DuPont was entirely engaged in the assignment they had given him. "Well," he thought, "maybe the assignment itself was a mistake. Why do we continue working with Farrell? Why not simply arrange our own security?"

After he considered that a bit, he came to the same conclusion that prompted the assignment in the first place. It was a matter of urgency. They all believed, and probably correctly, that Farrell could find security people to protect them right away. That's what they wanted. That's what they needed. Then, if there was an interest in changing security, they would have more time to consider hiring someone else.

He called his friend, Ruth. He called her chambers, her apartment, and her cell phone but could not reach her. He left voice messages. After ten minutes he called again. She did not answer. "Maybe she is in a conference," he thought. Still, always before she had returned the call, if only to say she could not talk at that time.

He decided to call DuPont again. This time it went to the hotel's voice-mail system. He called DuPont's cell-phone number, and that went to voice mail. He left a scathing message.

Why rely on DuPont for information? The Law Professor called Farrell. Cut to the chase. Get it done. No answer. He waited five minutes and called again. This time he left a detailed message.

He again called Bergman at the three numbers he had. No answer.

The Law Professor called the Supreme Court, this time speaking with Bergman's administrative assistant. She told him no one knew where Justice Bergman was, although they assumed she needed some rest following her husband's funeral. Since it was not a day for oral arguments, the fact that Justice Bergman was not in her office was of no immediate concern to anyone.

He wondered if he should go to her apartment. He could catch a flight later in the day. Or should he call her daughter who lived nearby in Maryland? Maybe call the police? No, probably not. His mind ran through all available options. Where was Ruth he wondered, now becoming a bit concerned. He had security on his mind. He was worried, profoundly worried.

Dead!

His mind raced to this worst conclusion. Could she be dead? He could feel his heart beating in his chest. He could not breathe deeply! Shallow breathing alarmed him. He knew he had to think like the lawyer he was. He needed to think clearly, analytically. But he was too disturbed to think clearly and analytically, much less devise a plan of action.

Gravity was taking him down. He could feel it pushing on him. He could feel the weight of past sins press on him.

"What if they plan to kill me?"

Did Ruth have anything in her apartment that might lead them to him? He thought not. She was always so careful.

"What am I thinking? They already know who we are. They know where we live. What if they are outside my house waiting for me?"

He decided not to go out. He would stay put until there was security in place.

"Where is our security?"

To occupy himself, he called all the others to let them know Ruth was missing and to share his fears that she might be dead. He worried that he might seem an alarmist. But, hell, this whole situation was quite alarming.

He changed his mind about staying home. He decided to go to Washington to find Ruth and to talk to Farrell about security.

106

THEY WERE RETURNING from the funeral services of the slain FBI agents. What a horrible way to spend this Christmas for those grieving families.

Blake looked out his car window. He saw Christmas decorations on the outside of commercial buildings, and he knew that inside there would be even more decorations. Federal office buildings had no Christmas decorations—and certainly nothing commemorating the birth of Jesus Christ, even though on those buildings the words "In God We Trust" were prominently inscribed.

Samantha thought how much she hated the fact that two wonderful men, men who had saved her life in Anguilla, were gone from this earth. What a tragedy.

She was also thinking that her assignment at the Justice Department would probably last only a few days more. Her thoughts turned to Blake and then to Leon and Sapphire. These people had become part of her daily life. She would miss them. She also thought of Jordan and her family, such loving and compassionate people. Her thoughts returned to Blake. She wondered if Blake...no, no, she tried to put it out of her mind. "Whatever happens, happens," she thought.

When they reached their conference-room office and opened the door, they discovered Sapphire and Leon had arrived first from the funeral services. They discussed the families of the FBI agents and how difficult it must be for them, especially this time of the year. Samantha commented on the heroic action of the men, saving her life but losing their own. She was in tears.

After a while they got down to business.

"What did the general say about Holly's story?" Sapphire inquired, referring to the telephone conversation Blake had with Tom Owens the night before.

"He found it as fascinating as we did," answered Blake, "especially her observations about Lawrence Perry."

The door opened and in walked Tom Owens, as if on cue. "Good morning. I just spoke with the White House about the conclusion to the ACLU investigation. The president seems pleased with the outcome, notwithstanding some minor open issues.

"My next assignment is to fly to San Francisco today to meet with the city officials out there and to prepare for a joint press conference tomorrow during which we will lay the blame on Lawrence Perry *for everything*. There is no limit to the number of crimes we can lay on one dead guy, apparently," Tom Owens said, half-facetiously, half-seriously.

Blake asked, "Will the incoming administration be satisfied?"

"As much as they can be, given their political DNA," Tom replied.

• • •

Carson Elliott and John Palmer were two men he greatly admired. What had happened to men like that? Where do you find them these days?

Tom Owens had one particular thought relating to John Palmer, a man every bit as clever as Carson Elliott. Tom wondered what John really knew about the nuclear device that exploded in San Francisco, especially after Blake found that postcard of the Bay View Brewery and Pub in John's bedroom. Could John have gone off in a sinister direction after his close friend Carson was murdered? Could John have had the device made and delivered? Was that why he was murdered?

Suddenly, Tom had another thought that brought a broad smile to his face. John worked for the Department of Defense, as part of the ACLU investigation. He was a member of the team investigating Eastern European scientists to find out if any of them could have been involved with making the nuclear device. Could John have planted misinformation or created disinformation, or any combination thereof, to prevent anyone from finding the source of the bomb in that part of the world? Could he have done that? Could he have deflected any closer investigation into the four nuclear scientists from Poland?

Tom, still smiling, shook his head, thinking about John Palmer, his former law professor. Smart. And what could he say about Holly? Brilliant, clever, determined. Along with Carson Elliott, the three of them were quite the force.

Gamesmanship.

You play the game, or it plays you.

What really happened?

"Who cares?" he thought.

"We have Lawrence Perry.

That is enough."

• • •

Holly met him in a private lounge for first-class passengers at Reagan National Airport an hour before his flight to the West Coast. "Tom, thank you for meeting me on such short notice," she said, as they embraced. Their relationship went way back. Tom's old law firm often worked closely with the Elliott and Morgan firm on commercial litigation. Over time, he became good friends with Holly and lawyers in that firm. Of course, he was already a close friend of Blake and was friends with Carson Elliott and John Palmer.

"I have something for you. Carson and John put it together, with the help of a Jesuit priest. I also assisted," Holly said, handing him a large envelope sealed with tape.

Tom did not ask what was in the envelope.

"Will there be more?"

Holly replied, "Yes. But it will go to the FBI. And to the media."

The two of them reminisced about simpler times, happier days. It was a brief meeting, Holly soon left. Tom got on his airplane headed to California. He would read what Holly gave him. It was a courtesy copy, he figured. The fact that she gave it to him first was a thoughtful gesture. That was Holly.

107

SHE STOOD NEXT to his bed, watching him sleep. The tiny room that was his world had two windows so he could look out at the sky. Today, the sky blended with the grayish-white walls. She looked around the room. Spartan. Very Spartan. Clean but drab. Well, at least it was clean. That, in itself, was something and spoke well of the housekeeping staff.

Angela was not so confident about the nursing staff, however, based on what she observed over the past three hours. She also thought the food service was horrible, especially since no one helped her brother eat his meal. She helped him because he had great physical difficulty just getting the food into his mouth. Surely, that must explain why he was so thin, the thinnest she had ever seen him in his adult life.

On his nightstand was a framed photo of Franco when he was much younger: Master Chief Petty Officer Franco Pacelli on board one of the many ships where he had spent a good portion of his life in service to his country. The younger Franco projected a powerful presence.

Not so today.

Angela held his hand. She tried to remember the last time she had seen him. Was it ten years ago? Longer? She had not seen him, or any family member, during the time she worked at the ACLU, with the exception of Dominic. She did not want to endanger them, in case she was being watched.

On his bed lay the rosary she brought him. Nothing religious adorned the walls. After all, she reminded herself, this is a government nursing home, operated by the Veterans Administration. Even though the occupants were veterans, many of whom had deep faith in God and thanked God for keeping them alive when they were in harm's way, their government would not permit any expression of religious belief to be attached to the walls or doors, not even with removable tape.

Angela knew this was because the ACLU assiduously attacked the Veterans Administration to ensure that no religious symbols would be permitted on government property, not even for the sake of the men and women who served their country: one nation, under God.

Dominic told her that Franco did not have long to live. It was for this reason that she came to visit him, even though he did not recognize her—heartbreaking for Angela…daily existence for Franco.

"A miserable existence," she thought.

She prayed for her brother's quick passage from this life.

108

THE LAW PROFESSOR walked briskly through the concourse at Reagan National Airport. His flight had landed a few minutes early. He stopped and called Bergman's cell phone. No answer. He left the message that he was in Washington and on his way to his hotel and asked her to please call him as soon as possible.

Next, he called DuPont at his hotel, only to discover that his younger colleague had checked out already. "Damn," thought the Law Professor. "Why didn't he call me before checking out? I'm here. Where the hell is he? What an inconsiderate bastard.

"Should I call Farrell?

"Not now. I will call him from my hotel."

The Law Professor was a creature of habit, of routine. He always stayed at the same hotel in Washington, DC, no matter where his business took him. Today was no different. He checked into The Four Seasons Hotel on Pennsylvania Avenue. He knew DuPont had stayed at the same hotel last night. How easy it could have been if only DuPont had waited and not rushed off somewhere.

After washing his face and hands in the bathroom of his hotel room, The Law Professor called Farrell.

"Hello?"

"Is this Mr. Farrell?" The Law Professor asked, not certain whether the voice belonged to the union leader.

"No it is not. Who is calling?"

It wasn't what the Law Professor anticipated. Every other time before, it was Farrell who had answered. After all, it was his cell phone. Who was this man? "Should I hang up?" he wondered. "No. I flew here to find Farrell. Why would I hang up? Maybe this man knows where Farrell is."

"My name is Justin Lowell," he said. "I was hoping to speak to Mr. Farrell. Is he available?"

"What is the nature of your business?" the voice asked.

The Law Professor raised his voice, "I want to speak with Mr. Farrell. If he is there, please put him on."

Seconds passed.

The Law Professor could hear people speaking in the background.

"You left a message for Mr. Farrell this morning, asking about security. Why do you need security?"

"Who is this?" The Law Professor demanded.

"I am Homicide Detective Howard Foreman. Mr. Farrell is dead. Murdered. More like tortured. I need to speak with you."

Tortured?

The Law Professor did not want to cooperate, but they had his name and cell-phone number. He had no choice. He gave Detective Foreman his personal information and said he could go downtown to Foreman's office tomorrow.

Farrell murdered!

"And now I am implicated."

• • •

Detective Foreman called the FBI and was routed to Leon Wilson. Foreman told him about the union leader's murder. The police had received an anonymous call that morning about a scuffle in Farrell's apartment and that the tenant wasn't answering his door. Foreman said they found blueprints of the three ACLU offices that had been destroyed by fire. They were on Farrell's desk.

Leon and an FBI tech went to Farrell's apartment to examine the blueprints and take photos. They found notes attached to each set. They assumed the dead man had written the notes, but that would be a matter for expert analysis. What interested Leon were the initials "LP" referenced in each note.

"LP" for Larry Perry? That was Leon's conclusion. If so, then Farrell must have been a middleman for Perry. Maybe Farrell found the arsonists for "LP."

Leon called Sapphire first because she had spent so much time working up a profile and history of Perry. He wanted her to know that the evidence found in Farrell's apartment possibly pointed to Larry Perry as the person responsible for the arson attacks and the murders. Sapphire was giddy.

He asked her to tell Blake, Samantha, and the general—especially, the general. He really should know this before the press conference in San Francisco. One big loose end tied down, Leon hoped.

109

"RUTH," EXCLAIMED THE Law Professor, his words rushing to escape his lips. He looked at his old friend and saw she was exhausted. It was late in the afternoon.

"I was so relieved when you finally called me," he said. "I was worried something had happened to you. It has been a miserable day. Farrell's been murdered, Ruth. Tortured! And now I have to meet with a homicide detective tomorrow.

"I can't find DuPont. I could not reach you at any of your phone numbers. I apologize, but I had to call your assistant to find out where you were, and when she didn't know…I thought the worst. That is why I left New Haven this morning to find you and to talk to Farrell myself."

They sat in a quiet area of The Four Seasons Hotel lobby. Bergman had called The Law Professor from the hotel's lobby, and he had hurried from his room to meet her there.

"It was so odd," he thought. "Definitely not like Ruth to be in a public place like this." But he dismissed the thought. He wanted to tell her more about Farrell and the detective who had questioned him, but before he could resume, Bergman grabbed his wrist.

"Justin, Holly Waters called me this morning. She wants to meet us, you and me.

"After she called, I left my apartment and walked for a long time. I was so disturbed after hearing her voice that I could not think clearly. It was such a shock."

"What did she say?"

"Just what I said, Justin. She wants to meet us."

"Meet us?" he repeated, stunned by this news. "Does she know we tried to kill her in Anguilla?"

"She knows," Bergman replied. "She did not say anything about it, but I picked it up in her voice."

"Why does she want to meet? So she can kill us?" The Law Professor ranted, thinking about how vulnerable they were with no security.

Ignoring him, Bergman said, "She wants to meet us tonight."

"*Tonight?* Why the hurry? Why now?"

"Justin, I do not know. It was a short call. It was not as if we were old friends catching up."

"What did you tell her?" The Law Professor became frantic at this turn of events.

"I told her we would meet her tonight. From my point of view, this is good. We can find out what she knows," Bergman said, but she hardly believed her own words.

"Where is the meeting?" asked The Law Professor, still concerned about his safety.

"Here. In the lobby. She wanted a public place."

"Here?" The Law Professor wondered if Holly Waters knew he was staying in this hotel.

"Yes. In two hours."

• • •

At six o'clock a long, black BMW sedan pulled in front of the hotel. Holly Waters got out of the back seat and walked into the lobby. She spotted them quickly. They were sitting together in an open area filled with greenery and flowers.

"I am on a mission," Holly told herself. "No emotions."

They did not stand up when she approached them. No handshakes. No civility.

"Perfect," Holly thought.

Holly sat down opposite them.

They eyed her keenly, but said nothing.

The elegantly appointed hotel lobby was huge. The area where they sat had no one close by. Still, Holly spoke softly, "I know that you had Carson killed. I know you had John Palmer killed and that you tried to kill Monsignor Pacelli. I also know you tried to kill Blake Elliott and me in Anguilla."

They tried to maintain poker faces, but it was difficult. How did she know all this? Or was she just bluffing…throwing out allegations to see how they might react? Was that it? Stone-faced, they said nothing in return.

Holly studied them. She had not seen them for a number of years. They were as she remembered. He was tall and slim, and she was short and emaciated looking. Bergman's face looked like it had been shrink-wrapped.

"You did not have to kill Carson. He was a lawyer doing his job."

Neither one of them responded, although their minds were racing back and forth on the topic of Carson Elliott. How many times had they discussed him? What difference did it make? They couldn't *unkill* him. It made no difference whether Holly was correct or not. Carson Elliott was *still* dead. They tried not to react. But Holly noticed the slightest acknowledgment in Bergman's body language.

Holly said, "I know you tried to kill the papal nuncio. But you failed."

This time, Bergman squirmed a bit. She moved around on the sofa, her feet not touching the floor. She was that short. The Law Professor did not squirm. He did not move. But his eyes twitched ever so slightly.

"I was the reason you failed," Holly said.

Finally, The Law Professor replied, "I do not know what you are talking about."

Holly focused on him. "I am talking about you, Professor. You are the one who arranged these things through your union man, James Farrell, and his colleague, The Fat Man," she explained. "I had them killed."

Fear ran across The Law Professor's face. An audible gasp left Bergman's mouth. They looked at each other. Their world was imploding.

"What do you want?" Bergman said, using her courtroom voice, trying to gain control.

"Actually, I do not want anything. I am here to tell you something," Holly replied, looking straight at Bergman.

"And what is that?" asked Bergman, not certain what was taking place.

"I own part of a very special company that does security work—including corporate espionage, cybersecurity, and so on. You may have heard of them? RavenRock. In fact, it was John Palmer who persuaded me to invest in them."

"We do not care about your business or your investments—or even you, for that matter. What is it you want to tell us?" The Law Professor arrogantly demanded.

"John and I thought it would be beneficial if we had more information about the select trustees and you, Ruth. So I prevailed on RavenRock to install electronic listening devices in your apartment, your chambers, and your landline phone, Ruth—and in your townhouse and office phone, Professor. They also bugged the conference room at Parton and Crownell that you select trustees use. They have been in place for about three years, monitored by RavenRock. I have hundreds of hours of tape, in which you discuss many, many things."

Bergman's eyes darted everywhere, except straight ahead. Suddenly, she felt the need to pee. She could not hold it. How embarrassing. She was already wet. Her mind leaked as much as her bladder…with memories of incriminating conversations spilling out, conversations that would condemn her.

But they had no search warrant, no court order.

Inadmissible evidence.

Except in the court of public opinion.

Guilty as charged. She knew it.

Bergman quickly reflected on her fleeting legacy. It had been her plan to retire from the Court next year, after the new president was sworn in. He was very progressive, so she felt confident that her successor would be a woman with the same judicial philosophy as hers. A woman not as intelligent or as accomplished probably, but someone worthy enough to follow in her footsteps. Someone younger to keep the dream alive.

Now this. Dammit!

The Law Professor considered what Holly Waters just said. *Hours of taped conversations.* In those conversations they plotted murder after murder, he knew. But did she really have tapes, or was this a game she was playing? Which was it? Truth or a bluff?

He had really never given Holly Waters much thought before. In his mind she was nothing more than a woman fawning after Carson Elliott. He was the lawyer for the Pope, after all. He had the track record and the brains. She lived in his shadow. "After we killed him, they did nothing. *She did nothing*," he thought. "No one ever contacted us again. Not even Palmer. Why should we believe her?"

Holly could tell they were struggling with their thoughts. Good. Let them struggle. Let their worlds collapse.

"I have the ACLU's written plans and networking strategy to destroy Christianity and patriotism in this country. That should make interesting reading. Before I came here, I distributed a hundred copies to newsrooms and news outlets around the country, along with transcripts of conversations I thought would be particularly interesting. The tapes themselves are on their way to the FBI and all network and cable-news outlets. The FBI will authenticate your voices, as well as those of your colleagues. All of this, of course, is provided anonymously. Call it a *public service*," Holly smiled.

From her purse she took out a couple pages of transcript. She gave them to Bergman. The topic discussed in the transcript was killing the papal nuncio.

Holly stood up. She felt exhilarated. Above all else, she felt vindicated. She looked down on them and said, "By the way, I am responsible for the explosion in San Francisco, with help from John Palmer and friends of Pope John Paul II. It took us a while to plan and execute. Almost three years, but it was time well spent."

"All because of Carson Elliott?" Bergman cried out.

"Yes. All because of Carson Elliott."

Without saying another word, Holly turned and walked through the lobby to the front door where her car and driver were waiting for her.

When she was seated inside the car, she handed the audio jamming device she had in her purse to her driver.

110

THEY SAT THERE not knowing what to do.

Their lives had just ended.

They were only drawing breath...empty human shells filling time and space.

"What should we do, Ruth?" The Law Professor asked.

After some reflection, she answered, "Go home, Justin. That is what I plan to do."

"But shouldn't we warn the others?"

"What difference would it make? However, if you feel compelled to do so, then please go ahead," Bergman said, as she slowly stood up. She took a quick peek behind her at the couch. She was worried it might be wet. All she wanted now was a ladies room and a cab to take her home.

The Law Professor stood as well. He bent and kissed his friend on her cheek. He knew he would never see her again.

"This is it?" he asked.

"Good night, Justin," was her sad reply.

• • •

Justin Addison Lowell decided to fly home that night. He gathered his things and checked out of The Four Seasons. He caught a late flight to New Haven. His vintage Volvo sedan was parked at the airport. He checked the fuel gauge as he drove home and then stopped at a gas station to fill the tank. Even though he was depressingly deep in troubled thought, he actually noticed that it was *not* snowing.

The Law Professor lived in a small townhouse not far from the Yale University campus. He had moved there after his wife and son passed. He pulled into the tiny single-car garage of his unit and closed the garage door. After taking everything from the car into the house, he used the bathroom and then went back to the garage.

He had not shut off the car. Fumes from the tired engine already filled the garage.

He got back in behind the steering wheel and lowered the windows. He pushed his seat as far back as it would go, and then he reclined the seat a little bit.

While sitting there, he thought of his wife and son. They would have been ashamed of him, no doubt. He reflected on the Lowell family in New England. Once they had been wealthy and influential, but now they were neither. He was the last Lowell: no children, hence, no progeny. The name would die with him, he knew. It was just as well; there would be no relatives living in disgrace.

He tried to recount the beginning of this day. It seemed so long ago. "Whatever happened to Andrew DuPont?" he wondered. And Farrell. Was he really tortured?

The garage was surprisingly airtight. In early November he had hired a handyman to insulate his garage door and add extra weather stripping to make it draft proof.

His eyelids started to close until they finally rested shut. His breathing slowed...and then it stopped.

• • •

"We all have to die someday," she thought. "Since I don't believe in God, there is no point in praying. Pray for what? Forgiveness? Really?"

She enjoyed using her legal mind to analyze these things, to stay mentally nimble even at the end. Still, her legal mind could not rationally explain this predicament she was in. Her situation was simply too overwhelming.

"Tomorrow my life will be in ruins. My achievements trashed. My legacy destroyed. How do I stop time? How do I stop tomorrow from coming?"

Her mind was quick to answer: today will be my day—my last day.

"Even if I did believe in God, I am still going to kill myself today," she thought. "That is how to stop time. For me, tomorrow will never come."

Bergman found the revolver her husband kept in the nightstand on his side of their bed. She was not familiar with the type of gun or the brand. She could see the bullets. It was fully loaded. But it made no difference. She was only going to use one bullet.

Confusion set in.

"Where do I sit…or should I stand? Do I put the barrel of the gun in my mouth? Maybe I should point it at my heart and pull the trigger. However, it might jerk, and I might just be wounded. I might live! That is not what I want. I want to die.

"How ludicrous," she thought, trying to figure out the best way to die. Most people do not have that option.

Finally, she chose her favorite chair in the living room. She elected to be properly seated for this last, major event of her life. She never gave her children a single thought. Why should she?

She decided to place the barrel in her mouth.

She practiced, wanting to ensure that the angle was correct—that the bullet would destroy her brain before it blasted through her skull. Then she realized how difficult it was to hold the gun. It was awkward. She did not think her finger was capable of pulling the trigger if the gun was upright. She practiced holding the gun on its side and then upside down.

She chose upside down. In this position she believed her hand and finger could do the job more easily—meticulous and detail-oriented to the end.

She was ready.

With the barrel in her mouth and the gun upside down, pointed at the angle she wanted to ensure brain penetration, she took a deep breath, exhaled slowly...and pulled the trigger.

For Ruth Adler Bergman, associate justice of the United States Supreme Court, time stopped.

111

EARLY THE NEXT morning, Holly electronically sent Monsignor Pacelli's analysis and copies of the information Angela had discovered in the national headquarters of the ACLU to one hundred media outlets and to the FBI. She included select transcripts of Ruth Adler Bergman and Justin Lowell discussing the murders of Carson Elliott, John Palmer, Father Leo, the attempted murder of Monsignor Pacelli and the papal nuncio, and the planned assassination of Pope Benedict in Washington, DC.

She sent select audio files of Bergman and Lowell's conversations to the FBI, along with audio files of phone conversations with the ACLU Select Board of Trustees, which the bugs in their phones had captured.

The day's breaking news sucked the air out of every other news story. News rooms scrambled to do their own investigative work. Talking heads multiplied across network and cable television like never before.

The remaining select trustees, under siege from reporters, went into seclusion with their personal attorneys since the law firm of Parton and Crownell informed them that they would no longer be representing them. The law firm itself started receiving hundreds of inquiries regarding its knowledge of these events.

A second round of breaking news limped across the airwaves and cyberspace informing the American people that, earlier in the day, the president-elect had named Zoe Levin as his choice to replace the outgoing attorney general.

• • •

At the Supreme Court, the administrative assistant to Justice Bergman told others about Mr. Lowell's phone call the day before. She tried to reach Justice Bergman, but she was unsuccessful; there was no answer. The phones at the office were ringing off the hook—reporters trying to reach Justice Bergman for comment.

The chief justice asked the US Marshals Service to take over. They went to Bergman's apartment and had the building superintendent open her door for them.

They found her sitting in a chair with part of her head sitting elsewhere—a grisly suicide with no note.

The marshal called the New Haven police to have them check on Professor Lowell. The police checked the garage of the professor's townhouse and found him permanently asleep in his vintage Volvo.

112

THE CHRISTMAS PAGEANT lasted all day: music, gifts, sermons, fund-raising, lots of children dressed for the Nativity program, live sheep and goats onstage. The fund-raising continued unabated because the Reverend Peterson wanted his faithful viewing audience to realize they had everyday responsibilities to help the poor and disadvantaged while spreading the Word of God. The prayer line was open for business.

Gorgeous Christmas decorations in tasteful measure added glorious color to the stage where the Reverend Peterson and Ruth Peterson presided—he still sitting in his stylish wheelchair and she at the end of the couch, close to him. Yes, they were holding hands like two people in love.

"We are here to celebrate the birthday of our Lord and Savior, Jesus Christ. King of Kings. The Lamb of God. Born in a stable to a virgin mother. Destined to die on the cross to save our souls. Today is the day it all began, for us and for our salvation.

"In a few minutes, our wonderful choir—under the direction of Sharon Lewis—will entertain us with traditional religious Christmas carols. Before the choir enchants us, I want to say a few words about the conclusion of the ACLU investigation. I want to thank our law-enforcement officials involved for their hard work. What a thankless task they had.

"Doesn't it seem perversely fitting, ladies and gentlemen, that one of the ACLU's own degenerate members, a pornography addict and AIDs-infected lunatic, was responsible for killing over four hundred ACLU sinners? Glory to God in the Highest.

"Now, let me introduce Sharon Lewis and our wonderful choir..."

• • •

Zoe Levin and Lester Zepester—one a nonobservant Jew and the other an atheist who preferred to be called a secular humanist—were on the least watched cable-news program, the one with progressive views. The host was the albino homosexual son of a wealthy mother with a famous name.

"Congratulations, Ms. Levin, on your nomination as attorney general. It must come as some relief that your predecessor has wrapped up the ACLU investigation in record time, so you won't have to deal with it next year."

"Thank you for your kind words," Levin said. She knew she had to bite her tongue and accept the fact that the ACLU investigation was concluded, with Larry Perry as the sole responsible person. She did not believe it for one minute, but she couldn't say that. So she said, "I applaud the men and women in law enforcement who investigated the horrible attack on the ACLU earlier this month. To think that one man alone was responsible is hard to digest, but it appears to be true."

"Appears to be true?" the host asked, picking up on Levin's choice of words. "Do you disagree with the findings of this investigation?"

Before Levin could respond, Lester Zepester interrupted. "As you know, Zoe and I have been quite busy of late. Each of us is gathering our own teams to hit the ground running next month. Neither of us has had the time to look at the investigative material and conclusions. We certainly are not in a position to second-guess the outgoing administration."

"Thanks, Mr. Zepester. Also, I want to congratulate you on your nomination as secretary of homeland security."

"Happy Holidays and Merry New Year" displayed in colorful script crept along the bottom of the television screen on the cable network no one watched.

113

"MERRY CHRISTMAS!" BLAKE and Samantha said to everyone. Jordan, David and their two children hugged them and wished them a Merry Christmas in return. Jennifer took their coats, and David and Paul took the presents they brought and put them under the tree.

Jordan stood back and watched. Her thoughts went to her father. How much he would have loved this moment. How much he would have enjoyed seeing Blake with a charming, intelligent woman who quite obviously enjoyed his company.

They all stood looking at the Christmas tree, the Nativity set, and the window beyond, which framed large snowflakes whirling through the afternoon air, seemingly never striking each other. Hardwood logs crackled in the fireplace, hissing occasionally. Embers popped now and then and were held in check by the brass fireplace screen.

Jordan noticed Blake and Samantha occasionally holding hands as they spoke to everyone. She smiled approvingly, as an older sister would.

• • •

Leon and Sapphire, family, and friends stood around the piano at Sapphire's parents' house, singing Christmas carols as her father played. It was like a variation of the old Volkswagen commercial about how many college students could fit in a Volkswagen Beetle. Today, how many people could fit around a piano?

Sapphire's mother and father had photocopied their favorite Christmas carols for everyone to sing. Leon and Sapphire held hands as their voices helped fill the room with Christmas joy:

> O little town of Bethlehem,
> How still we see thee lie!
> Above thy deep and dreamless sleep
> The silent stars go by;
> Yet in thy dark streets shineth
> The everlasting Light;
> The hopes and fears of all the years
> Are met in thee tonight.

• • •

Tom, Taryn, and Barbara sat at the table in his office. In the background, his tiny audio system played Christmas music. Tom produced very generous Christmas presents for them—and even more generous cash Christmas bonuses, from his own pocket. Taryn and Barbara, in turn, had thoughtful presents for him.

Tom had two bottles of elegant red wine decanted and ready for consumption, three wineglasses, some cheese, fruit, crackers, and chocolates. This was, blessedly, their last Christmas in this building. Certainly that was something to celebrate.

He thanked them for their friendship and their loyalty. He told them he could never have made it through his time at the Department of Justice without them and their support. He toasted them, and they all toasted each other. They even toasted Zoe Levin, the presumptive attorney general, and, they added, "God save our country."

After a few moments of reflection, Tom looked at them and asked, "Well, what do we do next?"

• • •

Cardinal Dominic Pacelli bent and kissed the main altar in the Church of the Most Holy Name of Jesus, located just outside the Vatican walls. This was the mother church of the Society of Jesus, designed by St. Ignatius of Loyola in 1551. All Jesuit churches worldwide are patterned after this particular church, in honor of their founder.

Under his Mass vestments, Cardinal Pacelli wore the red cassock that signified his status as a Prince of the Church and, on his head, the red skullcap. Assisting Cardinal Pacelli in the celebration of the Mass was Father Sabino Arana, superior general of the Society of Jesus, wearing his simple black cassock under his vestments.

This Mass was a hallmark event for this church. For, in its long history, this was the first time Mass had been offered there by a *Jesuit* cardinal. Neighbors, seminarians, tourists, priests, and nuns filled the church to capacity. The choir sang traditional religious carols in Latin.

Sitting in the very front pew was an American woman named Maria Angela Pacelli Carr. Her brother, the cardinal, was saying the Mass. Sitting next to her was Markus Roist.

• • •

She walked along the plowed road to a marker she knew by heart. As was her habit, she made a right turn toward the monument, which was not far from the road.

Her warm boots, long coat, scarf, gloves, and wool hat kept the cold at bay. In her gloved hands were freshly cut flowers: beautiful red roses braving the winter weather. The only sound came from her footsteps treading over the crusty snow, now being quietly blanketed with fresh snow.

She stood in front of the monument.

She said the same prayer she had been saying for the past few years, through every season, in all weather conditions.

It was *their* prayer for happiness together.

The names on the monument were Katherine Elliott, Wife, and Carson Elliott, Husband, followed by their birth dates and the date each died.

Holly's profound wish—silly under the circumstances, but always the same—was that her name be on the monument next to Carson's name, in place of Katherine's.

Not once did she regret the choices she had made in her life. Each day she and Carson were together was a day filled with promise and love...and more promise of love.

"How sad can I really be?" she pondered. "In an important way, I had Carson to myself for all those many years. Still, it was not what either of us wanted." But, in the end, it was enough. It had to be.

Holly laid the roses on the snow in front of the monument.

"At last, it is finished," she whispered. "I know you would not have approved, but John and I had to do it."

Holly looked at Carson Elliott's name one more time, turned, and walked away.

Made in the USA
Columbia, SC
10 May 2017